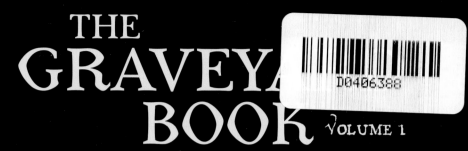

THE GRAVEYARD BOOK VOLUME 1

Based on the novel by: NEIL GAIMAN

Adapted by: P. CRAIG RUSSELL

Illustrated by: KEVIN NOWLAN P. CRAIG RUSSELL
TONY HARRIS SCOTT HAMPTON GALEN SHOWMAN
JILL THOMPSON STEPHEN B. SCOTT

Colorist: LOVERN KINDZIERSKI

Letterer: RICK PARKER

HARPER

An Imprint of HarperCollinsPublishers

D0406388

The Graveyard Book Graphic Novel, Volume 1

Text copyright © 2008 by Neil Gaiman

Illustrations copyright © 2014 by P. Craig Russell

All rights reserved. Printed in the U.S.A.

No part of this book may be used or reproduced in any manner
whatsoever without written permission except in the case of brief
quotations embodied in critical articles and reviews. For information
address HarperCollins Children's Books, a division of HarperCollins
Publishers, 195 Broadway, New York, NY 10007.

www.harpercollinschildrens.com

Library of Congress catalog card number: 2013953799

ISBN 978-0-06-219481-7 (trade bdg.)

ISBN 978-0-06-219482-4 (pbk.)

Lettering by Rick Parker

Typography by Brian Durniak

15 16 17 18 19   RRDC   10 9 8 7 6 5 4 3 2

First Edition

To Brooke and Andrew, Jadon and Josiah, and Naomi and Emmeline

(and special thanks to Galen Showman and Scott Hampton for service above and beyond)

—P.C.R.

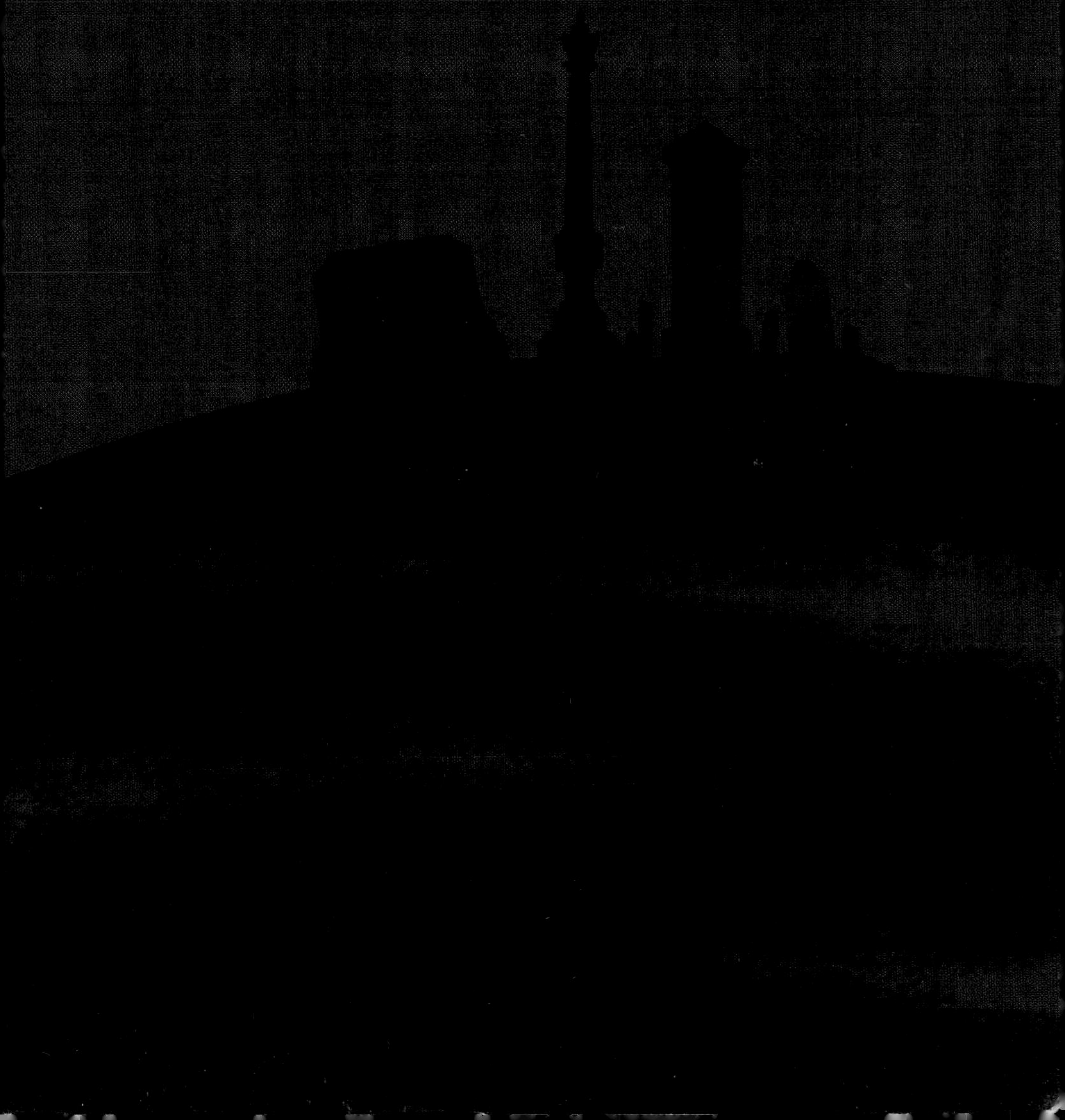

1
How Nobody Came to the Graveyard

Illustrated by Kevin Nowlan

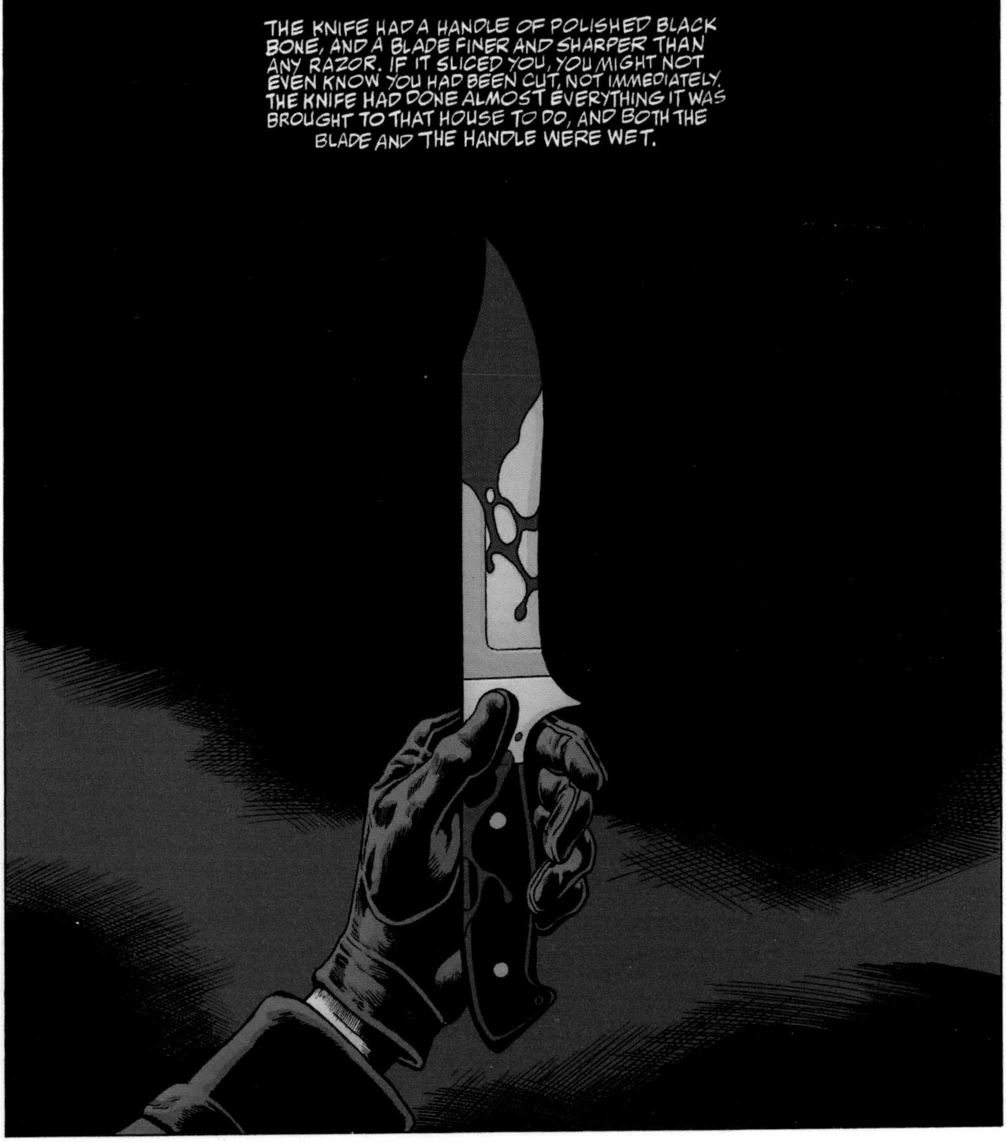
THE KNIFE HAD A HANDLE OF POLISHED BLACK BONE, AND A BLADE FINER AND SHARPER THAN ANY RAZOR. IF IT SLICED YOU, YOU MIGHT NOT EVEN KNOW YOU HAD BEEN CUT, NOT IMMEDIATELY. THE KNIFE HAD DONE ALMOST EVERYTHING IT WAS BROUGHT TO THAT HOUSE TO DO, AND BOTH THE BLADE AND THE HANDLE WERE WET.

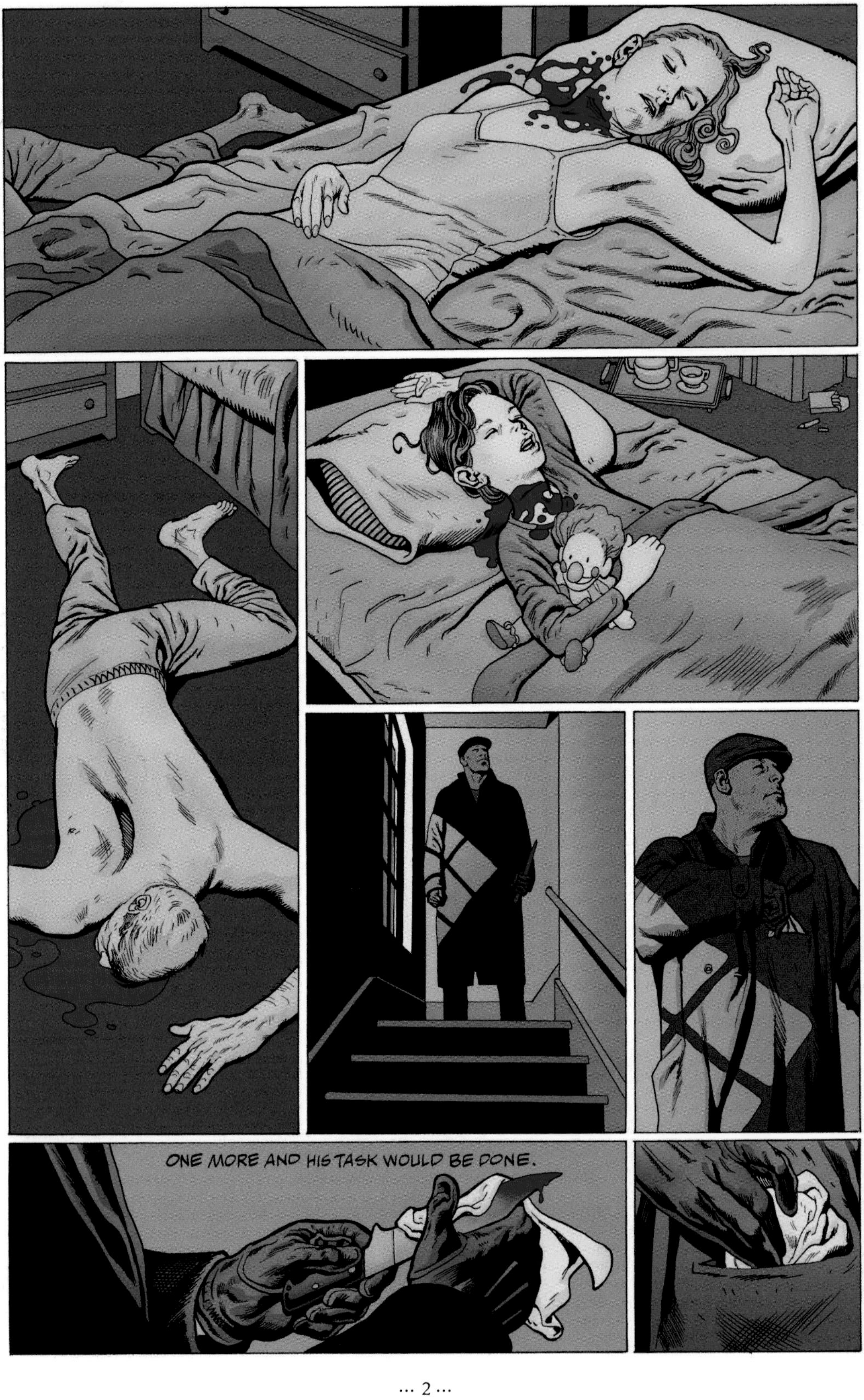
ONE MORE AND HIS TASK WOULD BE DONE.

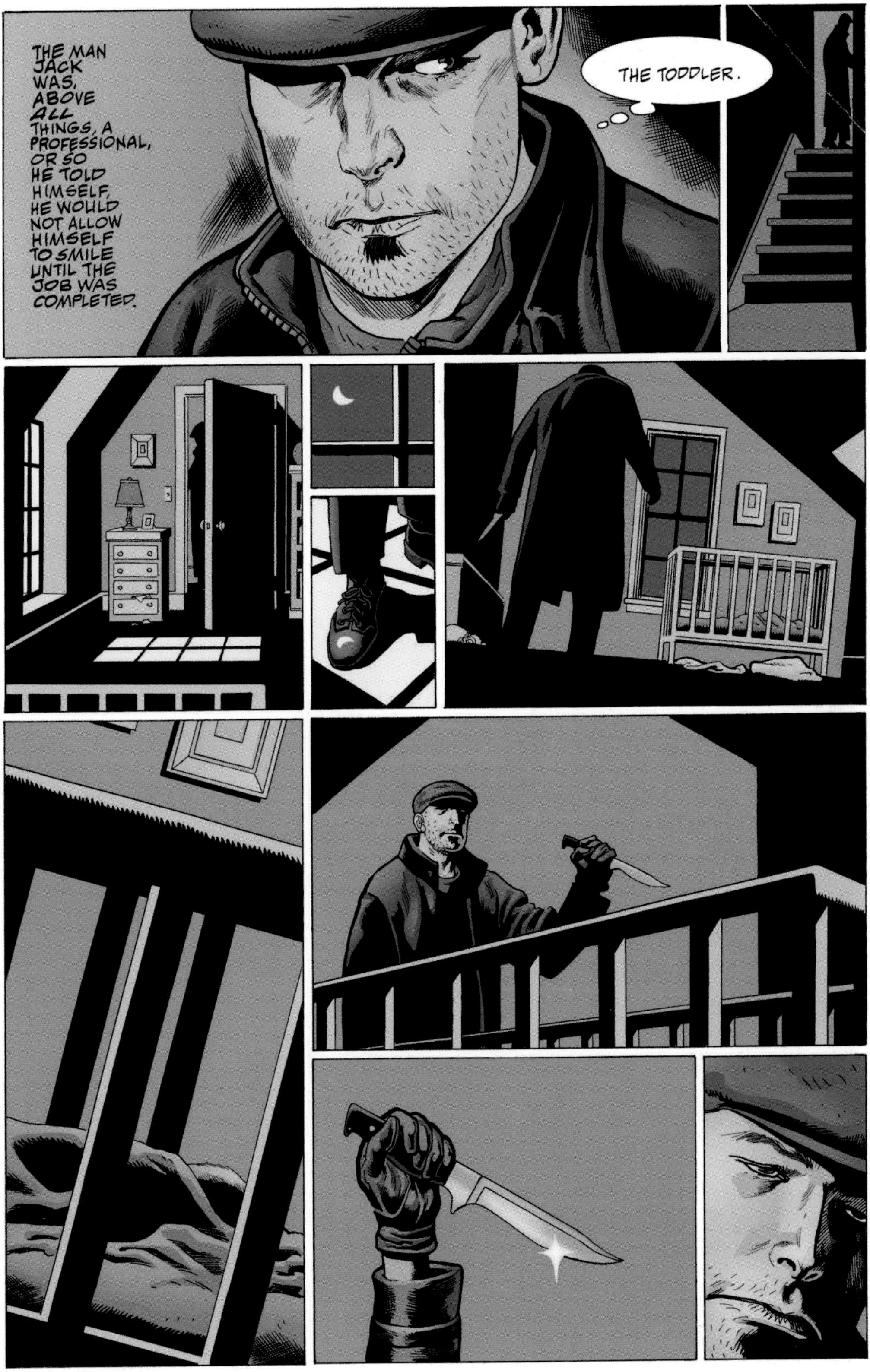
THE MAN JACK WAS, ABOVE ALL THINGS, A PROFESSIONAL, OR SO HE TOLD HIMSELF. HE WOULD NOT ALLOW HIMSELF TO SMILE UNTIL THE JOB WAS COMPLETED.
THE TODDLER.

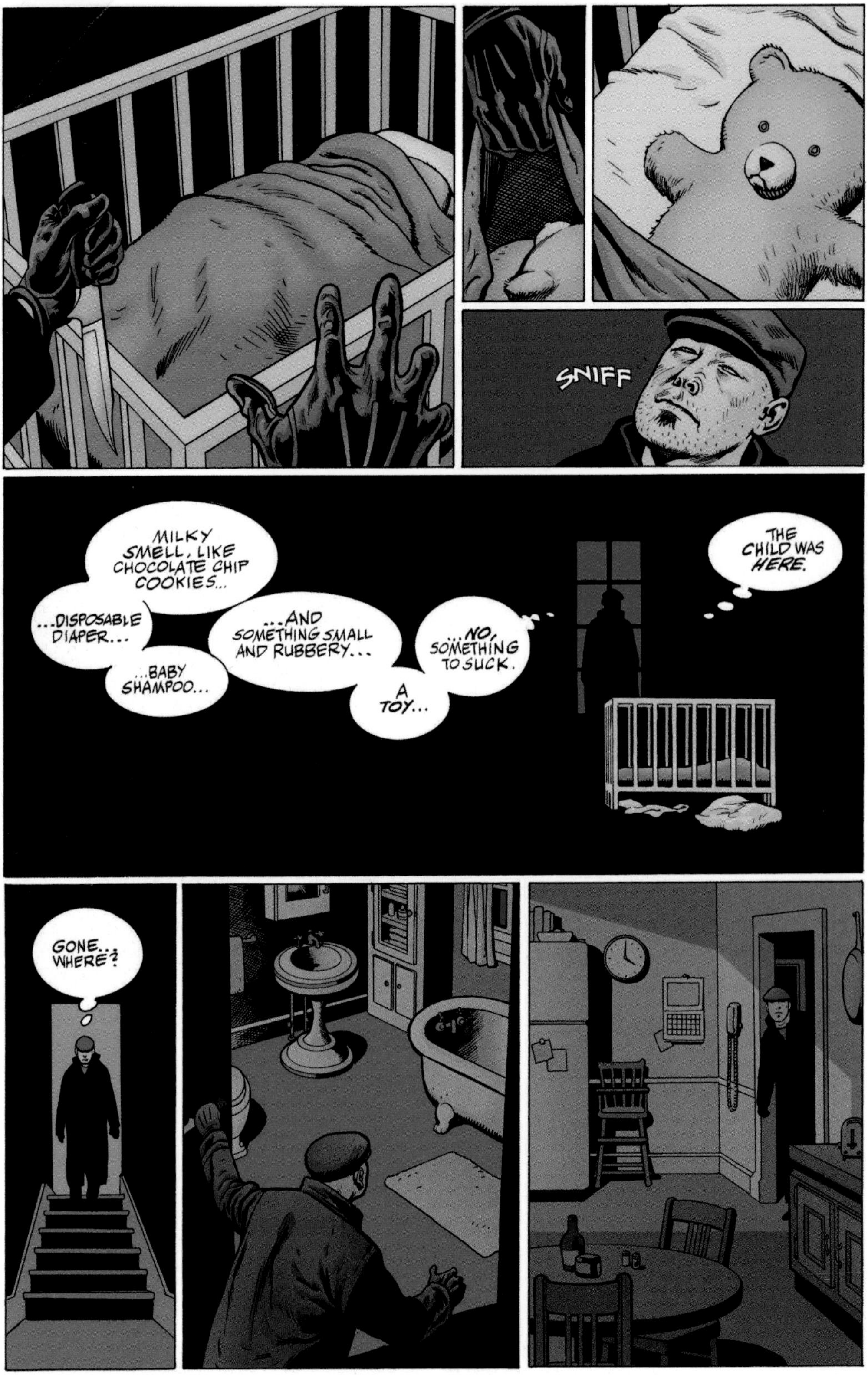
SNIFF
MILKY SMELL, LIKE CHOCOLATE CHIP COOKIES...
...DISPOSABLE DIAPER...
...BABY SHAMPOO...
...AND SOMETHING SMALL AND RUBBERY...
A TOY...
...NO, SOMETHING TO SUCK.
THE CHILD WAS HERE.
GONE... WHERE?

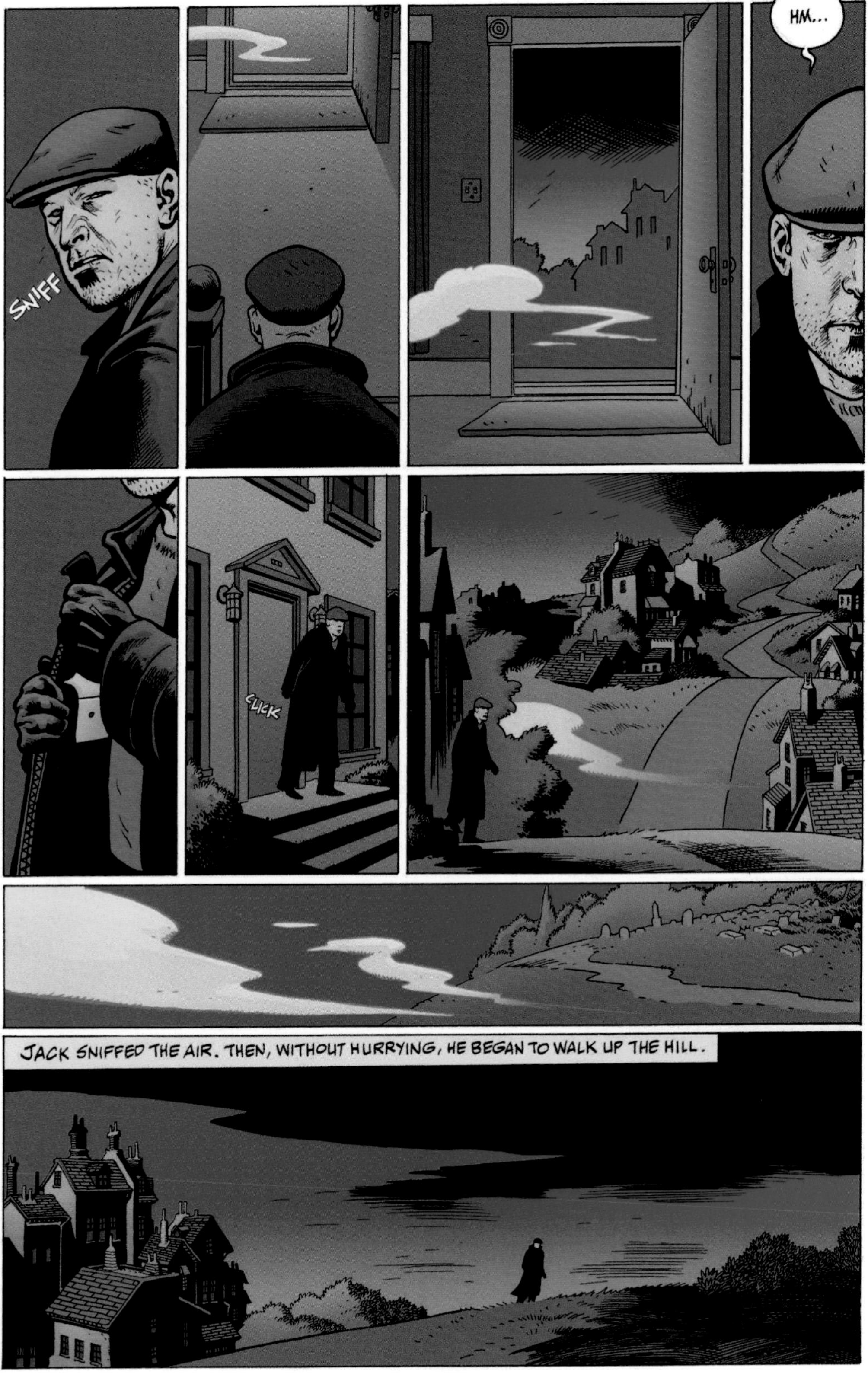
SNIFF
HM...
CLICK
JACK SNIFFED THE AIR. THEN, WITHOUT HURRYING, HE BEGAN TO WALK UP THE HILL.

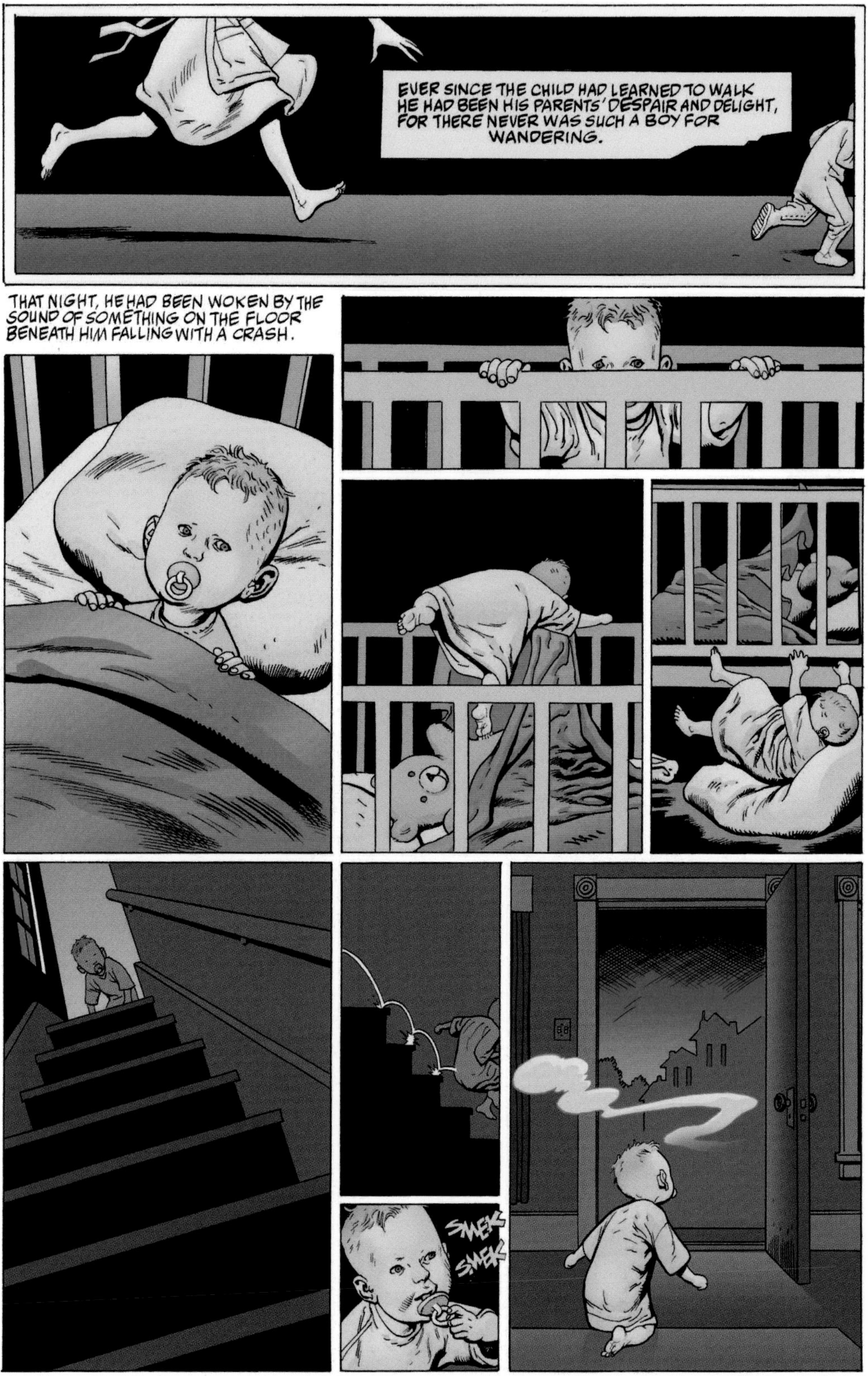
EVER SINCE THE CHILD HAD LEARNED TO WALK HE HAD BEEN HIS PARENTS' DESPAIR AND DELIGHT, FOR THERE NEVER WAS SUCH A BOY FOR WANDERING.
THAT NIGHT, HE HAD BEEN WOKEN BY THE SOUND OF SOMETHING ON THE FLOOR BENEATH HIM FALLING WITH A CRASH.
SMEK
SMEK

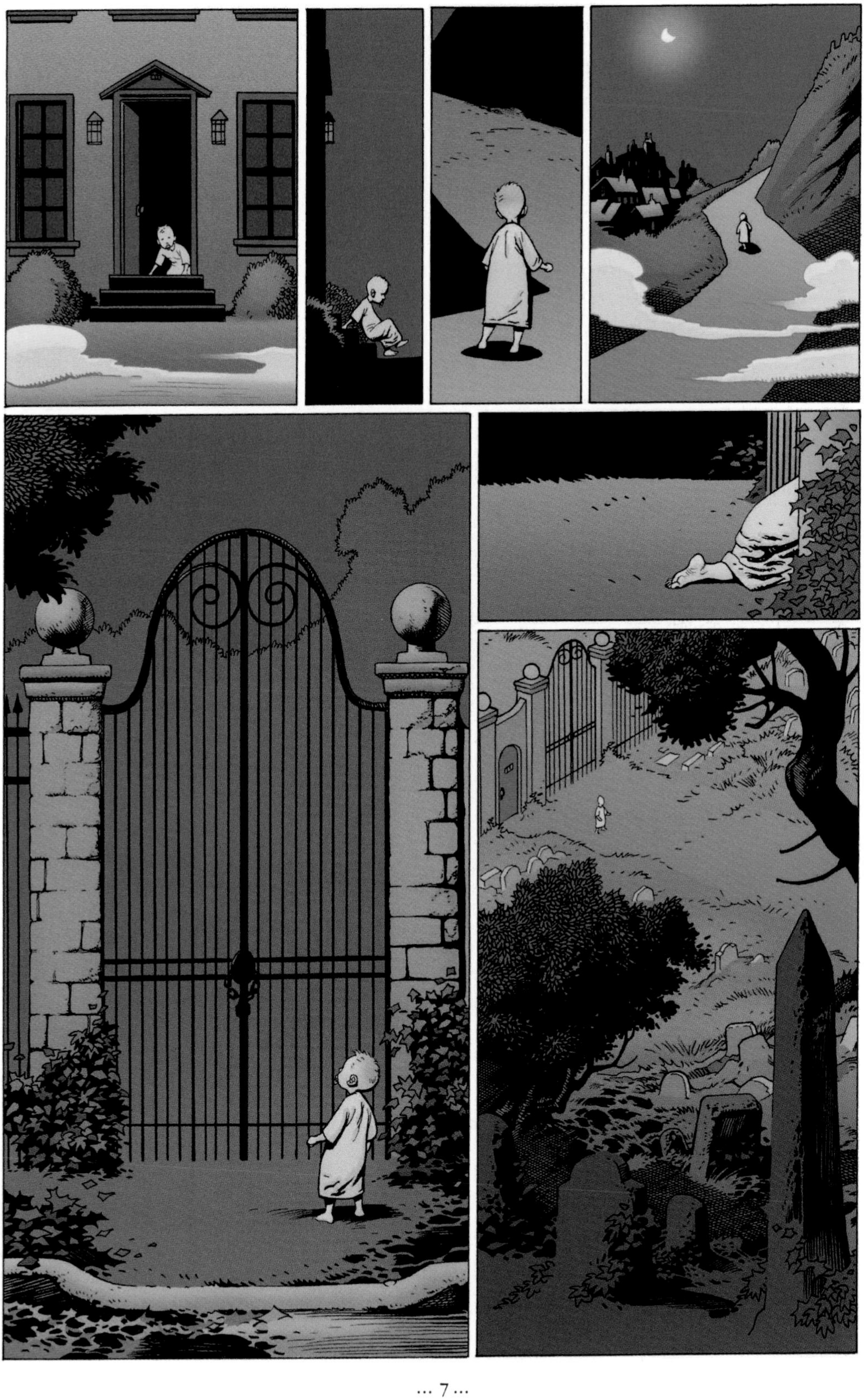

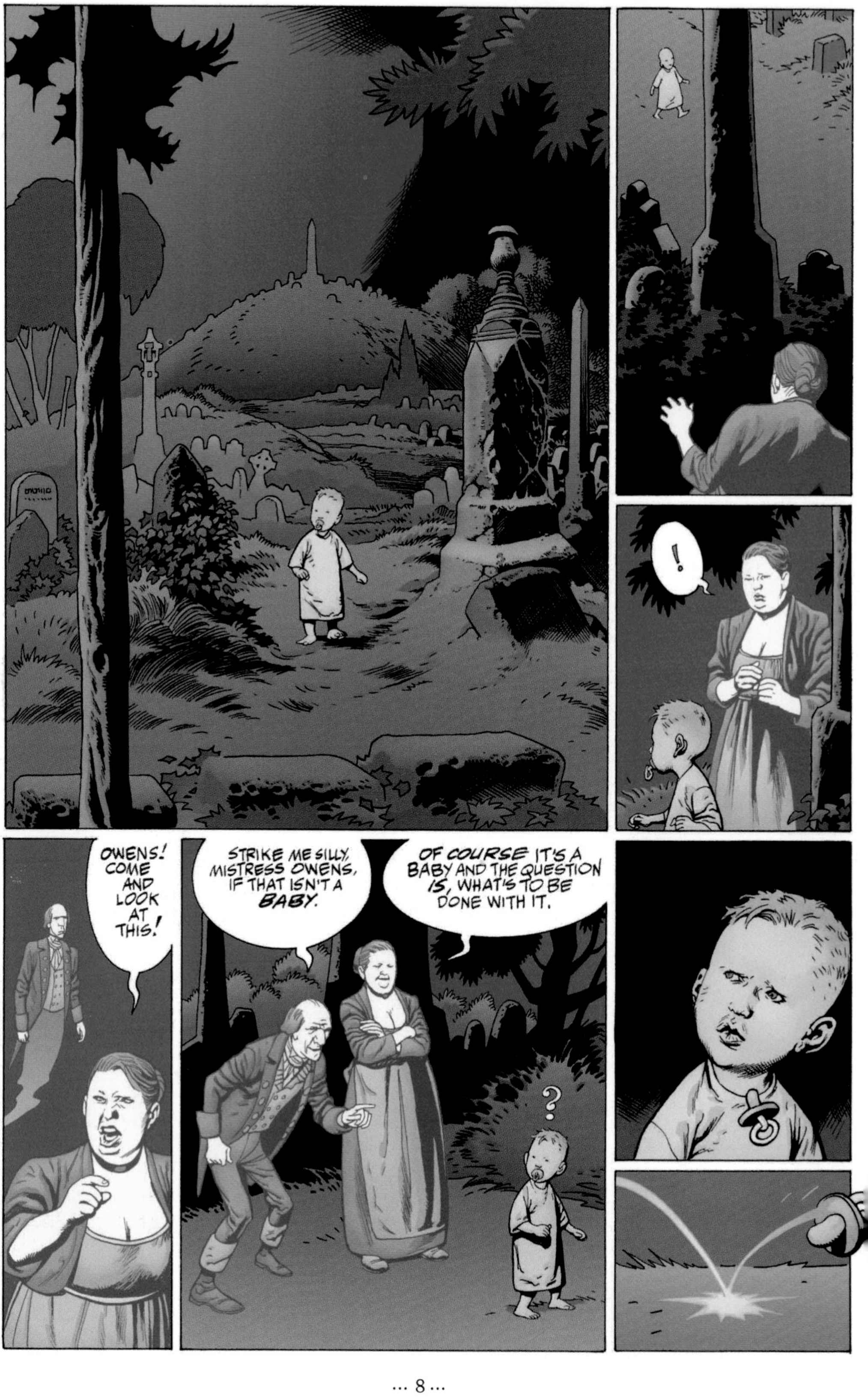
!
OWENS! COME AND LOOK AT THIS!
STRIKE ME SILLY, MISTRESS OWENS, IF THAT ISN'T A BABY.
OF COURSE IT'S A BABY AND THE QUESTION IS, WHAT'S TO BE DONE WITH IT.
?

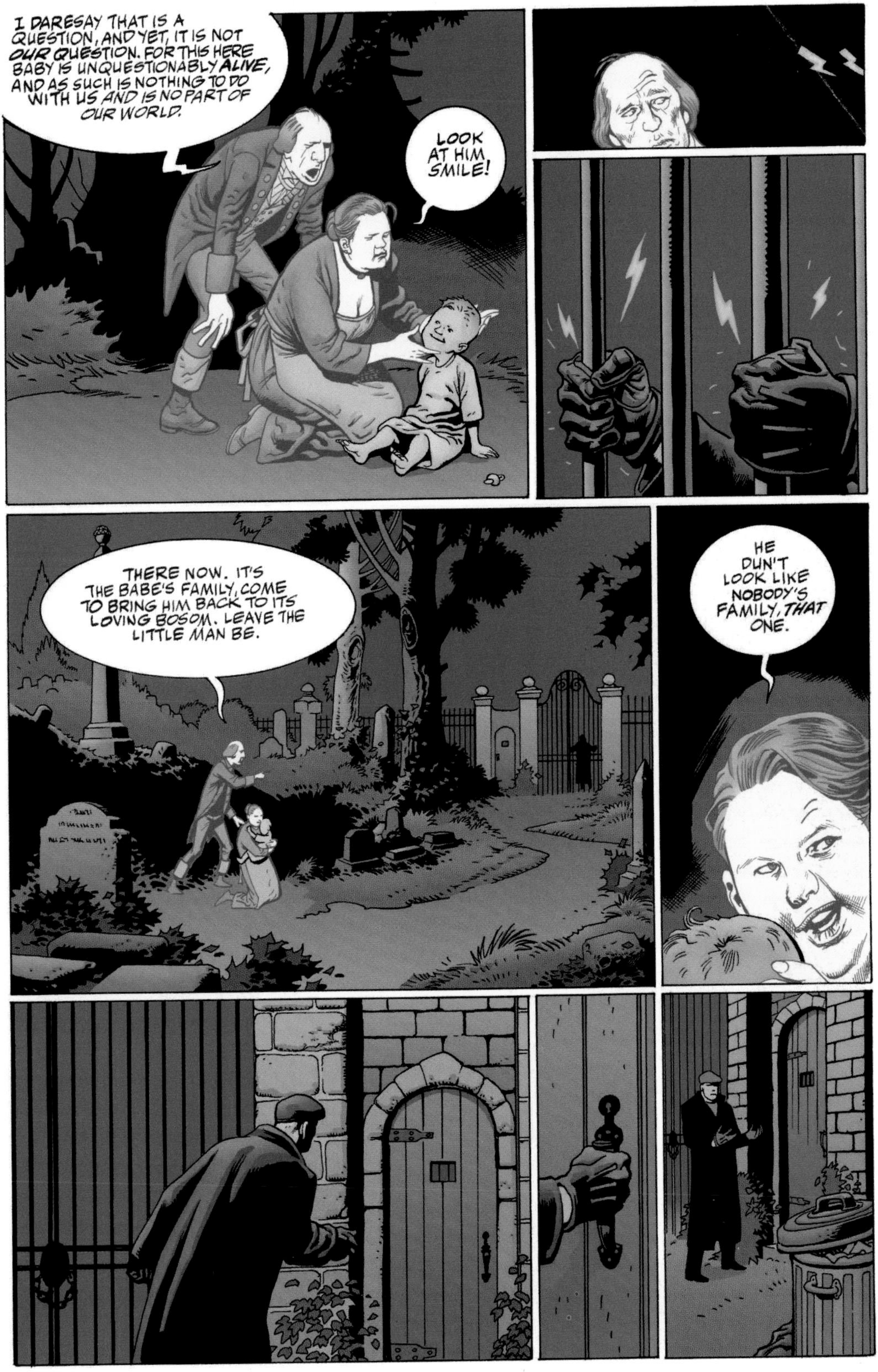
I DARESAY THAT IS A QUESTION, AND YET, IT IS NOT OUR QUESTION. FOR THIS HERE BABY IS UNQUESTIONABLY ALIVE, AND AS SUCH IS NOTHING TO DO WITH US AND IS NO PART OF OUR WORLD.
LOOK AT HIM SMILE!
THERE NOW. IT'S THE BABE'S FAMILY, COME TO BRING HIM BACK TO ITS LOVING BOSOM. LEAVE THE LITTLE MAN BE.
HE DUN'T LOOK LIKE NOBODY'S FAMILY, THAT ONE.

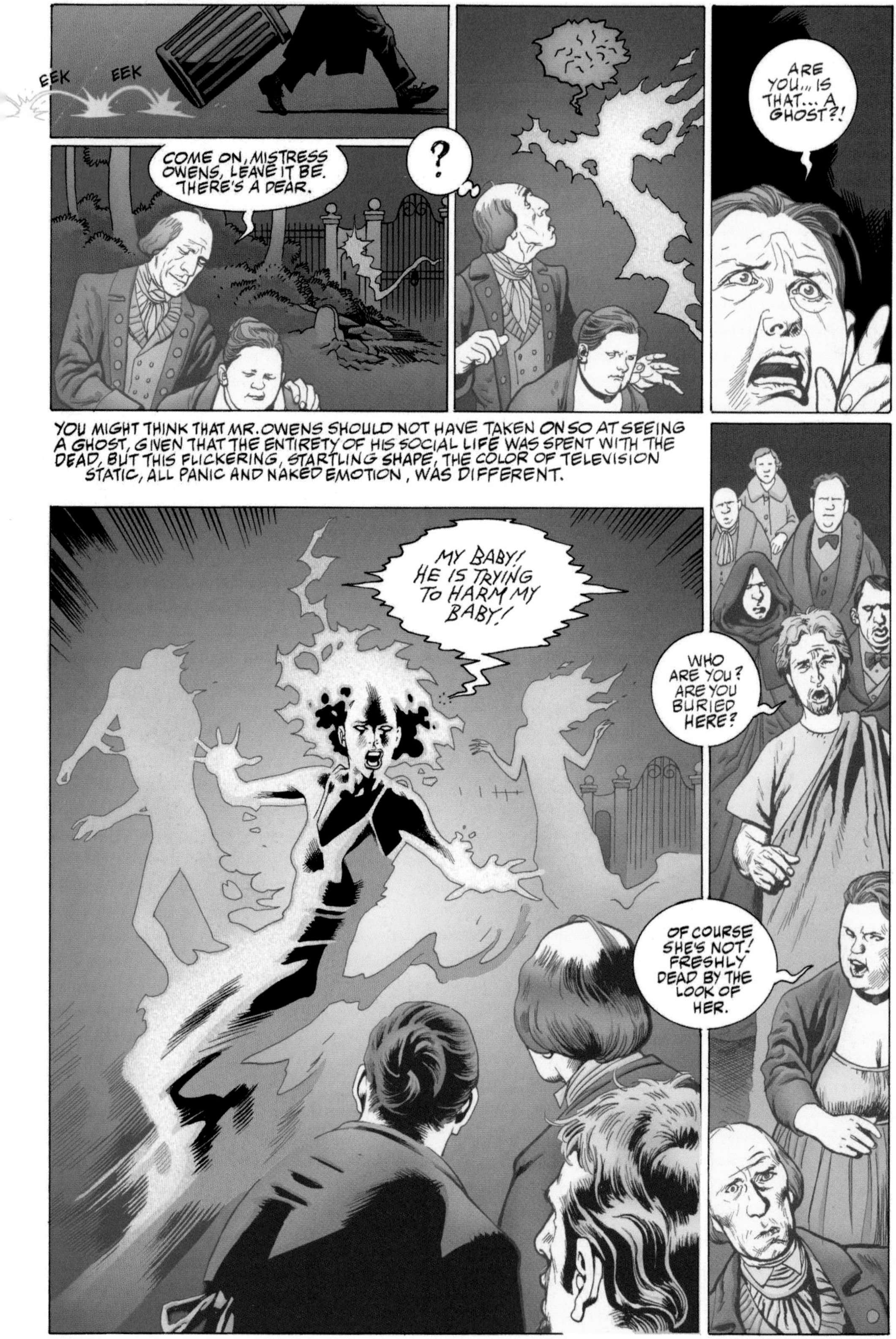
EEK
EEK
COME ON, MISTRESS OWENS, LEAVE IT BE. THERE'S A DEAR.
?
ARE YOU... IS THAT... A GHOST?!
YOU MIGHT THINK THAT MR. OWENS SHOULD NOT HAVE TAKEN ON SO AT SEEING A GHOST, GIVEN THAT THE ENTIRETY OF HIS SOCIAL LIFE WAS SPENT WITH THE DEAD, BUT THIS FLICKERING, STARTLING SHAPE, THE COLOR OF TELEVISION STATIC, ALL PANIC AND NAKED EMOTION, WAS DIFFERENT.
MY BABY! HE IS TRYING TO HARM MY BABY!
WHO ARE YOU? ARE YOU BURIED HERE?
OF COURSE SHE'S NOT! FRESHLY DEAD BY THE LOOK OF HER.

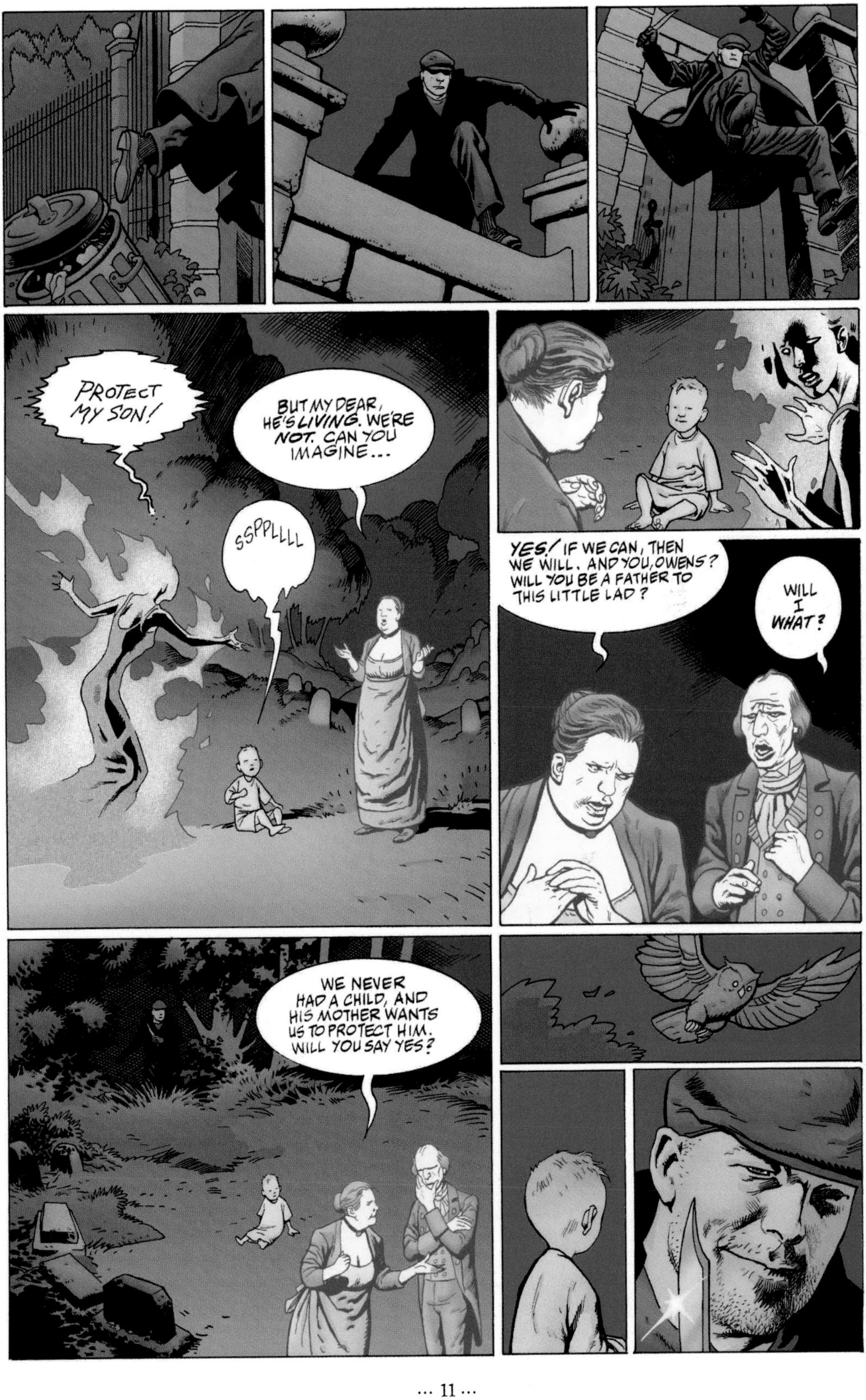
PROTECT MY SON!
BUT MY DEAR, HE'S LIVING. WE'RE NOT. CAN YOU IMAGINE...
SSPPLLLL
YES! IF WE CAN, THEN WE WILL. AND YOU, OWENS? WILL YOU BE A FATHER TO THIS LITTLE LAD?
WILL I WHAT?
WE NEVER HAD A CHILD, AND HIS MOTHER WANTS US TO PROTECT HIM. WILL YOU SAY YES?

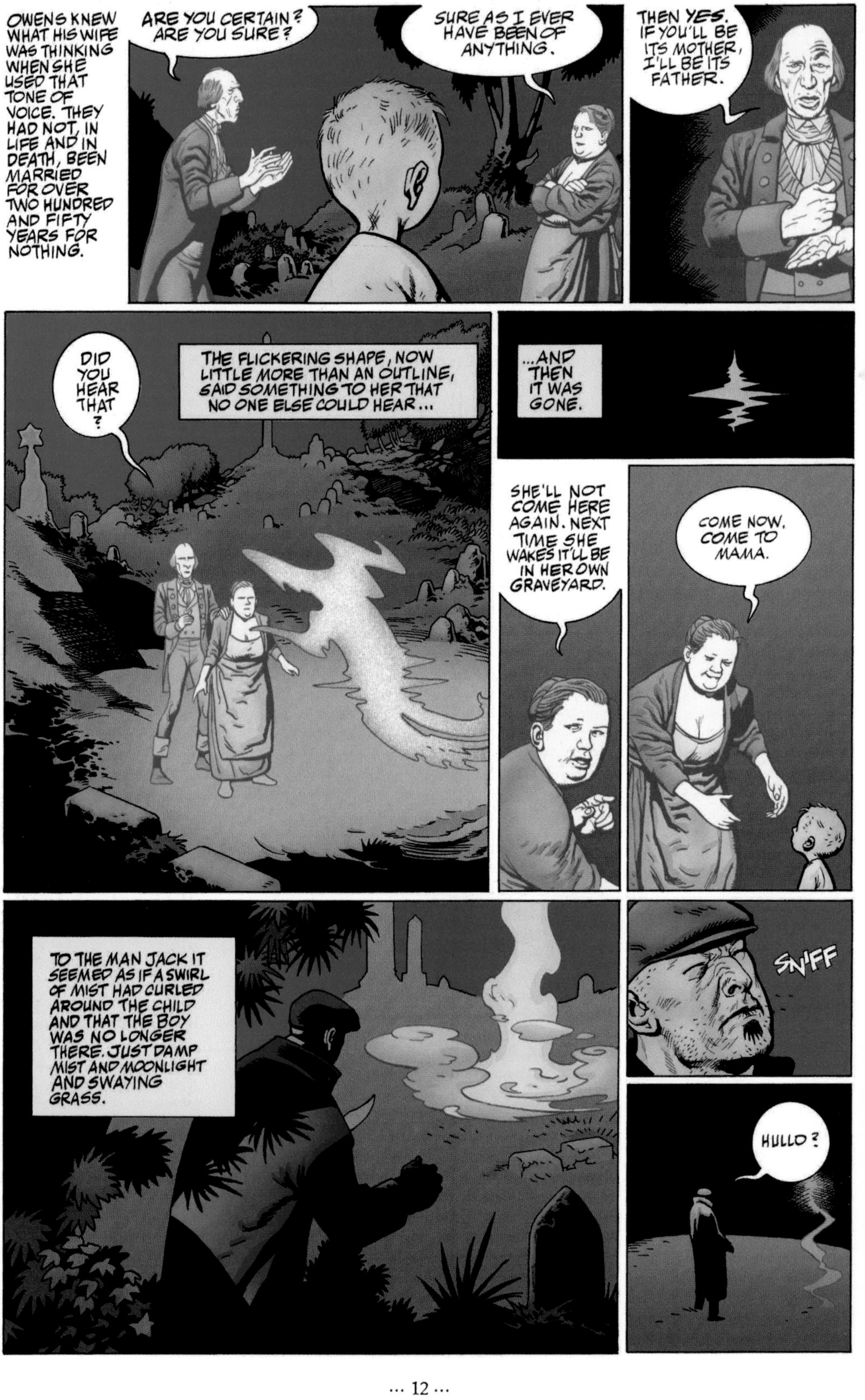
OWENS KNEW WHAT HIS WIFE WAS THINKING WHEN SHE USED THAT TONE OF VOICE. THEY HAD NOT, IN LIFE AND IN DEATH, BEEN MARRIED FOR OVER TWO HUNDRED AND FIFTY YEARS FOR NOTHING.
ARE YOU CERTAIN? ARE YOU SURE?
SURE AS I EVER HAVE BEEN OF ANYTHING.
THEN YES. IF YOU'LL BE ITS MOTHER, I'LL BE ITS FATHER.
THE FLICKERING SHAPE, NOW LITTLE MORE THAN AN OUTLINE, SAID SOMETHING TO HER THAT NO ONE ELSE COULD HEAR...
DID YOU HEAR THAT?
...AND THEN IT WAS GONE.
SHE'LL NOT COME HERE AGAIN. NEXT TIME SHE WAKES IT'LL BE IN HER OWN GRAVEYARD.
COME NOW. COME TO MAMA.
TO THE MAN JACK IT SEEMED AS IF A SWIRL OF MIST HAD CURLED AROUND THE CHILD AND THAT THE BOY WAS NO LONGER THERE. JUST DAMP MIST AND MOONLIGHT AND SWAYING GRASS.
SNIFF
HULLO?

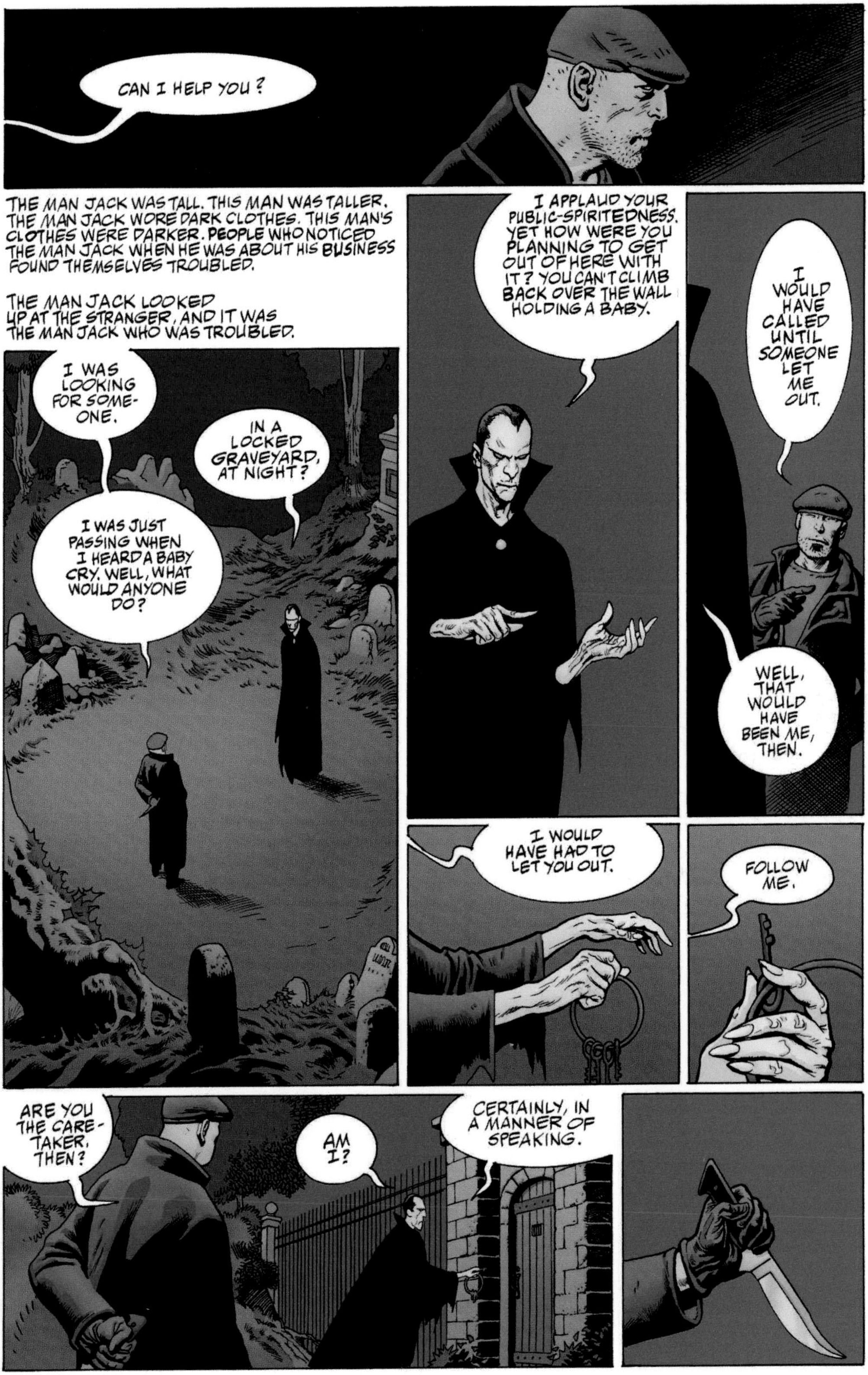
CAN I HELP YOU?
THE MAN JACK WAS TALL. THIS MAN WAS TALLER. THE MAN JACK WORE DARK CLOTHES. THIS MAN'S CLOTHES WERE DARKER. PEOPLE WHO NOTICED THE MAN JACK WHEN HE WAS ABOUT HIS BUSINESS FOUND THEMSELVES TROUBLED.
THE MAN JACK LOOKED UP AT THE STRANGER, AND IT WAS THE MAN JACK WHO WAS TROUBLED.
I WAS LOOKING FOR SOME-ONE.
IN A LOCKED GRAVEYARD, AT NIGHT?
I WAS JUST PASSING WHEN I HEARD A BABY CRY. WELL, WHAT WOULD ANYONE DO?
I APPLAUD YOUR PUBLIC-SPIRITEDNESS. YET HOW WERE YOU PLANNING TO GET OUT OF HERE WITH IT? YOU CAN'T CLIMB BACK OVER THE WALL HOLDING A BABY.
I WOULD HAVE CALLED UNTIL SOMEONE LET ME OUT.
WELL, THAT WOULD HAVE BEEN ME, THEN.
I WOULD HAVE HAD TO LET YOU OUT.
FOLLOW ME.
ARE YOU THE CARE-TAKER, THEN?
AM I?
CERTAINLY, IN A MANNER OF SPEAKING.

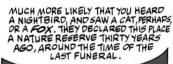

MUCH MORE LIKELY THAT YOU HEARD A NIGHTBIRD, AND SAW A CAT, PERHAPS, OR A *FOX*. THEY DECLARED THIS PLACE A NATURE RESERVE THIRTY YEARS AGO, AROUND THE TIME OF THE LAST FUNERAL.

IF THERE *WAS* A BABY, IT WOULDN'T HAVE BEEN HERE IN THE GRAVEYARD.

PERHAPS YOU WERE MISTAKEN.

NOW THINK CAREFULLY, AND TELL ME YOU ARE *CERTAIN* THAT IT WAS A CHILD THAT YOU SAW.

A *FOX*. THEY MAKE THE MOST UNCOMMON NOISES, NOT UNLIKE A PERSON CRYING.

NO, YOUR VISIT TO THE GRAVEYARD WAS A MIS-STEP. SOMEWHERE THE CHILD YOU SEEK AWAITS YOU...

...BUT HE IS NOT *HERE*.

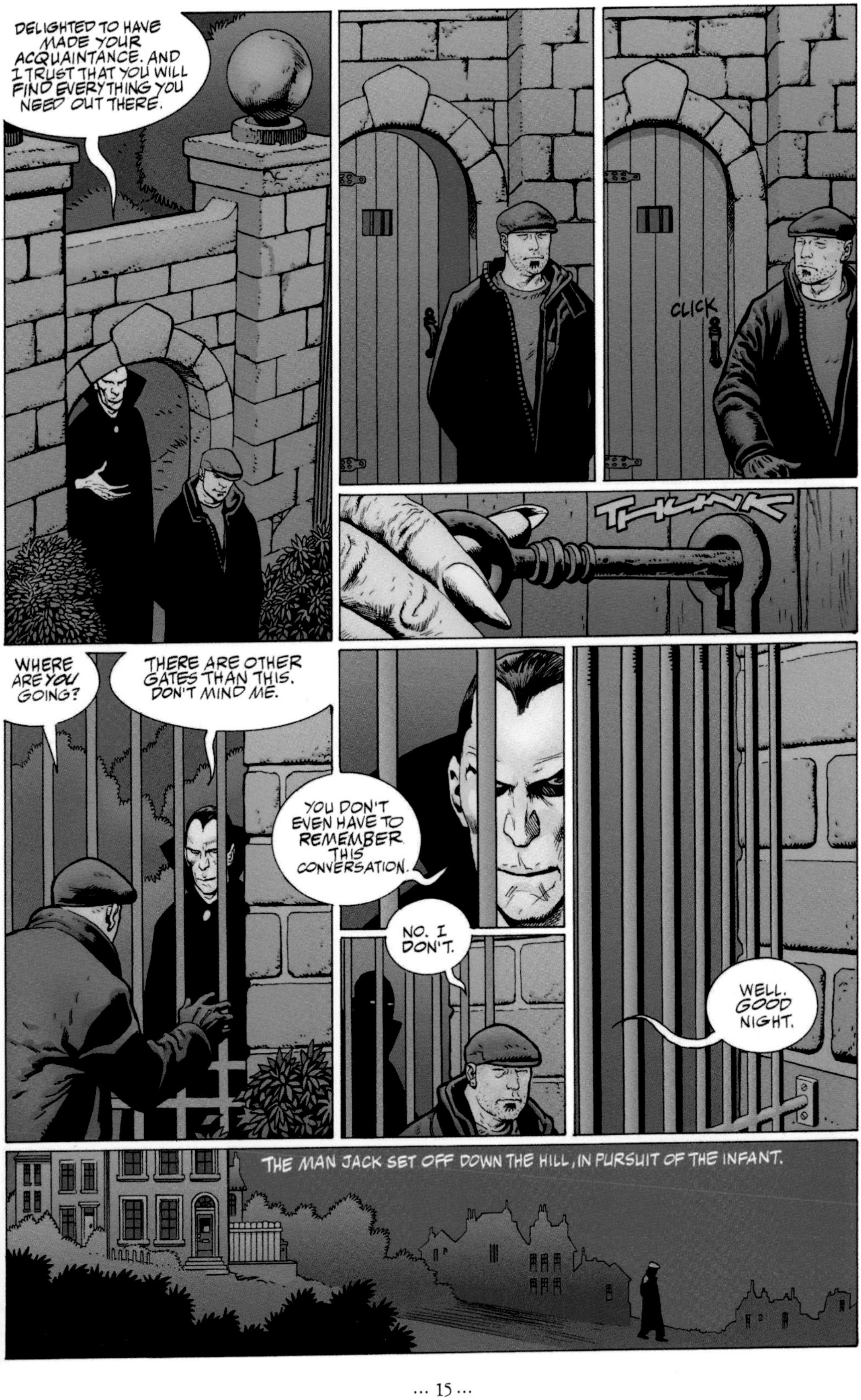
DELIGHTED TO HAVE MADE YOUR ACQUAINTANCE. AND I TRUST THAT YOU WILL FIND EVERYTHING YOU NEED OUT THERE.
CLICK
THUNK
WHERE ARE YOU GOING?
THERE ARE OTHER GATES THAN THIS. DON'T MIND ME.
YOU DON'T EVEN HAVE TO REMEMBER THIS CONVERSATION.
NO. I DON'T.
WELL. GOOD NIGHT.
THE MAN JACK SET OFF DOWN THE HILL, IN PURSUIT OF THE INFANT.

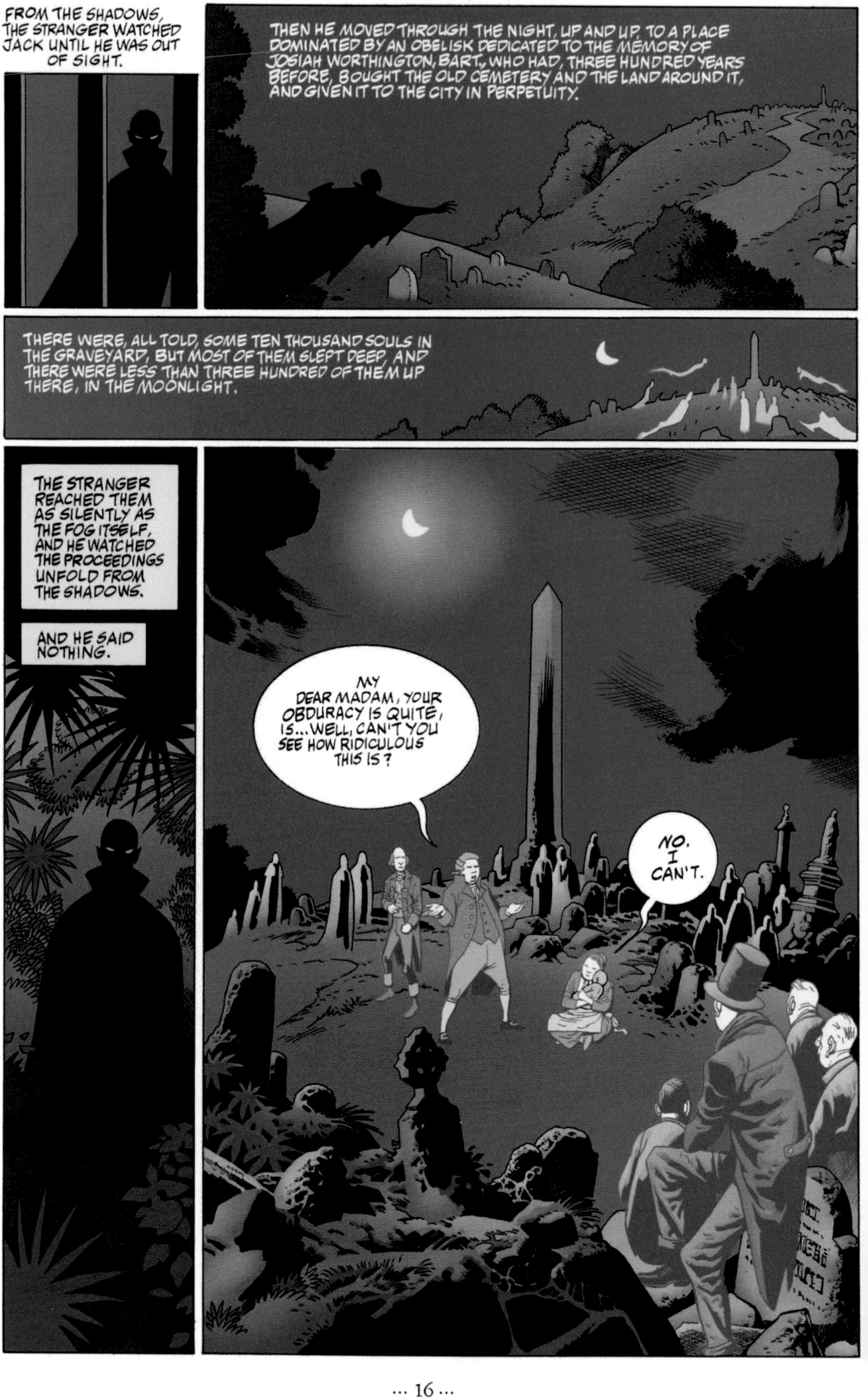
FROM THE SHADOWS, THE STRANGER WATCHED JACK UNTIL HE WAS OUT OF SIGHT.
THEN HE MOVED THROUGH THE NIGHT, UP AND UP, TO A PLACE DOMINATED BY AN OBELISK DEDICATED TO THE MEMORY OF JOSIAH WORTHINGTON, BART., WHO HAD, THREE HUNDRED YEARS BEFORE, BOUGHT THE OLD CEMETERY AND THE LAND AROUND IT, AND GIVEN IT TO THE CITY IN PERPETUITY.
THERE WERE, ALL TOLD, SOME TEN THOUSAND SOULS IN THE GRAVEYARD, BUT MOST OF THEM SLEPT DEEP, AND THERE WERE LESS THAN THREE HUNDRED OF THEM UP THERE, IN THE MOONLIGHT.
THE STRANGER REACHED THEM AS SILENTLY AS THE FOG ITSELF, AND HE WATCHED THE PROCEEDINGS UNFOLD FROM THE SHADOWS.
AND HE SAID NOTHING.
MY DEAR MADAM, YOUR OBDURACY IS QUITE, IS...WELL, CAN'T YOU SEE HOW RIDICULOUS THIS IS?
NO. I CAN'T.

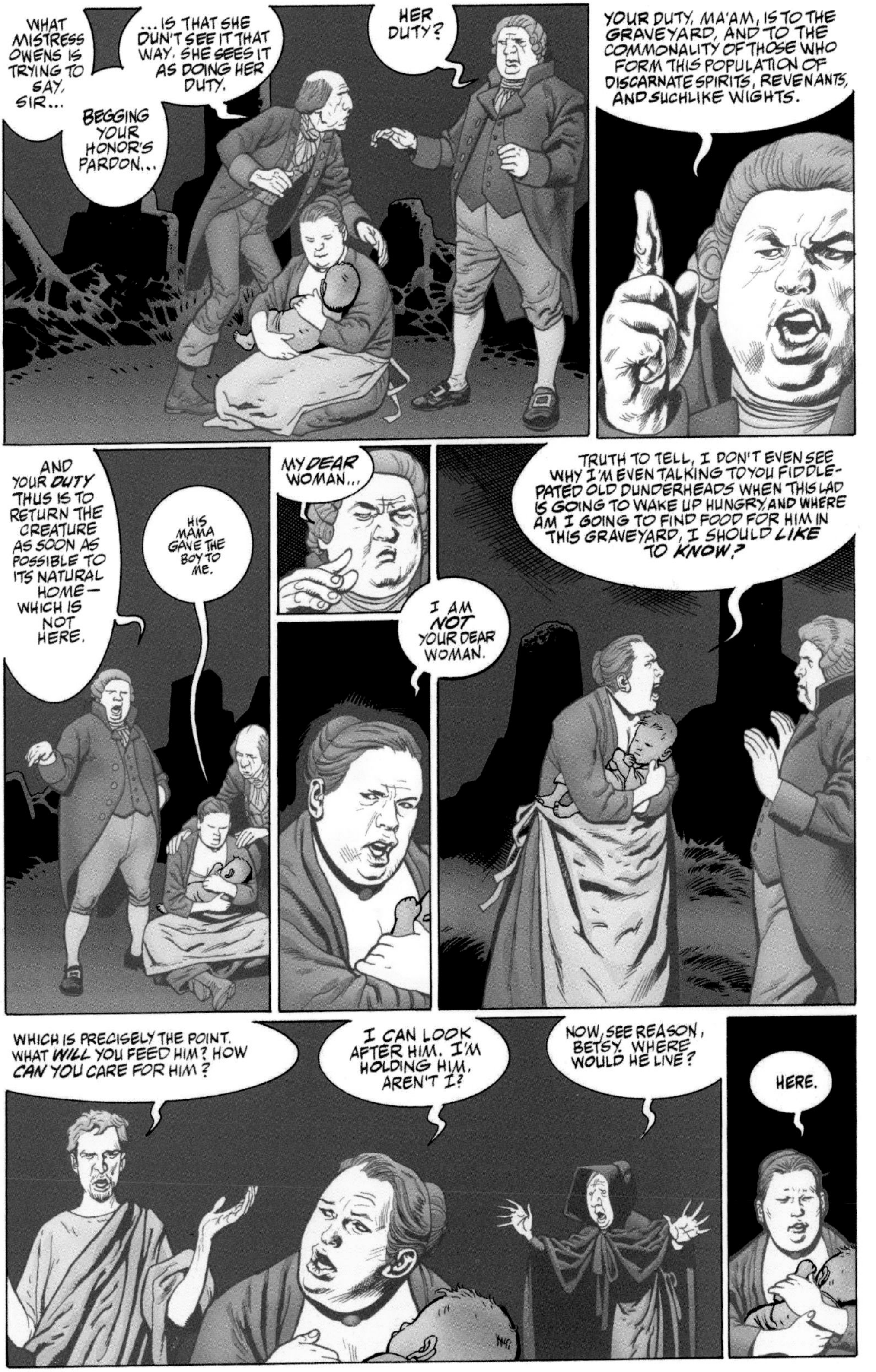
WHAT MISTRESS OWENS IS TRYING TO SAY, SIR...
...IS THAT SHE DON'T SEE IT THAT WAY. SHE SEES IT AS DOING HER DUTY.
BEGGING YOUR HONOR'S PARDON...
HER DUTY?
YOUR DUTY, MA'AM, IS TO THE GRAVEYARD, AND TO THE COMMONALITY OF THOSE WHO FORM THIS POPULATION OF DISCARNATE SPIRITS, REVENANTS, AND SUCHLIKE WIGHTS.
AND YOUR DUTY THUS IS TO RETURN THE CREATURE AS SOON AS POSSIBLE TO ITS NATURAL HOME—WHICH IS NOT HERE.
HIS MAMA GAVE THE BOY TO ME.
MY DEAR WOMAN...
I AM NOT YOUR DEAR WOMAN.
TRUTH TO TELL, I DON'T EVEN SEE WHY I'M EVEN TALKING TO YOU FIDDLE-PATED OLD DUNDERHEADS WHEN THIS LAD IS GOING TO WAKE UP HUNGRY, AND WHERE AM I GOING TO FIND FOOD FOR HIM IN THIS GRAVEYARD, I SHOULD LIKE TO KNOW?
WHICH IS PRECISELY THE POINT. WHAT WILL YOU FEED HIM? HOW CAN YOU CARE FOR HIM?
I CAN LOOK AFTER HIM. I'M HOLDING HIM, AREN'T I?
NOW, SEE REASON, BETSY. WHERE WOULD HE LIVE?
HERE.

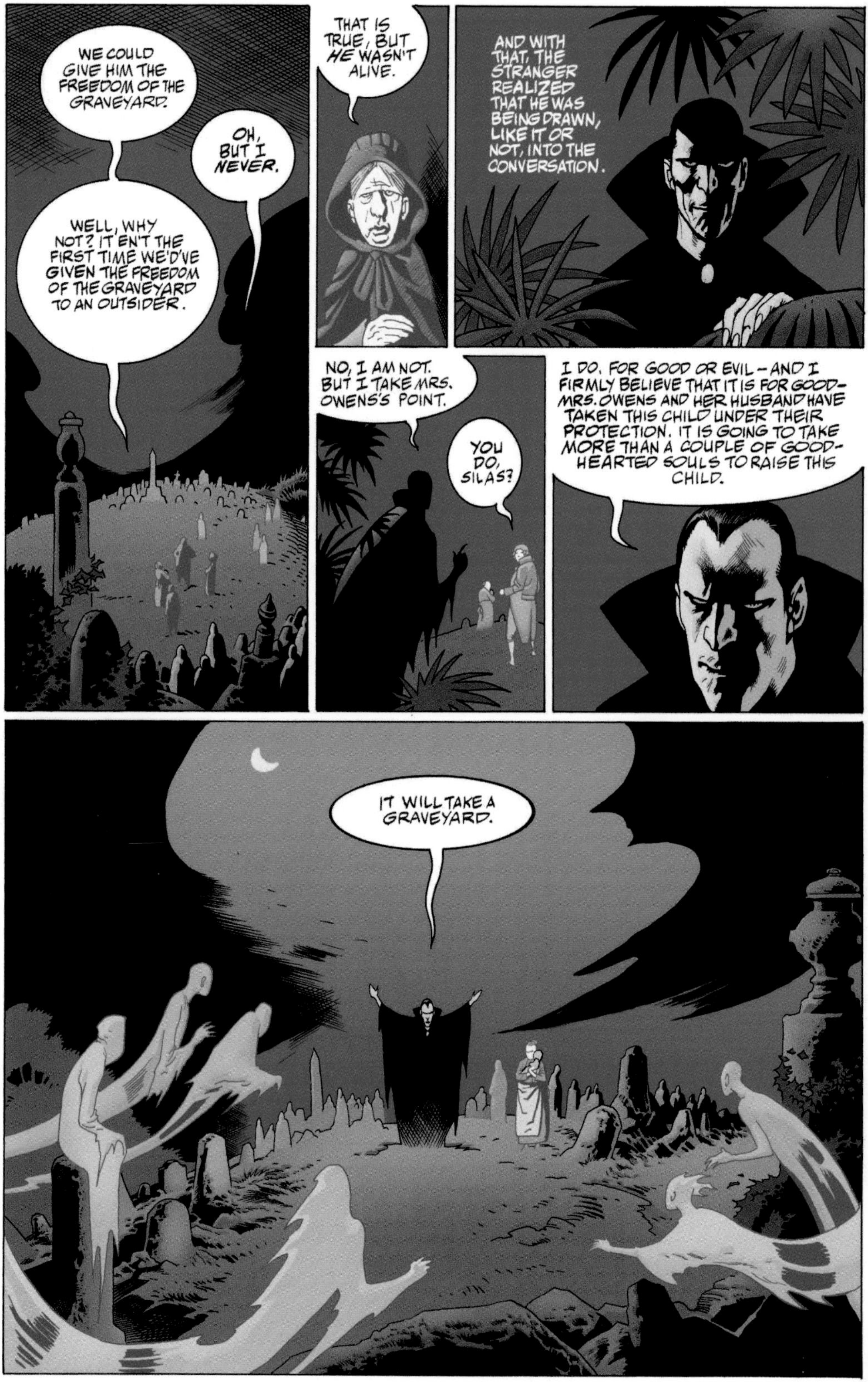
WE COULD GIVE HIM THE FREEDOM OF THE GRAVEYARD.
OH, BUT I NEVER.
WELL, WHY NOT? IT EN'T THE FIRST TIME WE'D'VE GIVEN THE FREEDOM OF THE GRAVEYARD TO AN OUTSIDER.
THAT IS TRUE, BUT HE WASN'T ALIVE.
AND WITH THAT, THE STRANGER REALIZED THAT HE WAS BEING DRAWN, LIKE IT OR NOT, INTO THE CONVERSATION.
NO, I AM NOT. BUT I TAKE MRS. OWENS'S POINT.
YOU DO, SILAS?
I DO. FOR GOOD OR EVIL — AND I FIRMLY BELIEVE THAT IT IS FOR GOOD — MRS. OWENS AND HER HUSBAND HAVE TAKEN THIS CHILD UNDER THEIR PROTECTION. IT IS GOING TO TAKE MORE THAN A COUPLE OF GOOD-HEARTED SOULS TO RAISE THIS CHILD.
IT WILL TAKE A GRAVEYARD.

AND WHAT OF FOOD, AND THE REST OF IT?

I CAN LEAVE THE GRAVEYARD AND RETURN. I CAN BRING HIM FOOD.

THAT'S ALL VERY WELL YOU SAYING THAT, BUT YOU COMES AND GOES AND NOBODY KEEPS TRACK OF YOU. IF YOU WENT OFF FOR A WEEK, THE BOY COULD *DIE.*

YOU ARE A WISE WOMAN. I SEE WHY THEY SPEAK SO HIGHLY OF YOU.

SILAS COULDN'T PUSH THE MINDS OF THE DEAD AS HE COULD THE LIVING, BUT HE COULD USE ALL THE TOOLS OF FLATTERY AND PERSUASION, FOR THE DEAD ARE NOT IMMUNE TO EITHER.

VERY WELL. IF MR. AND MRS. OWENS WILL BE HIS PARENTS, I SHALL BE HIS GUARDIAN. I SHALL REMAIN HERE, AND IF I NEED TO LEAVE I SHALL ENSURE THAT SOMEONE TAKES MY PLACE, LOOKING AFTER THE CHILD. WE CAN USE THE CRYPT OF THE CHAPEL.

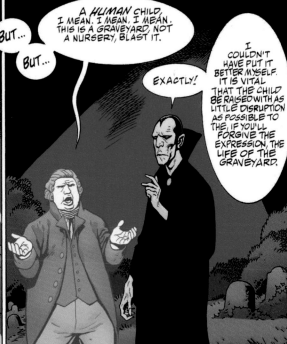

BUT...

BUT...

A *HUMAN* CHILD, I MEAN. I MEAN, I MEAN. THIS IS A GRAVEYARD, NOT A NURSERY, BLAST IT.

EXACTLY!

I COULDN'T HAVE PUT IT BETTER MYSELF. IT IS VITAL THAT THE CHILD BE RAISED WITH AS LITTLE DISRUPTION AS POSSIBLE TO THE, IF YOU'LL FORGIVE THE EXPRESSION, LIFE OF THE GRAVEYARD.

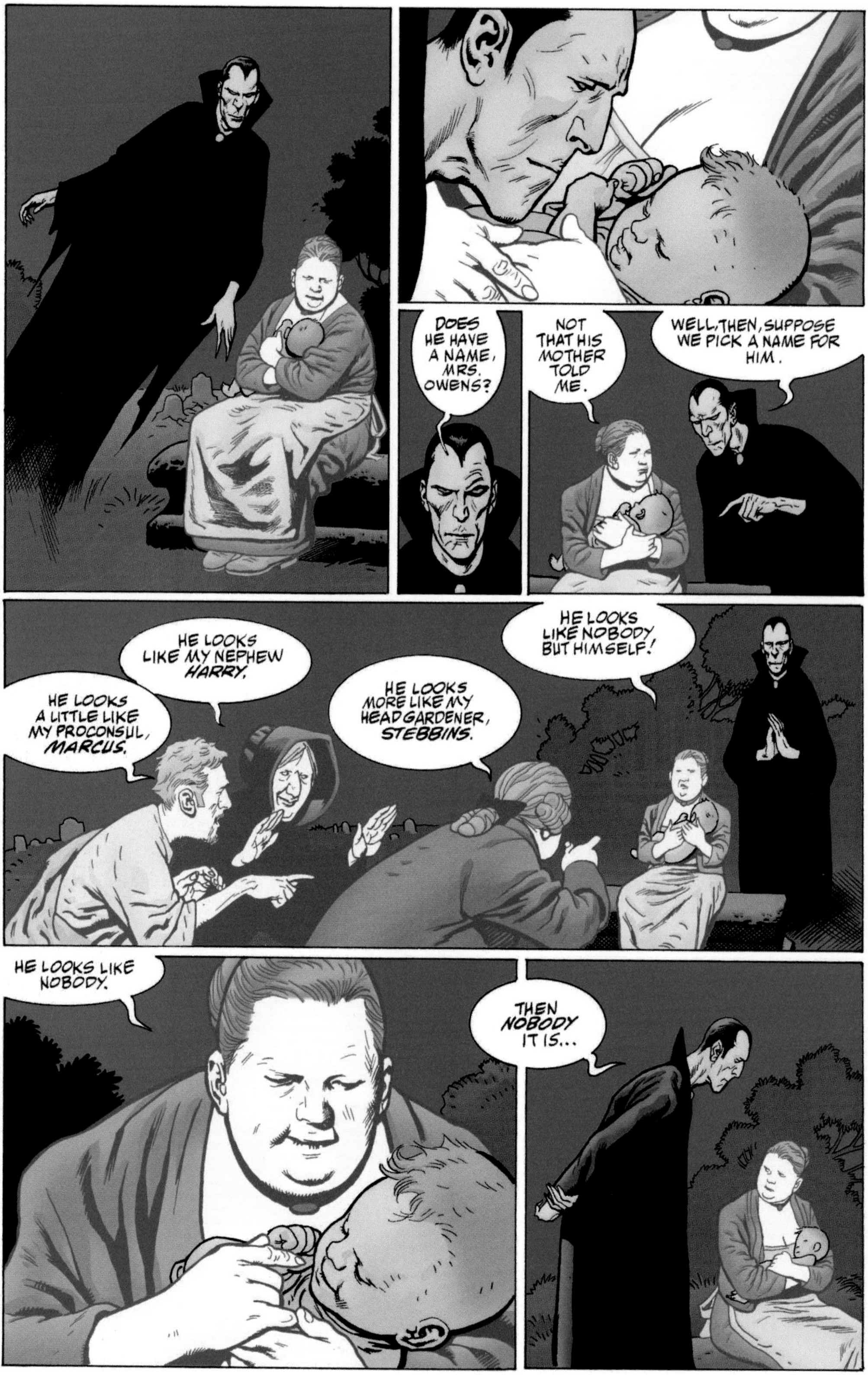
DOES HE HAVE A NAME, MRS. OWENS?
NOT THAT HIS MOTHER TOLD ME.
WELL, THEN, SUPPOSE WE PICK A NAME FOR HIM.
HE LOOKS A LITTLE LIKE MY PROCONSUL, MARCUS.
HE LOOKS LIKE MY NEPHEW HARRY.
HE LOOKS MORE LIKE MY HEAD GARDENER, STEBBINS.
HE LOOKS LIKE NOBODY BUT HIMSELF!
HE LOOKS LIKE NOBODY.
THEN NOBODY IT IS...

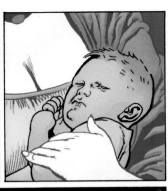

...NOBODY OWENS.

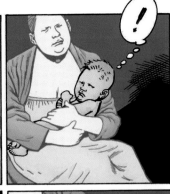

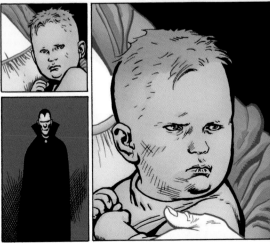

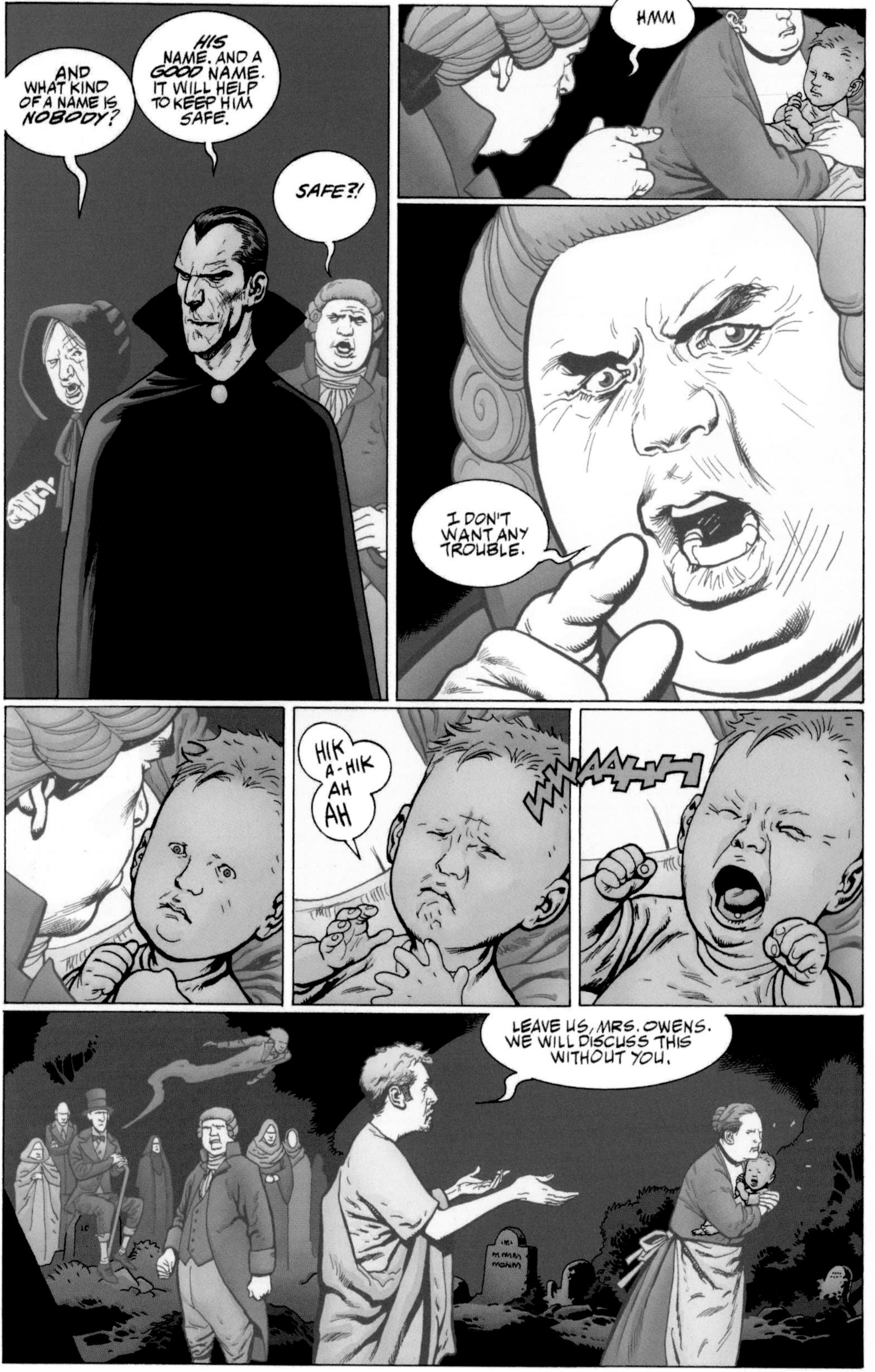
AND WHAT KIND OF A NAME IS NOBODY?
HIS NAME. AND A GOOD NAME. IT WILL HELP TO KEEP HIM SAFE.
SAFE?!
HMM
I DON'T WANT ANY TROUBLE.
HIK A-HIK AH AH
WAAHH
LEAVE US, MRS. OWENS. WE WILL DISCUSS THIS WITHOUT YOU.

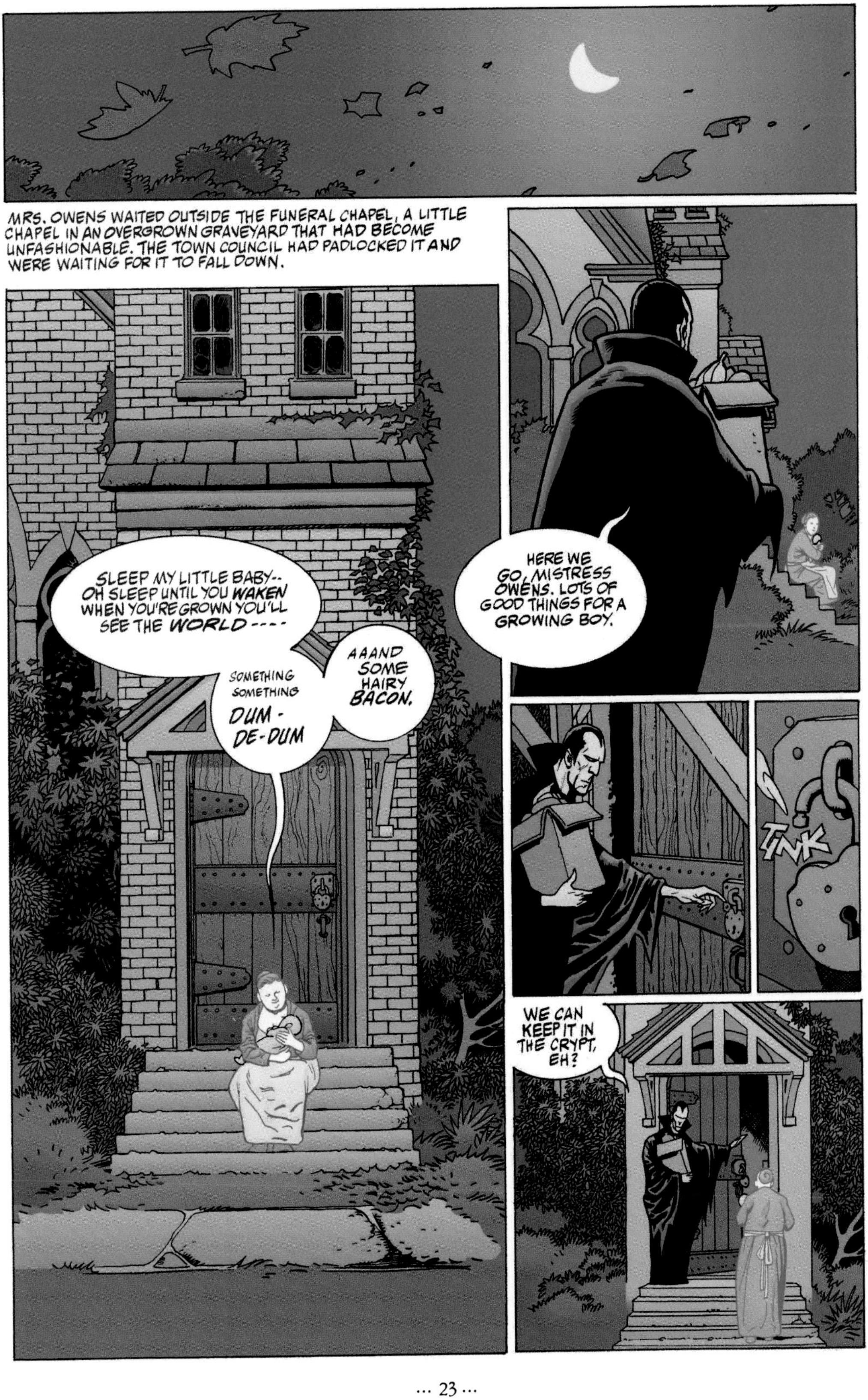
MRS. OWENS WAITED OUTSIDE THE FUNERAL CHAPEL, A LITTLE CHAPEL IN AN OVERGROWN GRAVEYARD THAT HAD BECOME UNFASHIONABLE. THE TOWN COUNCIL HAD PADLOCKED IT AND WERE WAITING FOR IT TO FALL DOWN.
SLEEP MY LITTLE BABY-- OH SLEEP UNTIL YOU WAKEN WHEN YOU'RE GROWN YOU'LL SEE THE WORLD----
SOMETHING SOMETHING DUM-DE-DUM
AAAND SOME HAIRY BACON.
HERE WE GO, MISTRESS OWENS. LOTS OF GOOD THINGS FOR A GROWING BOY.
TINK
WE CAN KEEP IT IN THE CRYPT, EH?

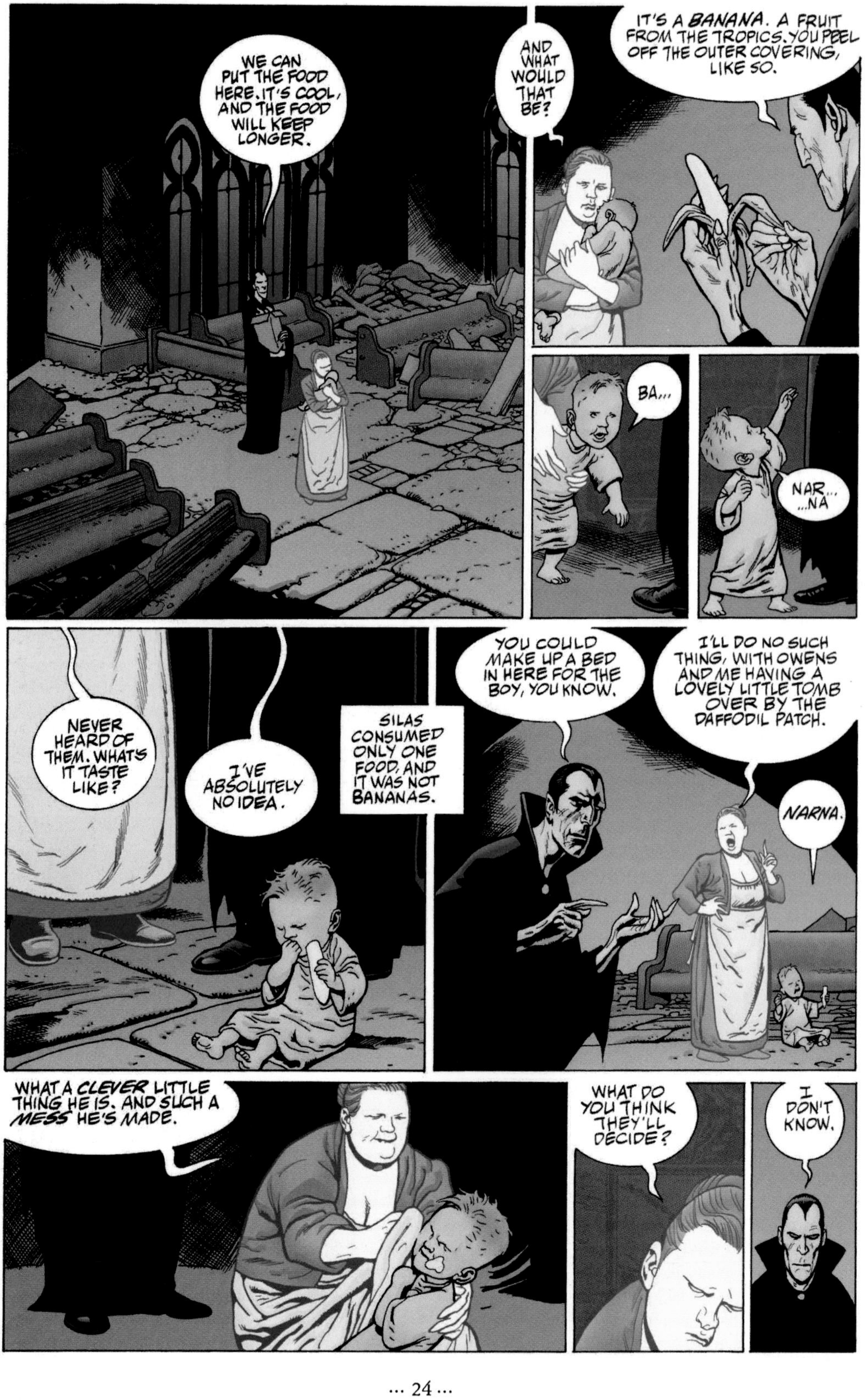
WE CAN PUT THE FOOD HERE. IT'S COOL, AND THE FOOD WILL KEEP LONGER.
AND WHAT WOULD THAT BE?
IT'S A BANANA. A FRUIT FROM THE TROPICS. YOU PEEL OFF THE OUTER COVERING, LIKE SO.
BA...
NAR... ...NA
NEVER HEARD OF THEM. WHAT'S IT TASTE LIKE?
I'VE ABSOLUTELY NO IDEA.
SILAS CONSUMED ONLY ONE FOOD, AND IT WAS NOT BANANAS.
YOU COULD MAKE UP A BED IN HERE FOR THE BOY, YOU KNOW.
I'LL DO NO SUCH THING, WITH OWENS AND ME HAVING A LOVELY LITTLE TOMB OVER BY THE DAFFODIL PATCH.
NARNA.
WHAT A CLEVER LITTLE THING HE IS. AND SUCH A MESS HE'S MADE.
WHAT DO YOU THINK THEY'LL DECIDE?
I DON'T KNOW.

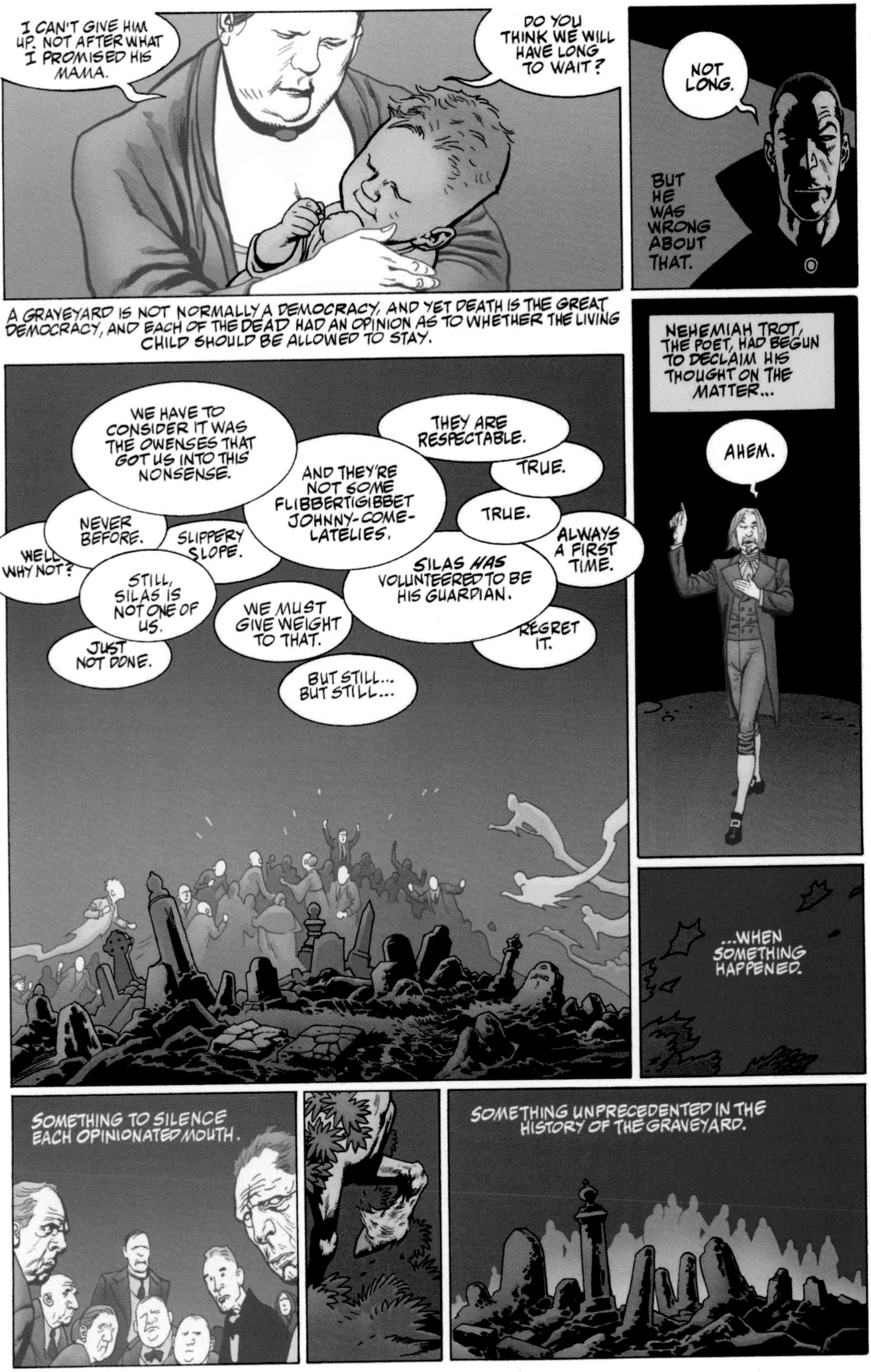
I CAN'T GIVE HIM UP. NOT AFTER WHAT I PROMISED HIS MAMA.
DO YOU THINK WE WILL HAVE LONG TO WAIT?
NOT LONG.
BUT HE WAS WRONG ABOUT THAT.
A GRAVEYARD IS NOT NORMALLY A DEMOCRACY, AND YET DEATH IS THE GREAT DEMOCRACY, AND EACH OF THE DEAD HAD AN OPINION AS TO WHETHER THE LIVING CHILD SHOULD BE ALLOWED TO STAY.
WE HAVE TO CONSIDER IT WAS THE OWENSES THAT GOT US INTO THIS NONSENSE.
THEY ARE RESPECTABLE.
TRUE.
AND THEY'RE NOT SOME FLIBBERTIGIBBET JOHNNY-COME-LATELIES.
TRUE.
NEVER BEFORE.
SLIPPERY SLOPE.
WELL, WHY NOT?
ALWAYS A FIRST TIME.
STILL, SILAS IS NOT ONE OF US.
SILAS HAS VOLUNTEERED TO BE HIS GUARDIAN.
WE MUST GIVE WEIGHT TO THAT.
REGRET IT.
JUST NOT DONE.
BUT STILL... BUT STILL...
NEHEMIAH TROT, THE POET, HAD BEGUN TO DECLAIM HIS THOUGHT ON THE MATTER...
AHEM.
...WHEN SOMETHING HAPPENED.
SOMETHING TO SILENCE EACH OPINIONATED MOUTH.
SOMETHING UNPRECEDENTED IN THE HISTORY OF THE GRAVEYARD.

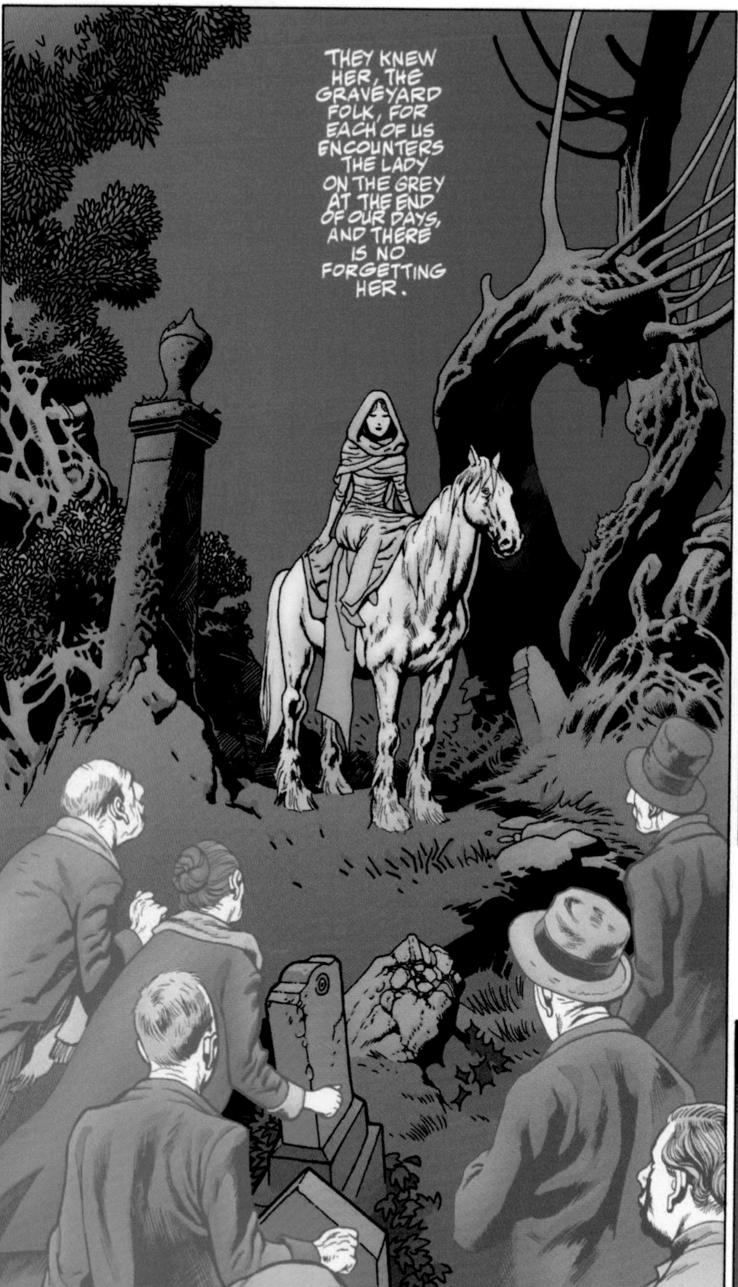
THEY KNEW HER, THE GRAVEYARD FOLK, FOR EACH OF US ENCOUNTERS THE LADY ON THE GREY AT THE END OF OUR DAYS, AND THERE IS NO FORGETTING HER.

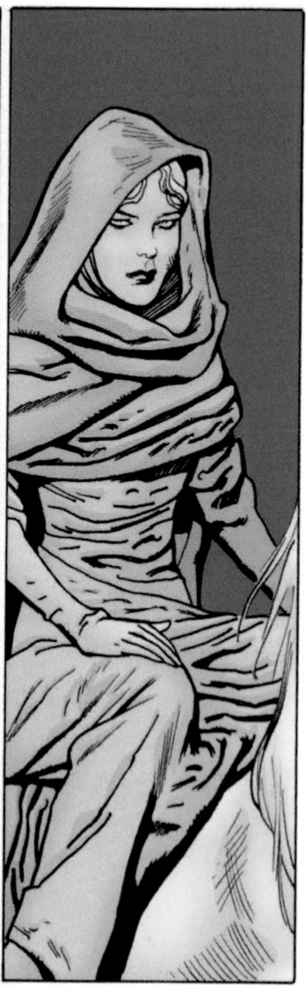

THE DEAD ARE NOT SUPERSTITIOUS, NOT AS A RULE, BUT THEY WATCHED HER AS A ROMAN AUGER MIGHT HAVE WATCHED THE SACRED CROWS CIRCLE, SEEKING WISDOM, SEEKING A CLUE.

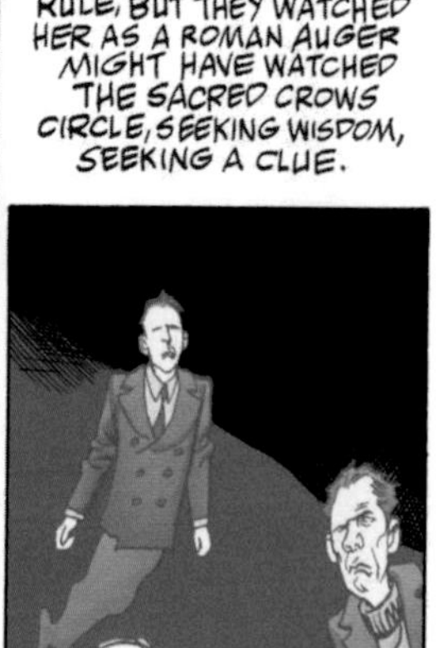

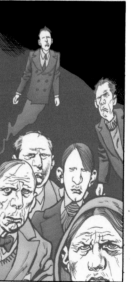

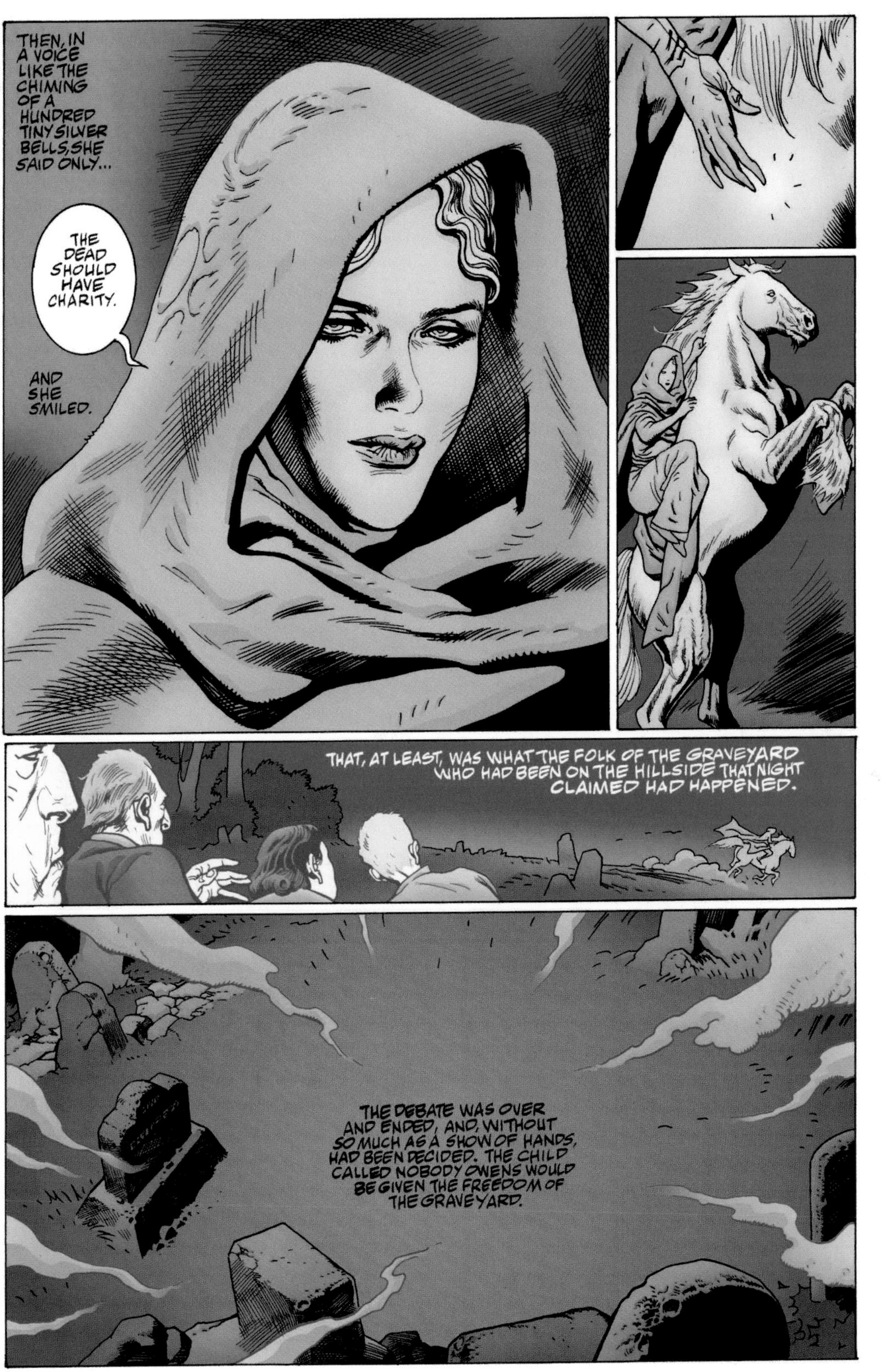
THEN, IN A VOICE LIKE THE CHIMING OF A HUNDRED TINY SILVER BELLS, SHE SAID ONLY...
THE DEAD SHOULD HAVE CHARITY.
AND SHE SMILED.
THAT, AT LEAST, WAS WHAT THE FOLK OF THE GRAVEYARD WHO HAD BEEN ON THE HILLSIDE THAT NIGHT CLAIMED HAD HAPPENED.
THE DEBATE WAS OVER AND ENDED, AND, WITHOUT SO MUCH AS A SHOW OF HANDS, HAD BEEN DECIDED. THE CHILD CALLED NOBODY OWENS WOULD BE GIVEN THE FREEDOM OF THE GRAVEYARD.

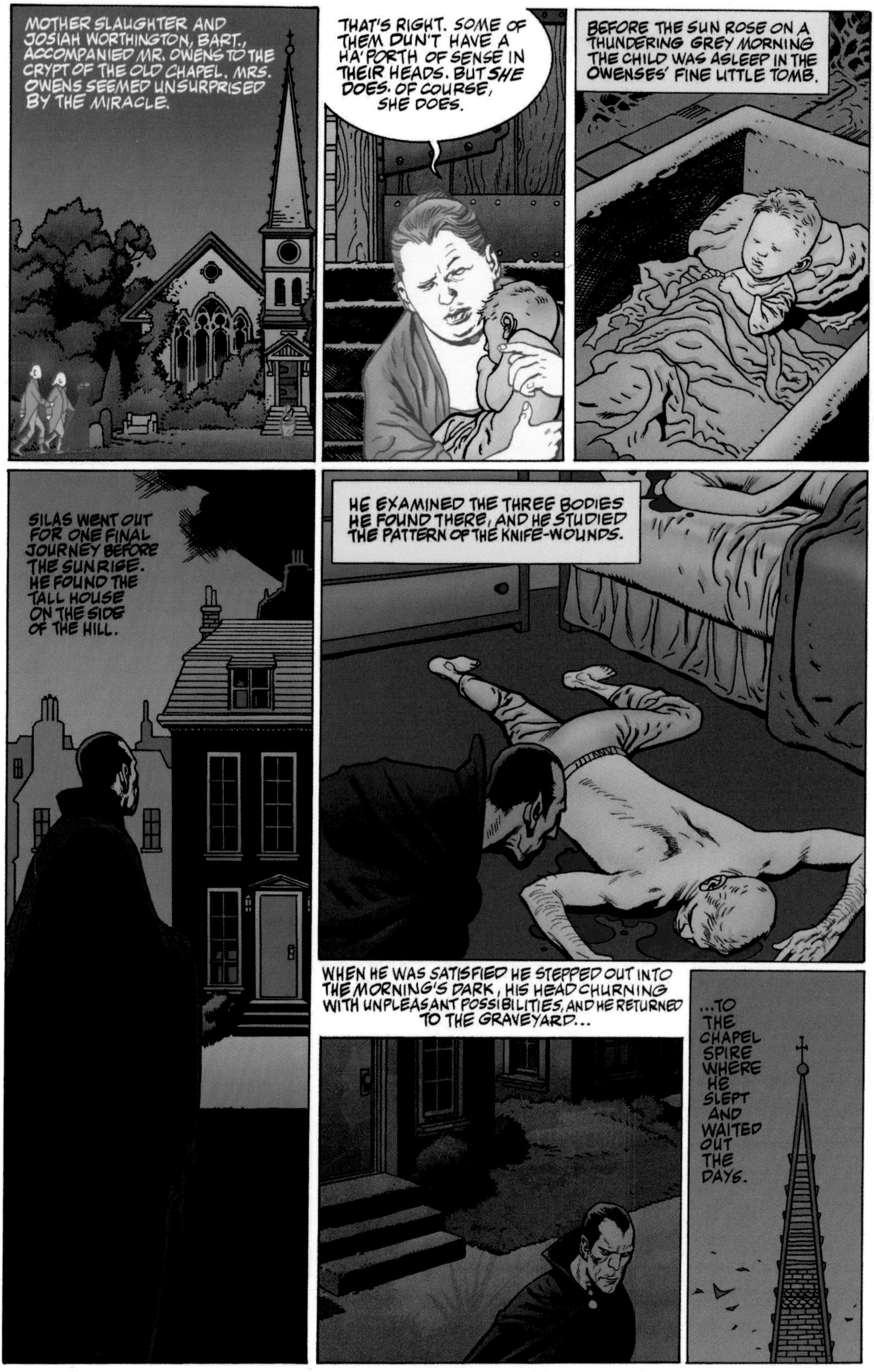
MOTHER SLAUGHTER AND JOSIAH WORTHINGTON, BART., ACCOMPANIED MR. OWENS TO THE CRYPT OF THE OLD CHAPEL. MRS. OWENS SEEMED UNSURPRISED BY THE MIRACLE.
THAT'S RIGHT. SOME OF THEM DUN'T HAVE A HA'PORTH OF SENSE IN THEIR HEADS. BUT SHE DOES. OF COURSE, SHE DOES.
BEFORE THE SUN ROSE ON A THUNDERING GREY MORNING THE CHILD WAS ASLEEP IN THE OWENSES' FINE LITTLE TOMB.
SILAS WENT OUT FOR ONE FINAL JOURNEY BEFORE THE SUNRISE. HE FOUND THE TALL HOUSE ON THE SIDE OF THE HILL.
HE EXAMINED THE THREE BODIES HE FOUND THERE, AND HE STUDIED THE PATTERN OF THE KNIFE-WOUNDS.
WHEN HE WAS SATISFIED HE STEPPED OUT INTO THE MORNING'S DARK, HIS HEAD CHURNING WITH UNPLEASANT POSSIBILITIES, AND HE RETURNED TO THE GRAVEYARD...
...TO THE CHAPEL SPIRE WHERE HE SLEPT AND WAITED OUT THE DAYS.

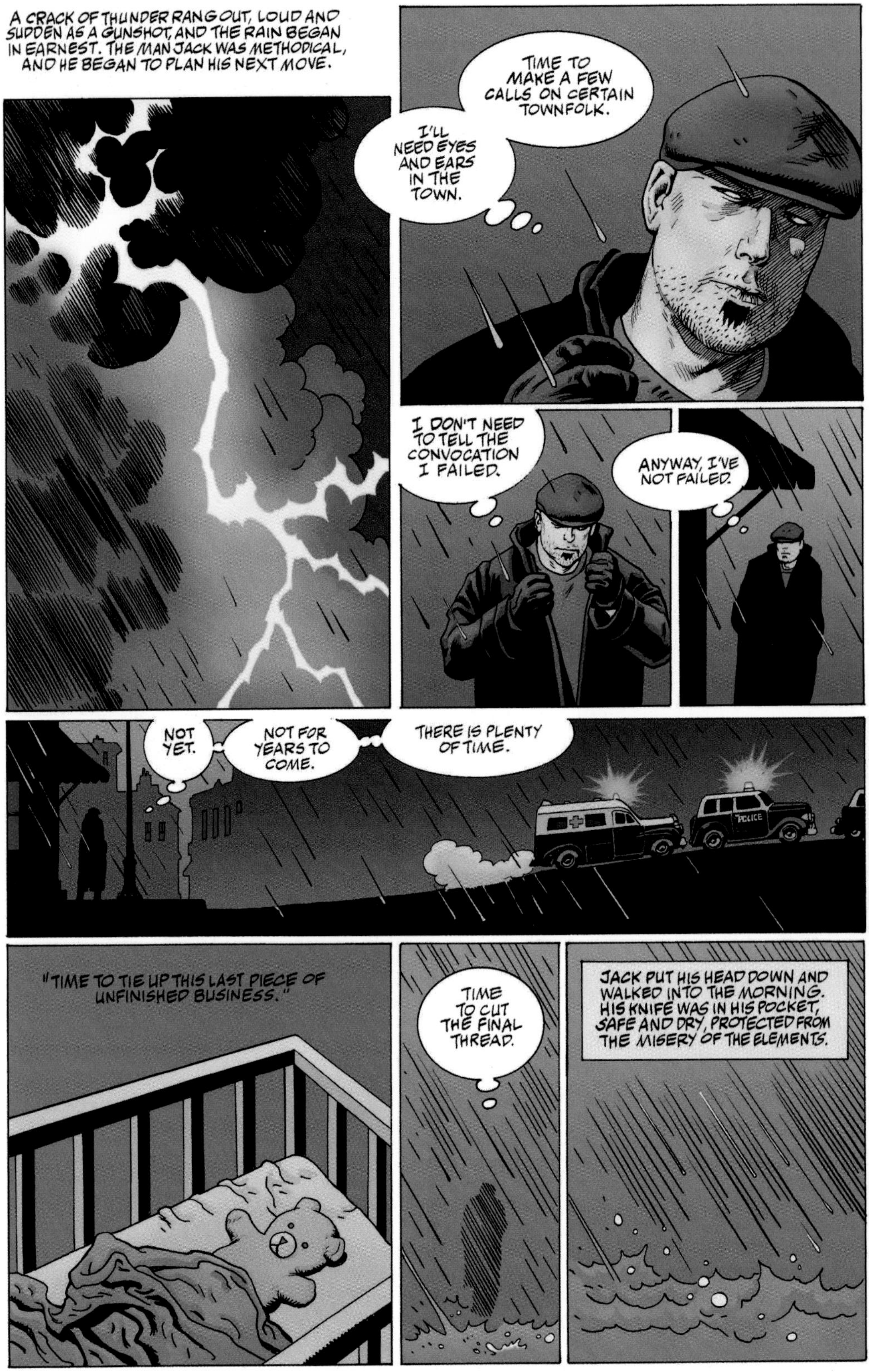
A CRACK OF THUNDER RANG OUT, LOUD AND SUDDEN AS A GUNSHOT, AND THE RAIN BEGAN IN EARNEST. THE MAN JACK WAS METHODICAL, AND HE BEGAN TO PLAN HIS NEXT MOVE.
TIME TO MAKE A FEW CALLS ON CERTAIN TOWNFOLK.
I'LL NEED EYES AND EARS IN THE TOWN.
I DON'T NEED TO TELL THE CONVOCATION I FAILED.
ANYWAY, I'VE NOT FAILED.
NOT YET.
NOT FOR YEARS TO COME.
THERE IS PLENTY OF TIME.
POLICE
"TIME TO TIE UP THIS LAST PIECE OF UNFINISHED BUSINESS."
TIME TO CUT THE FINAL THREAD.
JACK PUT HIS HEAD DOWN AND WALKED INTO THE MORNING. HIS KNIFE WAS IN HIS POCKET, SAFE AND DRY, PROTECTED FROM THE MISERY OF THE ELEMENTS.

2
The New Friend

Illustrated by P. Craig Russell

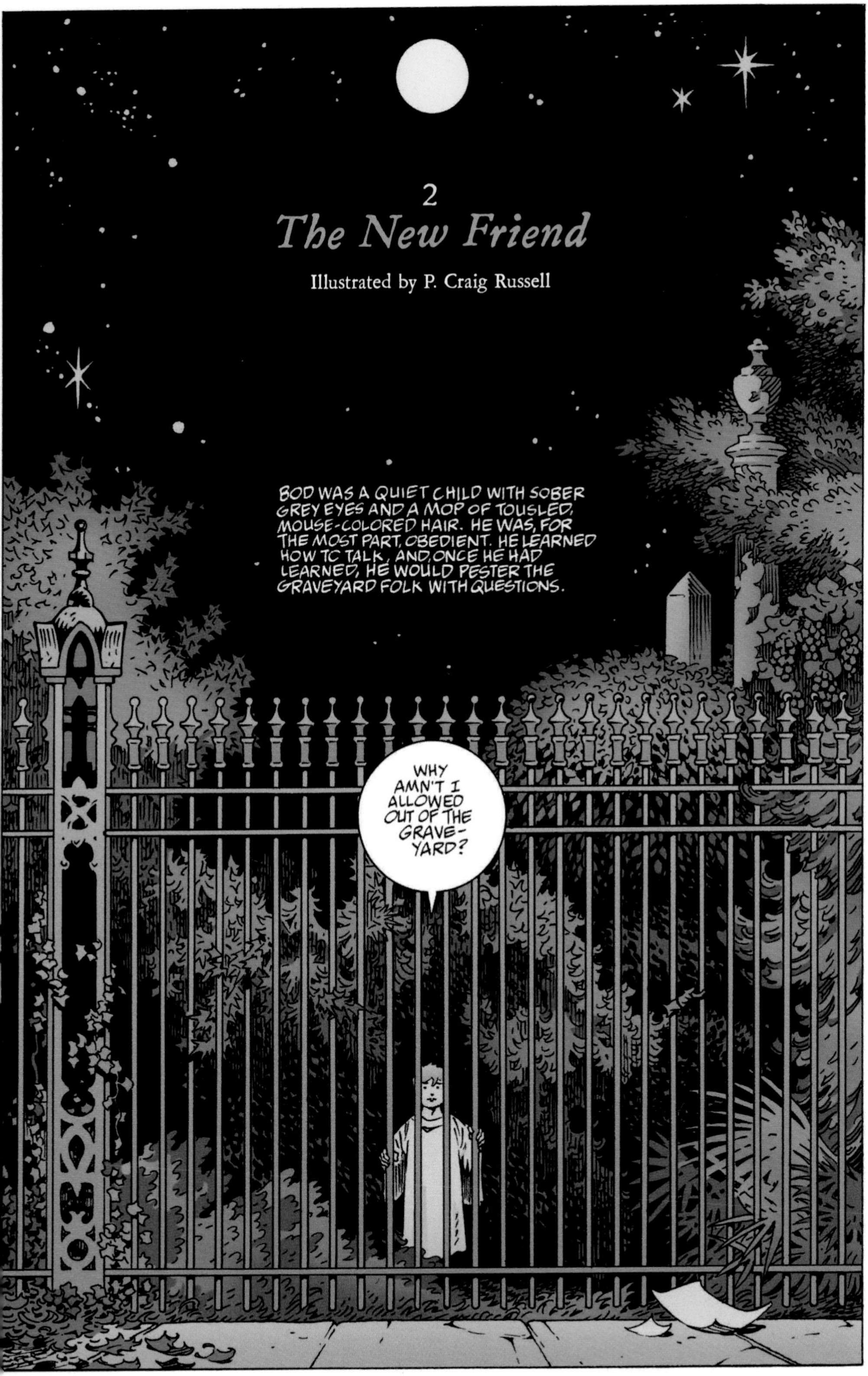
BOD WAS A QUIET CHILD WITH SOBER GREY EYES AND A MOP OF TOUSLED, MOUSE-COLORED HAIR. HE WAS, FOR THE MOST PART, OBEDIENT. HE LEARNED HOW TO TALK, AND, ONCE HE HAD LEARNED, HE WOULD PESTER THE GRAVEYARD FOLK WITH QUESTIONS.
WHY AMN'T I ALLOWED OUT OF THE GRAVE-YARD?

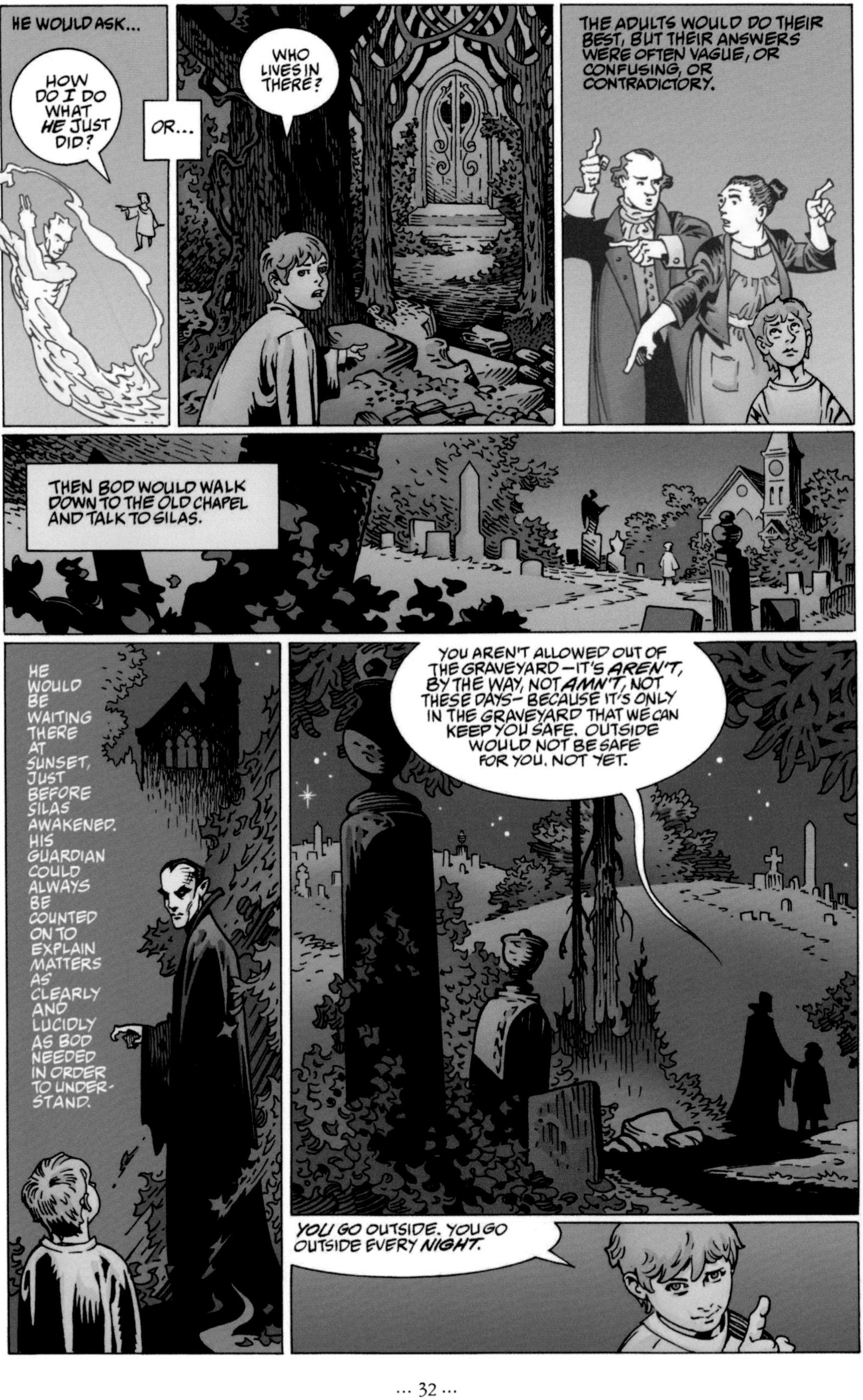
HE WOULD ASK...
HOW DO I DO WHAT HE JUST DID?
OR...
WHO LIVES IN THERE?
THE ADULTS WOULD DO THEIR BEST, BUT THEIR ANSWERS WERE OFTEN VAGUE, OR CONFUSING, OR CONTRADICTORY.
THEN BOD WOULD WALK DOWN TO THE OLD CHAPEL AND TALK TO SILAS.
HE WOULD BE WAITING THERE AT SUNSET, JUST BEFORE SILAS AWAKENED. HIS GUARDIAN COULD ALWAYS BE COUNTED ON TO EXPLAIN MATTERS AS CLEARLY AND LUCIDLY AS BOD NEEDED IN ORDER TO UNDER-STAND.
YOU AREN'T ALLOWED OUT OF THE GRAVEYARD—IT'S AREN'T, BY THE WAY, NOT AMN'T, NOT THESE DAYS—BECAUSE IT'S ONLY IN THE GRAVEYARD THAT WE CAN KEEP YOU SAFE. OUTSIDE WOULD NOT BE SAFE FOR YOU. NOT YET.
YOU GO OUTSIDE. YOU GO OUTSIDE EVERY NIGHT.

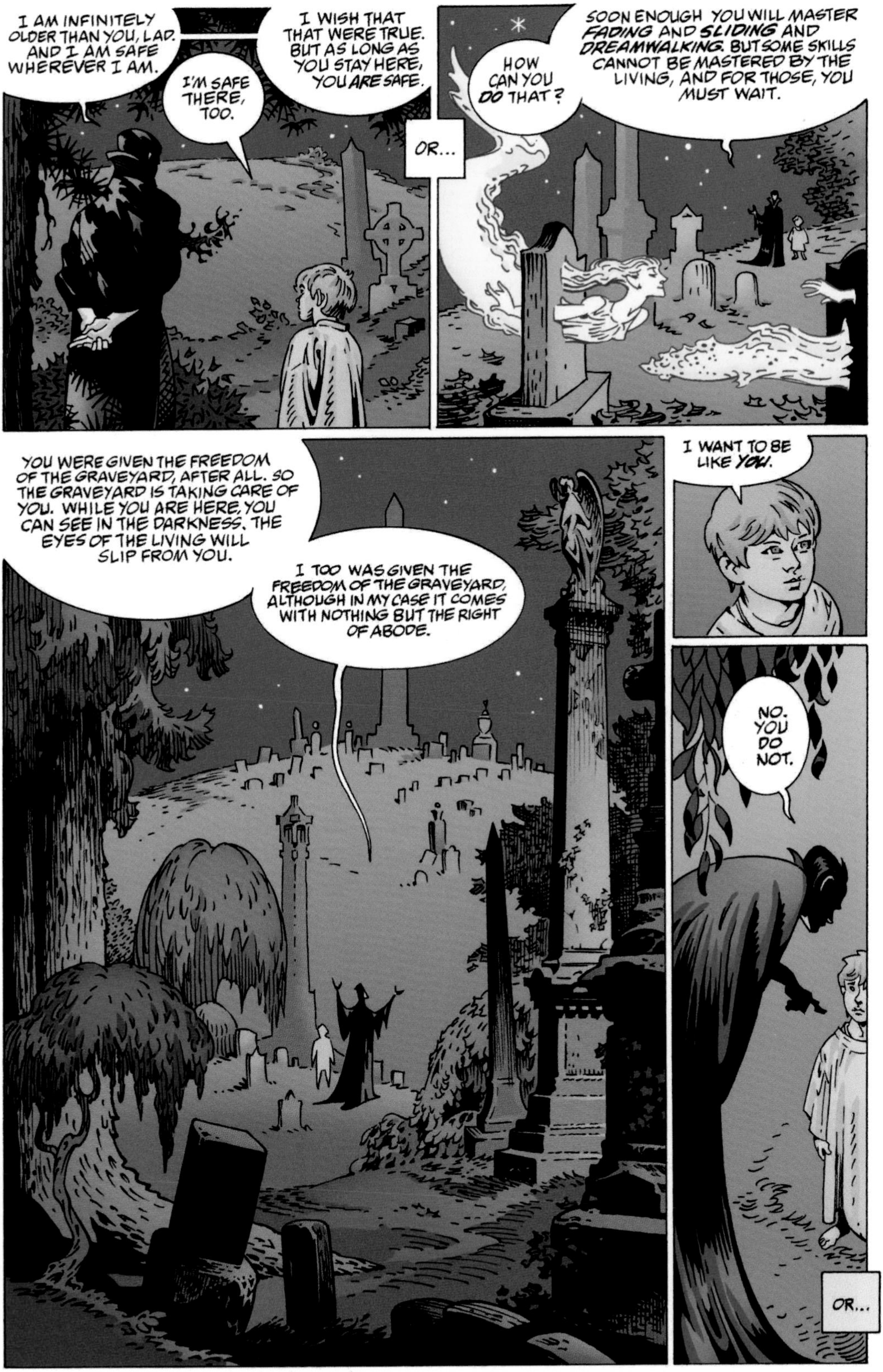
I AM INFINITELY OLDER THAN YOU, LAD. AND I AM SAFE WHEREVER I AM.
I'M SAFE THERE, TOO.
I WISH THAT THAT WERE TRUE. BUT AS LONG AS YOU STAY HERE, YOU *ARE* SAFE.
OR...
HOW CAN YOU *DO* THAT?
SOON ENOUGH YOU WILL MASTER *FADING* AND *SLIDING* AND *DREAMWALKING*. BUT SOME SKILLS CANNOT BE MASTERED BY THE LIVING, AND FOR THOSE, YOU MUST WAIT.
YOU WERE GIVEN THE FREEDOM OF THE GRAVEYARD, AFTER ALL. SO THE GRAVEYARD IS TAKING CARE OF YOU. WHILE YOU ARE HERE, YOU CAN SEE IN THE DARKNESS. THE EYES OF THE LIVING WILL SLIP FROM YOU.
I TOO WAS GIVEN THE FREEDOM OF THE GRAVEYARD, ALTHOUGH IN MY CASE IT COMES WITH NOTHING BUT THE RIGHT OF ABODE.
I WANT TO BE LIKE *YOU*.
NO. YOU DO NOT.
OR...

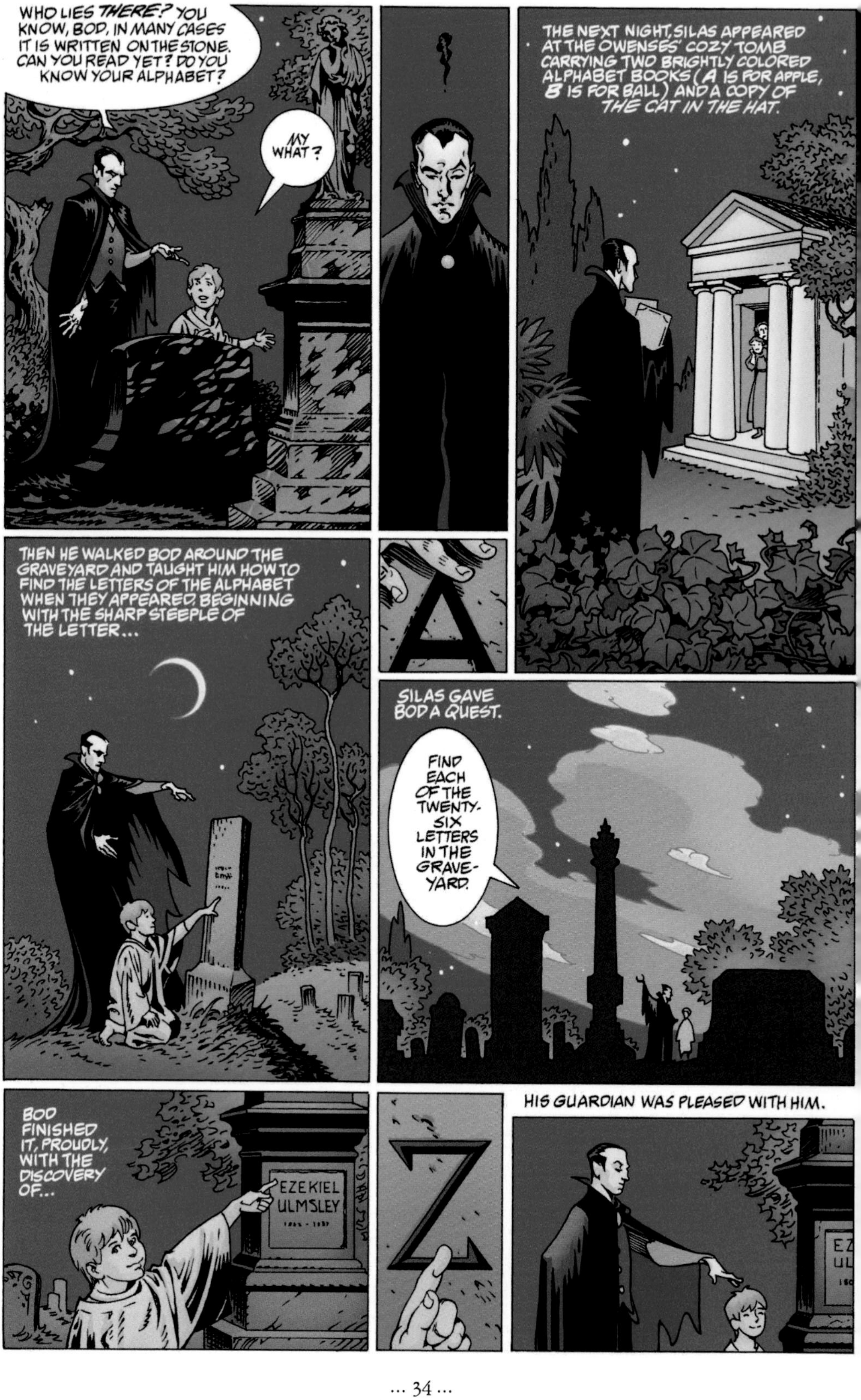
WHO LIES THERE? YOU KNOW, BOD, IN MANY CASES IT IS WRITTEN ON THE STONE. CAN YOU READ YET? DO YOU KNOW YOUR ALPHABET?
MY WHAT?
THE NEXT NIGHT, SILAS APPEARED AT THE OWENSES' COZY TOMB CARRYING TWO BRIGHTLY COLORED ALPHABET BOOKS (A IS FOR APPLE, B IS FOR BALL) AND A COPY OF THE CAT IN THE HAT.
THEN HE WALKED BOD AROUND THE GRAVEYARD AND TAUGHT HIM HOW TO FIND THE LETTERS OF THE ALPHABET WHEN THEY APPEARED, BEGINNING WITH THE SHARP STEEPLE OF THE LETTER...
A
SILAS GAVE BOD A QUEST.
FIND EACH OF THE TWENTY-SIX LETTERS IN THE GRAVEYARD.
BOD FINISHED IT, PROUDLY, WITH THE DISCOVERY OF...
EZEKIEL ULMSLEY
Z
HIS GUARDIAN WAS PLEASED WITH HIM.

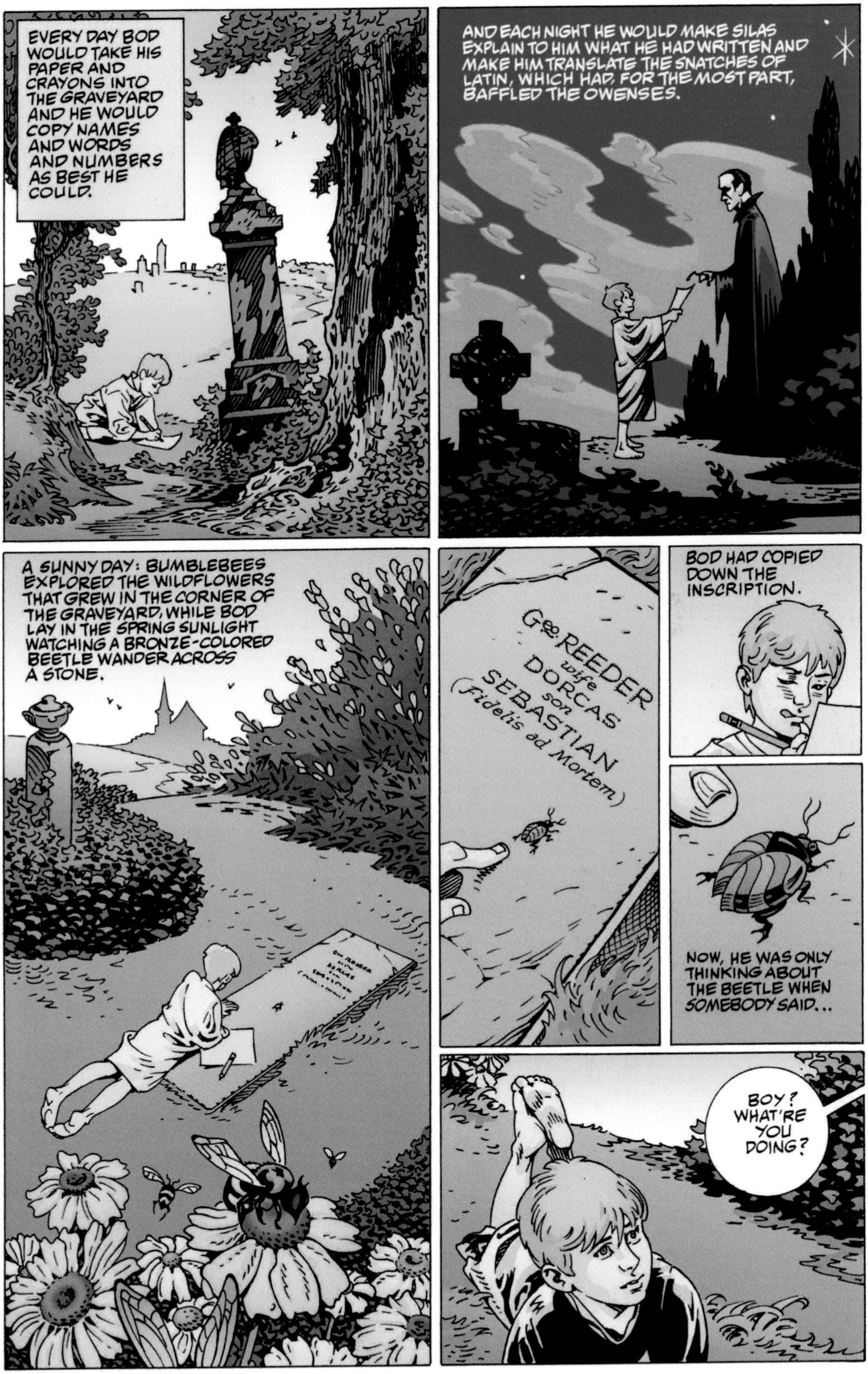
EVERY DAY BOD WOULD TAKE HIS PAPER AND CRAYONS INTO THE GRAVEYARD AND HE WOULD COPY NAMES AND WORDS AND NUMBERS AS BEST HE COULD.
AND EACH NIGHT HE WOULD MAKE SILAS EXPLAIN TO HIM WHAT HE HAD WRITTEN AND MAKE HIM TRANSLATE THE SNATCHES OF LATIN, WHICH HAD, FOR THE MOST PART, BAFFLED THE OWENSES.
A SUNNY DAY: BUMBLEBEES EXPLORED THE WILDFLOWERS THAT GREW IN THE CORNER OF THE GRAVEYARD, WHILE BOD LAY IN THE SPRING SUNLIGHT WATCHING A BRONZE-COLORED BEETLE WANDER ACROSS A STONE.
Geo. REEDER
wife
DORCAS
son
SEBASTIAN
(Fidelis ad Mortem)
BOD HAD COPIED DOWN THE INSCRIPTION.
NOW, HE WAS ONLY THINKING ABOUT THE BEETLE WHEN SOMEBODY SAID...
BOY? WHAT'RE YOU DOING?

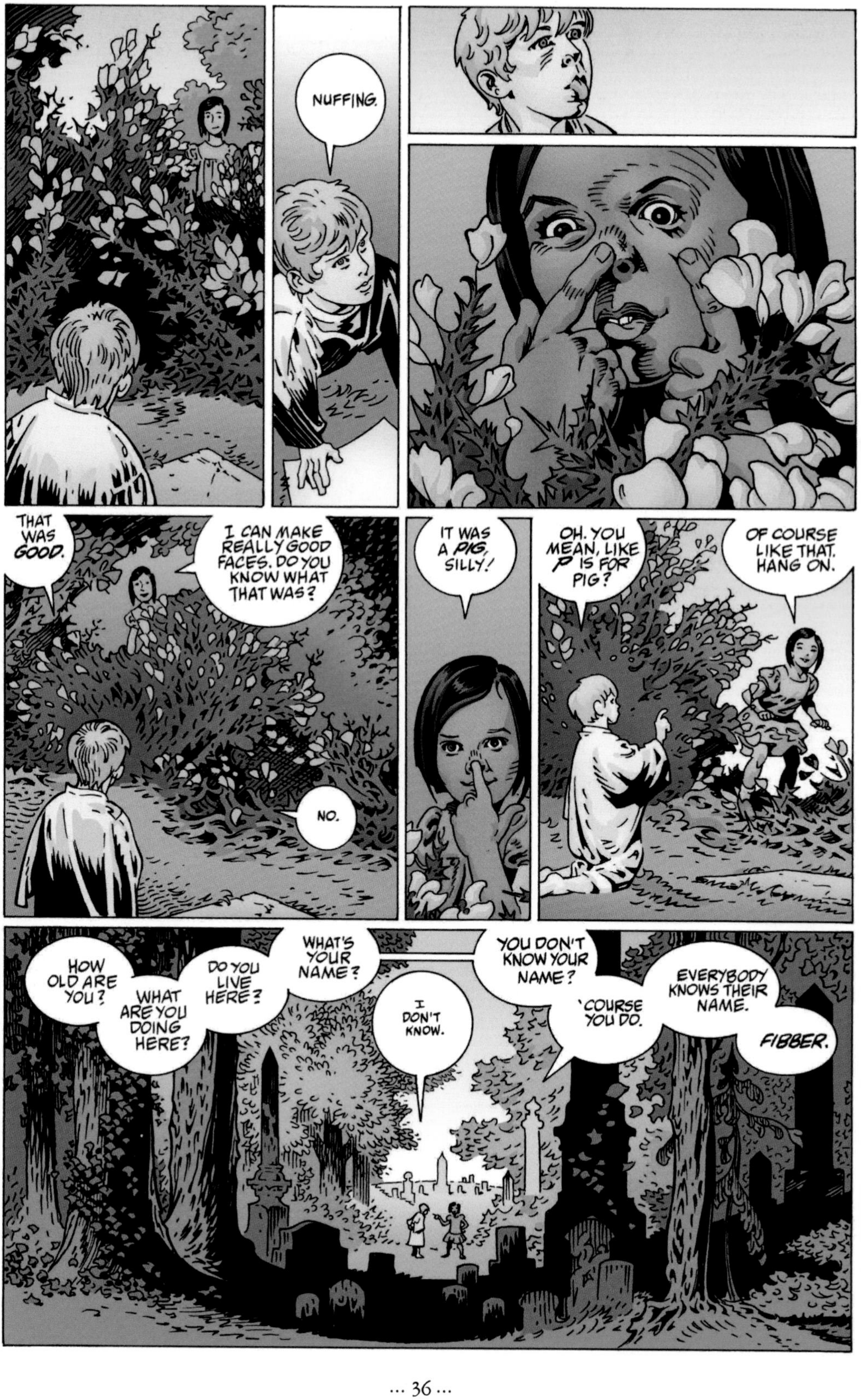
NUFFING.
THAT WAS GOOD.
I CAN MAKE REALLY GOOD FACES. DO YOU KNOW WHAT THAT WAS?
NO.
IT WAS A PIG, SILLY!
OH. YOU MEAN, LIKE P IS FOR PIG?
OF COURSE LIKE THAT. HANG ON.
HOW OLD ARE YOU?
WHAT ARE YOU DOING HERE?
DO YOU LIVE HERE?
WHAT'S YOUR NAME?
I DON'T KNOW.
YOU DON'T KNOW YOUR NAME?
`COURSE YOU DO.
EVERYBODY KNOWS THEIR NAME.
FIBBER.

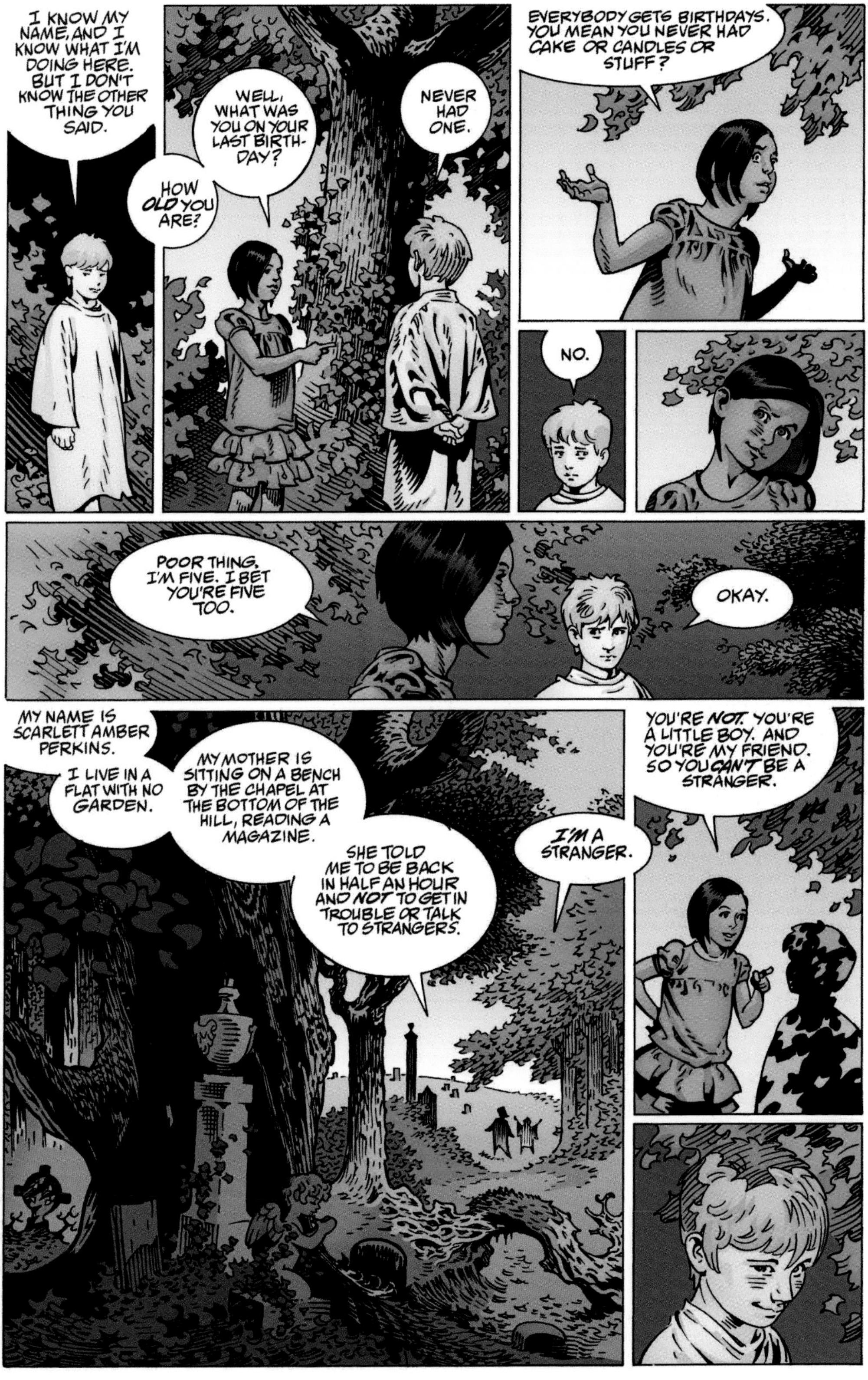
I KNOW MY NAME, AND I KNOW WHAT I'M DOING HERE. BUT I DON'T KNOW THE OTHER THING YOU SAID.
HOW OLD YOU ARE?
WELL, WHAT WAS YOU ON YOUR LAST BIRTH-DAY?
NEVER HAD ONE.
EVERYBODY GETS BIRTHDAYS. YOU MEAN YOU NEVER HAD CAKE OR CANDLES OR STUFF?
NO.
POOR THING. I'M FIVE. I BET YOU'RE FIVE TOO.
OKAY.
MY NAME IS SCARLETT AMBER PERKINS.
I LIVE IN A FLAT WITH NO GARDEN.
MY MOTHER IS SITTING ON A BENCH BY THE CHAPEL AT THE BOTTOM OF THE HILL, READING A MAGAZINE.
SHE TOLD ME TO BE BACK IN HALF AN HOUR AND NOT TO GET IN TROUBLE OR TALK TO STRANGERS.
I'M A STRANGER.
YOU'RE NOT. YOU'RE A LITTLE BOY. AND YOU'RE MY FRIEND. SO YOU CAN'T BE A STRANGER.

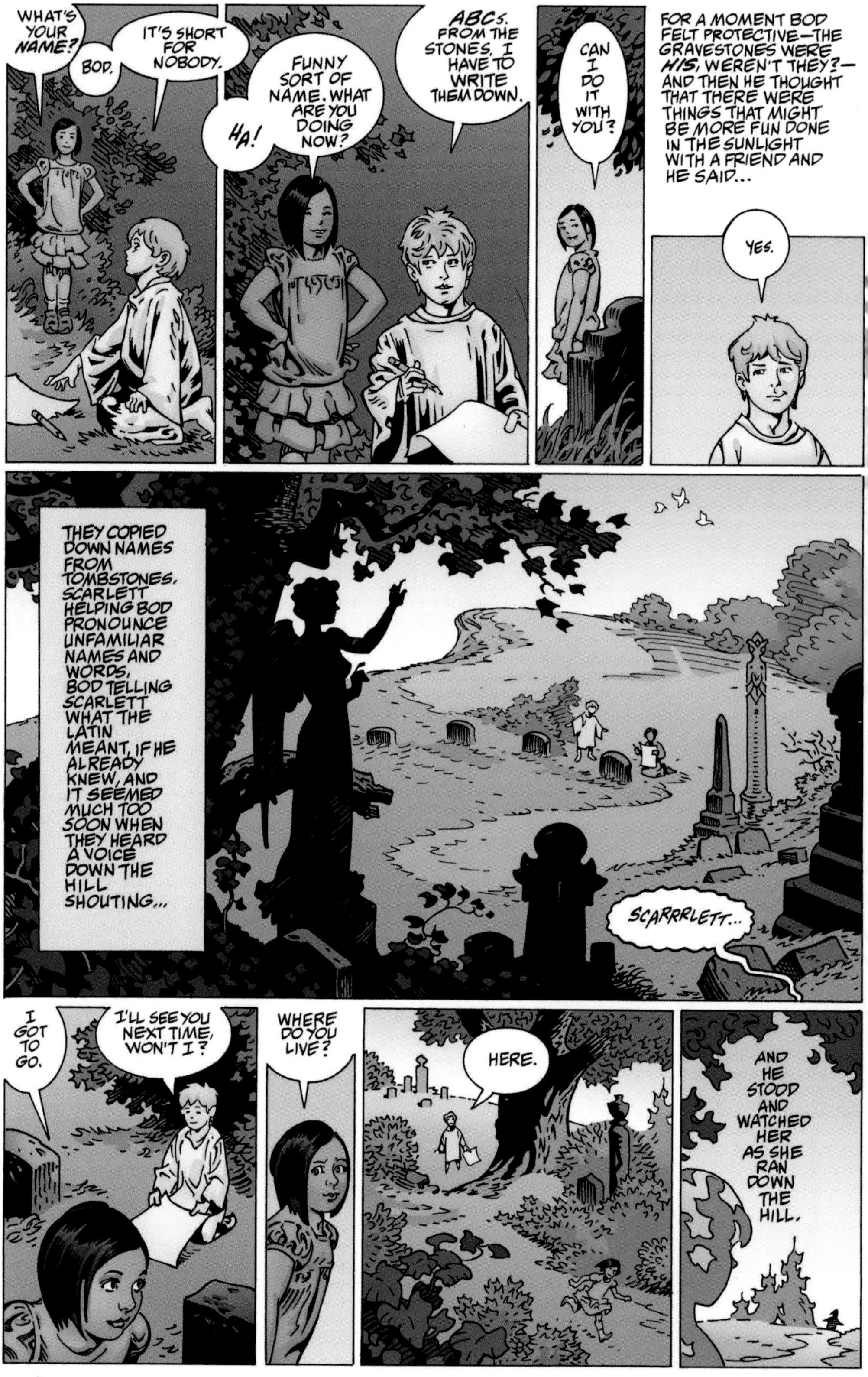
WHAT'S YOUR NAME?
BOD.
IT'S SHORT FOR NOBODY.
HA!
FUNNY SORT OF NAME. WHAT ARE YOU DOING NOW?
ABCs. FROM THE STONES. I HAVE TO WRITE THEM DOWN.
CAN I DO IT WITH YOU?
FOR A MOMENT BOD FELT PROTECTIVE—THE GRAVESTONES WERE HIS, WEREN'T THEY?—AND THEN HE THOUGHT THAT THERE WERE THINGS THAT MIGHT BE MORE FUN DONE IN THE SUNLIGHT WITH A FRIEND AND HE SAID...
YES.
THEY COPIED DOWN NAMES FROM TOMBSTONES, SCARLETT HELPING BOD PRONOUNCE UNFAMILIAR NAMES AND WORDS, BOD TELLING SCARLETT WHAT THE LATIN MEANT, IF HE ALREADY KNEW, AND IT SEEMED MUCH TOO SOON WHEN THEY HEARD A VOICE DOWN THE HILL SHOUTING...
SCARRRLETT...
I GOT TO GO.
I'LL SEE YOU NEXT TIME, WON'T I?
WHERE DO YOU LIVE?
HERE.
AND HE STOOD AND WATCHED HER AS SHE RAN DOWN THE HILL.

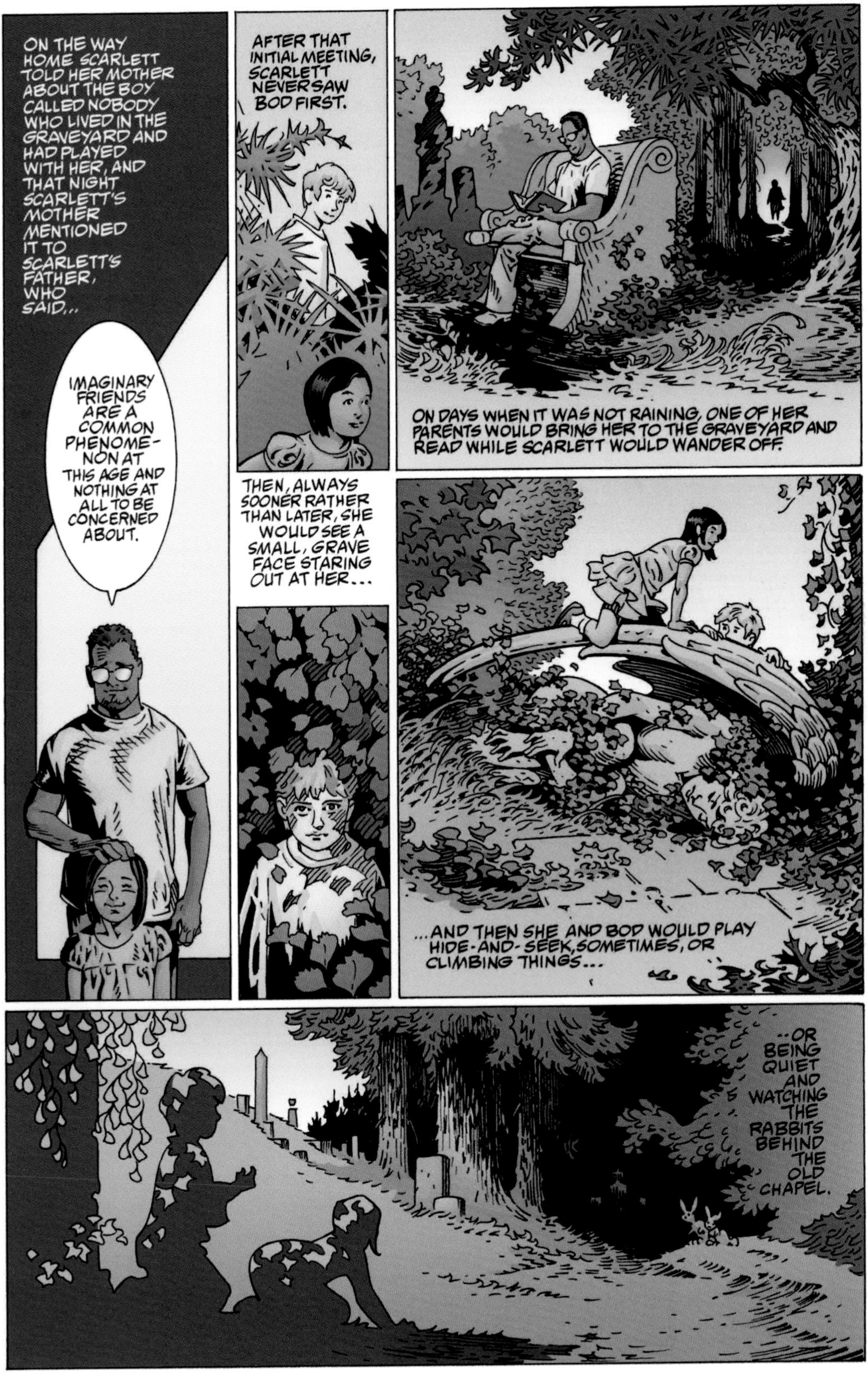
ON THE WAY HOME SCARLETT TOLD HER MOTHER ABOUT THE BOY CALLED NOBODY WHO LIVED IN THE GRAVEYARD AND HAD PLAYED WITH HER, AND THAT NIGHT SCARLETT'S MOTHER MENTIONED IT TO SCARLETT'S FATHER, WHO SAID...
IMAGINARY FRIENDS ARE A COMMON PHENOMENON AT THIS AGE AND NOTHING AT ALL TO BE CONCERNED ABOUT.
AFTER THAT INITIAL MEETING, SCARLETT NEVER SAW BOD FIRST.
ON DAYS WHEN IT WAS NOT RAINING, ONE OF HER PARENTS WOULD BRING HER TO THE GRAVEYARD AND READ WHILE SCARLETT WOULD WANDER OFF.
THEN, ALWAYS SOONER RATHER THAN LATER, SHE WOULD SEE A SMALL, GRAVE FACE STARING OUT AT HER...
...AND THEN SHE AND BOD WOULD PLAY HIDE-AND-SEEK, SOMETIMES, OR CLIMBING THINGS...
...OR BEING QUIET AND WATCHING THE RABBITS BEHIND THE OLD CHAPEL.

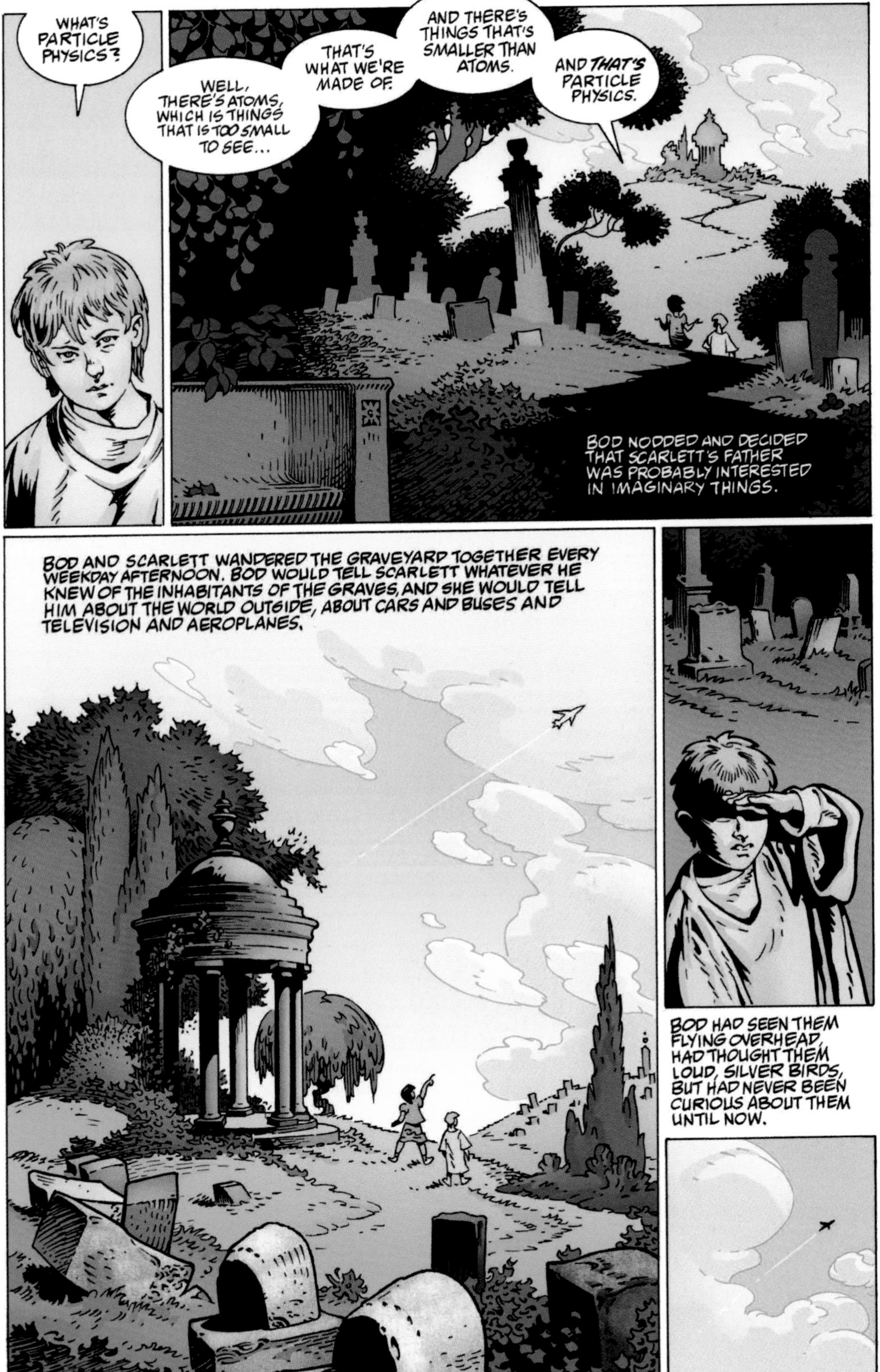
WHAT'S PARTICLE PHYSICS?
WELL, THERE'S ATOMS, WHICH IS THINGS THAT IS TOO SMALL TO SEE...
THAT'S WHAT WE'RE MADE OF.
AND THERE'S THINGS THAT'S SMALLER THAN ATOMS.
AND THAT'S PARTICLE PHYSICS.
BOD NODDED AND DECIDED THAT SCARLETT'S FATHER WAS PROBABLY INTERESTED IN IMAGINARY THINGS.
BOD AND SCARLETT WANDERED THE GRAVEYARD TOGETHER EVERY WEEKDAY AFTERNOON. BOD WOULD TELL SCARLETT WHATEVER HE KNEW OF THE INHABITANTS OF THE GRAVES, AND SHE WOULD TELL HIM ABOUT THE WORLD OUTSIDE, ABOUT CARS AND BUSES AND TELEVISION AND AEROPLANES.
BOD HAD SEEN THEM FLYING OVERHEAD, HAD THOUGHT THEM LOUD, SILVER BIRDS, BUT HAD NEVER BEEN CURIOUS ABOUT THEM UNTIL NOW.

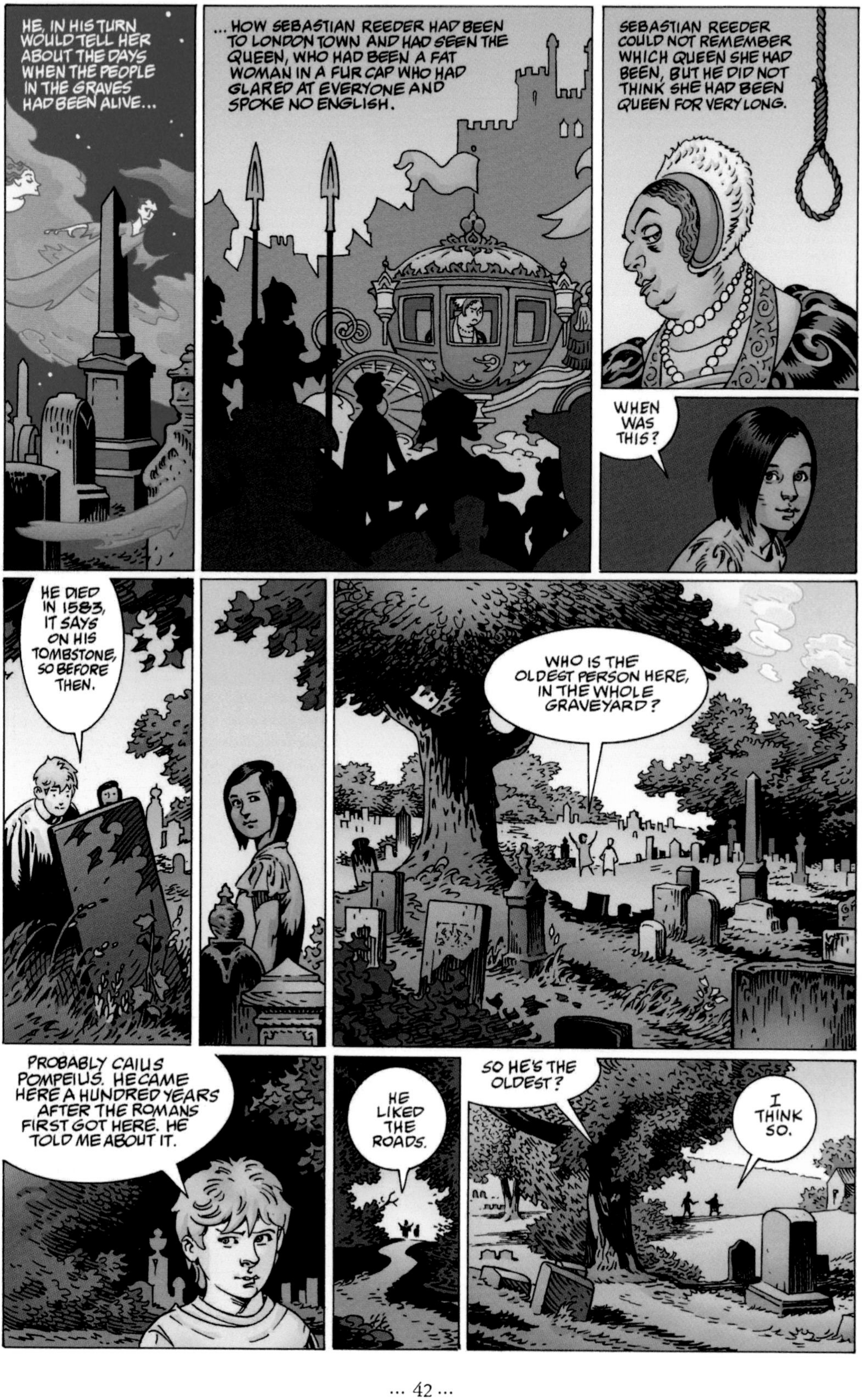
HE, IN HIS TURN WOULD TELL HER ABOUT THE DAYS WHEN THE PEOPLE IN THE GRAVES HAD BEEN ALIVE...
...HOW SEBASTIAN REEDER HAD BEEN TO LONDON TOWN AND HAD SEEN THE QUEEN, WHO HAD BEEN A FAT WOMAN IN A FUR CAP WHO HAD GLARED AT EVERYONE AND SPOKE NO ENGLISH.
SEBASTIAN REEDER COULD NOT REMEMBER WHICH QUEEN SHE HAD BEEN, BUT HE DID NOT THINK SHE HAD BEEN QUEEN FOR VERY LONG.
WHEN WAS THIS?
HE DIED IN 1583, IT SAYS ON HIS TOMBSTONE, SO BEFORE THEN.
WHO IS THE OLDEST PERSON HERE, IN THE WHOLE GRAVEYARD?
PROBABLY CAIUS POMPEIUS. HE CAME HERE A HUNDRED YEARS AFTER THE ROMANS FIRST GOT HERE. HE TOLD ME ABOUT IT.
HE LIKED THE ROADS.
SO HE'S THE OLDEST?
I THINK SO.

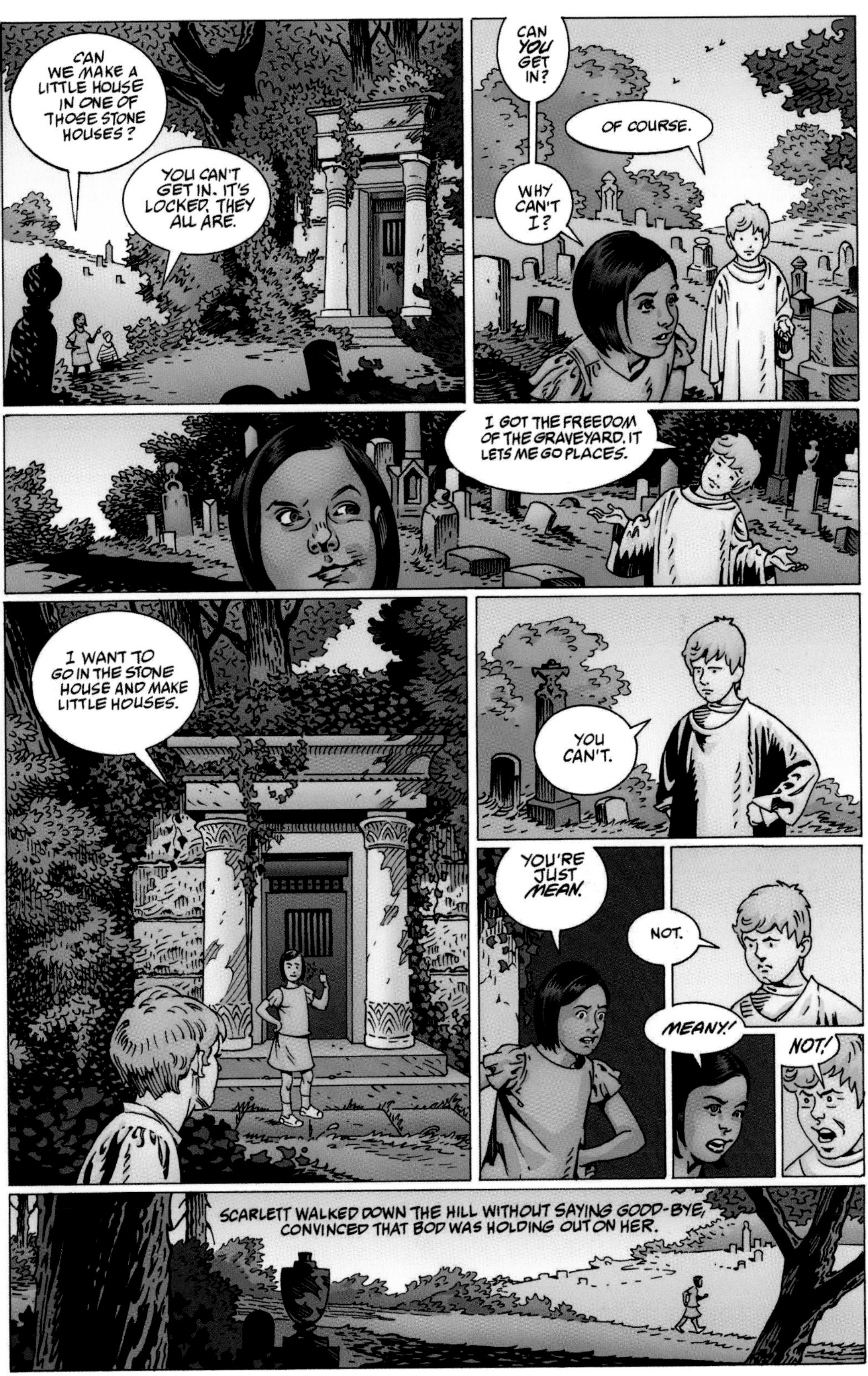
CAN WE MAKE A LITTLE HOUSE IN ONE OF THOSE STONE HOUSES?
YOU CAN'T GET IN. IT'S LOCKED. THEY ALL ARE.
CAN YOU GET IN?
OF COURSE.
WHY CAN'T I?
I GOT THE FREEDOM OF THE GRAVEYARD. IT LETS ME GO PLACES.
I WANT TO GO IN THE STONE HOUSE AND MAKE LITTLE HOUSES.
YOU CAN'T.
YOU'RE JUST MEAN.
NOT.
MEANY!
NOT!
SCARLETT WALKED DOWN THE HILL WITHOUT SAYING GOOD-BYE, CONVINCED THAT BOD WAS HOLDING OUT ON HER.

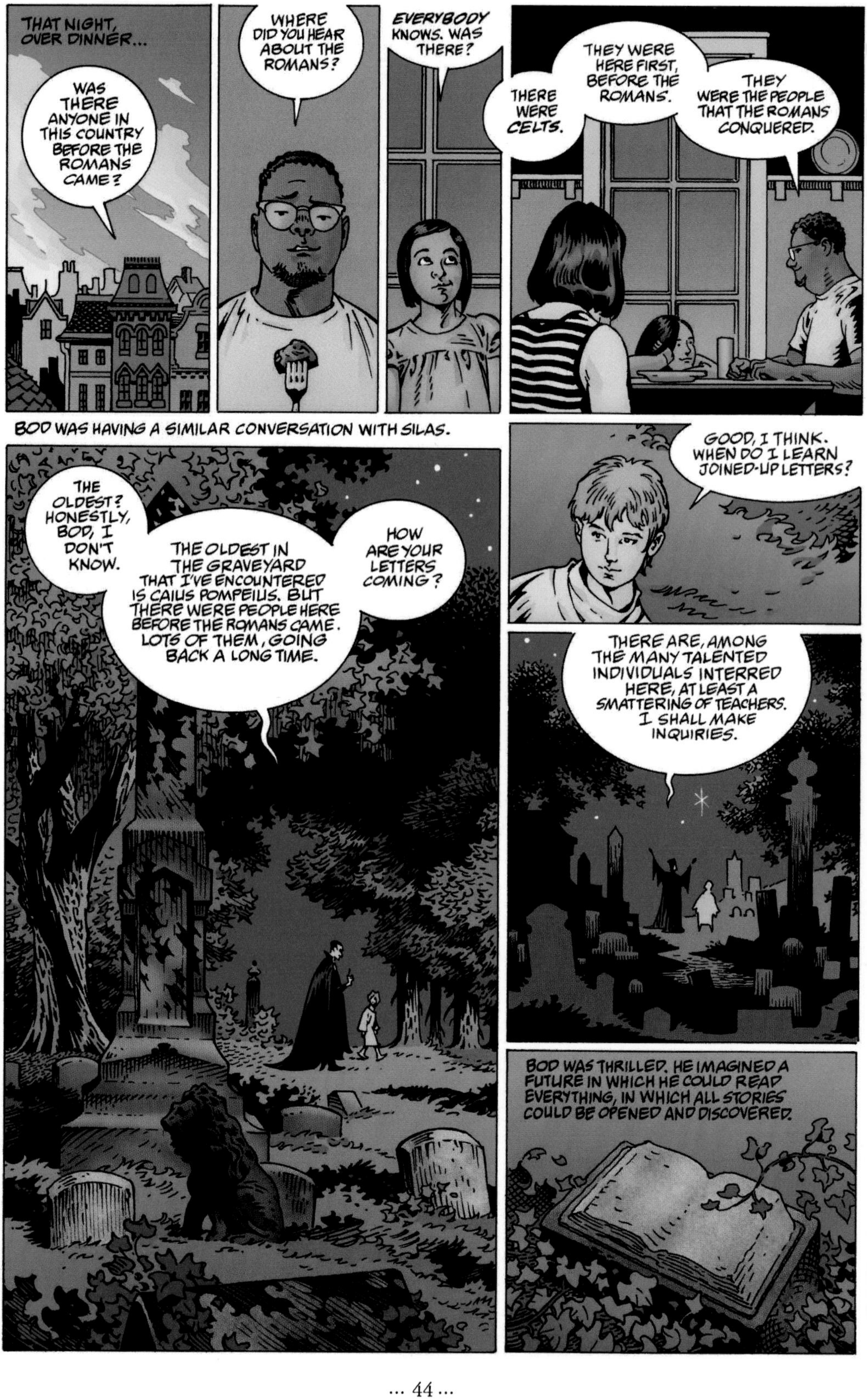
THAT NIGHT, OVER DINNER...
WAS THERE ANYONE IN THIS COUNTRY BEFORE THE ROMANS CAME?
WHERE DID YOU HEAR ABOUT THE ROMANS?
EVERYBODY KNOWS. WAS THERE?
THERE WERE CELTS.
THEY WERE HERE FIRST, BEFORE THE ROMANS.
THEY WERE THE PEOPLE THAT THE ROMANS CONQUERED.
BOD WAS HAVING A SIMILAR CONVERSATION WITH SILAS.
THE OLDEST? HONESTLY, BOD, I DON'T KNOW.
THE OLDEST IN THE GRAVEYARD THAT I'VE ENCOUNTERED IS CAIUS POMPEIUS. BUT THERE WERE PEOPLE HERE BEFORE THE ROMANS CAME. LOTS OF THEM, GOING BACK A LONG TIME.
HOW ARE YOUR LETTERS COMING?
GOOD, I THINK. WHEN DO I LEARN JOINED-UP LETTERS?
THERE ARE, AMONG THE MANY TALENTED INDIVIDUALS INTERRED HERE, AT LEAST A SMATTERING OF TEACHERS. I SHALL MAKE INQUIRIES.
BOD WAS THRILLED. HE IMAGINED A FUTURE IN WHICH HE COULD READ EVERYTHING, IN WHICH ALL STORIES COULD BE OPENED AND DISCOVERED.

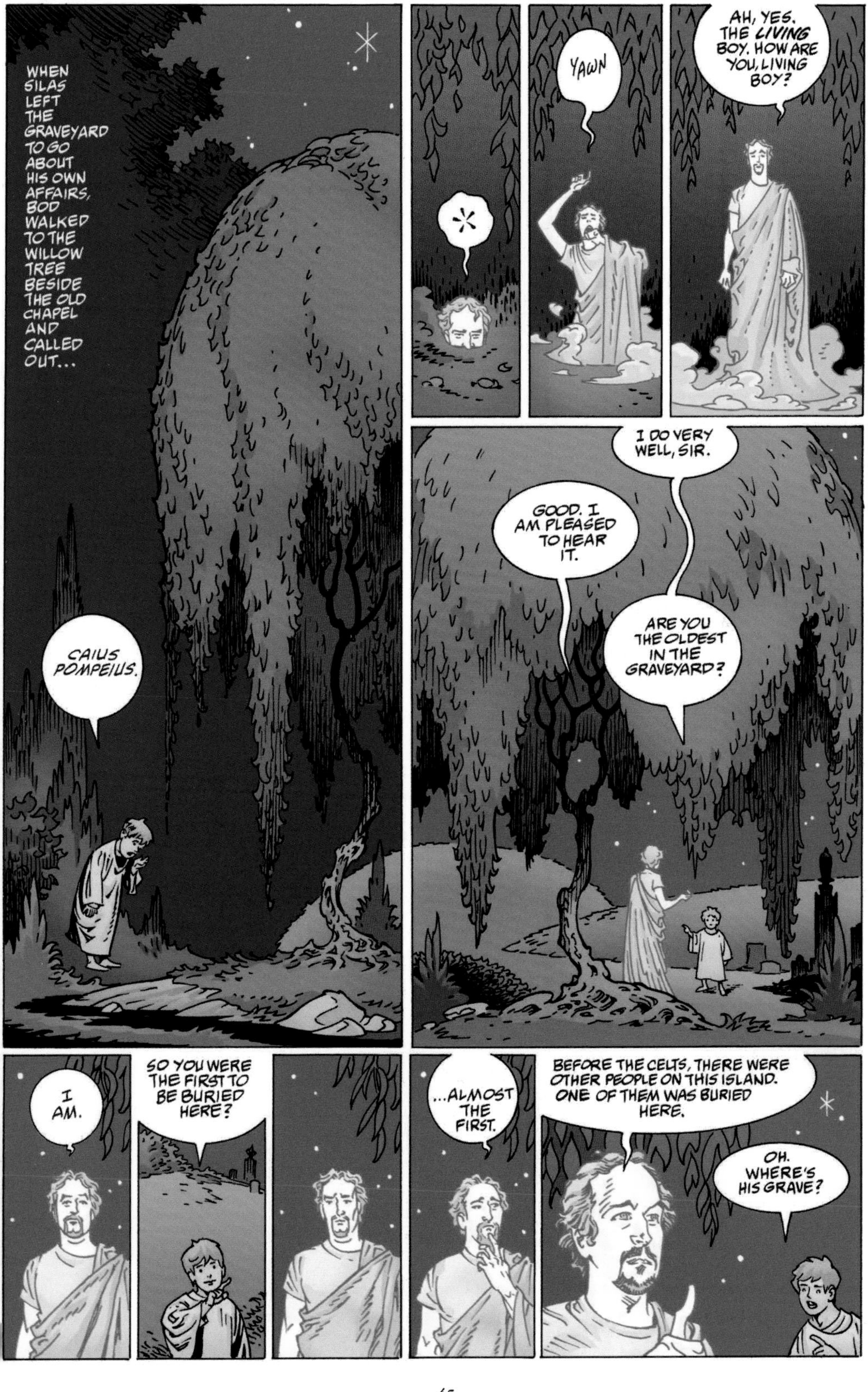
WHEN SILAS LEFT THE GRAVEYARD TO GO ABOUT HIS OWN AFFAIRS, BOD WALKED TO THE WILLOW TREE BESIDE THE OLD CHAPEL AND CALLED OUT...
CAIUS POMPEIUS.
YAWN
AH, YES. THE LIVING BOY. HOW ARE YOU, LIVING BOY?
I DO VERY WELL, SIR.
GOOD. I AM PLEASED TO HEAR IT.
ARE YOU THE OLDEST IN THE GRAVEYARD?
I AM.
SO YOU WERE THE FIRST TO BE BURIED HERE?
...ALMOST THE FIRST.
BEFORE THE CELTS, THERE WERE OTHER PEOPLE ON THIS ISLAND. ONE OF THEM WAS BURIED HERE.
OH. WHERE'S HIS GRAVE?

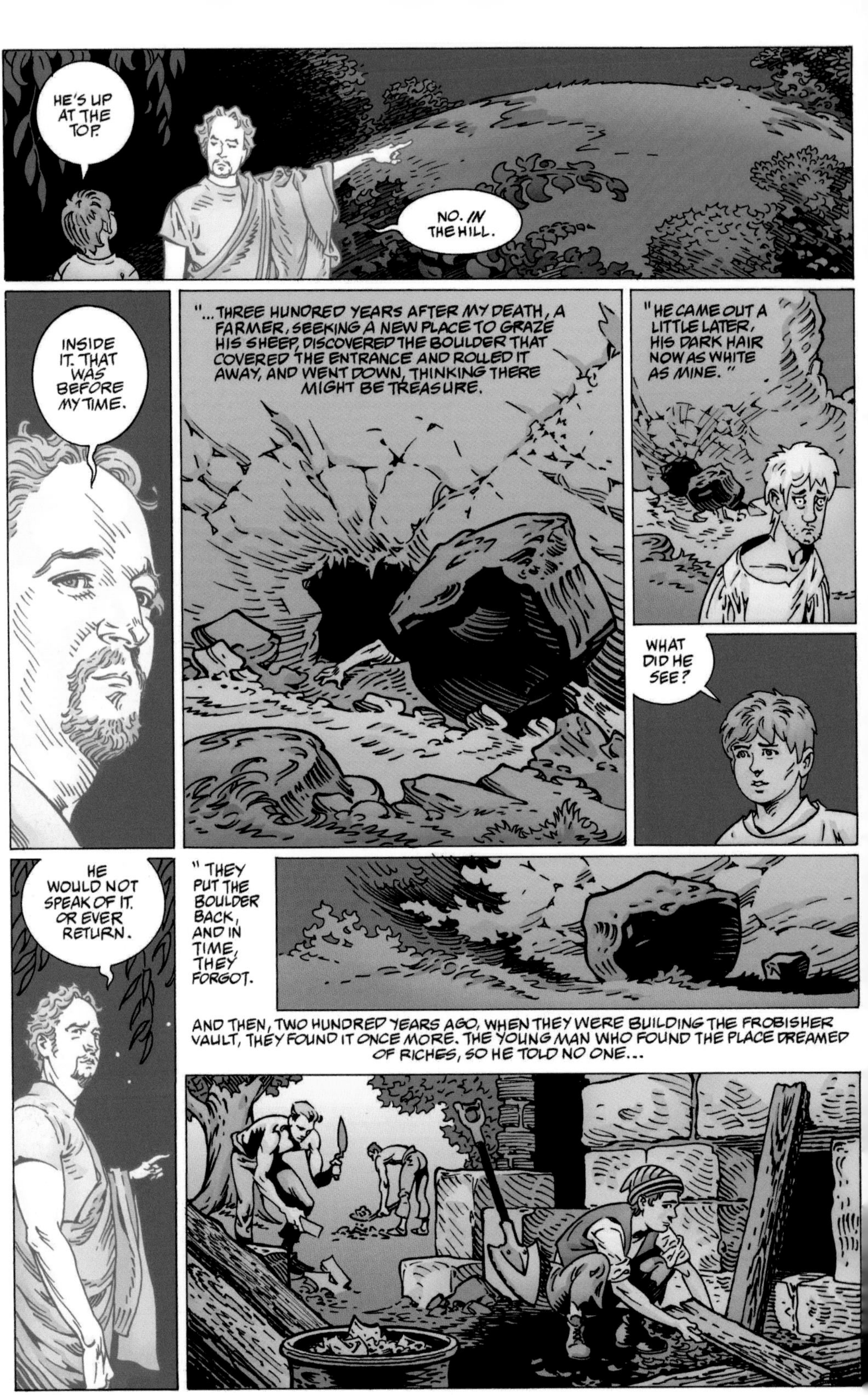
HE'S UP AT THE TOP?
NO. IN THE HILL.
INSIDE IT. THAT WAS BEFORE MY TIME.
"...THREE HUNDRED YEARS AFTER MY DEATH, A FARMER, SEEKING A NEW PLACE TO GRAZE HIS SHEEP, DISCOVERED THE BOULDER THAT COVERED THE ENTRANCE AND ROLLED IT AWAY, AND WENT DOWN, THINKING THERE MIGHT BE TREASURE.
"HE CAME OUT A LITTLE LATER, HIS DARK HAIR NOW AS WHITE AS MINE."
WHAT DID HE SEE?
HE WOULD NOT SPEAK OF IT. OR EVER RETURN.
"THEY PUT THE BOULDER BACK, AND IN TIME, THEY FORGOT.
AND THEN, TWO HUNDRED YEARS AGO, WHEN THEY WERE BUILDING THE FROBISHER VAULT, THEY FOUND IT ONCE MORE. THE YOUNG MAN WHO FOUND THE PLACE DREAMED OF RICHES, SO HE TOLD NO ONE...

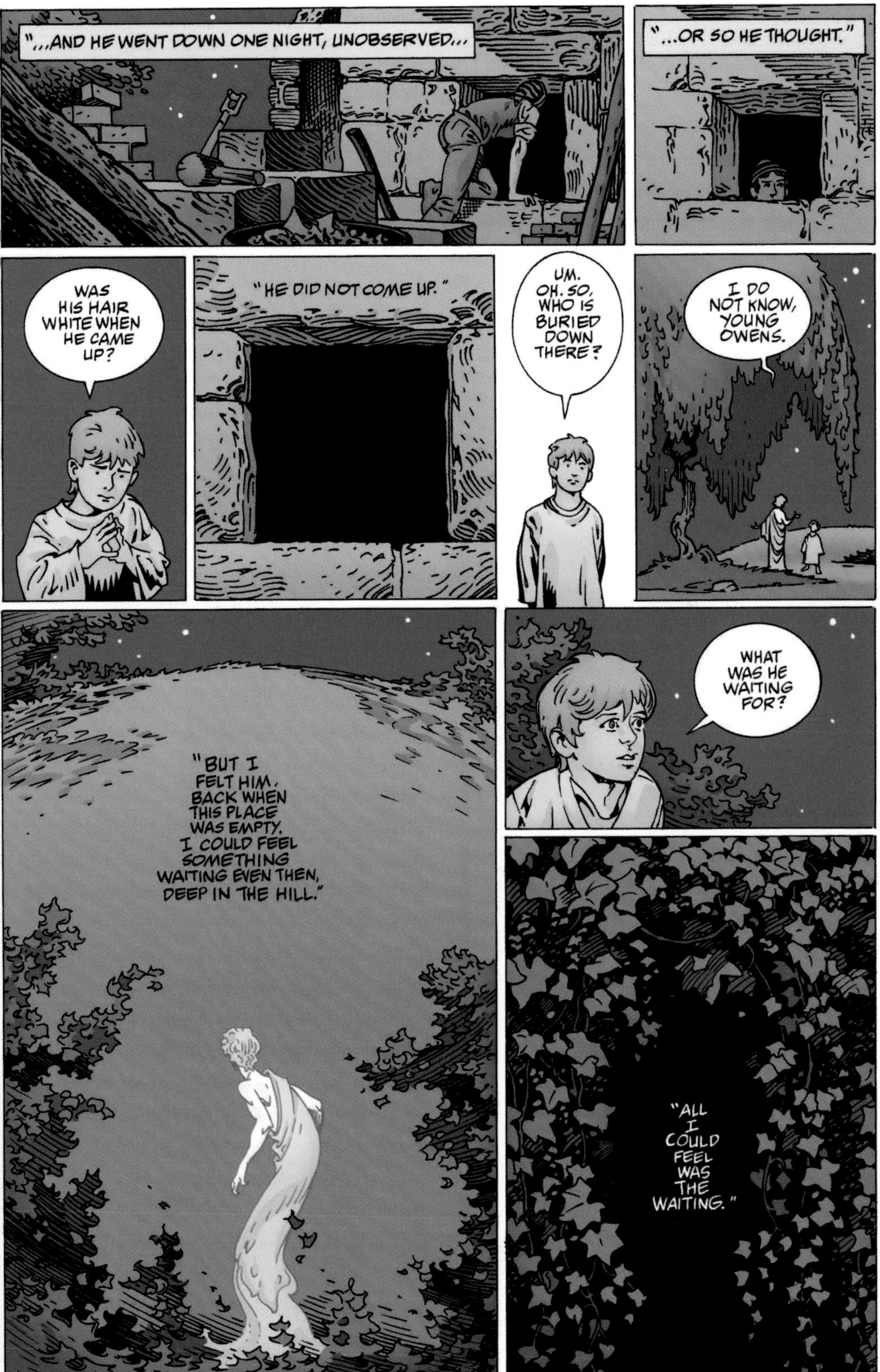
"...AND HE WENT DOWN ONE NIGHT, UNOBSERVED...
"...OR SO HE THOUGHT."
WAS HIS HAIR WHITE WHEN HE CAME UP?
"HE DID NOT COME UP."
UM. OH. SO, WHO IS BURIED DOWN THERE?
I DO NOT KNOW, YOUNG OWENS.
"BUT I FELT HIM, BACK WHEN THIS PLACE WAS EMPTY. I COULD FEEL SOMETHING WAITING EVEN THEN, DEEP IN THE HILL."
WHAT WAS HE WAITING FOR?
"ALL I COULD FEEL WAS THE WAITING."

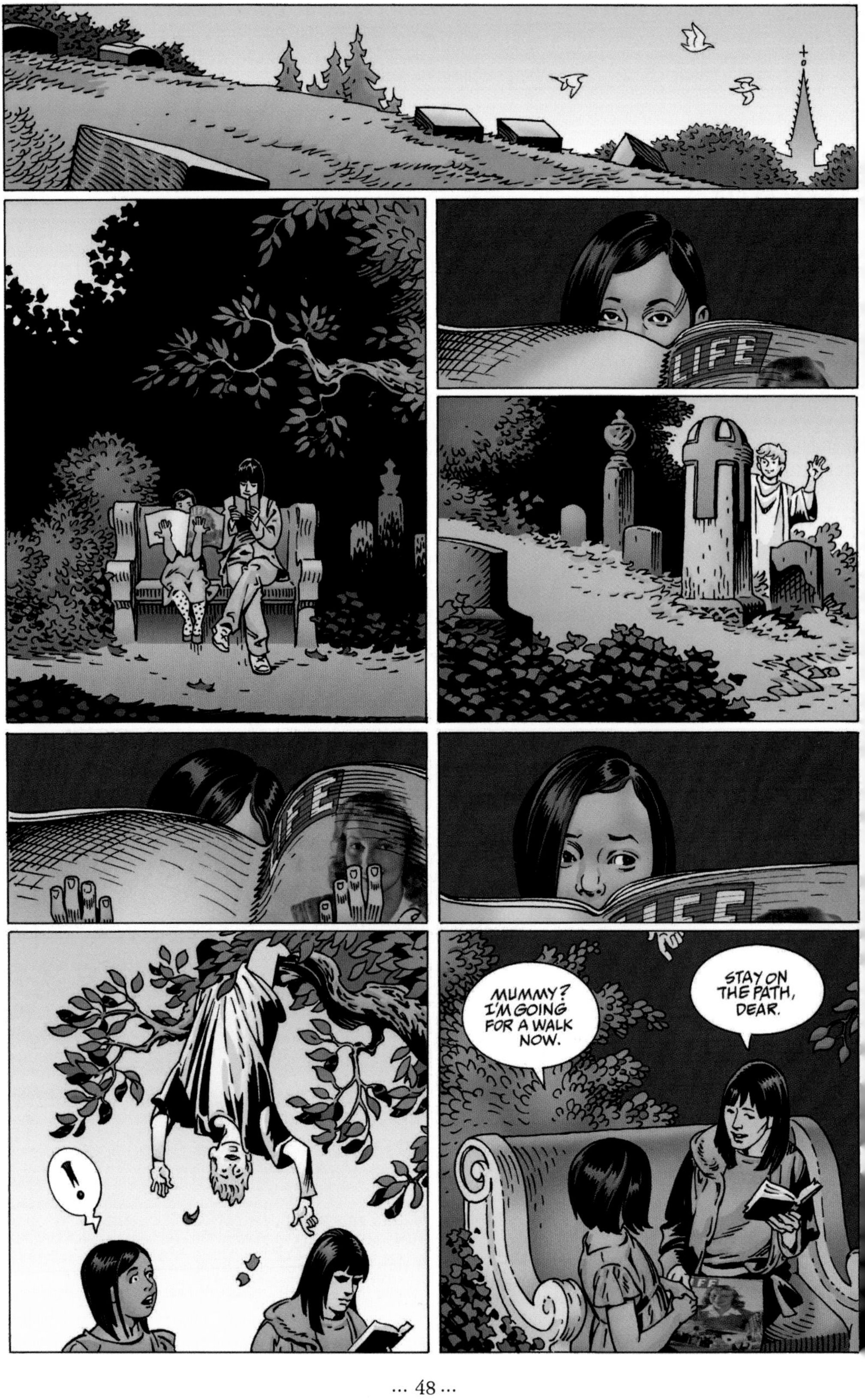
LIFE
!
MUMMY? I'M GOING FOR A WALK NOW.
STAY ON THE PATH, DEAR.

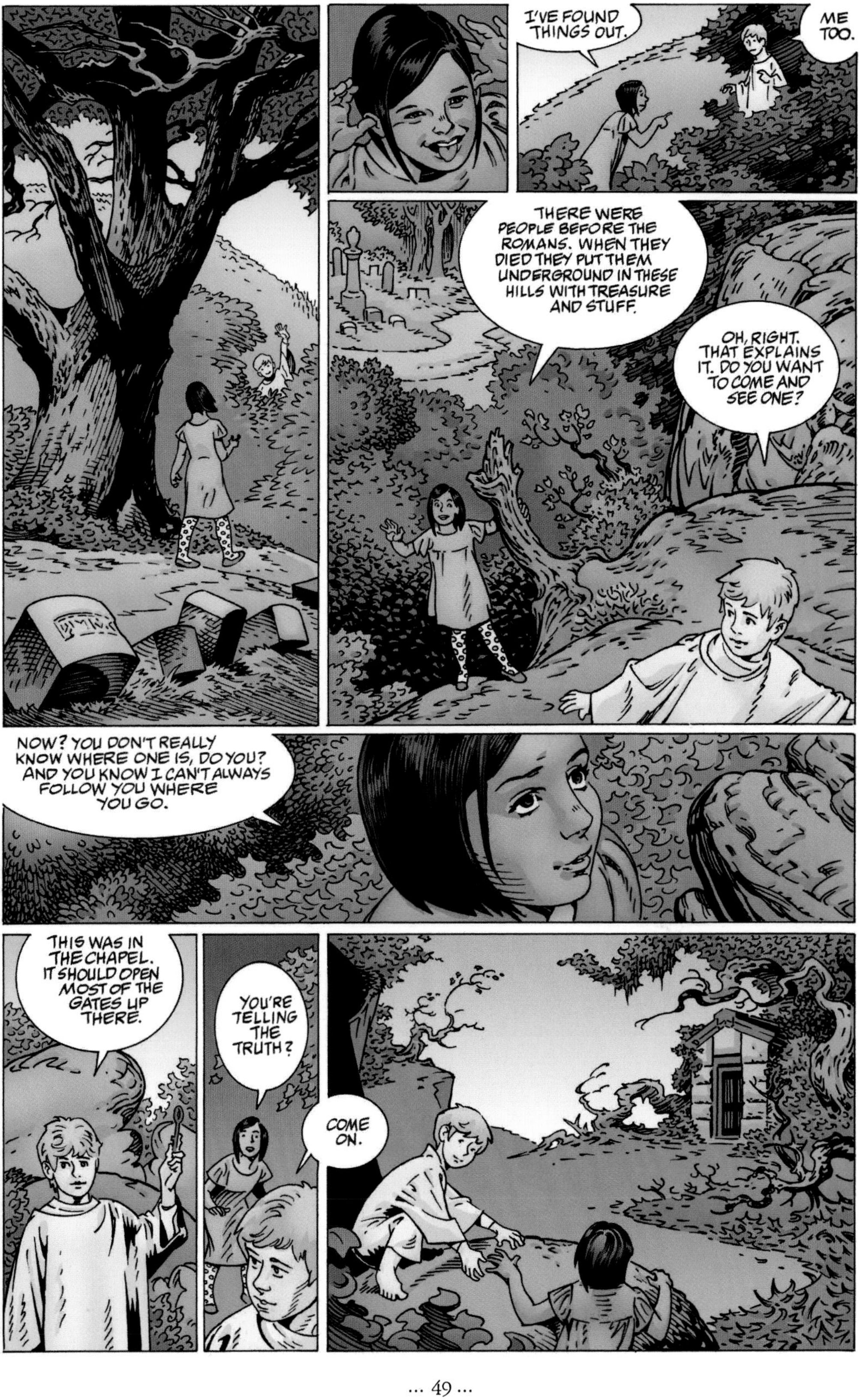
I'VE FOUND THINGS OUT.
ME TOO.
THERE WERE PEOPLE BEFORE THE ROMANS. WHEN THEY DIED THEY PUT THEM UNDERGROUND IN THESE HILLS WITH TREASURE AND STUFF.
OH, RIGHT. THAT EXPLAINS IT. DO YOU WANT TO COME AND SEE ONE?
NOW? YOU DON'T REALLY KNOW WHERE ONE IS, DO YOU? AND YOU KNOW I CAN'T ALWAYS FOLLOW YOU WHERE YOU GO.
THIS WAS IN THE CHAPEL. IT SHOULD OPEN MOST OF THE GATES UP THERE.
YOU'RE TELLING THE TRUTH?
COME ON.

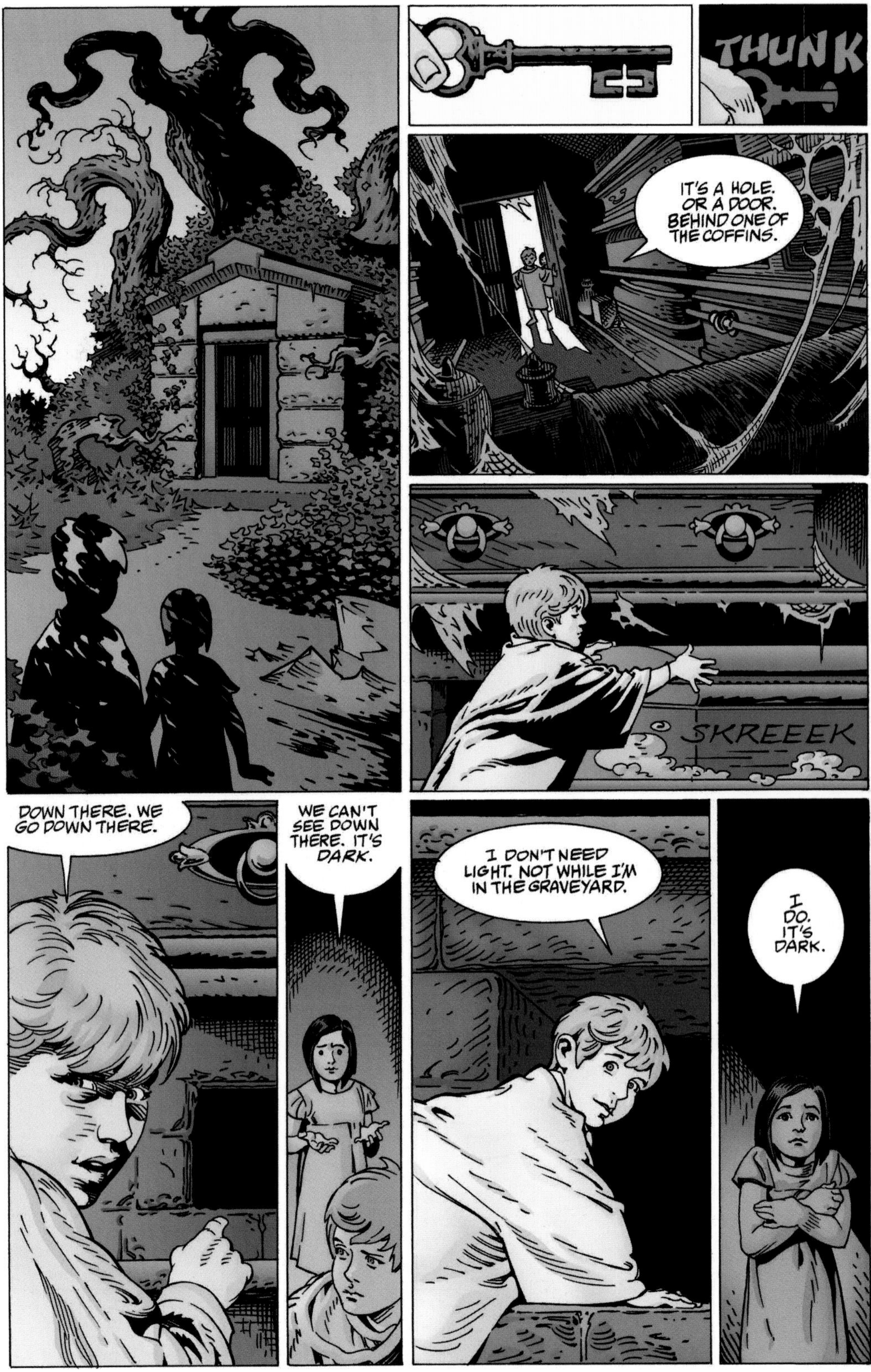
THUNK
IT'S A HOLE. OR A DOOR. BEHIND ONE OF THE COFFINS.
SKREEEK
DOWN THERE. WE GO DOWN THERE.
WE CAN'T SEE DOWN THERE. IT'S DARK.
I DON'T NEED LIGHT. NOT WHILE I'M IN THE GRAVEYARD.
I DO. IT'S DARK.

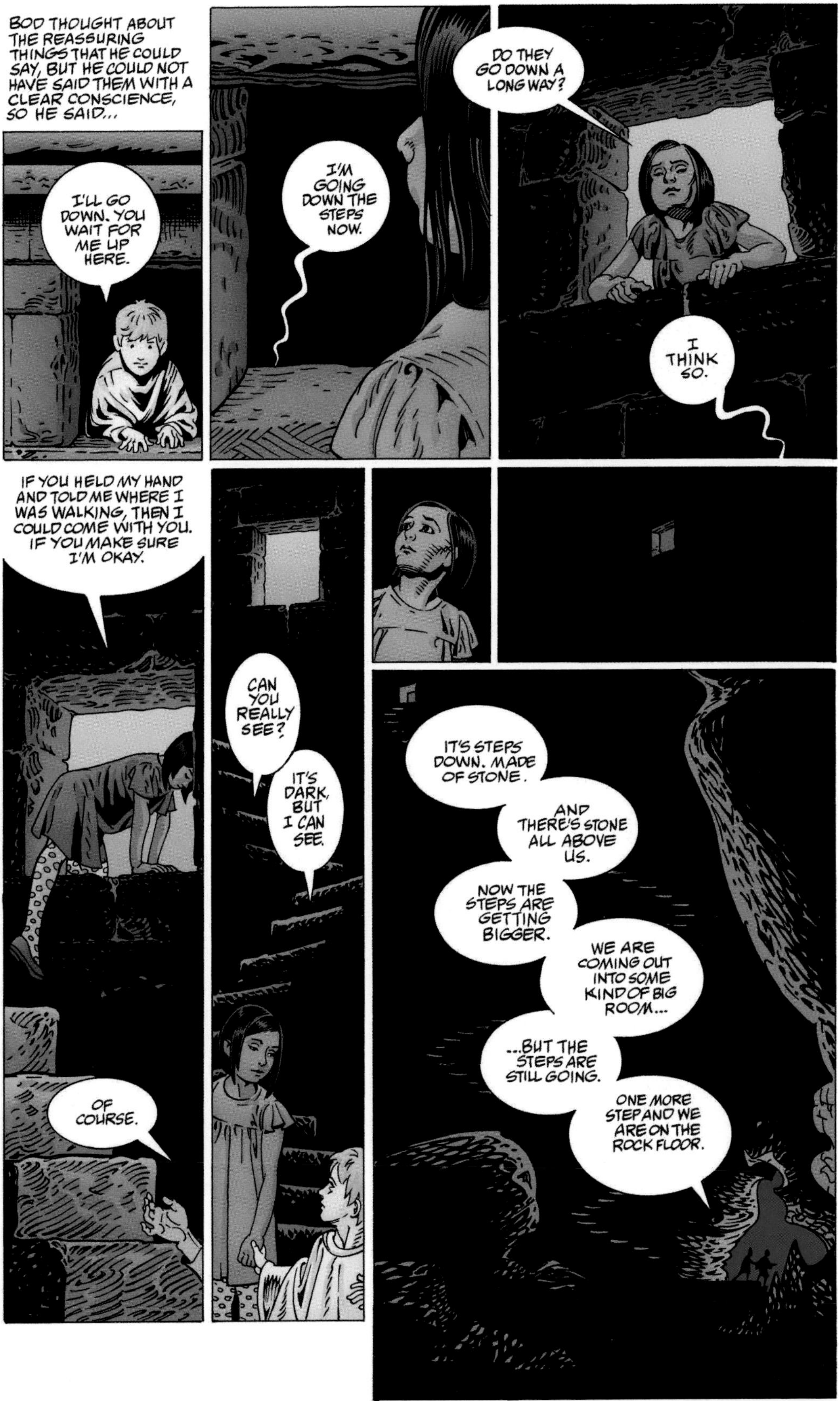
BOD THOUGHT ABOUT THE REASSURING THINGS THAT HE COULD SAY, BUT HE COULD NOT HAVE SAID THEM WITH A CLEAR CONSCIENCE, SO HE SAID...
I'LL GO DOWN. YOU WAIT FOR ME UP HERE.
I'M GOING DOWN THE STEPS NOW.
DO THEY GO DOWN A LONG WAY?
I THINK SO.
IF YOU HELD MY HAND AND TOLD ME WHERE I WAS WALKING, THEN I COULD COME WITH YOU. IF YOU MAKE SURE I'M OKAY.
OF COURSE.
CAN YOU REALLY SEE?
IT'S DARK, BUT I CAN SEE.
IT'S STEPS DOWN. MADE OF STONE.
AND THERE'S STONE ALL ABOVE US.
NOW THE STEPS ARE GETTING BIGGER.
WE ARE COMING OUT INTO SOME KIND OF BIG ROOM...
...BUT THE STEPS ARE STILL GOING.
ONE MORE STEP AND WE ARE ON THE ROCK FLOOR.

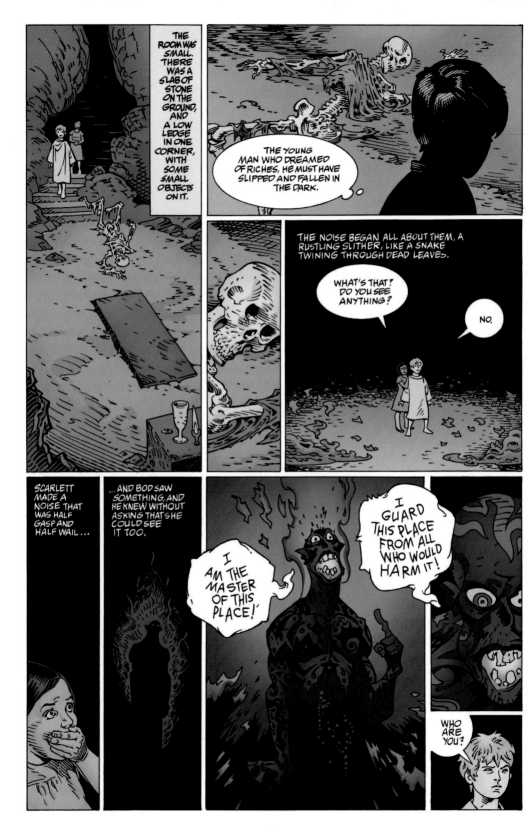

THE ROOM WAS SMALL. THERE WAS A SLAB OF STONE ON THE GROUND, AND A LOW LEDGE IN ONE CORNER, WITH SOME SMALL OBJECTS ON IT.

THE YOUNG MAN WHO DREAMED OF RICHES, HE MUST HAVE SLIPPED AND FALLEN IN THE DARK.

THE NOISE BEGAN ALL ABOUT THEM, A RUSTLING SLITHER, LIKE A SNAKE TWINING THROUGH DEAD LEAVES.

WHAT'S THAT? DO YOU SEE ANYTHING?

NO.

SCARLETT MADE A NOISE THAT WAS HALF GASP AND HALF WAIL...

...AND BOD SAW SOMETHING, AND HE KNEW WITHOUT ASKING THAT'S HE COULD SEE IT TOO.

I AM THE MASTER OF THIS PLACE!

I GUARD THIS PLACE FROM ALL WHO WOULD HARM IT!

WHO ARE YOU?

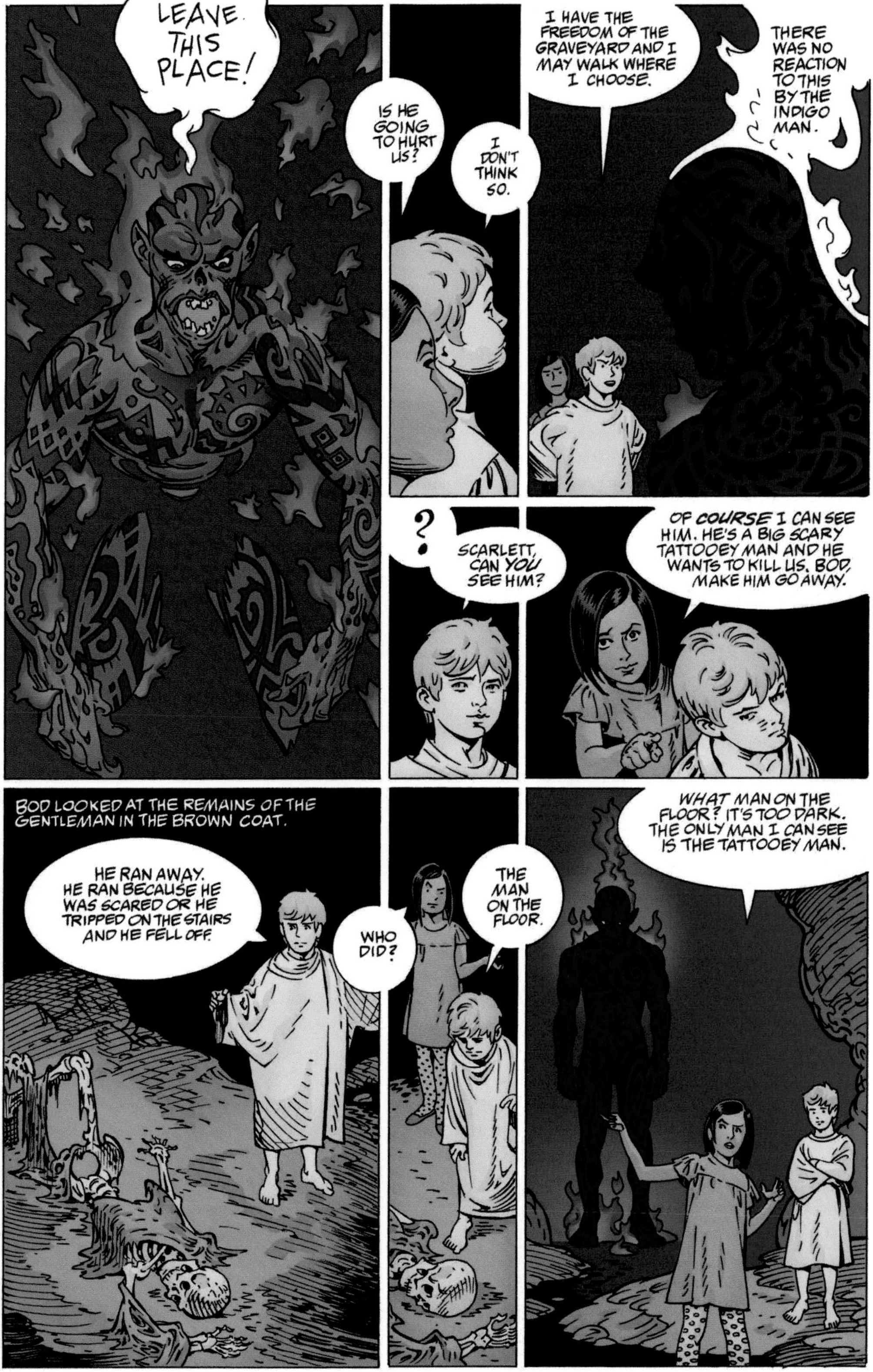
LEAVE THIS PLACE!
IS HE GOING TO HURT US?
I DON'T THINK SO.
I HAVE THE FREEDOM OF THE GRAVEYARD AND I MAY WALK WHERE I CHOOSE.
THERE WAS NO REACTION TO THIS BY THE INDIGO MAN.
?
SCARLETT, CAN YOU SEE HIM?
OF COURSE I CAN SEE HIM. HE'S A BIG SCARY TATTOOEY MAN AND HE WANTS TO KILL US. BOD, MAKE HIM GO AWAY.
BOD LOOKED AT THE REMAINS OF THE GENTLEMAN IN THE BROWN COAT.
HE RAN AWAY. HE RAN BECAUSE HE WAS SCARED OR HE TRIPPED ON THE STAIRS AND HE FELL OFF.
WHO DID?
THE MAN ON THE FLOOR.
WHAT MAN ON THE FLOOR? IT'S TOO DARK. THE ONLY MAN I CAN SEE IS THE TATTOOEY MAN.

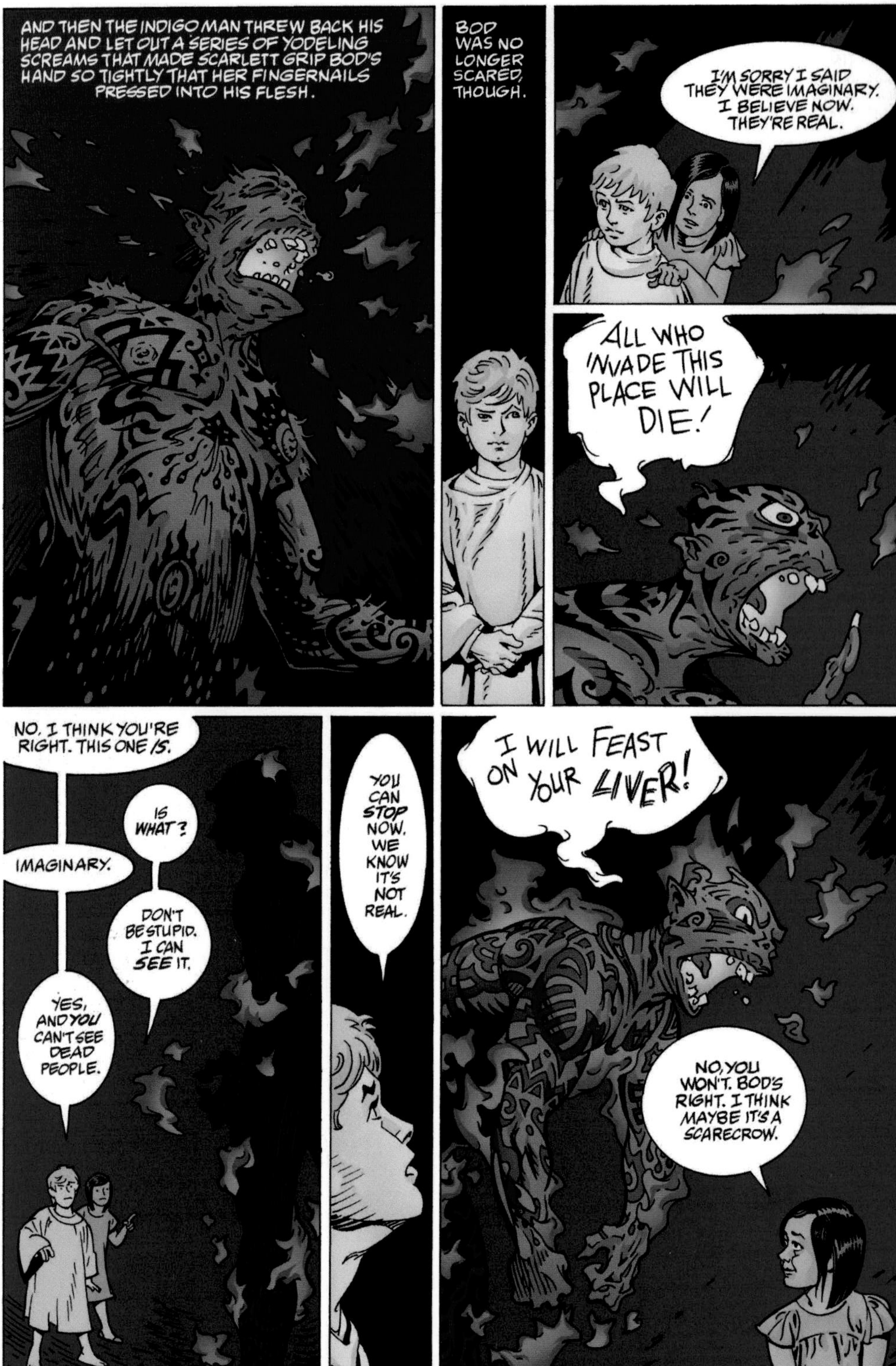
AND THEN THE INDIGO MAN THREW BACK HIS HEAD AND LET OUT A SERIES OF YODELING SCREAMS THAT MADE SCARLETT GRIP BOD'S HAND SO TIGHTLY THAT HER FINGERNAILS PRESSED INTO HIS FLESH.
BOD WAS NO LONGER SCARED, THOUGH.
I'M SORRY I SAID THEY WERE IMAGINARY. I BELIEVE NOW. THEY'RE REAL.
ALL WHO INVADE THIS PLACE WILL DIE!
NO, I THINK YOU'RE RIGHT. THIS ONE IS.
IS WHAT?
IMAGINARY.
DON'T BE STUPID. I CAN SEE IT.
YES, AND YOU CAN'T SEE DEAD PEOPLE.
YOU CAN STOP NOW. WE KNOW IT'S NOT REAL.
I WILL FEAST ON YOUR LIVER!
NO, YOU WON'T. BOD'S RIGHT. I THINK MAYBE IT'S A SCARECROW.

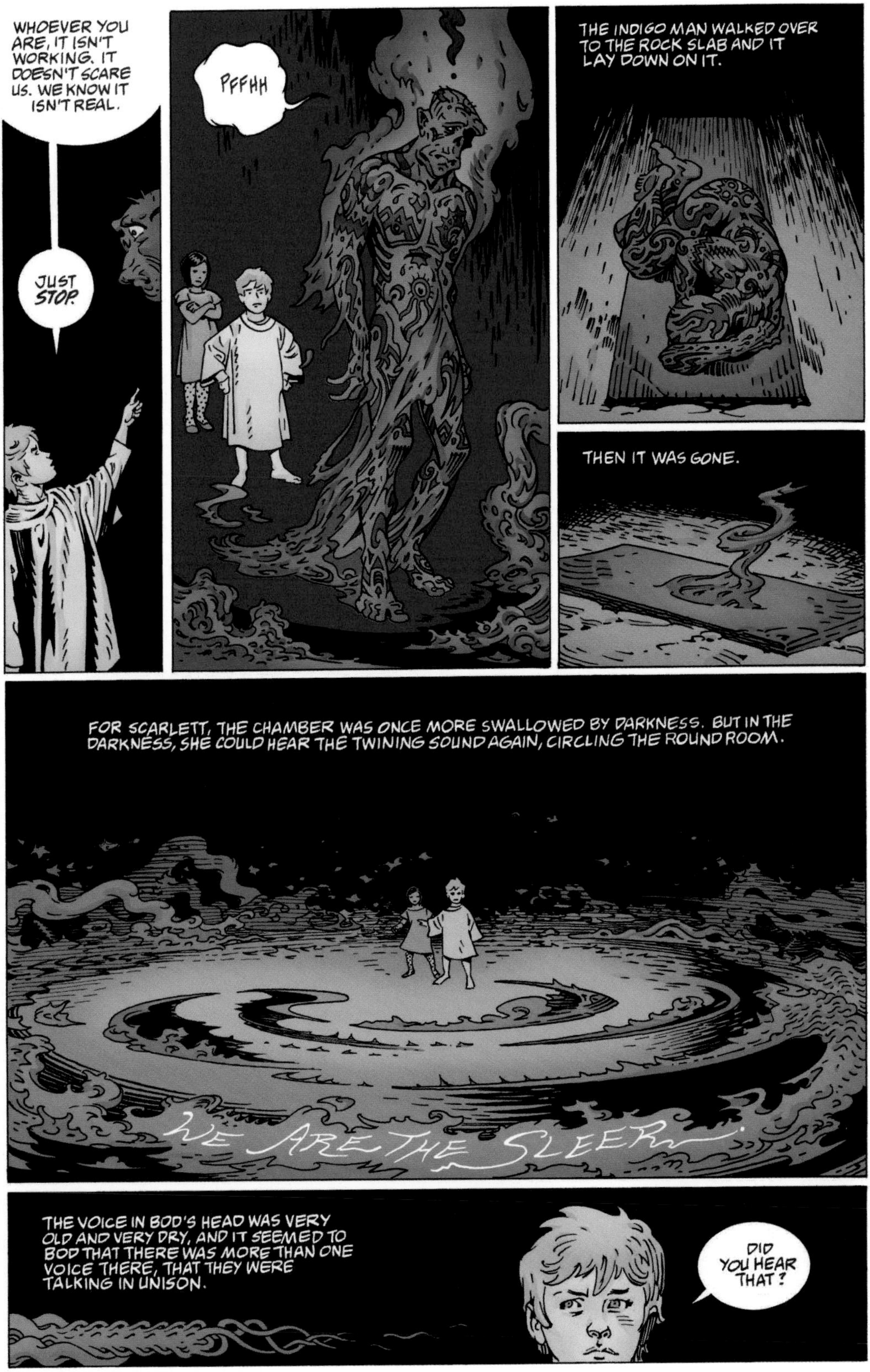
WHOEVER YOU ARE, IT ISN'T WORKING. IT DOESN'T SCARE US. WE KNOW IT ISN'T REAL.
JUST STOP.
PFFHH
THE INDIGO MAN WALKED OVER TO THE ROCK SLAB AND IT LAY DOWN ON IT.
THEN IT WAS GONE.
FOR SCARLETT, THE CHAMBER WAS ONCE MORE SWALLOWED BY DARKNESS. BUT IN THE DARKNESS, SHE COULD HEAR THE TWINING SOUND AGAIN, CIRCLING THE ROUND ROOM.
WE ARE THE SLEER.
THE VOICE IN BOD'S HEAD WAS VERY OLD AND VERY DRY, AND IT SEEMED TO BOD THAT THERE WAS MORE THAN ONE VOICE THERE, THAT THEY WERE TALKING IN UNISON.
DID YOU HEAR THAT?

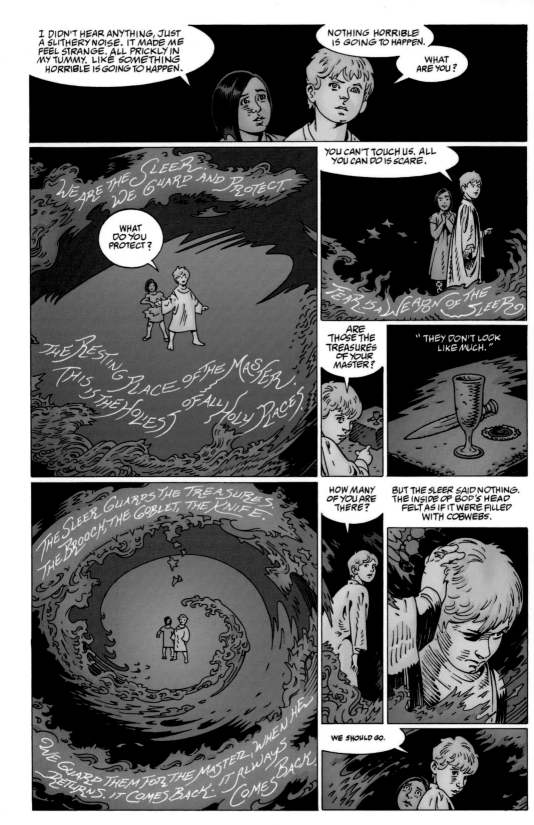

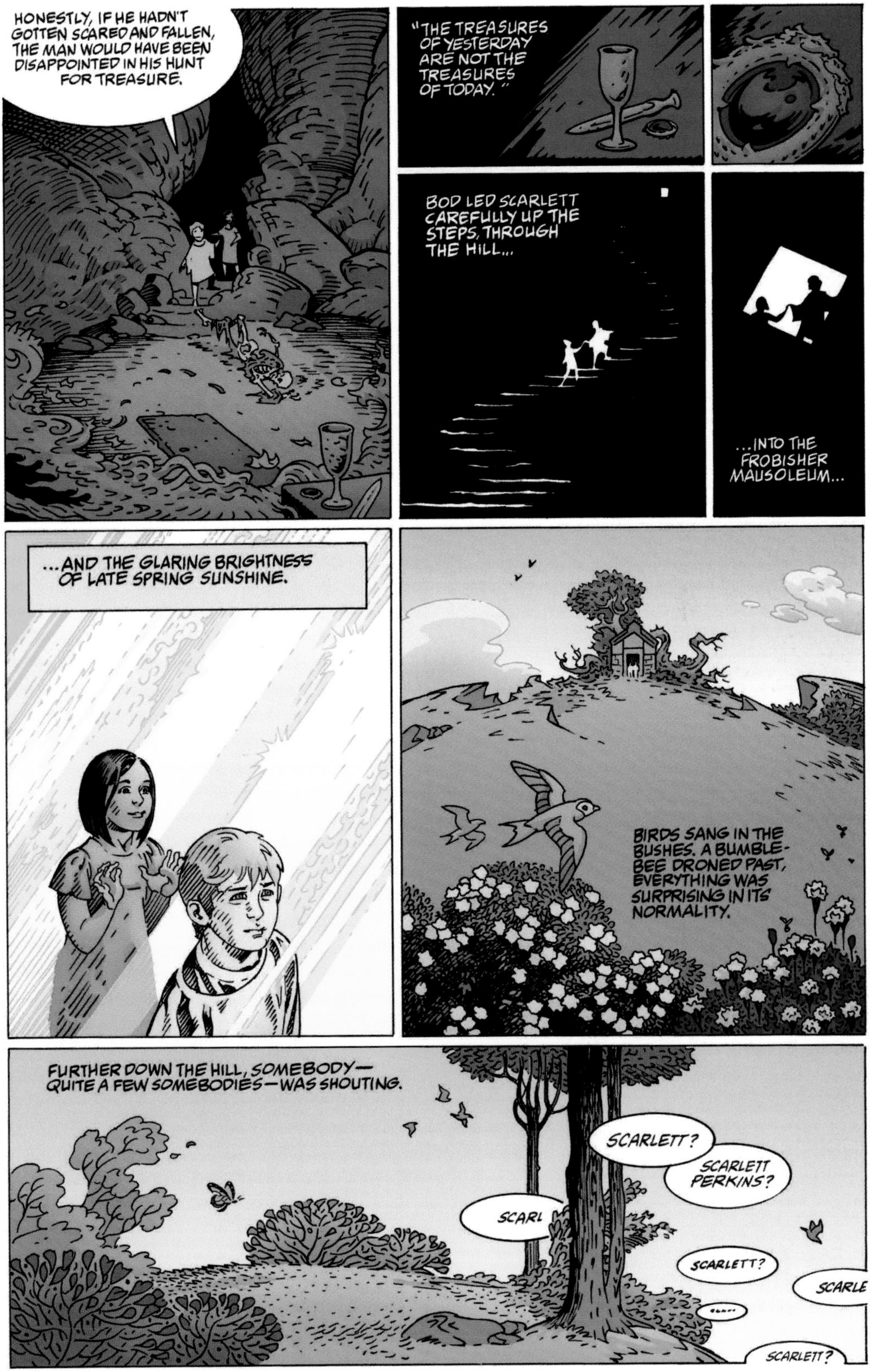
HONESTLY, IF HE HADN'T GOTTEN SCARED AND FALLEN, THE MAN WOULD HAVE BEEN DISAPPOINTED IN HIS HUNT FOR TREASURE.
"THE TREASURES OF YESTERDAY ARE NOT THE TREASURES OF TODAY."
BOD LED SCARLETT CAREFULLY UP THE STEPS, THROUGH THE HILL...
...INTO THE FROBISHER MAUSOLEUM...
...AND THE GLARING BRIGHTNESS OF LATE SPRING SUNSHINE.
BIRDS SANG IN THE BUSHES. A BUMBLE-BEE DRONED PAST, EVERYTHING WAS SURPRISING IN ITS NORMALITY.
FURTHER DOWN THE HILL, SOMEBODY—QUITE A FEW SOMEBODIES—WAS SHOUTING.
SCARLETT?
SCARLETT PERKINS?
SCARL
SCARLETT?
SCARLE
SCARLETT?

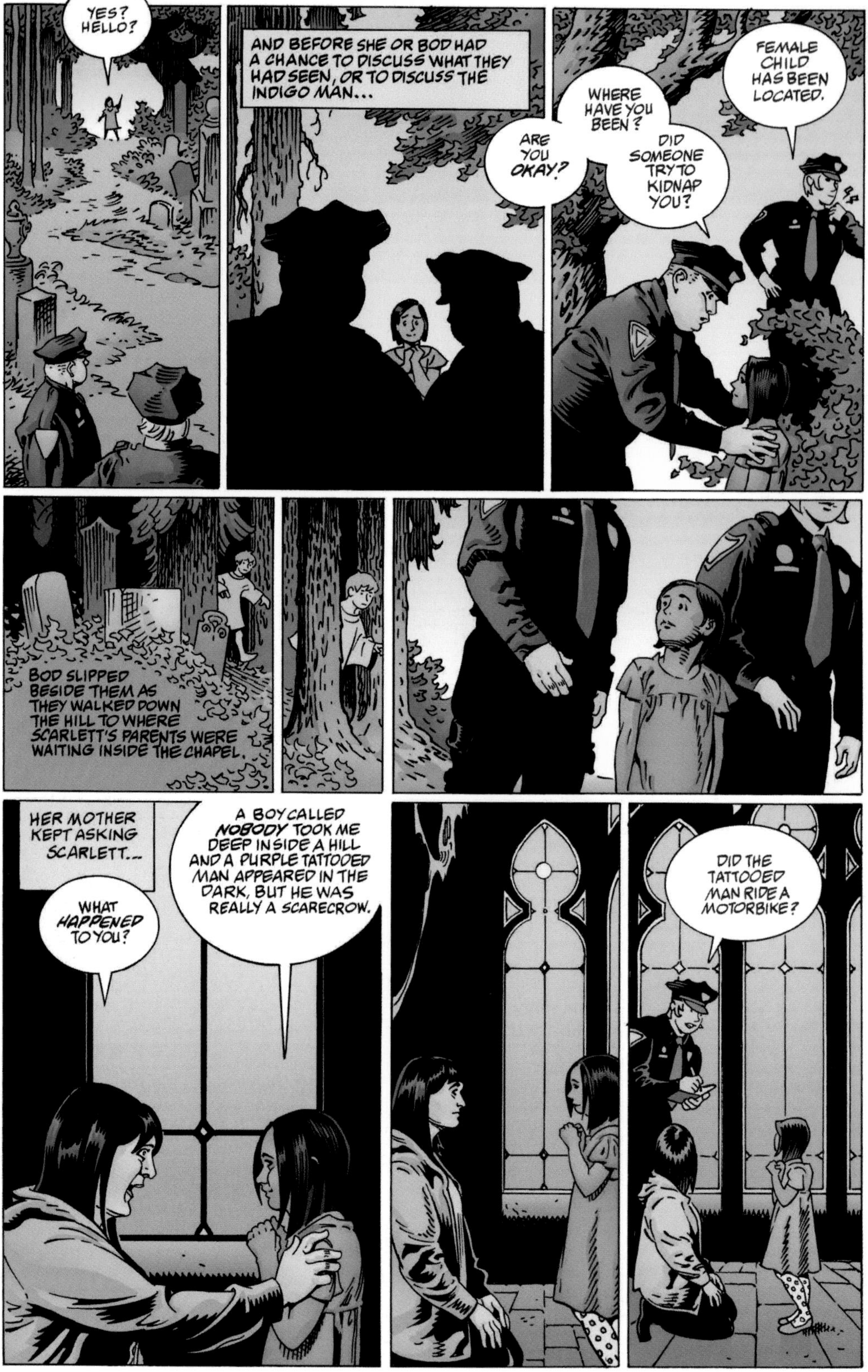
YES? HELLO?
AND BEFORE SHE OR BOD HAD A CHANCE TO DISCUSS WHAT THEY HAD SEEN, OR TO DISCUSS THE INDIGO MAN...
FEMALE CHILD HAS BEEN LOCATED.
WHERE HAVE YOU BEEN?
ARE YOU OKAY?
DID SOMEONE TRY TO KIDNAP YOU?
BOD SLIPPED BESIDE THEM AS THEY WALKED DOWN THE HILL TO WHERE SCARLETT'S PARENTS WERE WAITING INSIDE THE CHAPEL.
HER MOTHER KEPT ASKING SCARLETT...
WHAT HAPPENED TO YOU?
A BOY CALLED NOBODY TOOK ME DEEP INSIDE A HILL AND A PURPLE TATTOOED MAN APPEARED IN THE DARK, BUT HE WAS REALLY A SCARECROW.
DID THE TATTOOED MAN RIDE A MOTORBIKE?

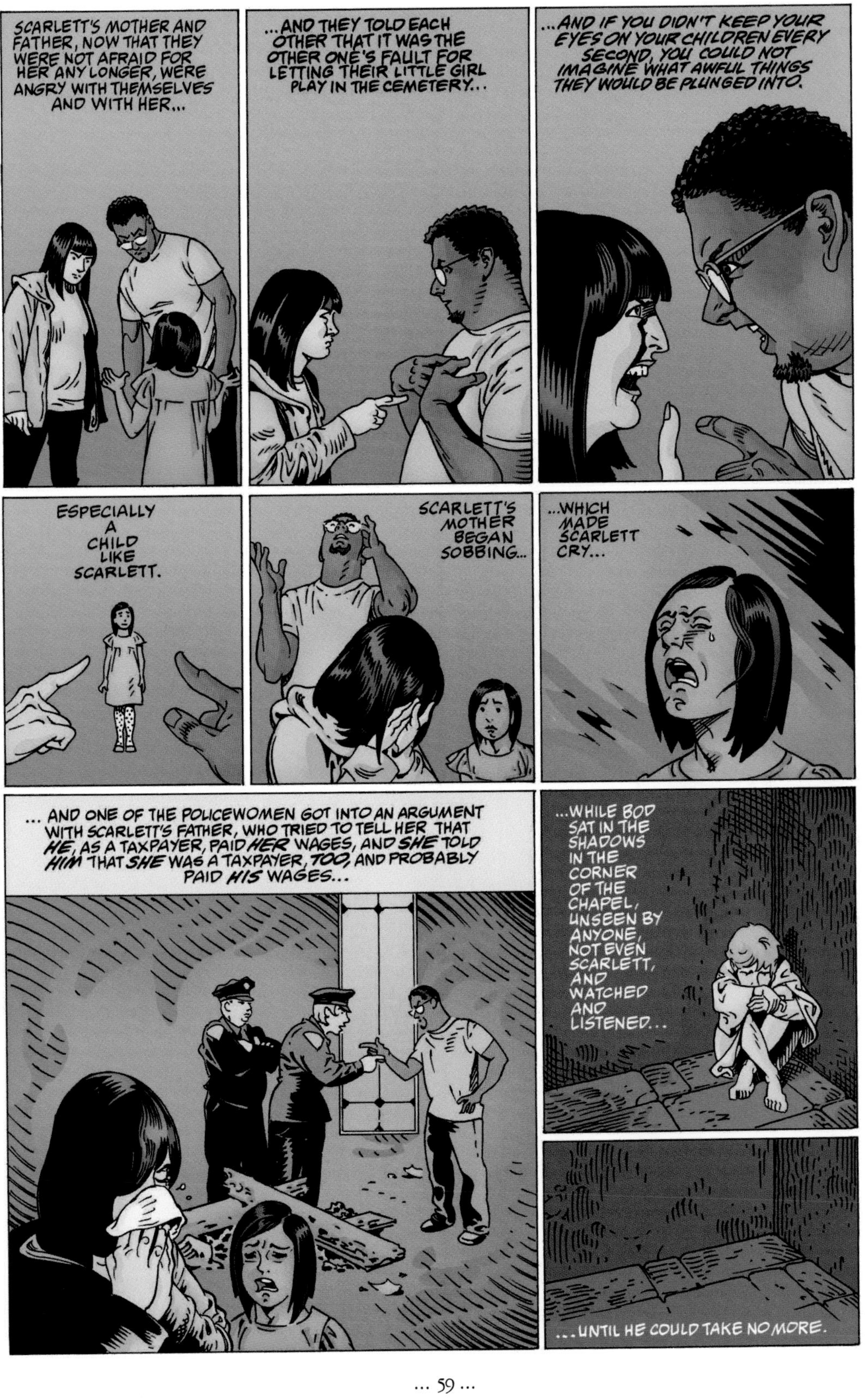
SCARLETT'S MOTHER AND FATHER, NOW THAT THEY WERE NOT AFRAID FOR HER ANY LONGER, WERE ANGRY WITH THEMSELVES AND WITH HER...
...AND THEY TOLD EACH OTHER THAT IT WAS THE OTHER ONE'S FAULT FOR LETTING THEIR LITTLE GIRL PLAY IN THE CEMETERY...
...AND IF YOU DIDN'T KEEP YOUR EYES ON YOUR CHILDREN EVERY SECOND, YOU COULD NOT IMAGINE WHAT AWFUL THINGS THEY WOULD BE PLUNGED INTO.
ESPECIALLY A CHILD LIKE SCARLETT.
SCARLETT'S MOTHER BEGAN SOBBING...
...WHICH MADE SCARLETT CRY...
... AND ONE OF THE POLICEWOMEN GOT INTO AN ARGUMENT WITH SCARLETT'S FATHER, WHO TRIED TO TELL HER THAT HE, AS A TAXPAYER, PAID HER WAGES, AND SHE TOLD HIM THAT SHE WAS A TAXPAYER, TOO, AND PROBABLY PAID HIS WAGES...
...WHILE BOD SAT IN THE SHADOWS IN THE CORNER OF THE CHAPEL, UNSEEN BY ANYONE, NOT EVEN SCARLETT, AND WATCHED AND LISTENED...
...UNTIL HE COULD TAKE NO MORE.

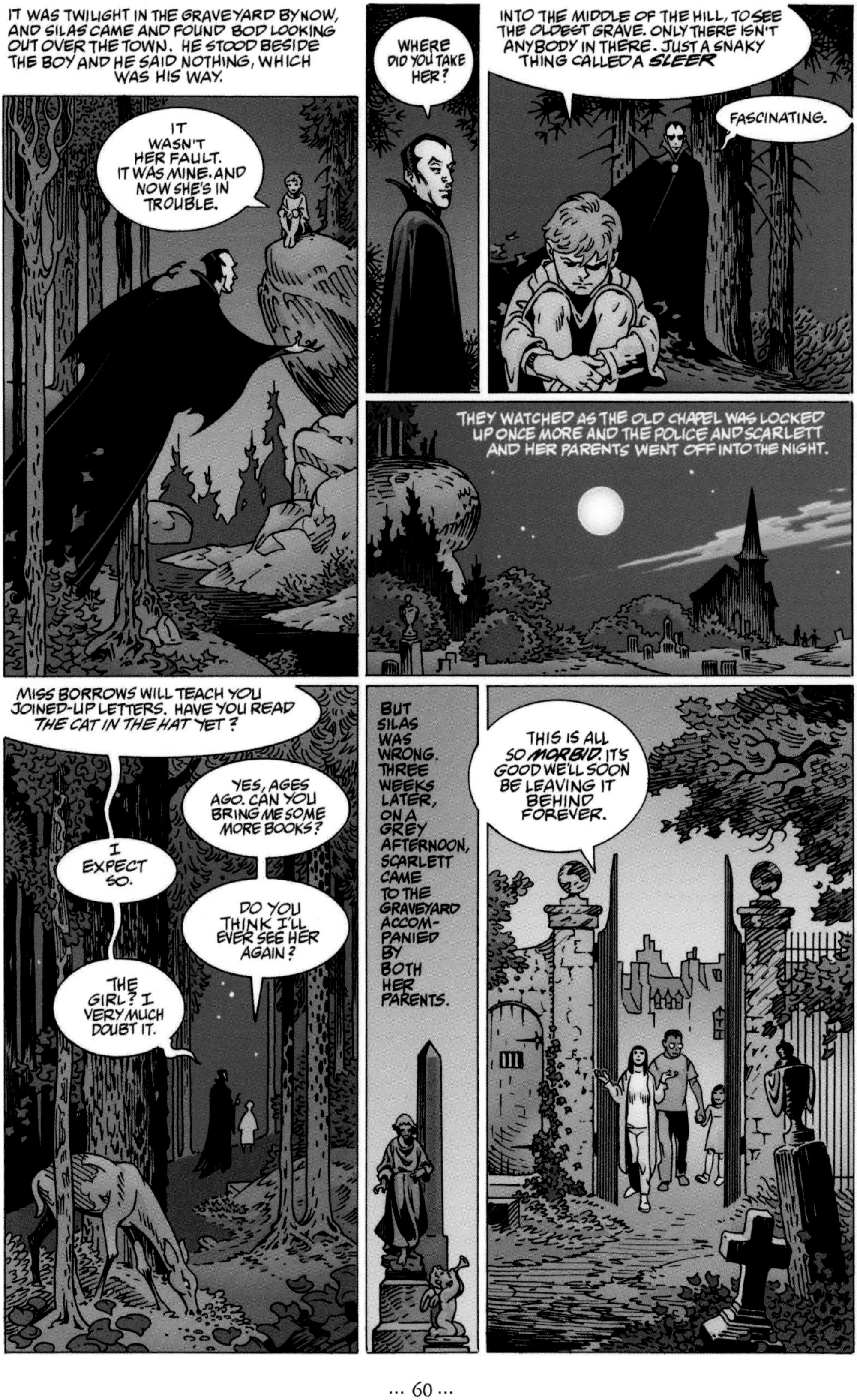
IT WAS TWILIGHT IN THE GRAVEYARD BY NOW, AND SILAS CAME AND FOUND BOD LOOKING OUT OVER THE TOWN. HE STOOD BESIDE THE BOY AND HE SAID NOTHING, WHICH WAS HIS WAY.
IT WASN'T HER FAULT. IT WAS MINE. AND NOW SHE'S IN TROUBLE.
WHERE DID YOU TAKE HER?
INTO THE MIDDLE OF THE HILL, TO SEE THE OLDEST GRAVE. ONLY THERE ISN'T ANYBODY IN THERE. JUST A SNAKY THING CALLED A SLEER
FASCINATING.
THEY WATCHED AS THE OLD CHAPEL WAS LOCKED UP ONCE MORE AND THE POLICE AND SCARLETT AND HER PARENTS WENT OFF INTO THE NIGHT.
MISS BORROWS WILL TEACH YOU JOINED-UP LETTERS. HAVE YOU READ THE CAT IN THE HAT YET?
YES, AGES AGO. CAN YOU BRING ME SOME MORE BOOKS?
I EXPECT SO.
DO YOU THINK I'LL EVER SEE HER AGAIN?
THE GIRL? I VERY MUCH DOUBT IT.
BUT SILAS WAS WRONG. THREE WEEKS LATER, ON A GREY AFTERNOON, SCARLETT CAME TO THE GRAVEYARD ACCOM-PANIED BY BOTH HER PARENTS.
THIS IS ALL SO MORBID. IT'S GOOD WE'LL SOON BE LEAVING IT BEHIND FOREVER.

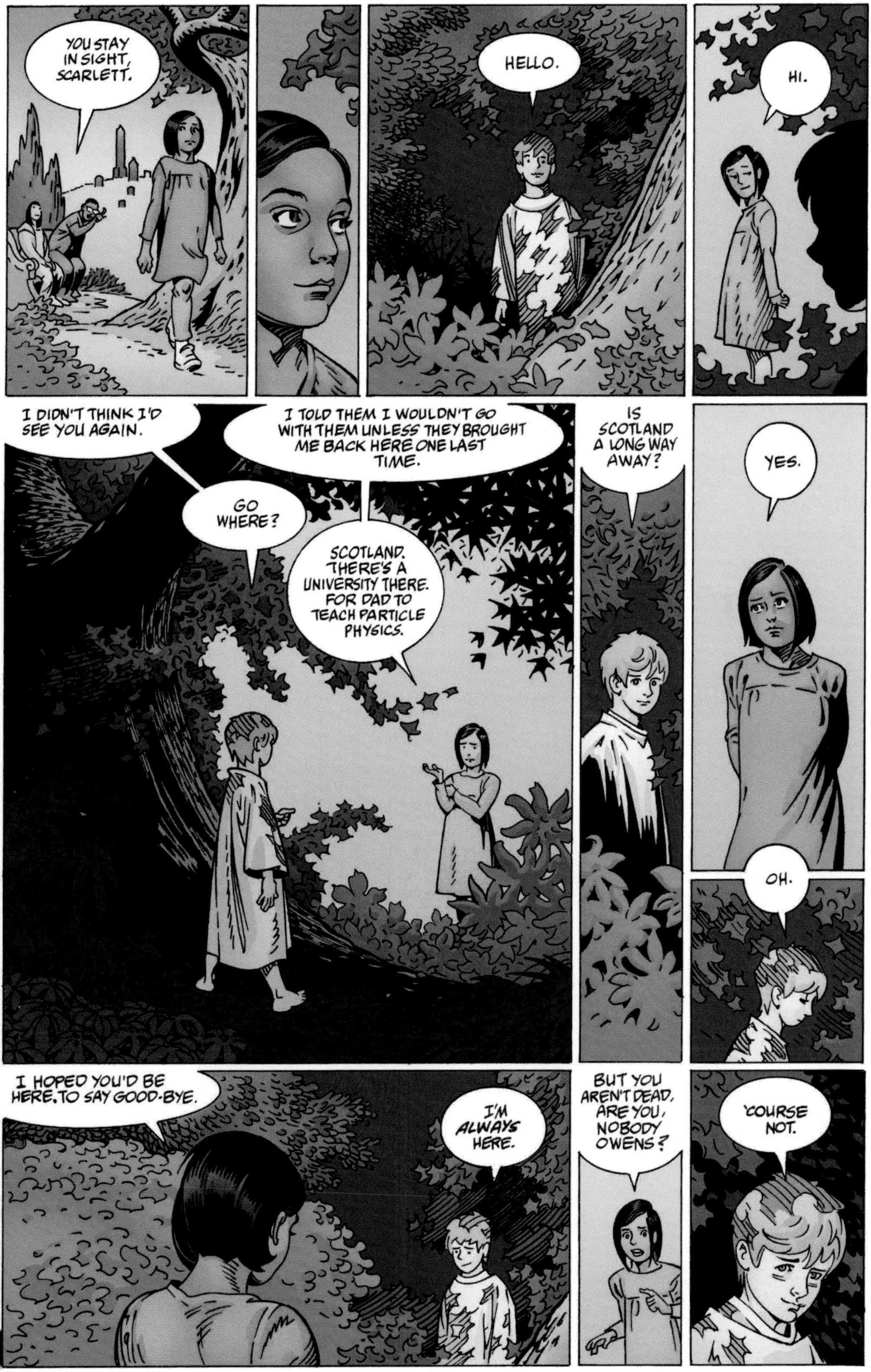
YOU STAY IN SIGHT, SCARLETT.
HELLO.
HI.
I DIDN'T THINK I'D SEE YOU AGAIN.
I TOLD THEM I WOULDN'T GO WITH THEM UNLESS THEY BROUGHT ME BACK HERE ONE LAST TIME.
GO WHERE?
SCOTLAND. THERE'S A UNIVERSITY THERE. FOR DAD TO TEACH PARTICLE PHYSICS.
IS SCOTLAND A LONG WAY AWAY?
YES.
OH.
I HOPED YOU'D BE HERE. TO SAY GOOD-BYE.
I'M *ALWAYS* HERE.
BUT YOU AREN'T DEAD, ARE YOU, NOBODY OWENS?
'COURSE NOT.

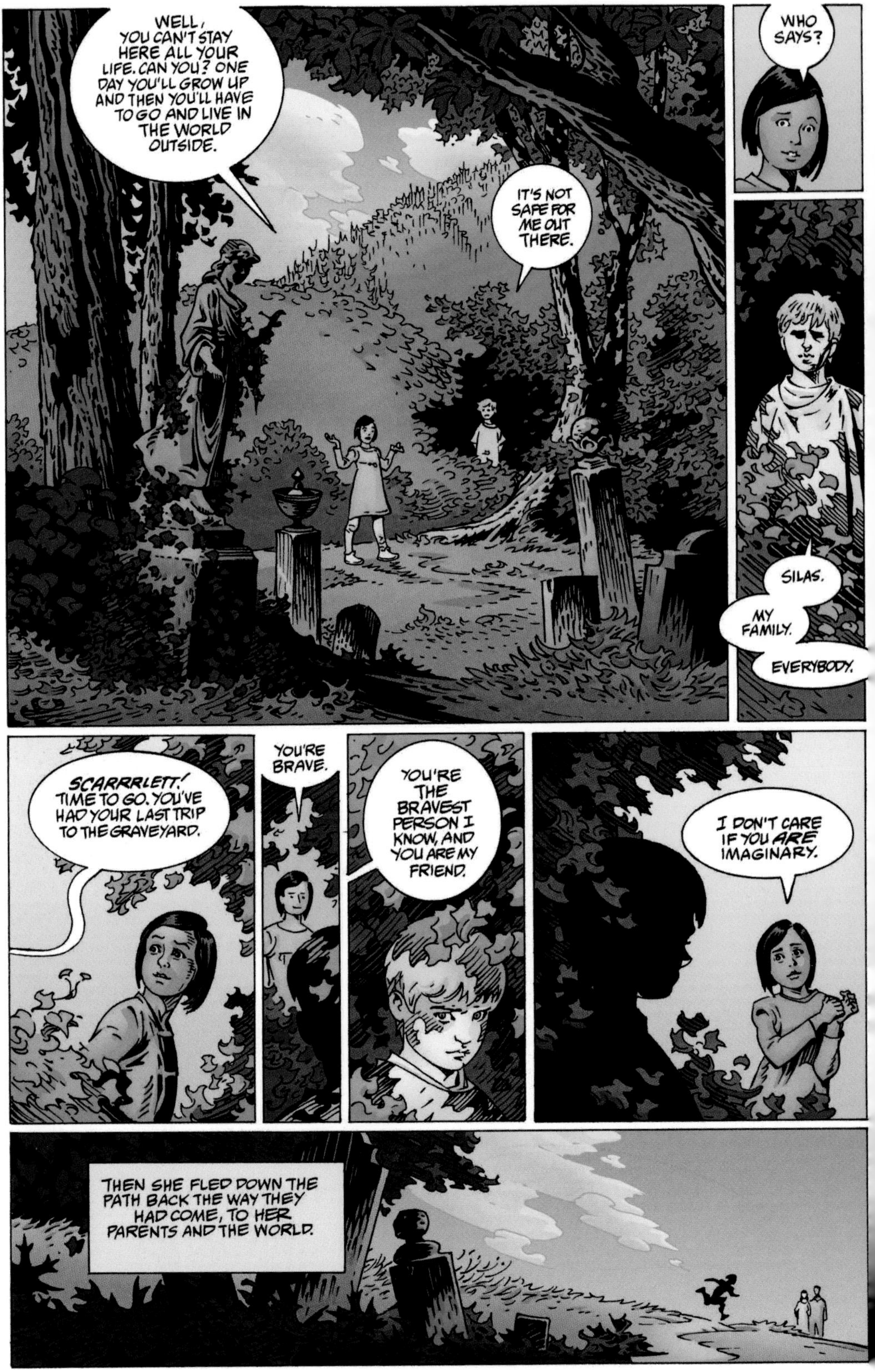
WELL, YOU CAN'T STAY HERE ALL YOUR LIFE. CAN YOU? ONE DAY YOU'LL GROW UP AND THEN YOU'LL HAVE TO GO AND LIVE IN THE WORLD OUTSIDE.
IT'S NOT SAFE FOR ME OUT THERE.
WHO SAYS?
SILAS.
MY FAMILY.
EVERYBODY.
SCARRRLETT! TIME TO GO. YOU'VE HAD YOUR LAST TRIP TO THE GRAVEYARD.
YOU'RE BRAVE.
YOU'RE THE BRAVEST PERSON I KNOW, AND YOU ARE MY FRIEND.
I DON'T CARE IF YOU *ARE* IMAGINARY.
THEN SHE FLED DOWN THE PATH BACK THE WAY THEY HAD COME, TO HER PARENTS AND THE WORLD.

3
The Hounds of God

Illustrated by Tony Harris and Scott Hampton

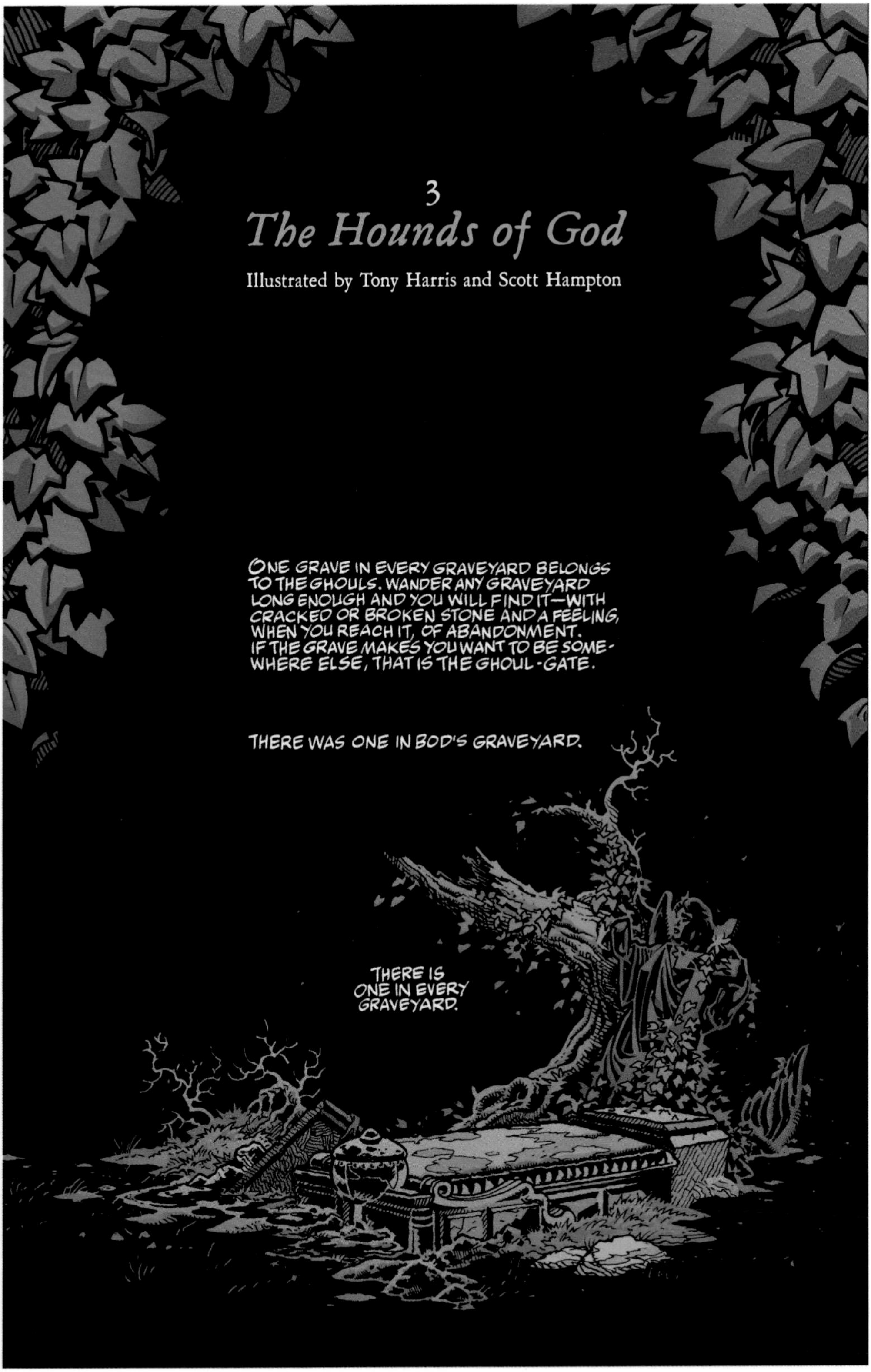
ONE GRAVE IN EVERY GRAVEYARD BELONGS TO THE GHOULS. WANDER ANY GRAVEYARD LONG ENOUGH AND YOU WILL FIND IT—WITH CRACKED OR BROKEN STONE AND A FEELING, WHEN YOU REACH IT, OF ABANDONMENT. IF THE GRAVE MAKES YOU WANT TO BE SOMEWHERE ELSE, THAT IS THE GHOUL-GATE.
THERE WAS ONE IN BOD'S GRAVEYARD.
THERE IS ONE IN EVERY GRAVEYARD.

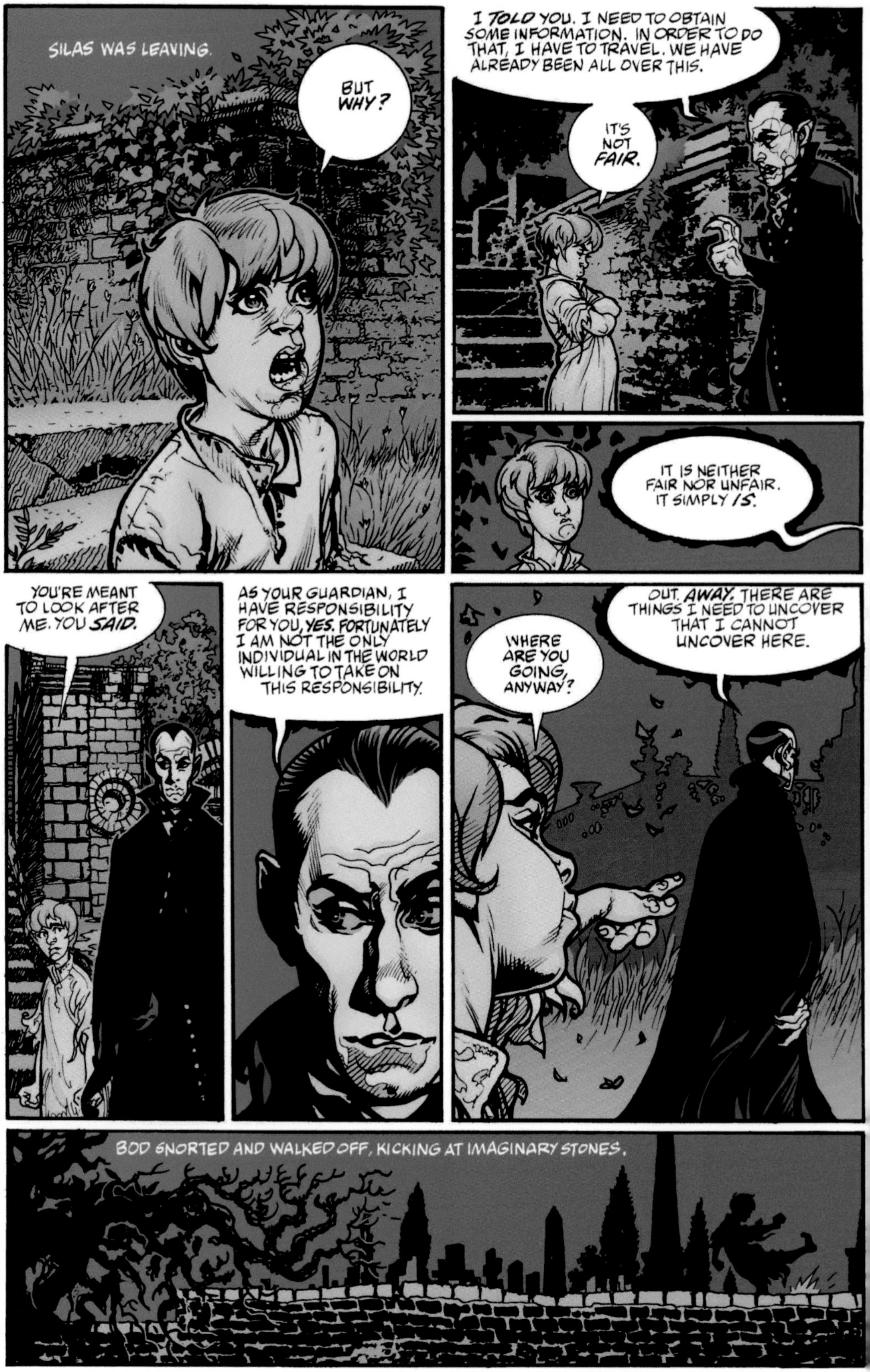
SILAS WAS LEAVING.
BUT WHY?
I TOLD YOU. I NEED TO OBTAIN SOME INFORMATION. IN ORDER TO DO THAT, I HAVE TO TRAVEL. WE HAVE ALREADY BEEN ALL OVER THIS.
IT'S NOT FAIR.
IT IS NEITHER FAIR NOR UNFAIR. IT SIMPLY IS.
YOU'RE MEANT TO LOOK AFTER ME. YOU SAID.
AS YOUR GUARDIAN, I HAVE RESPONSIBILITY FOR YOU, YES. FORTUNATELY I AM NOT THE ONLY INDIVIDUAL IN THE WORLD WILLING TO TAKE ON THIS RESPONSIBILITY.
WHERE ARE YOU GOING, ANYWAY?
OUT. AWAY. THERE ARE THINGS I NEED TO UNCOVER THAT I CANNOT UNCOVER HERE.
BOD SNORTED AND WALKED OFF, KICKING AT IMAGINARY STONES.

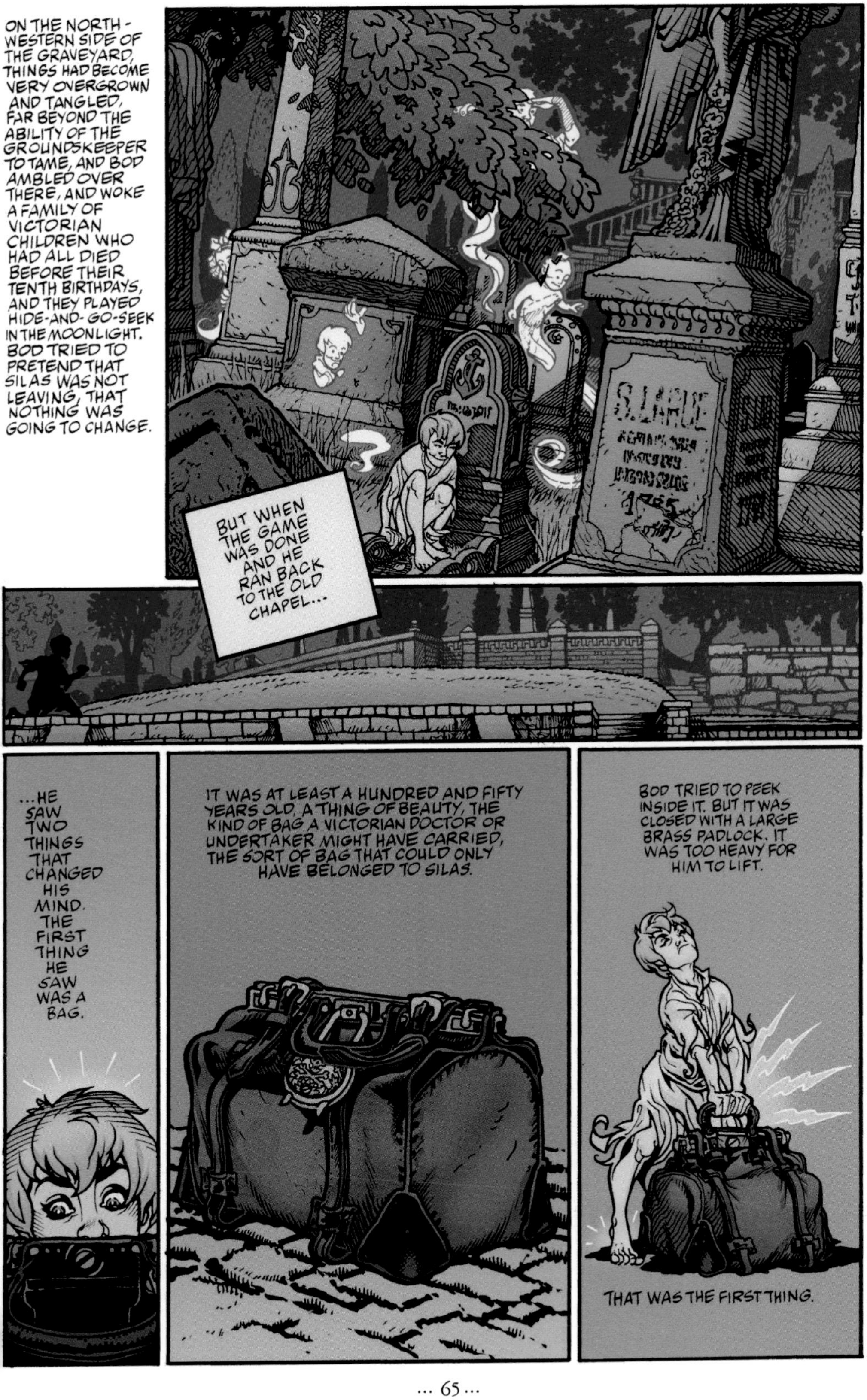
ON THE NORTH-WESTERN SIDE OF THE GRAVEYARD, THINGS HAD BECOME VERY OVERGROWN AND TANGLED, FAR BEYOND THE ABILITY OF THE GROUNDSKEEPER TO TAME, AND BOD AMBLED OVER THERE, AND WOKE A FAMILY OF VICTORIAN CHILDREN WHO HAD ALL DIED BEFORE THEIR TENTH BIRTHDAYS, AND THEY PLAYED HIDE-AND-GO-SEEK IN THE MOONLIGHT. BOD TRIED TO PRETEND THAT SILAS WAS NOT LEAVING, THAT NOTHING WAS GOING TO CHANGE.
BUT WHEN THE GAME WAS DONE AND HE RAN BACK TO THE OLD CHAPEL...
...HE SAW TWO THINGS THAT CHANGED HIS MIND. THE FIRST THING HE SAW WAS A BAG.
IT WAS AT LEAST A HUNDRED AND FIFTY YEARS OLD, A THING OF BEAUTY, THE KIND OF BAG A VICTORIAN DOCTOR OR UNDERTAKER MIGHT HAVE CARRIED, THE SORT OF BAG THAT COULD ONLY HAVE BELONGED TO SILAS.
BOD TRIED TO PEEK INSIDE IT. BUT IT WAS CLOSED WITH A LARGE BRASS PADLOCK. IT WAS TOO HEAVY FOR HIM TO LIFT.
THAT WAS THE FIRST THING.

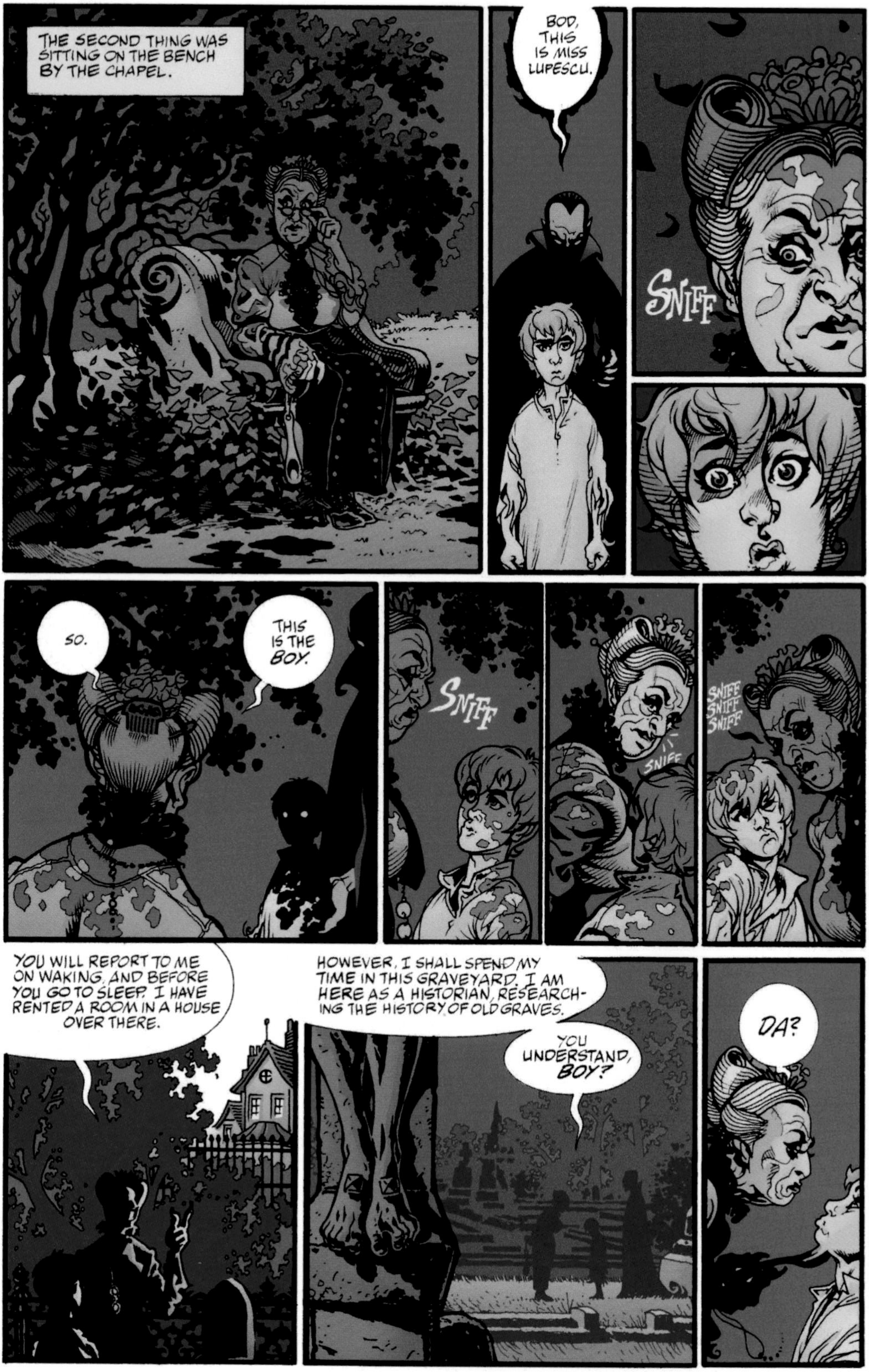
THE SECOND THING WAS SITTING ON THE BENCH BY THE CHAPEL.
BOD, THIS IS MISS LUPESCU.
SNIFF
SO.
THIS IS THE BOY.
SNIFF
SNIFF
SNIFF SNIFF SNIFF
YOU WILL REPORT TO ME ON WAKING, AND BEFORE YOU GO TO SLEEP. I HAVE RENTED A ROOM IN A HOUSE OVER THERE.
HOWEVER, I SHALL SPEND MY TIME IN THIS GRAVEYARD. I AM HERE AS A HISTORIAN, RESEARCHING THE HISTORY OF OLD GRAVES.
YOU UNDERSTAND, BOY?
DA?

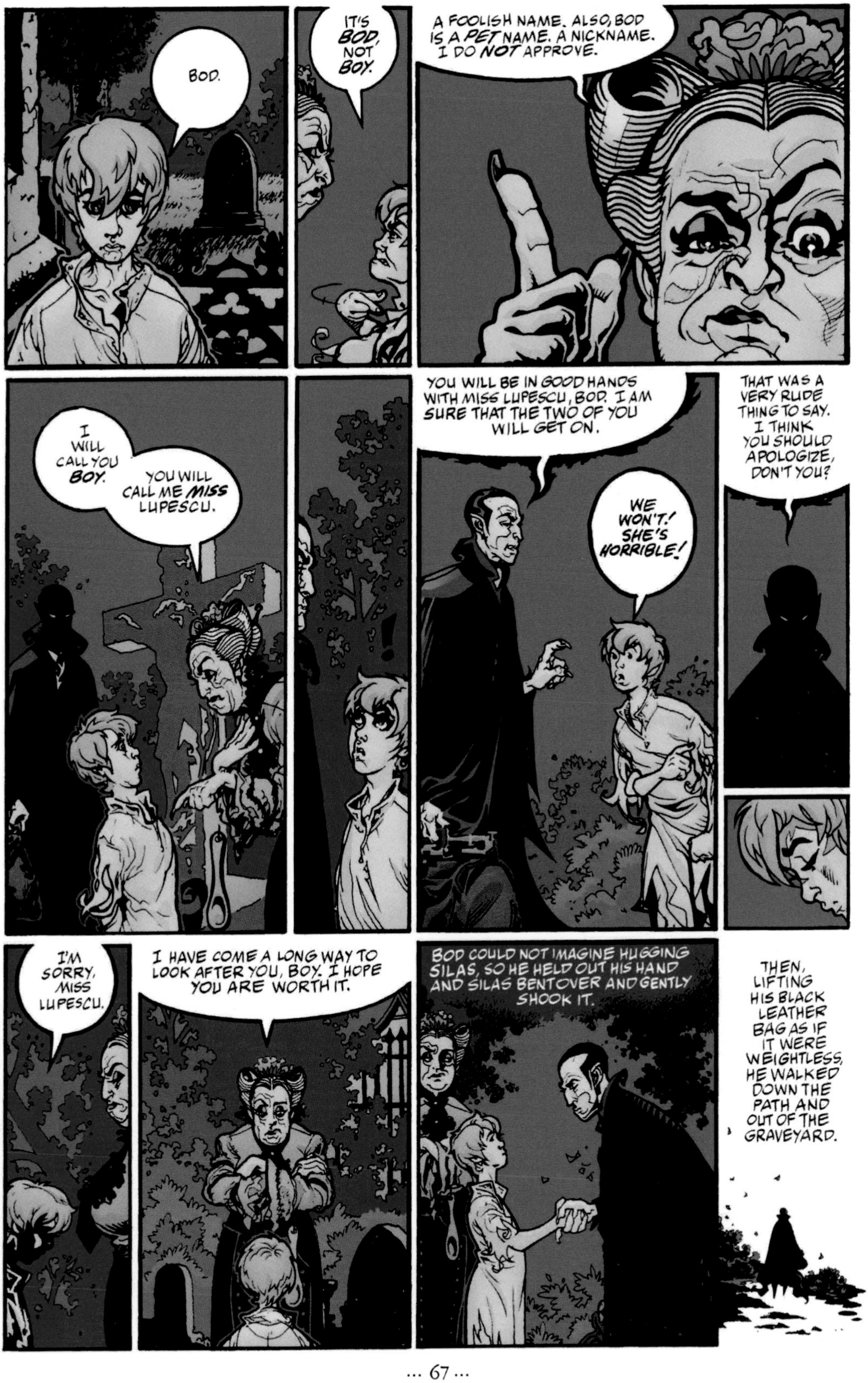
BOD.
IT'S BOD, NOT BOY.
A FOOLISH NAME. ALSO, BOD IS A PET NAME. A NICKNAME. I DO NOT APPROVE.
I WILL CALL YOU BOY.
YOU WILL CALL ME MISS LUPESCU.
!
YOU WILL BE IN GOOD HANDS WITH MISS LUPESCU, BOD. I AM SURE THAT THE TWO OF YOU WILL GET ON.
WE WON'T! SHE'S HORRIBLE!
THAT WAS A VERY RUDE THING TO SAY. I THINK YOU SHOULD APOLOGIZE, DON'T YOU?
I'M SORRY, MISS LUPESCU.
I HAVE COME A LONG WAY TO LOOK AFTER YOU, BOY. I HOPE YOU ARE WORTH IT.
BOD COULD NOT IMAGINE HUGGING SILAS, SO HE HELD OUT HIS HAND AND SILAS BENT OVER AND GENTLY SHOOK IT.
THEN, LIFTING HIS BLACK LEATHER BAG AS IF IT WERE WEIGHTLESS, HE WALKED DOWN THE PATH AND OUT OF THE GRAVEYARD.

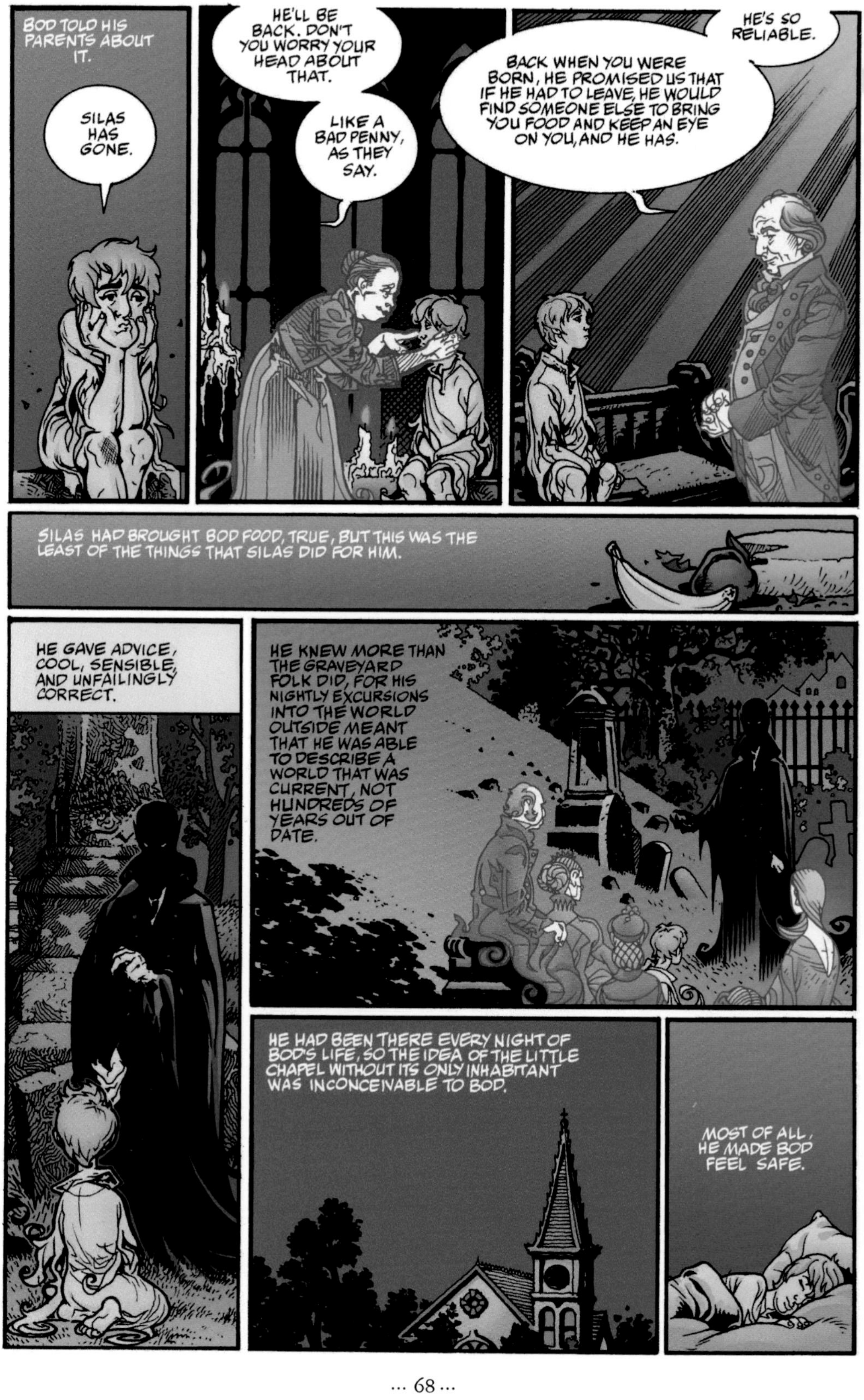
BOD TOLD HIS PARENTS ABOUT IT.
SILAS HAS GONE.
HE'LL BE BACK. DON'T YOU WORRY YOUR HEAD ABOUT THAT.
LIKE A BAD PENNY, AS THEY SAY.
BACK WHEN YOU WERE BORN, HE PROMISED US THAT IF HE HAD TO LEAVE, HE WOULD FIND SOMEONE ELSE TO BRING YOU FOOD AND KEEP AN EYE ON YOU, AND HE HAS.
HE'S SO RELIABLE.
SILAS HAD BROUGHT BOD FOOD, TRUE, BUT THIS WAS THE LEAST OF THE THINGS THAT SILAS DID FOR HIM.
HE GAVE ADVICE, COOL, SENSIBLE, AND UNFAILINGLY CORRECT.
HE KNEW MORE THAN THE GRAVEYARD FOLK DID, FOR HIS NIGHTLY EXCURSIONS INTO THE WORLD OUTSIDE MEANT THAT HE WAS ABLE TO DESCRIBE A WORLD THAT WAS CURRENT, NOT HUNDREDS OF YEARS OUT OF DATE.
HE HAD BEEN THERE EVERY NIGHT OF BOD'S LIFE, SO THE IDEA OF THE LITTLE CHAPEL WITHOUT ITS ONLY INHABITANT WAS INCONCEIVABLE TO BOD.
MOST OF ALL, HE MADE BOD FEEL SAFE.

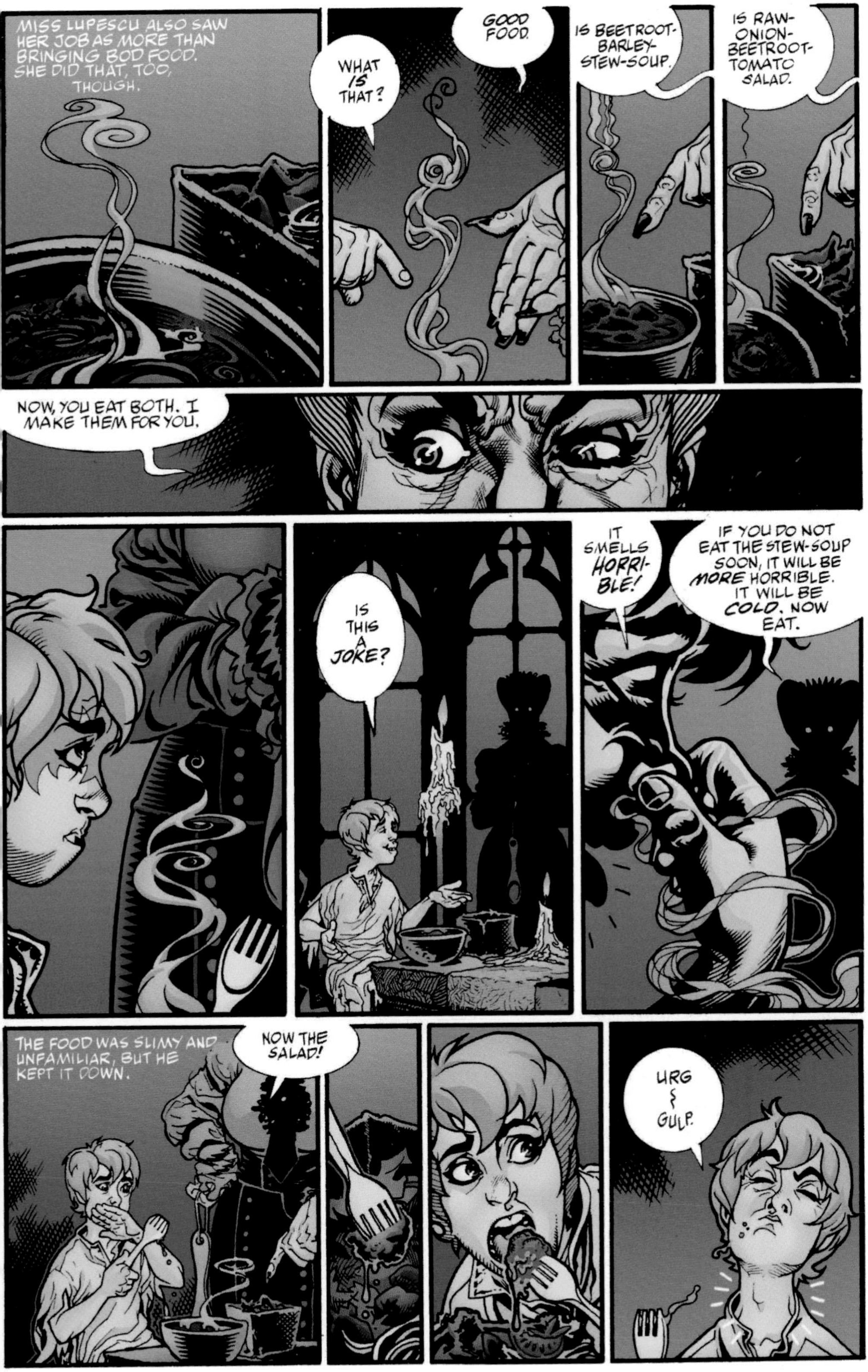
MISS LUPESCU ALSO SAW HER JOB AS MORE THAN BRINGING BOD FOOD. SHE DID THAT, TOO, THOUGH.
WHAT IS THAT?
GOOD FOOD.
IS BEETROOT-BARLEY-STEW-SOUP.
IS RAW-ONION-BEETROOT-TOMATO SALAD.
NOW, YOU EAT BOTH. I MAKE THEM FOR YOU.
IS THIS A JOKE?
IT SMELLS HORRIBLE!
IF YOU DO NOT EAT THE STEW-SOUP SOON, IT WILL BE MORE HORRIBLE. IT WILL BE COLD. NOW EAT.
THE FOOD WAS SLIMY AND UNFAMILIAR, BUT HE KEPT IT DOWN.
NOW THE SALAD!
URG & GULP.

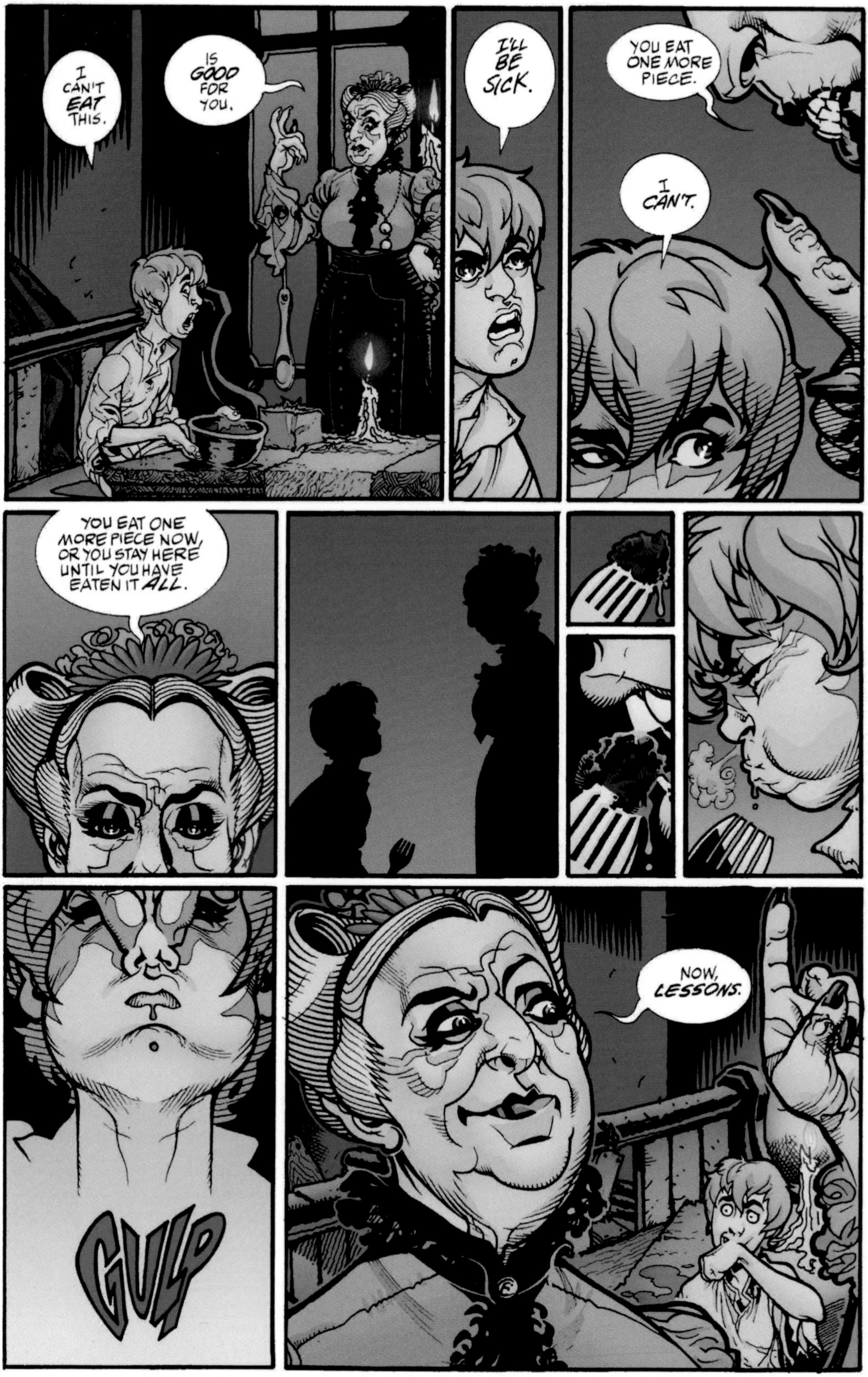
I CAN'T EAT THIS.
IS GOOD FOR YOU.
I'LL BE SICK.
YOU EAT ONE MORE PIECE.
I CAN'T.
YOU EAT ONE MORE PIECE NOW, OR YOU STAY HERE UNTIL YOU HAVE EATEN IT ALL.
GULP
NOW, LESSONS.

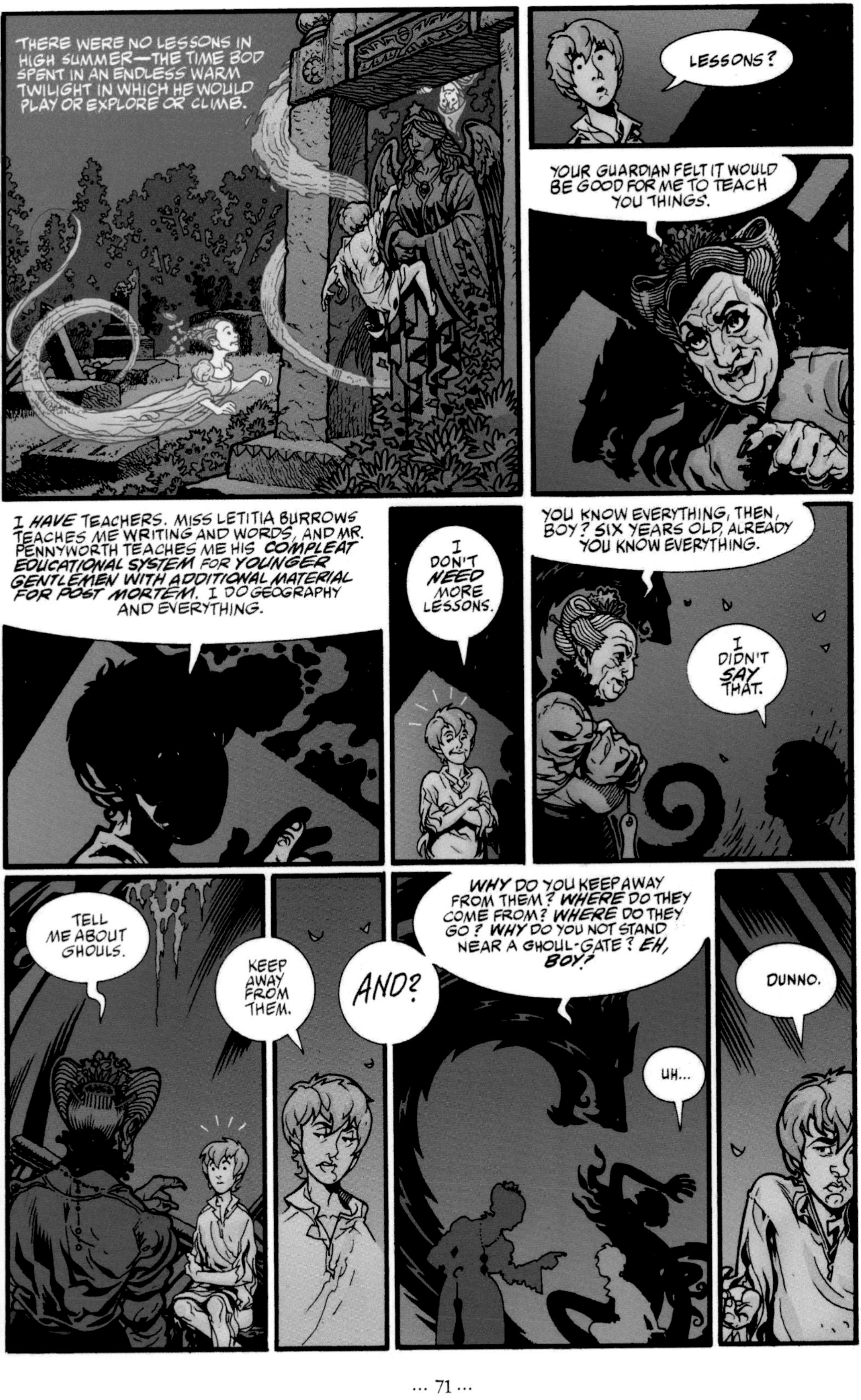
THERE WERE NO LESSONS IN HIGH SUMMER—THE TIME BOD SPENT IN AN ENDLESS WARM TWILIGHT IN WHICH HE WOULD PLAY OR EXPLORE OR CLIMB.
LESSONS?
YOUR GUARDIAN FELT IT WOULD BE GOOD FOR ME TO TEACH YOU THINGS.
I HAVE TEACHERS. MISS LETITIA BURROWS TEACHES ME WRITING AND WORDS, AND MR. PENNYWORTH TEACHES ME HIS COMPLEAT EDUCATIONAL SYSTEM FOR YOUNGER GENTLEMEN WITH ADDITIONAL MATERIAL FOR POST MORTEM. I DO GEOGRAPHY AND EVERYTHING.
I DON'T NEED MORE LESSONS.
YOU KNOW EVERYTHING, THEN, BOY? SIX YEARS OLD, ALREADY YOU KNOW EVERYTHING.
I DIDN'T SAY THAT.
TELL ME ABOUT GHOULS.
KEEP AWAY FROM THEM.
AND?
WHY DO YOU KEEP AWAY FROM THEM? WHERE DO THEY COME FROM? WHERE DO THEY GO? WHY DO YOU NOT STAND NEAR A GHOUL-GATE? EH, BOY?
UH...
DUNNO.

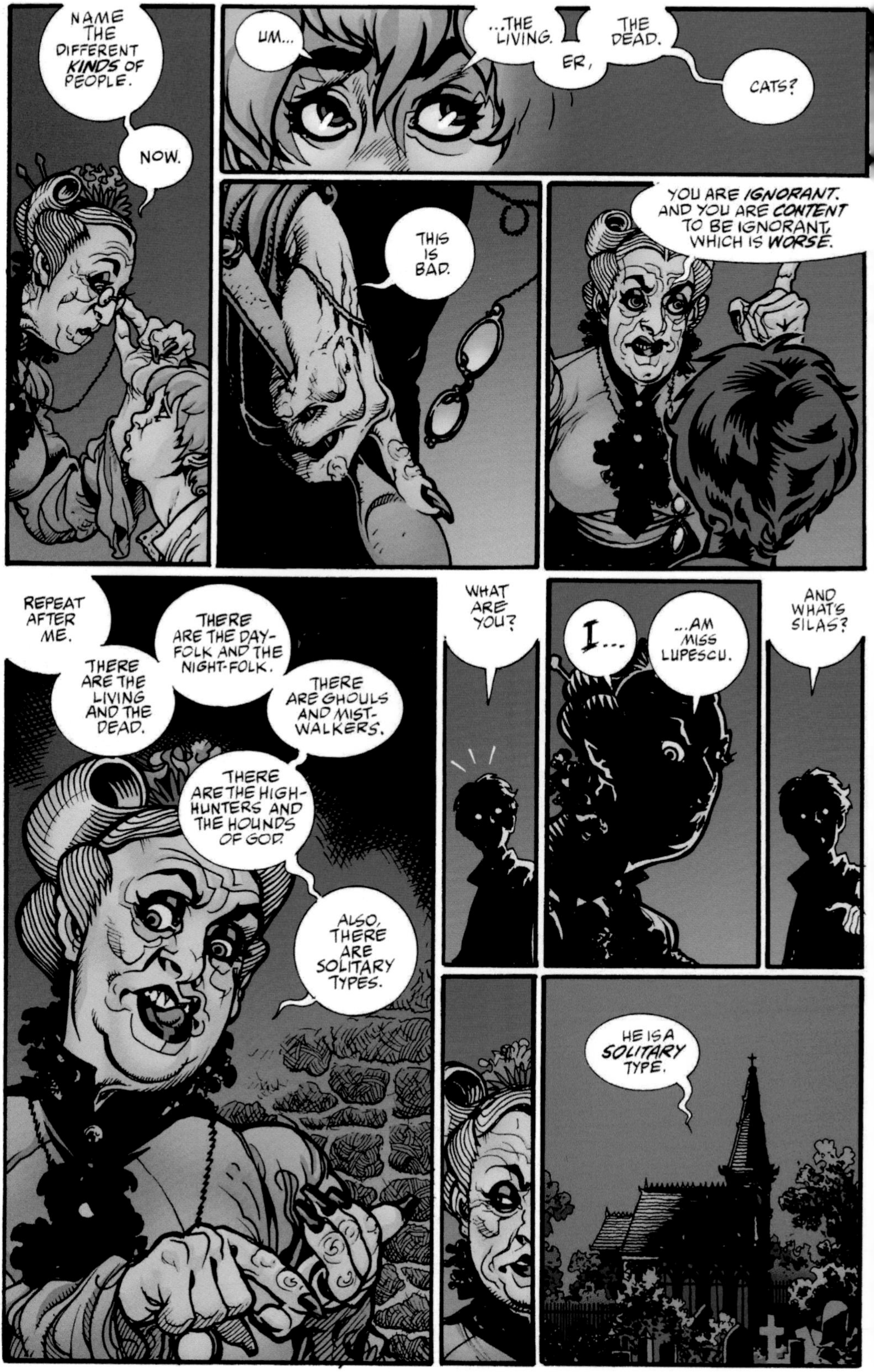
NAME THE DIFFERENT KINDS OF PEOPLE.
NOW.
UM...
...THE LIVING.
ER,
THE DEAD.
CATS?
THIS IS BAD.
YOU ARE IGNORANT. AND YOU ARE CONTENT TO BE IGNORANT, WHICH IS WORSE.
REPEAT AFTER ME.
THERE ARE THE LIVING AND THE DEAD.
THERE ARE THE DAY-FOLK AND THE NIGHT-FOLK.
THERE ARE GHOULS AND MIST-WALKERS.
THERE ARE THE HIGH-HUNTERS AND THE HOUNDS OF GOD.
ALSO, THERE ARE SOLITARY TYPES.
WHAT ARE YOU?
I...
...AM MISS LUPESCU.
AND WHAT'S SILAS?
HE IS A SOLITARY TYPE.

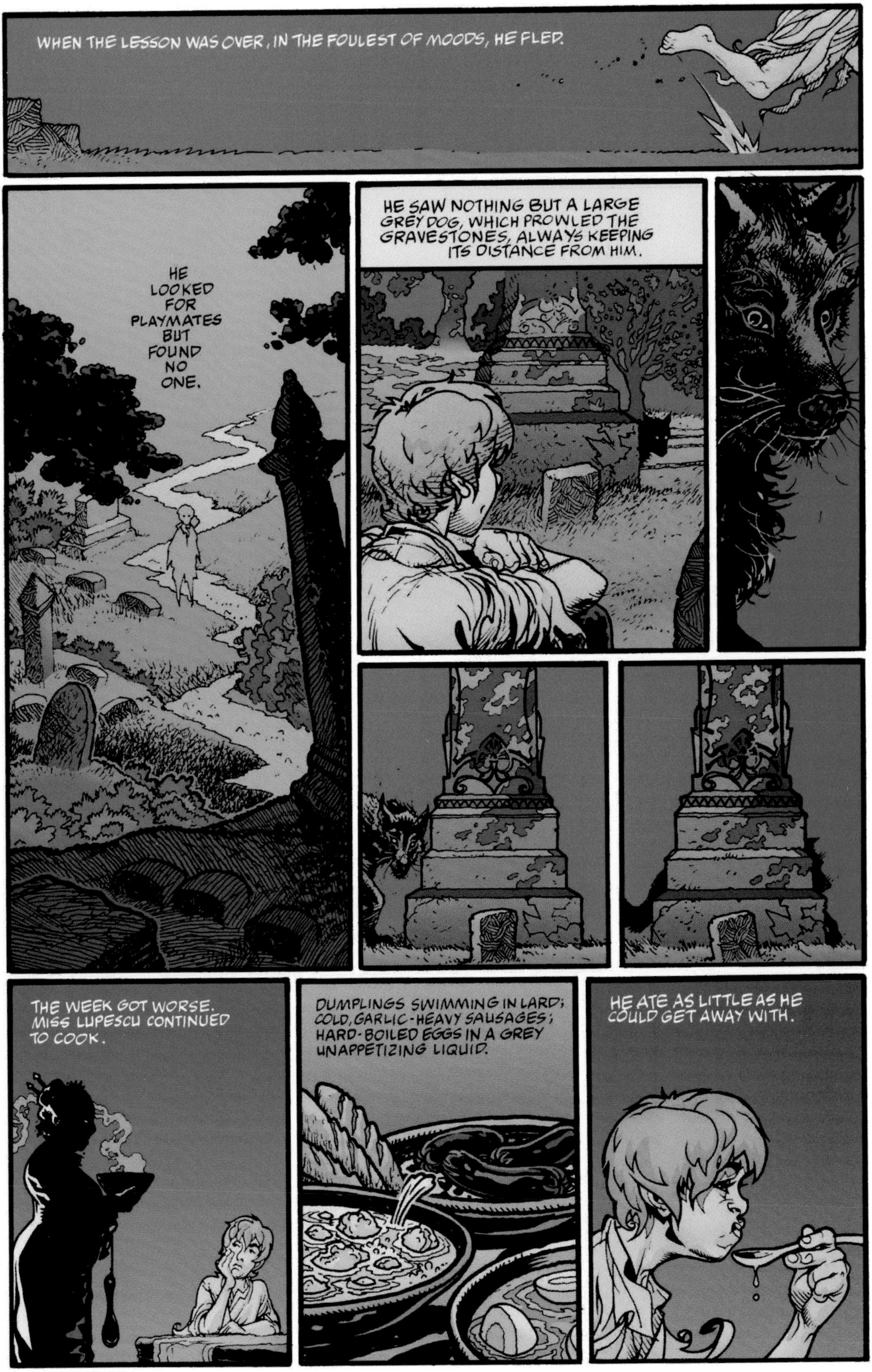
WHEN THE LESSON WAS OVER, IN THE FOULEST OF MOODS, HE FLED.
HE LOOKED FOR PLAYMATES BUT FOUND NO ONE.
HE SAW NOTHING BUT A LARGE GREY DOG, WHICH PROWLED THE GRAVESTONES, ALWAYS KEEPING ITS DISTANCE FROM HIM.
THE WEEK GOT WORSE. MISS LUPESCU CONTINUED TO COOK.
DUMPLINGS SWIMMING IN LARD; COLD, GARLIC-HEAVY SAUSAGES; HARD-BOILED EGGS IN A GREY UNAPPETIZING LIQUID.
HE ATE AS LITTLE AS HE COULD GET AWAY WITH.

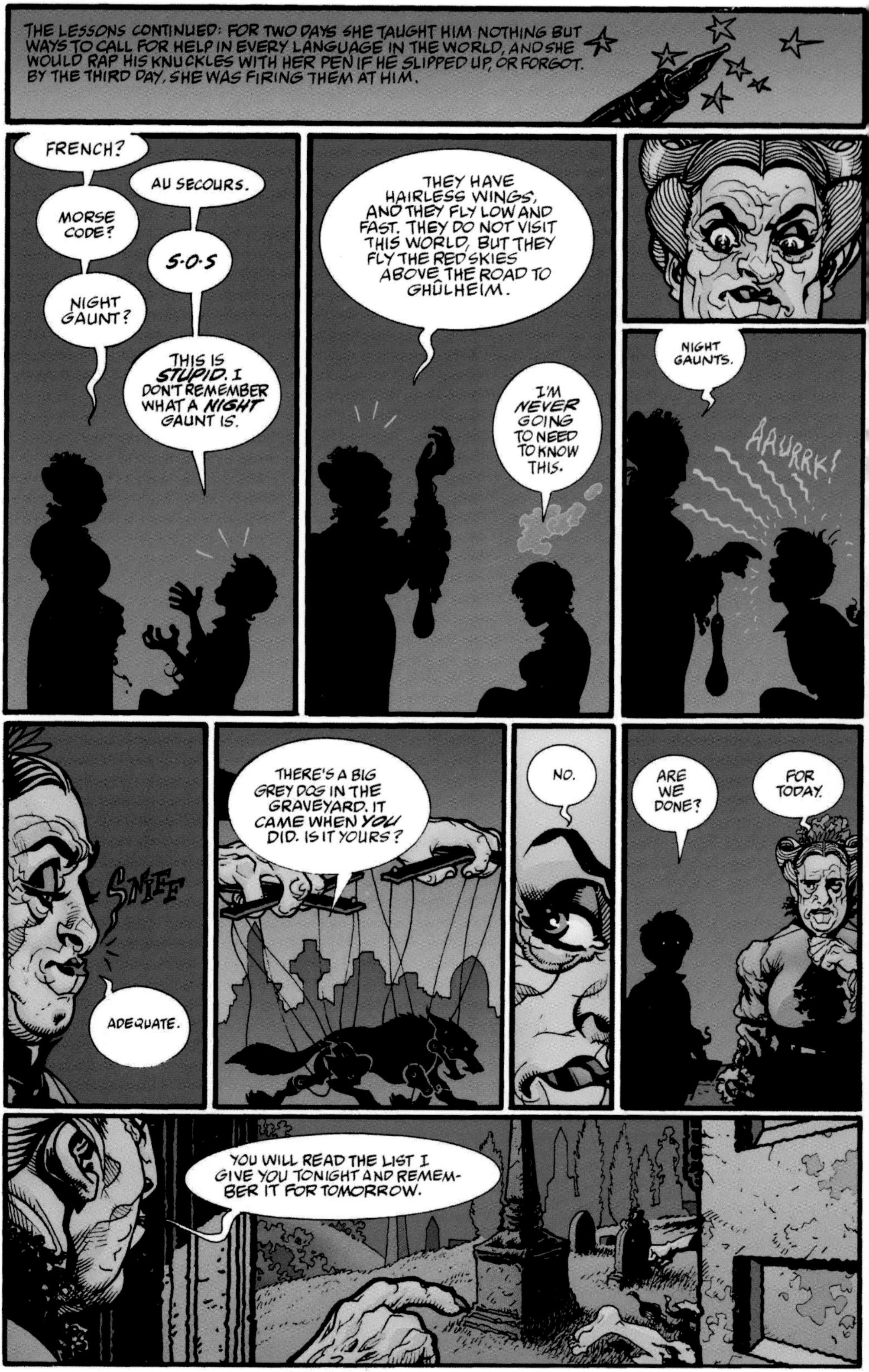
THE LESSONS CONTINUED: FOR TWO DAYS SHE TAUGHT HIM NOTHING BUT WAYS TO CALL FOR HELP IN EVERY LANGUAGE IN THE WORLD, AND SHE WOULD RAP HIS KNUCKLES WITH HER PEN IF HE SLIPPED UP, OR FORGOT. BY THE THIRD DAY, SHE WAS FIRING THEM AT HIM.
FRENCH?
AU SECOURS.
MORSE CODE?
S·O·S
NIGHT GAUNT?
THIS IS STUPID. I DON'T REMEMBER WHAT A NIGHT GAUNT IS.
THEY HAVE HAIRLESS WINGS, AND THEY FLY LOW AND FAST. THEY DO NOT VISIT THIS WORLD, BUT THEY FLY THE RED SKIES ABOVE THE ROAD TO GHÛLHEIM.
I'M NEVER GOING TO NEED TO KNOW THIS.
NIGHT GAUNTS.
AAURRK!
SNIFF
ADEQUATE.
THERE'S A BIG GREY DOG IN THE GRAVEYARD. IT CAME WHEN YOU DID. IS IT YOURS?
NO.
ARE WE DONE?
FOR TODAY.
YOU WILL READ THE LIST I GIVE YOU TONIGHT AND REMEMBER IT FOR TOMORROW.

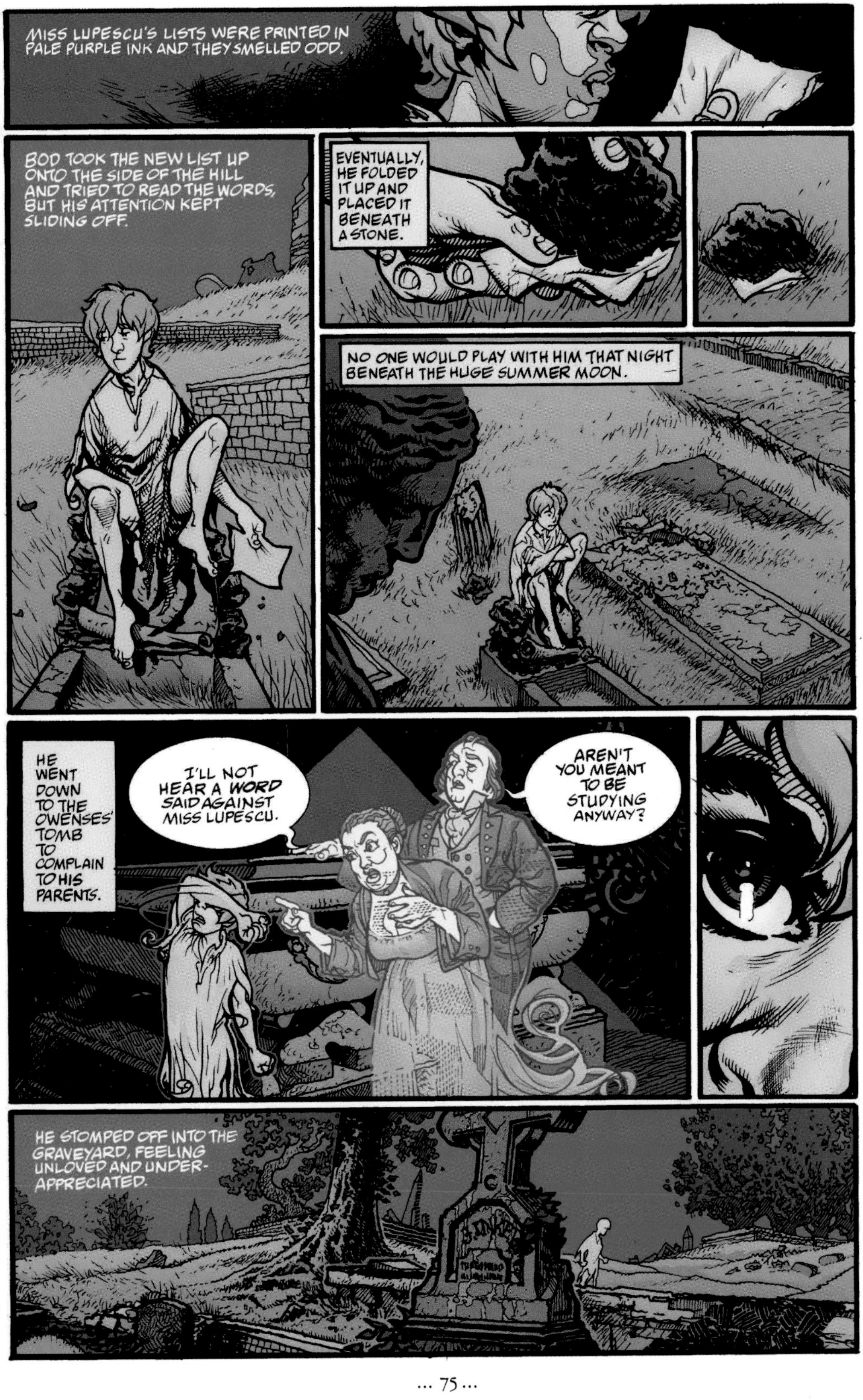
MISS LUPESCU'S LISTS WERE PRINTED IN PALE PURPLE INK AND THEY SMELLED ODD.
BOD TOOK THE NEW LIST UP ONTO THE SIDE OF THE HILL AND TRIED TO READ THE WORDS, BUT HIS ATTENTION KEPT SLIDING OFF.
EVENTUALLY, HE FOLDED IT UP AND PLACED IT BENEATH A STONE.
NO ONE WOULD PLAY WITH HIM THAT NIGHT BENEATH THE HUGE SUMMER MOON.
HE WENT DOWN TO THE OWENSES' TOMB TO COMPLAIN TO HIS PARENTS.
I'LL NOT HEAR A WORD SAID AGAINST MISS LUPESCU.
AREN'T YOU MEANT TO BE STUDYING ANYWAY?
HE STOMPED OFF INTO THE GRAVEYARD, FEELING UNLOVED AND UNDER-APPRECIATED.

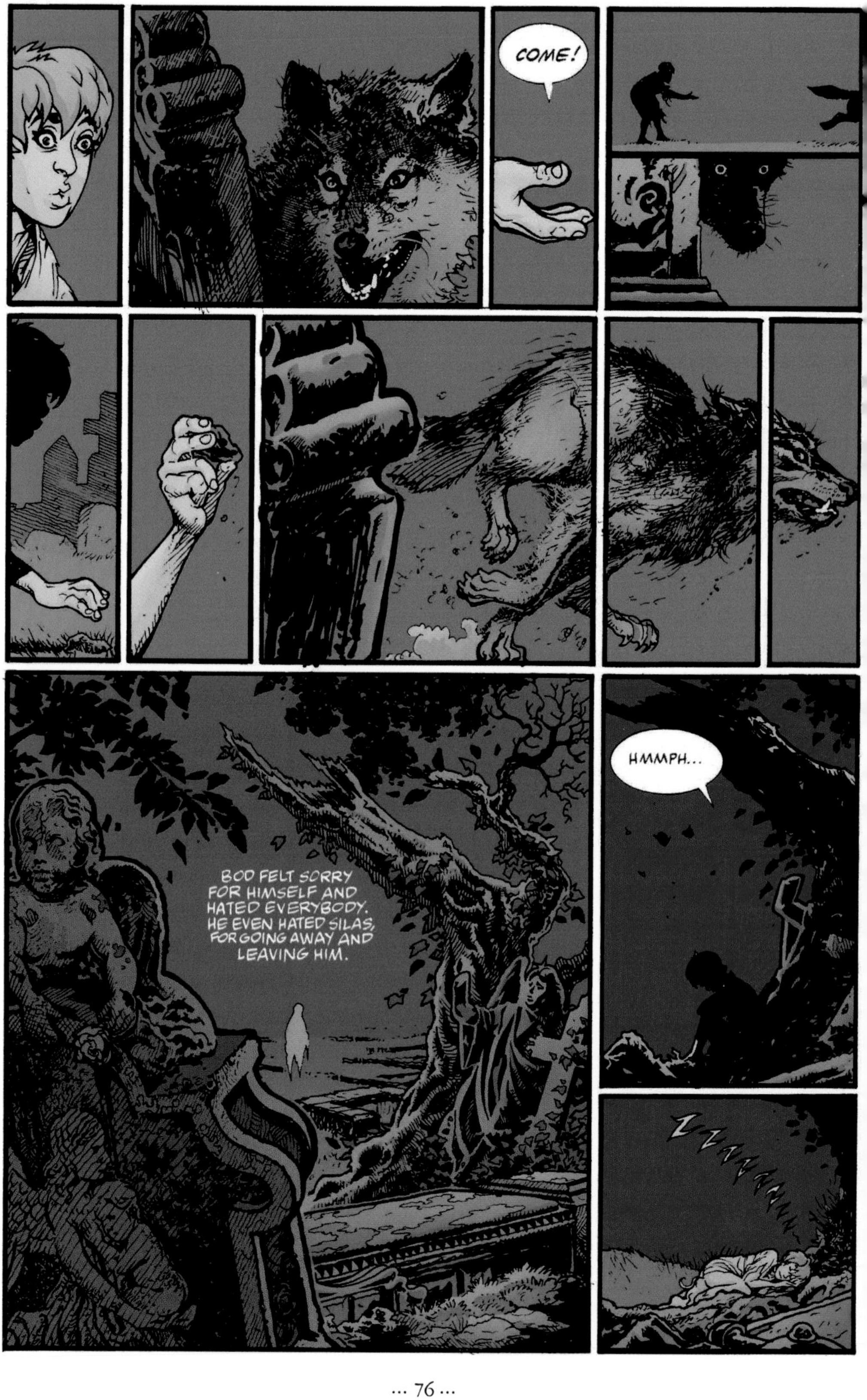
COME!
BOD FELT SORRY FOR HIMSELF AND HATED EVERYBODY. HE EVEN HATED SILAS, FOR GOING AWAY AND LEAVING HIM.
HMMPH...
ZZZZZZZ

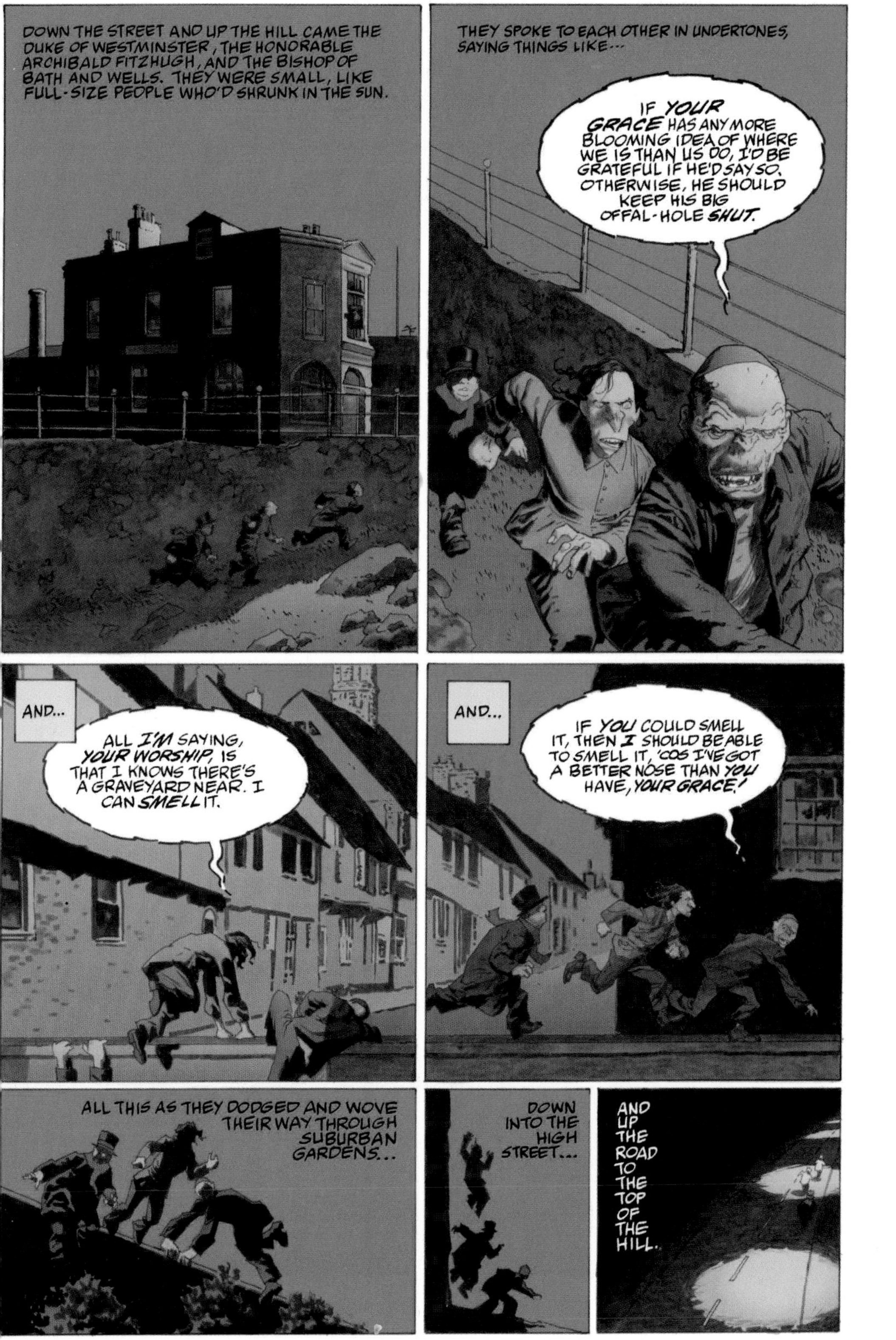
DOWN THE STREET AND UP THE HILL CAME THE DUKE OF WESTMINSTER, THE HONORABLE ARCHIBALD FITZHUGH, AND THE BISHOP OF BATH AND WELLS. THEY WERE SMALL, LIKE FULL-SIZE PEOPLE WHO'D SHRUNK IN THE SUN.
THEY SPOKE TO EACH OTHER IN UNDERTONES, SAYING THINGS LIKE...
IF YOUR GRACE HAS ANY MORE BLOOMING IDEA OF WHERE WE IS THAN US DO, I'D BE GRATEFUL IF HE'D SAY SO. OTHERWISE, HE SHOULD KEEP HIS BIG OFFAL-HOLE SHUT.
AND...
ALL I'M SAYING, YOUR WORSHIP, IS THAT I KNOWS THERE'S A GRAVEYARD NEAR. I CAN SMELL IT.
AND...
IF YOU COULD SMELL IT, THEN I SHOULD BE ABLE TO SMELL IT, 'COS I'VE GOT A BETTER NOSE THAN YOU HAVE, YOUR GRACE!
ALL THIS AS THEY DODGED AND WOVE THEIR WAY THROUGH SUBURBAN GARDENS...
DOWN INTO THE HIGH STREET...
AND UP THE ROAD TO THE TOP OF THE HILL.

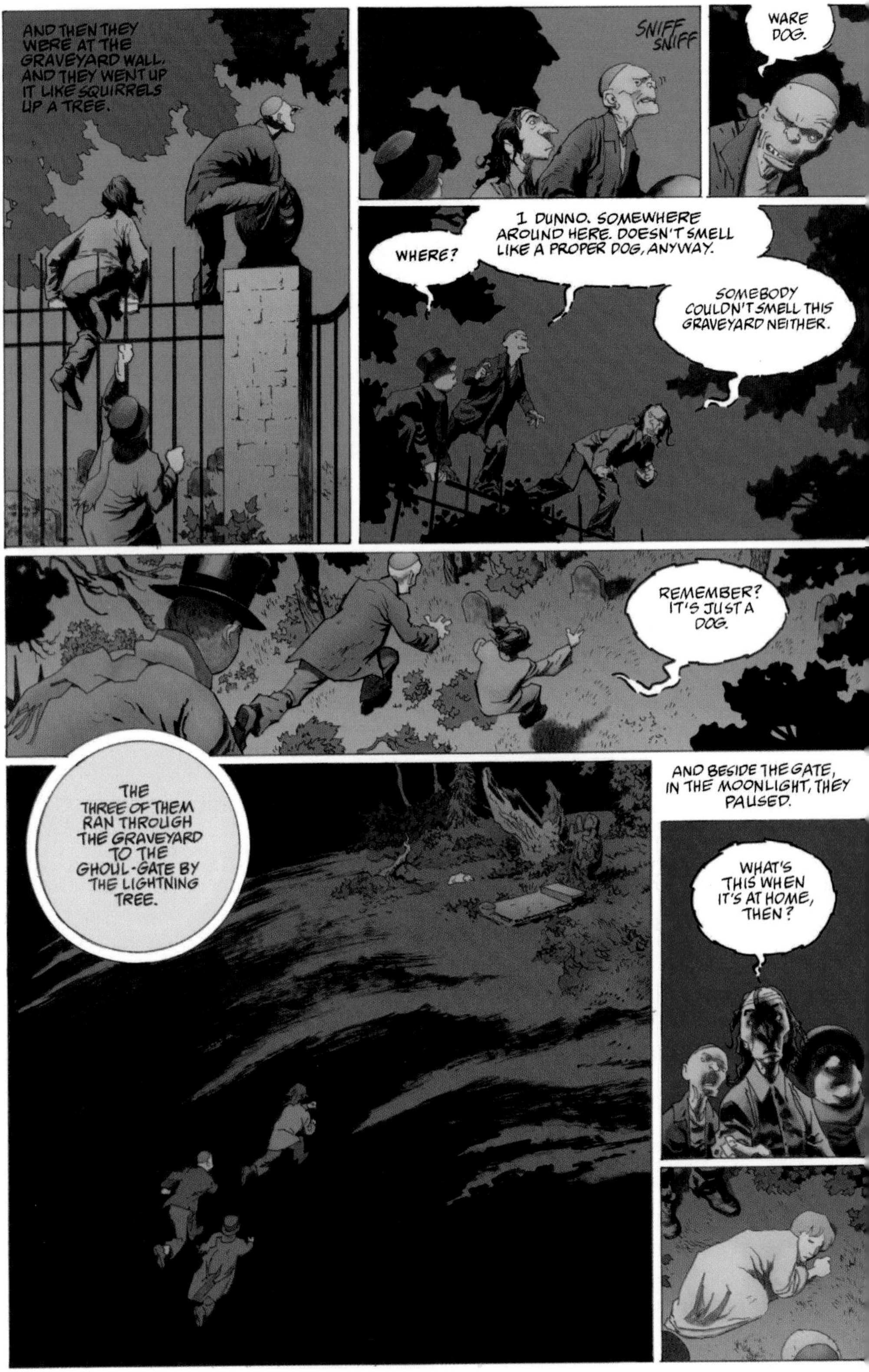
AND THEN THEY WERE AT THE GRAVEYARD WALL. AND THEY WENT UP IT LIKE SQUIRRELS UP A TREE.
SNIFF SNIFF
WARE DOG.
WHERE?
I DUNNO. SOMEWHERE AROUND HERE. DOESN'T SMELL LIKE A PROPER DOG, ANYWAY.
SOMEBODY COULDN'T SMELL THIS GRAVEYARD NEITHER.
REMEMBER? IT'S JUST A DOG.
THE THREE OF THEM RAN THROUGH THE GRAVEYARD TO THE GHOUL-GATE BY THE LIGHTNING TREE.
AND BESIDE THE GATE, IN THE MOONLIGHT, THEY PAUSED.
WHAT'S THIS WHEN IT'S AT HOME, THEN?

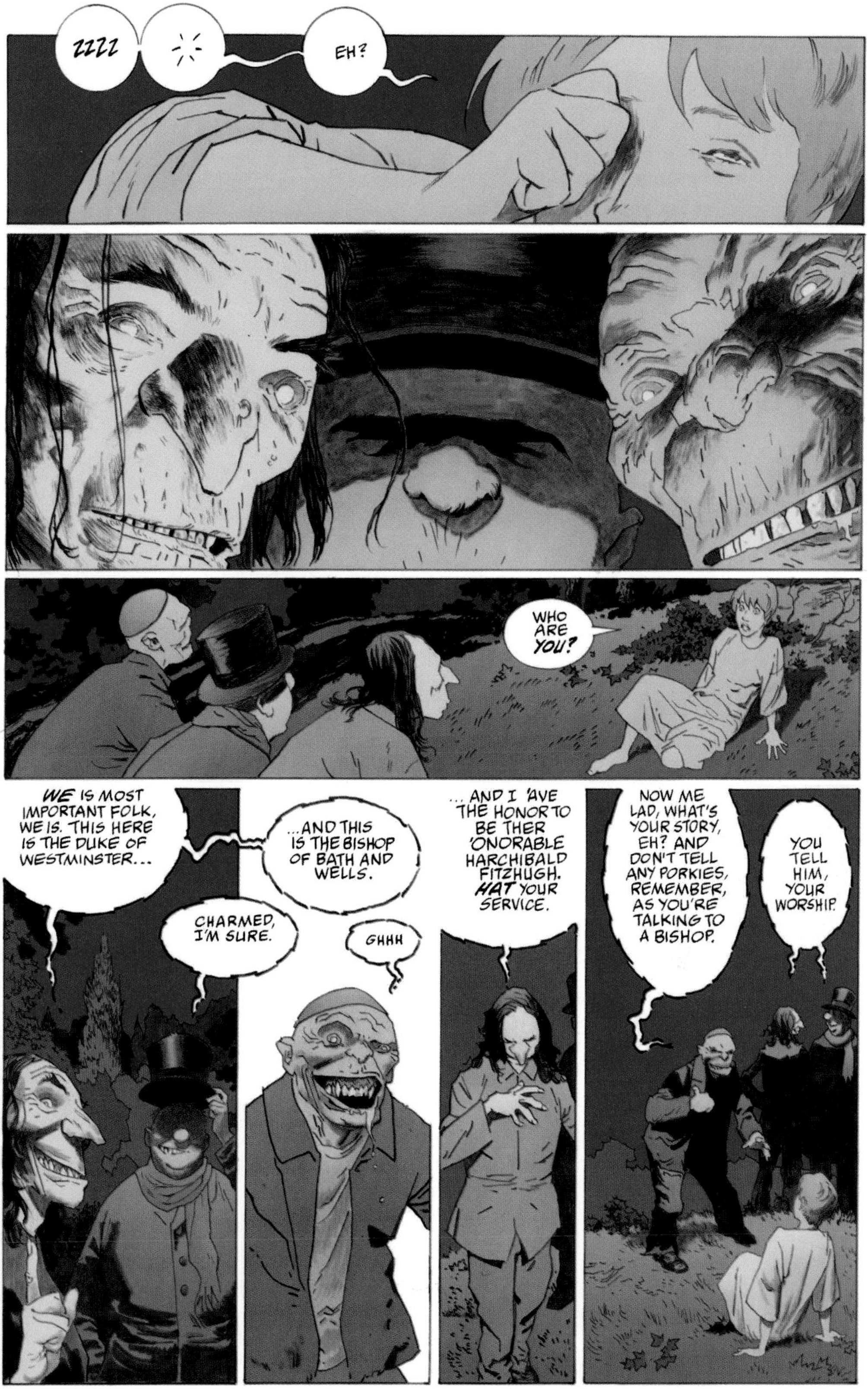
ZZZZ
EH?
WHO ARE YOU?
WE IS MOST IMPORTANT FOLK, WE IS. THIS HERE IS THE DUKE OF WESTMINSTER...
...AND THIS IS THE BISHOP OF BATH AND WELLS.
CHARMED, I'M SURE.
GHHH
...AND I 'AVE THE HONOR TO BE THER 'ONORABLE HARCHIBALD FITZHUGH. HAT YOUR SERVICE.
NOW ME LAD, WHAT'S YOUR STORY, EH? AND DON'T TELL ANY PORKIES, REMEMBER, AS YOU'RE TALKING TO A BISHOP.
YOU TELL HIM, YOUR WORSHIP.

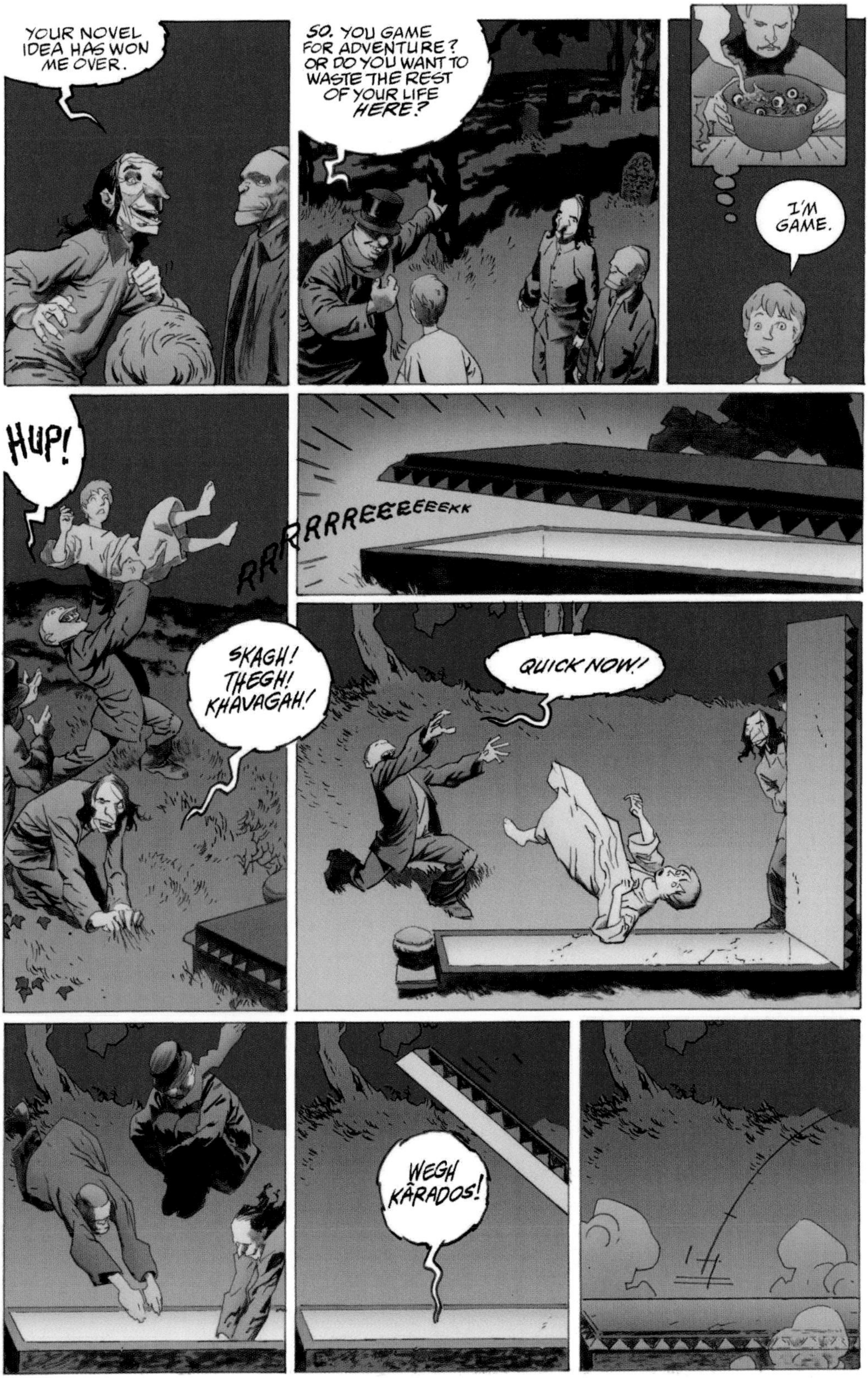
YOUR NOVEL IDEA HAS WON ME OVER.
SO. YOU GAME FOR ADVENTURE? OR DO YOU WANT TO WASTE THE REST OF YOUR LIFE HERE?
I'M GAME.
HUP!
RRRRRREEEEEEEEKK
SKAGH! THEGH! KHAVAGAH!
QUICK NOW!
WEGH KÃRADOS!

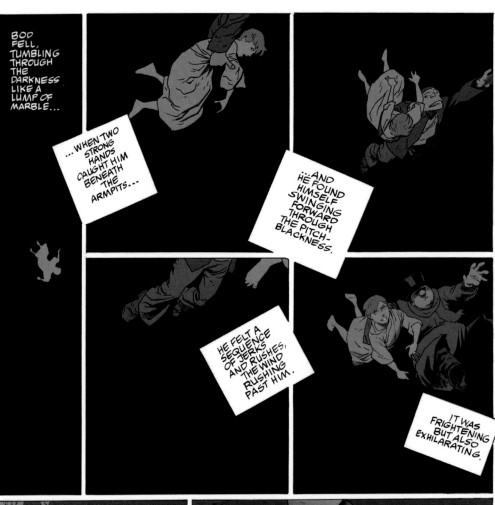

BOD FELL, TUMBLING THROUGH THE DARKNESS LIKE A LUMP OF MARBLE...

...WHEN TWO STRONG HANDS CAUGHT HIM BENEATH THE ARMPITS...

...AND HE FOUND HIMSELF SWINGING FORWARD THROUGH THE PITCH-BLACKNESS.

HE FELT A SEQUENCE OF JERKS, AND RUSHES, THE WIND RUSHING PAST HIM.

IT WAS FRIGHTENING BUT ALSO EXHILARATING.

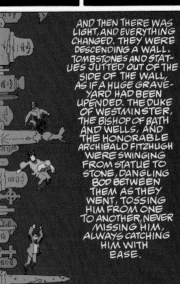

AND THEN THERE WAS LIGHT, AND EVERYTHING CHANGED. THEY WERE DESCENDING A WALL. TOMBSTONES AND STATUES JUTTED OUT OF THE SIDE OF THE WALL, AS IF A HUGE GRAVEYARD HAD BEEN UPENDED. THE DUKE OF WESTMINSTER, THE BISHOP OF BATH AND WELLS, AND THE HONORABLE ARCHIBALD FITZHUGH WERE SWINGING FROM STATUE TO STONE, DANGLING BOD BETWEEN THEM AS THEY WENT, TOSSING HIM FROM ONE TO ANOTHER, NEVER MISSING HIM, ALWAYS CATCHING HIM WITH EASE.

WHERE ARE WE GOING?

BUT BOD'S VOICE WAS WHIPPED AWAY BY THE WIND.

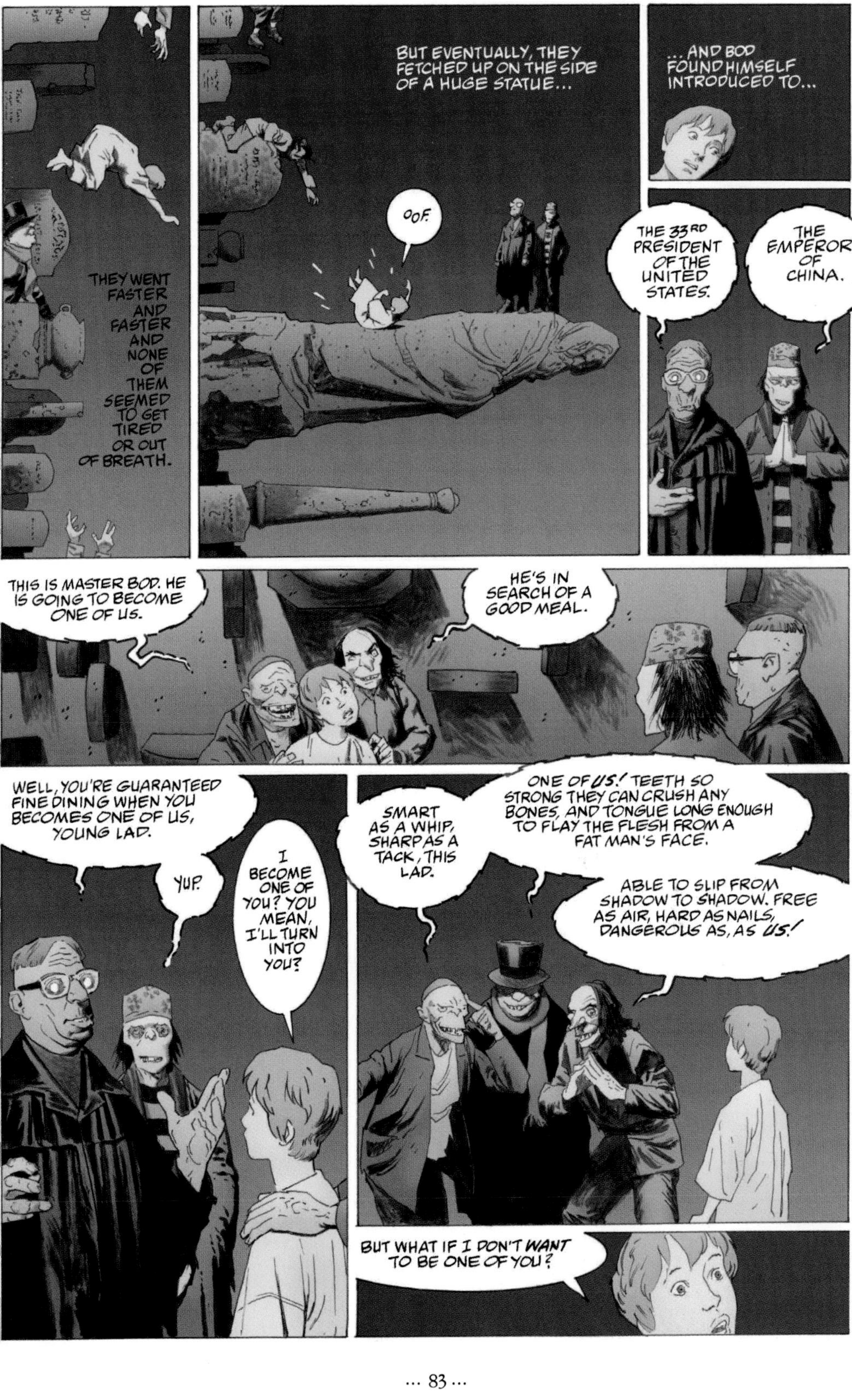

THEY WENT FASTER AND FASTER AND NONE OF THEM SEEMED TO GET TIRED OR OUT OF BREATH.
BUT EVENTUALLY, THEY FETCHED UP ON THE SIDE OF A HUGE STATUE...
OOF.
...AND BOD FOUND HIMSELF INTRODUCED TO...
THE 33RD PRESIDENT OF THE UNITED STATES.
THE EMPEROR OF CHINA.
THIS IS MASTER BOD. HE IS GOING TO BECOME ONE OF US.
HE'S IN SEARCH OF A GOOD MEAL.
WELL, YOU'RE GUARANTEED FINE DINING WHEN YOU BECOMES ONE OF US, YOUNG LAD.
YUP.
I BECOME ONE OF YOU? YOU MEAN, I'LL TURN INTO YOU?
SMART AS A WHIP, SHARP AS A TACK, THIS LAD.
ONE OF US! TEETH SO STRONG THEY CAN CRUSH ANY BONES, AND TONGUE LONG ENOUGH TO FLAY THE FLESH FROM A FAT MAN'S FACE.
ABLE TO SLIP FROM SHADOW TO SHADOW. FREE AS AIR, HARD AS NAILS, DANGEROUS AS, AS US!
BUT WHAT IF I DON'T WANT TO BE ONE OF YOU?

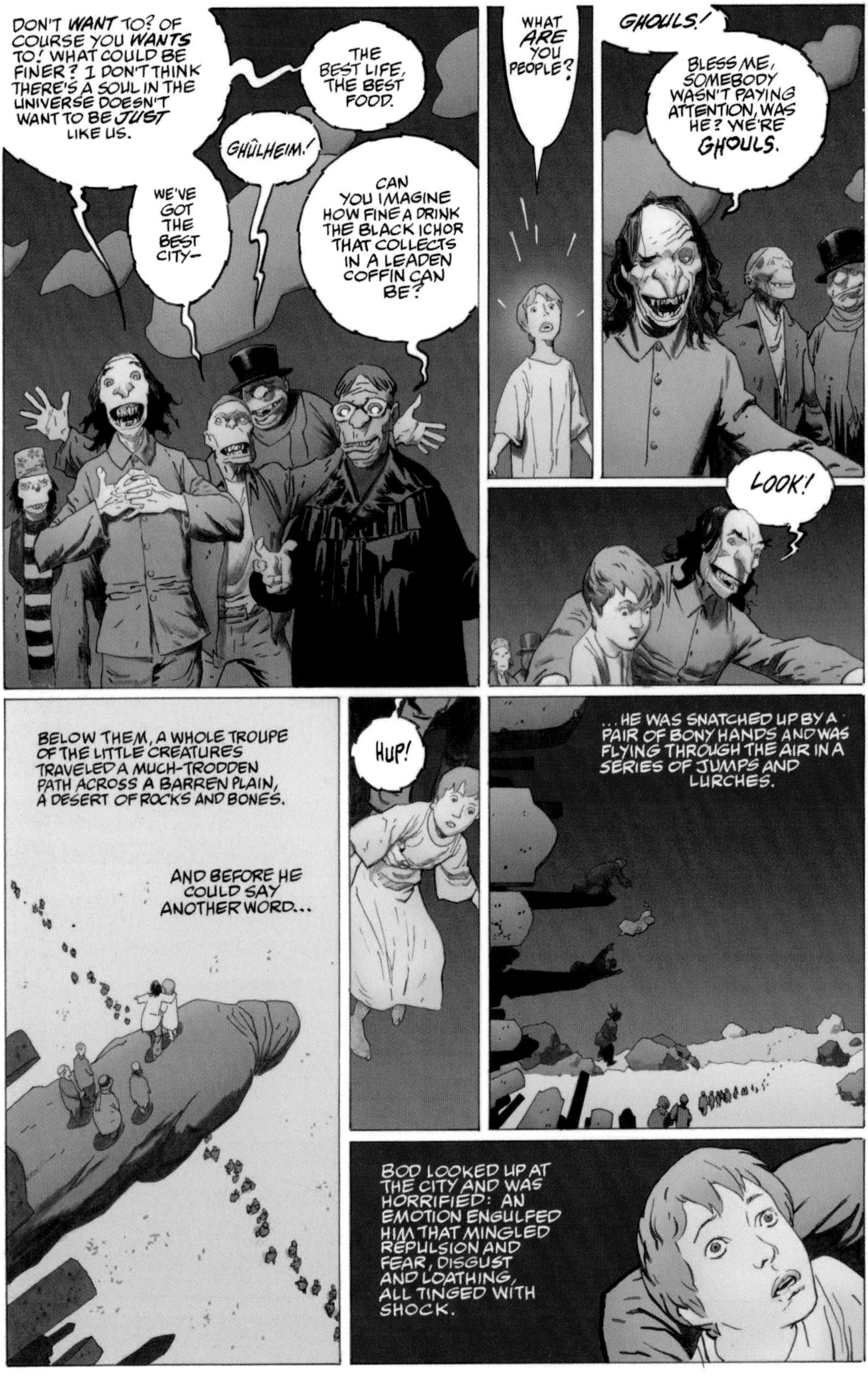
DON'T WANT TO? OF COURSE YOU WANTS TO! WHAT COULD BE FINER? I DON'T THINK THERE'S A SOUL IN THE UNIVERSE DOESN'T WANT TO BE JUST LIKE US.
WE'VE GOT THE BEST CITY-
GHÛLHEIM!
THE BEST LIFE, THE BEST FOOD.
CAN YOU IMAGINE HOW FINE A DRINK THE BLACK ICHOR THAT COLLECTS IN A LEADEN COFFIN CAN BE?
WHAT ARE YOU PEOPLE?
GHOULS!
BLESS ME, SOMEBODY WASN'T PAYING ATTENTION, WAS HE? WE'RE GHOULS.
LOOK!
BELOW THEM, A WHOLE TROUPE OF THE LITTLE CREATURES TRAVELED A MUCH-TRODDEN PATH ACROSS A BARREN PLAIN, A DESERT OF ROCKS AND BONES.
AND BEFORE HE COULD SAY ANOTHER WORD...
HUP!
...HE WAS SNATCHED UP BY A PAIR OF BONY HANDS AND WAS FLYING THROUGH THE AIR IN A SERIES OF JUMPS AND LURCHES.
BOD LOOKED UP AT THE CITY AND WAS HORRIFIED: AN EMOTION ENGULFED HIM THAT MINGLED REPULSION AND FEAR, DISGUST AND LOATHING, ALL TINGED WITH SHOCK.

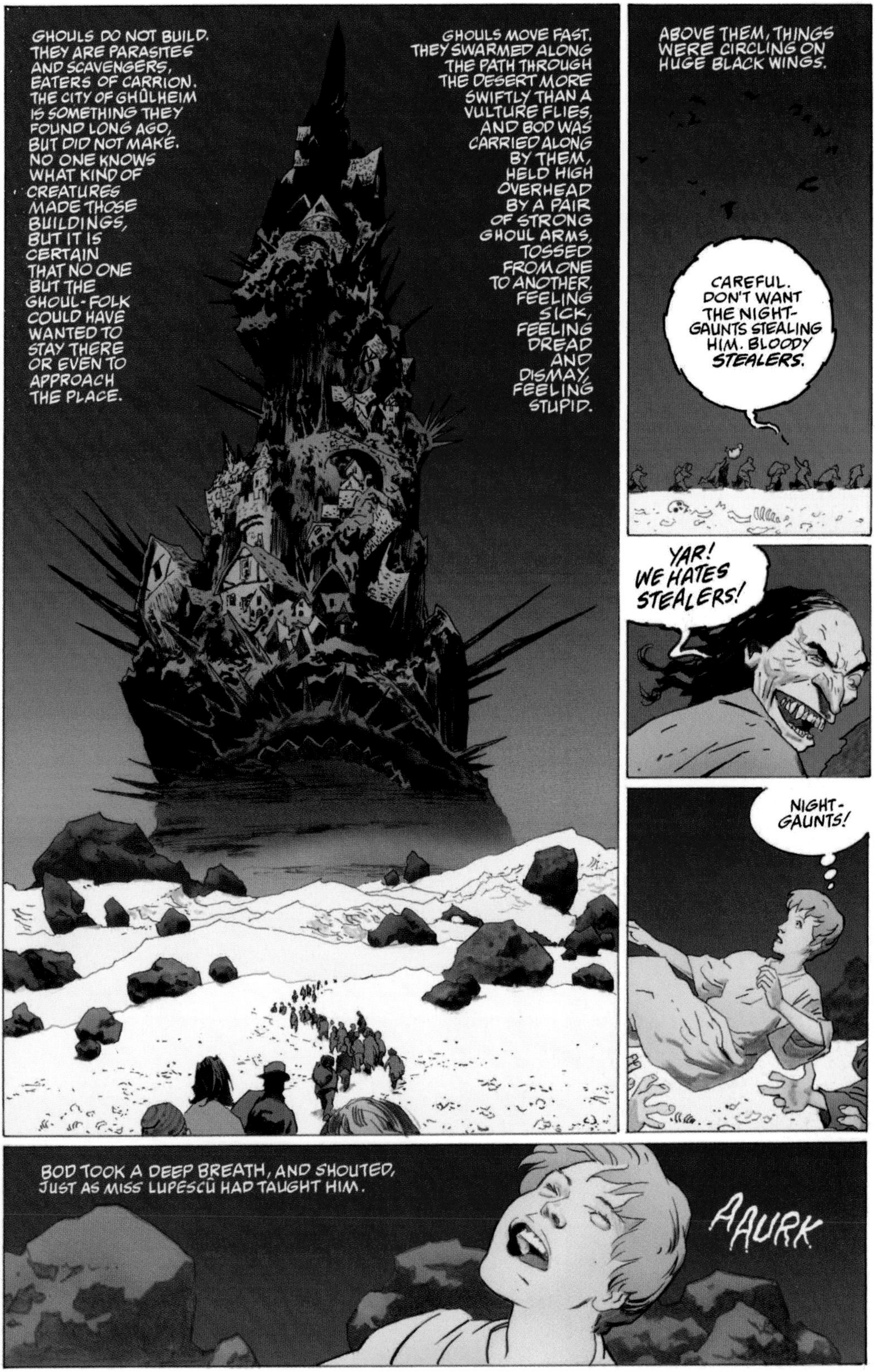
GHOULS DO NOT BUILD. THEY ARE PARASITES AND SCAVENGERS, EATERS OF CARRION. THE CITY OF GHÛLHEIM IS SOMETHING THEY FOUND LONG AGO, BUT DID NOT MAKE. NO ONE KNOWS WHAT KIND OF CREATURES MADE THOSE BUILDINGS, BUT IT IS CERTAIN THAT NO ONE BUT THE GHOUL-FOLK COULD HAVE WANTED TO STAY THERE OR EVEN TO APPROACH THE PLACE.
GHOULS MOVE FAST. THEY SWARMED ALONG THE PATH THROUGH THE DESERT MORE SWIFTLY THAN A VULTURE FLIES, AND BOD WAS CARRIED ALONG BY THEM, HELD HIGH OVERHEAD BY A PAIR OF STRONG GHOUL ARMS, TOSSED FROM ONE TO ANOTHER, FEELING SICK, FEELING DREAD AND DISMAY, FEELING STUPID.
ABOVE THEM, THINGS WERE CIRCLING ON HUGE BLACK WINGS.
CAREFUL. DON'T WANT THE NIGHT-GAUNTS STEALING HIM. BLOODY STEALERS.
YAR! WE HATES STEALERS!
NIGHT-GAUNTS!
BOD TOOK A DEEP BREATH, AND SHOUTED, JUST AS MISS LUPESCU HAD TAUGHT HIM.
AAURK

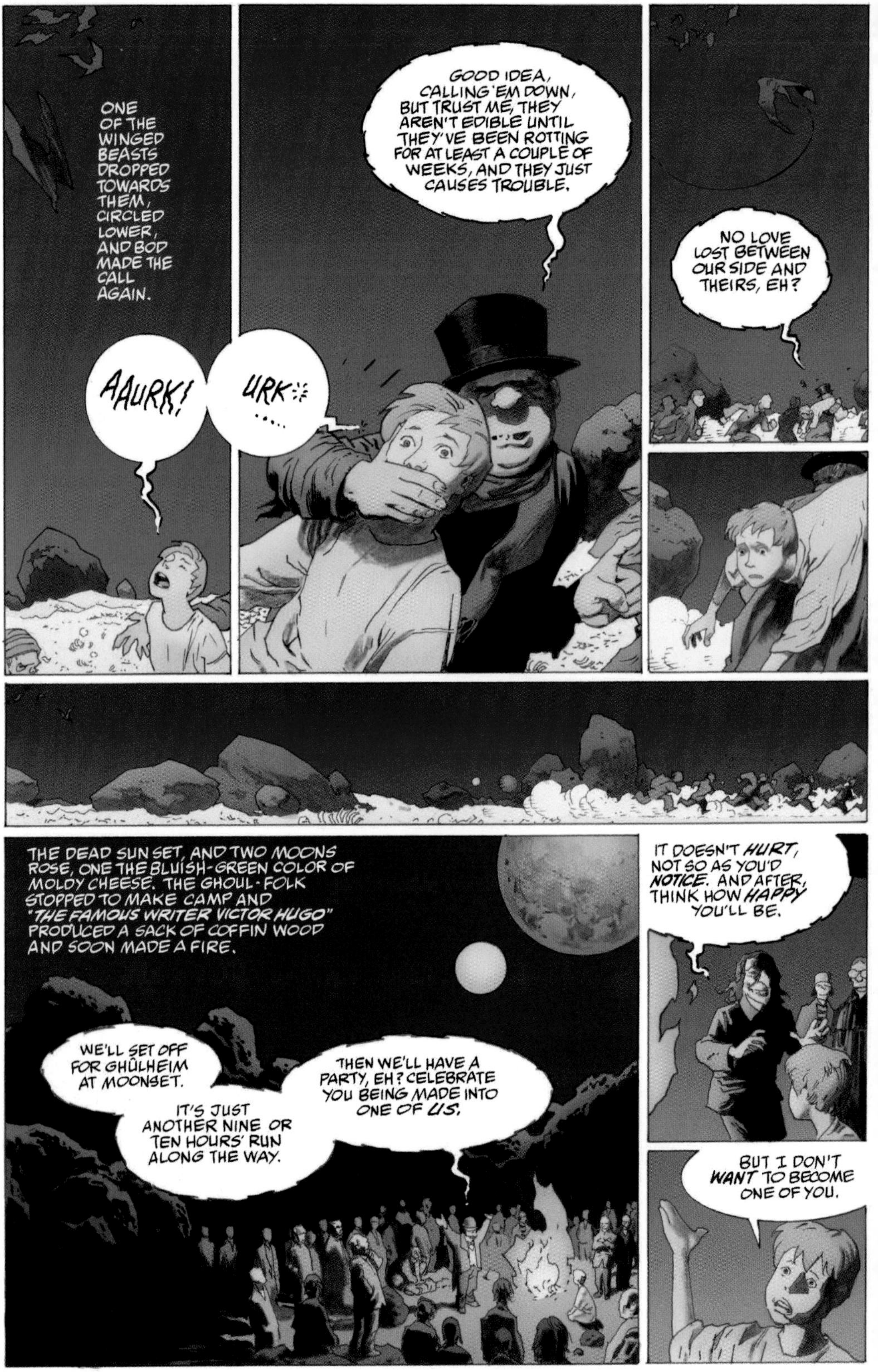
ONE OF THE WINGED BEASTS DROPPED TOWARDS THEM, CIRCLED LOWER, AND BOD MADE THE CALL AGAIN.
AAURK!
URK
GOOD IDEA, CALLING 'EM DOWN, BUT TRUST ME, THEY AREN'T EDIBLE UNTIL THEY'VE BEEN ROTTING FOR AT LEAST A COUPLE OF WEEKS, AND THEY JUST CAUSES TROUBLE.
NO LOVE LOST BETWEEN OUR SIDE AND THEIRS, EH?
THE DEAD SUN SET, AND TWO MOONS ROSE, ONE THE BLUISH-GREEN COLOR OF MOLDY CHEESE. THE GHOUL-FOLK STOPPED TO MAKE CAMP AND "THE FAMOUS WRITER VICTOR HUGO" PRODUCED A SACK OF COFFIN WOOD AND SOON MADE A FIRE.
WE'LL SET OFF FOR GHÛLHEIM AT MOONSET.
IT'S JUST ANOTHER NINE OR TEN HOURS' RUN ALONG THE WAY.
THEN WE'LL HAVE A PARTY, EH? CELEBRATE YOU BEING MADE INTO ONE OF US.
IT DOESN'T HURT, NOT SO AS YOU'D NOTICE. AND AFTER, THINK HOW HAPPY YOU'LL BE.
BUT I DON'T WANT TO BECOME ONE OF YOU.

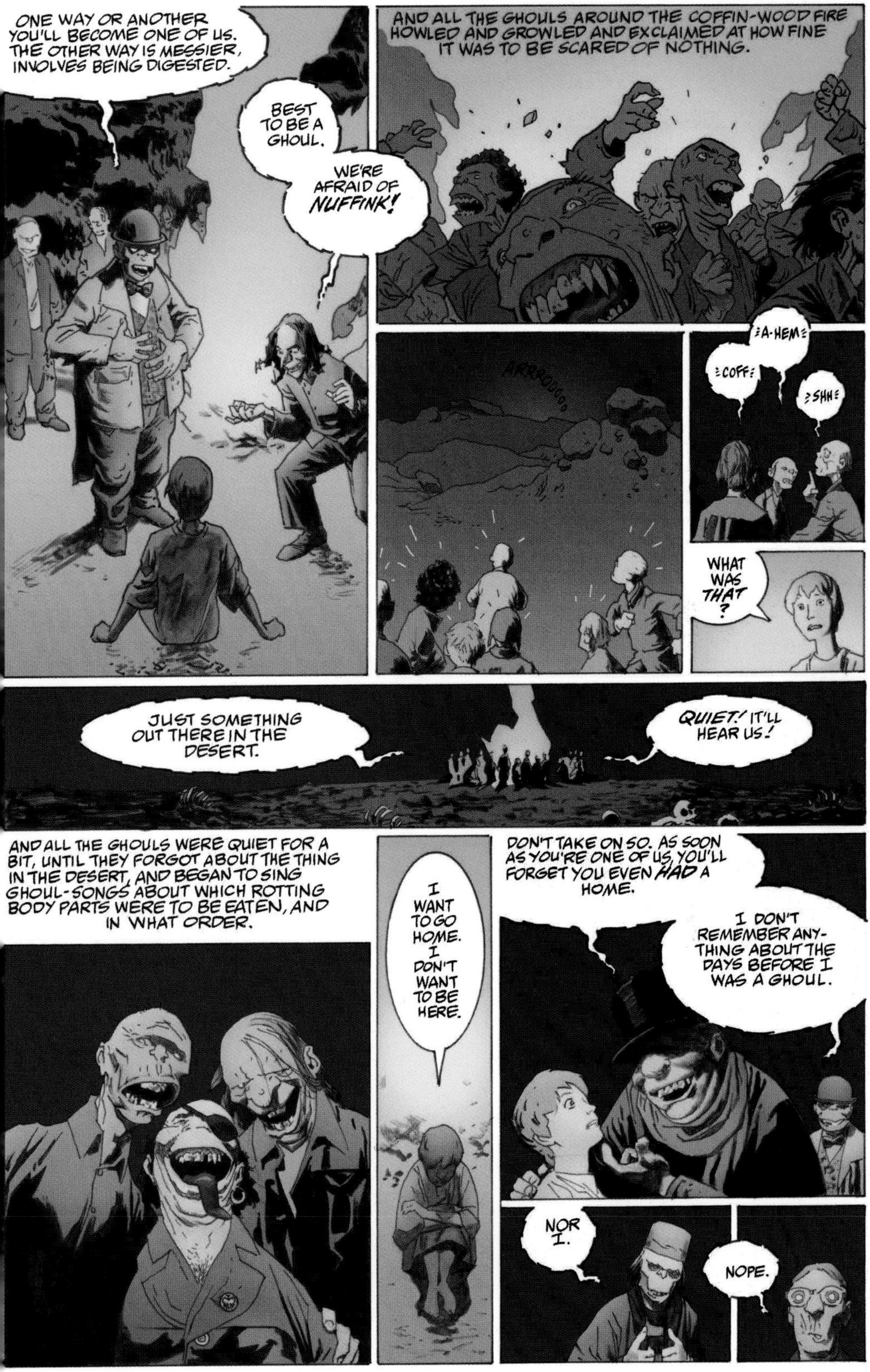
ONE WAY OR ANOTHER YOU'LL BECOME ONE OF US. THE OTHER WAY IS MESSIER, INVOLVES BEING DIGESTED.
BEST TO BE A GHOUL.
WE'RE AFRAID OF NUFFINK!
AND ALL THE GHOULS AROUND THE COFFIN-WOOD FIRE HOWLED AND GROWLED AND EXCLAIMED AT HOW FINE IT WAS TO BE SCARED OF NOTHING.
ARRROOOOO
A-HEM
COFF
SHH
WHAT WAS THAT?
JUST SOMETHING OUT THERE IN THE DESERT.
QUIET! IT'LL HEAR US!
AND ALL THE GHOULS WERE QUIET FOR A BIT, UNTIL THEY FORGOT ABOUT THE THING IN THE DESERT, AND BEGAN TO SING GHOUL-SONGS ABOUT WHICH ROTTING BODY PARTS WERE TO BE EATEN, AND IN WHAT ORDER.
I WANT TO GO HOME. I DON'T WANT TO BE HERE.
DON'T TAKE ON SO. AS SOON AS YOU'RE ONE OF US, YOU'LL FORGET YOU EVEN HAD A HOME.
I DON'T REMEMBER ANYTHING ABOUT THE DAYS BEFORE I WAS A GHOUL.
NOR I.
NOPE.

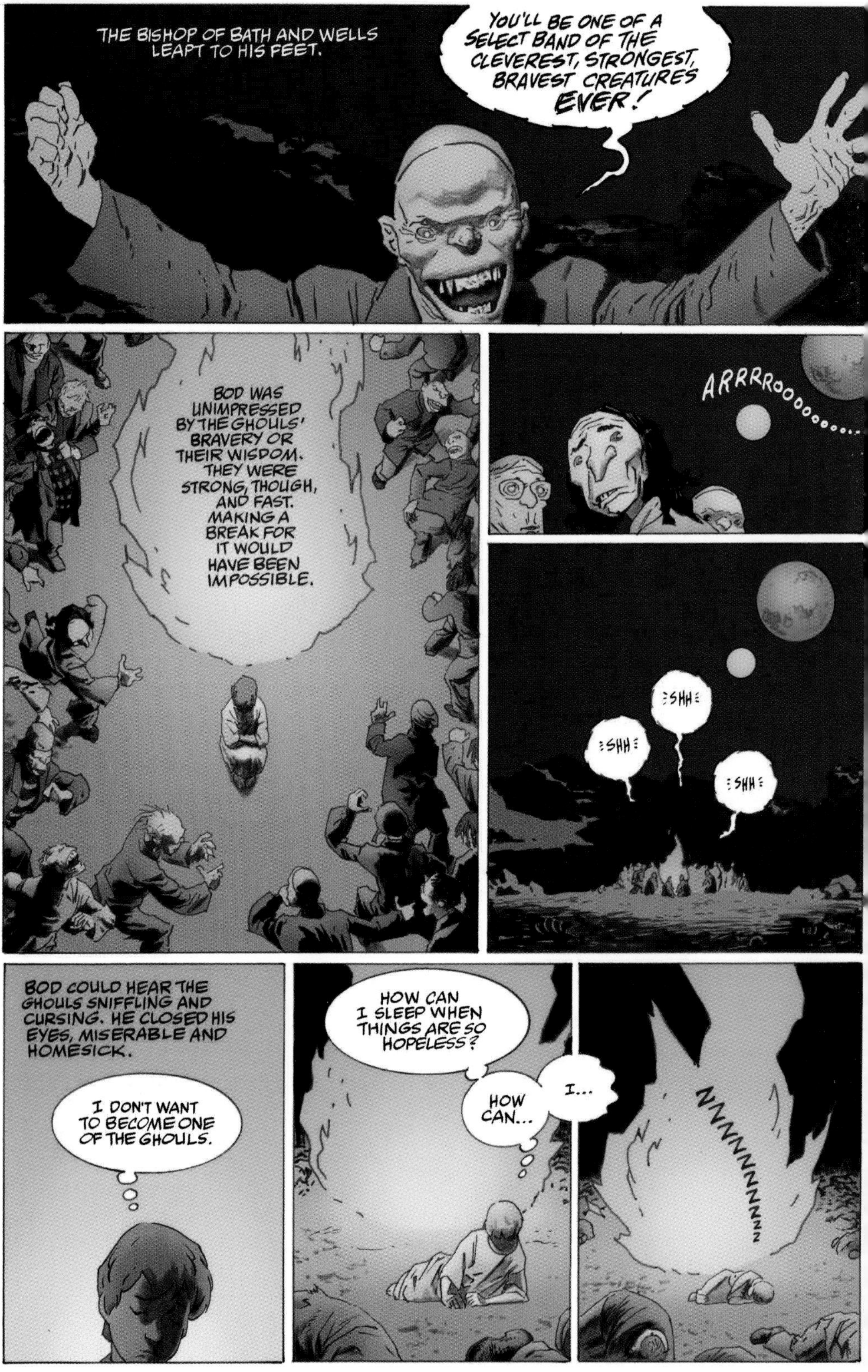
THE BISHOP OF BATH AND WELLS LEAPT TO HIS FEET.
YOU'LL BE ONE OF A SELECT BAND OF THE CLEVEREST, STRONGEST, BRAVEST CREATURES EVER!
BOD WAS UNIMPRESSED BY THE GHOULS' BRAVERY OR THEIR WISDOM. THEY WERE STRONG, THOUGH, AND FAST. MAKING A BREAK FOR IT WOULD HAVE BEEN IMPOSSIBLE.
ARRRROOOOOOOO.....
SHH
SHH
SHH
BOD COULD HEAR THE GHOULS SNIFFLING AND CURSING. HE CLOSED HIS EYES, MISERABLE AND HOMESICK.
I DON'T WANT TO BECOME ONE OF THE GHOULS.
HOW CAN I SLEEP WHEN THINGS ARE SO HOPELESS?
HOW CAN...
I...
NNNNNNNNNzzz

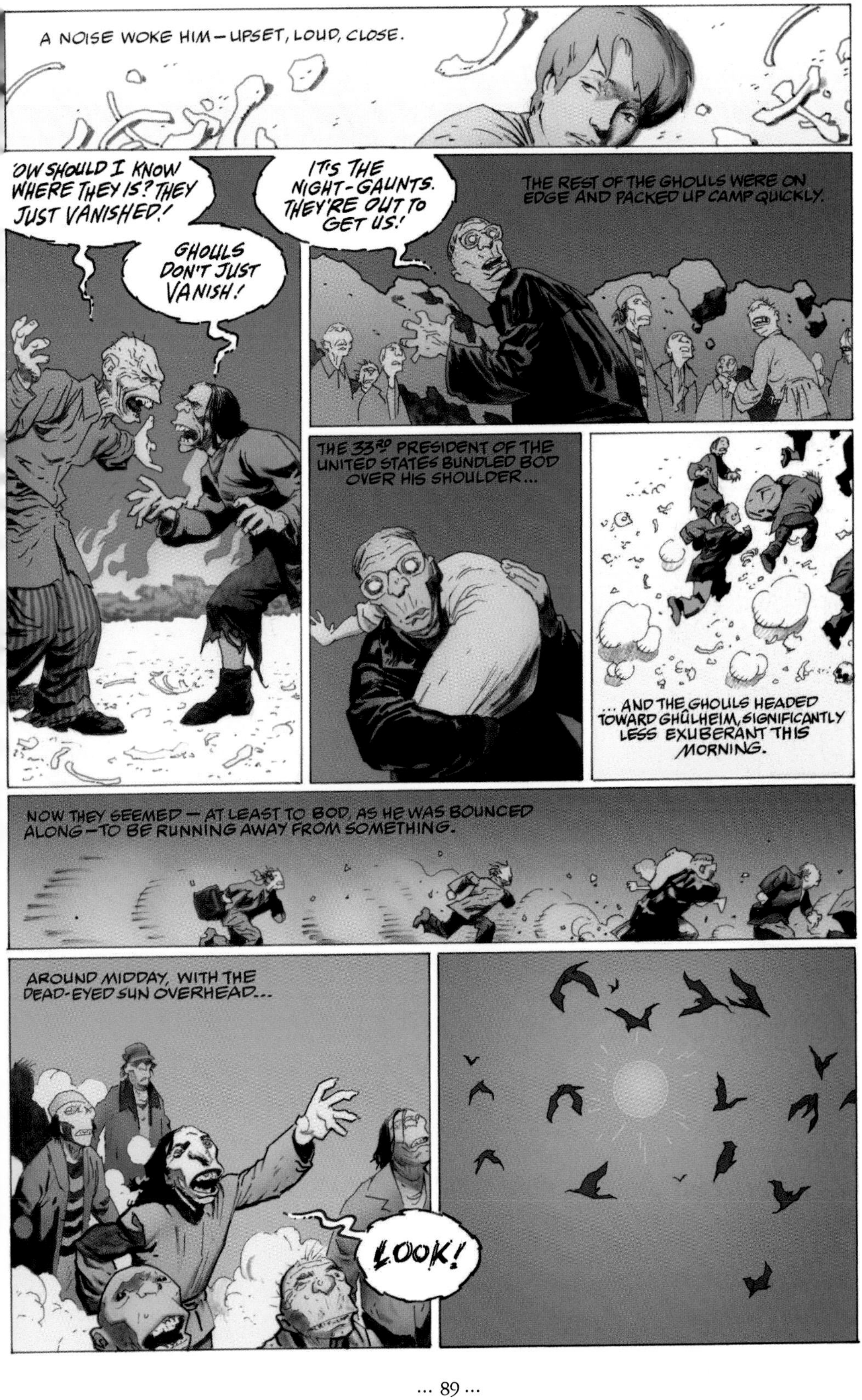
A NOISE WOKE HIM—UPSET, LOUD, CLOSE.
'OW SHOULD I KNOW WHERE THEY IS? THEY JUST VANISHED!
GHOULS DON'T JUST VANISH!
IT'S THE NIGHT-GAUNTS. THEY'RE OUT TO GET US!
THE REST OF THE GHOULS WERE ON EDGE AND PACKED UP CAMP QUICKLY.
THE 33RD PRESIDENT OF THE UNITED STATES BUNDLED BOD OVER HIS SHOULDER...
...AND THE GHOULS HEADED TOWARD GHÛLHEIM, SIGNIFICANTLY LESS EXUBERANT THIS MORNING.
NOW THEY SEEMED—AT LEAST TO BOD, AS HE WAS BOUNCED ALONG—TO BE RUNNING AWAY FROM SOMETHING.
AROUND MIDDAY, WITH THE DEAD-EYED SUN OVERHEAD...
LOOK!

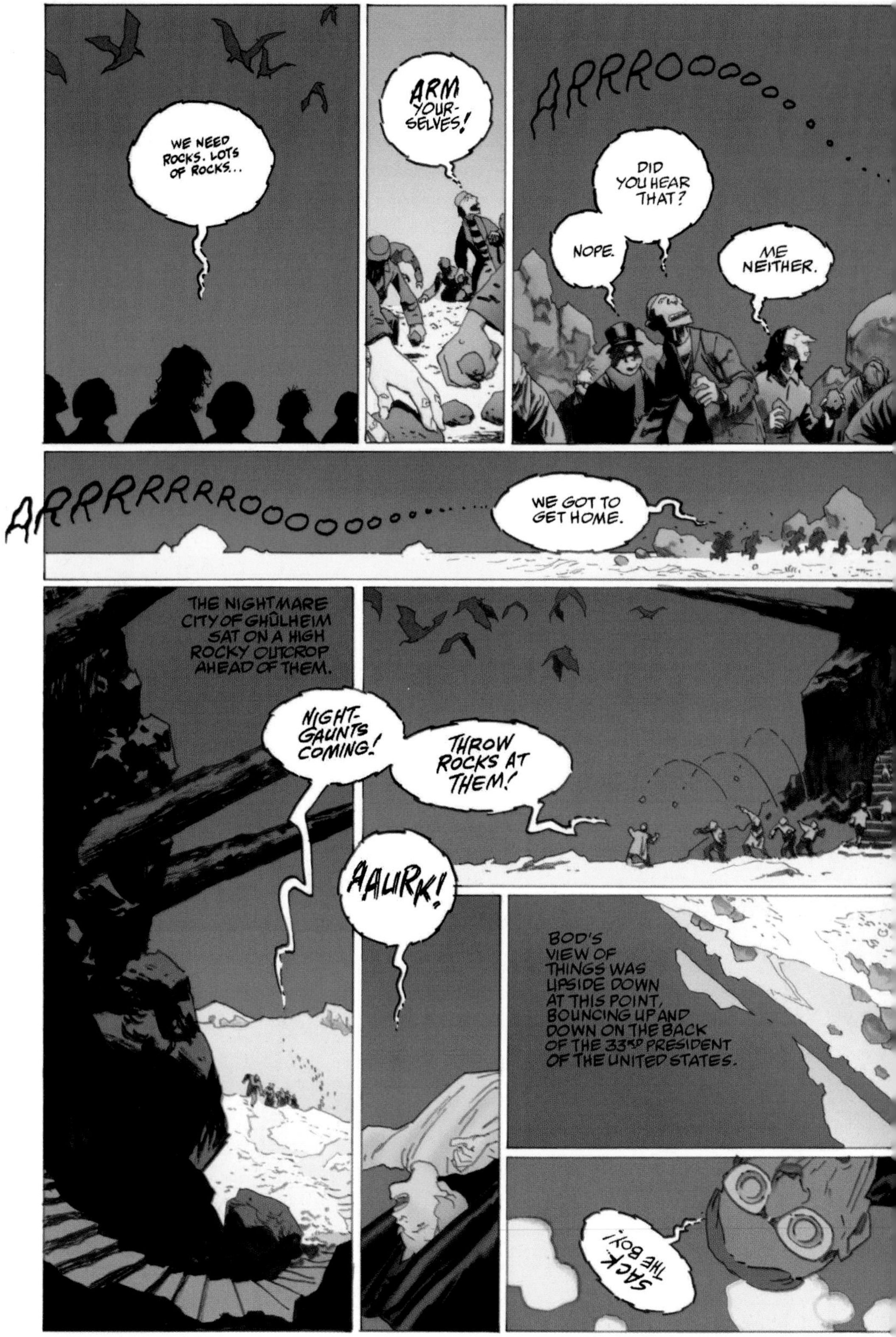
WE NEED ROCKS. LOTS OF ROCKS...
ARM YOUR-SELVES!
ARRROooooo...
DID YOU HEAR THAT?
NOPE.
ME NEITHER.
ARRRRRRROOOOOOOOoo.....
WE GOT TO GET HOME.
THE NIGHTMARE CITY OF GHÛLHEIM SAT ON A HIGH ROCKY OUTCROP AHEAD OF THEM.
NIGHT-GAUNTS COMING!
THROW ROCKS AT THEM!
AAURK!
BOD'S VIEW OF THINGS WAS UPSIDE DOWN AT THIS POINT, BOUNCING UP AND DOWN ON THE BACK OF THE 33RD PRESIDENT OF THE UNITED STATES.
SACK THE BOY!

THE 33RD PRESIDENT OF THE UNITED STATES HANDED BOD OVER TO THE FAMOUS WRITER VICTOR HUGO.

DON'T YOU WORRY, BOY. THERE WON'T BE ANY OF THIS NONSENSE WHEN WE GET YOU TO GHÛLHEIM. IT'S IMPENETRABLE.

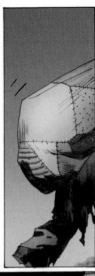

QUICKLY!

BOD WAS BEING PAINFULLY SLAMMED AGAINST THE FAMOUS WRITER VICTOR HUGO'S BACK AND OCCASIONALLY BANGED ON THE GROUND.

TO MAKE MATTERS WORSE THERE WERE, IN THERE WITH HIM, THE FINAL REMNANTS OF THE COFFIN-BASED FIREWOOD.

A SCREW WAS JUST UNDER HIS HAND, DIGGING INTO HIM.

BOD MANAGED TO GRASP THE SCREW IN HIS RIGHT HAND.

HE FELT THE TIP OF IT, SHARP TO THE TOUCH.

THEN HE PUSHED THE SCREW INTO
THE FABRIC OF THE SACK...

...WORKING
THE
SHARP
END
IN...

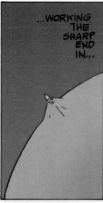

...THEN
PULLING
IT
BACK...

...AND MAKING
ANOTHER HOLE
A LITTLE WAY
BELOW THE
FIRST.

FROM BEHIND, HE HEARD SOME-
THING HOWL ONCE MORE.

ANYTHING THAT CAN TERRIFY
THE GHOUL-FOLK MUST BE
EVEN MORE TERRIFYING
THAN THEY ARE.

WHAT IF
I FALL FROM
THE SACK INTO
THE ARMS OF
SOME VICIOUS
BEAST?

I WILL
HAVE DIED
WITH ALL MY
MEMORIES. I
KNOW WHO MY
PARENTS ARE,
WHO SILAS
IS...

BUT
AT LEAST
IF I DIE, I
WILL HAVE
DIED AS
MYSELF.

I
EVEN
KNOW
WHO
MISS
LUPESCU
IS.

HE ATTACKED THE SACKING AGAIN,
JABBING AND PUSHING.

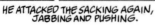

THAT
WAS
GOOD.

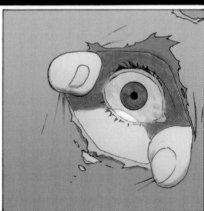

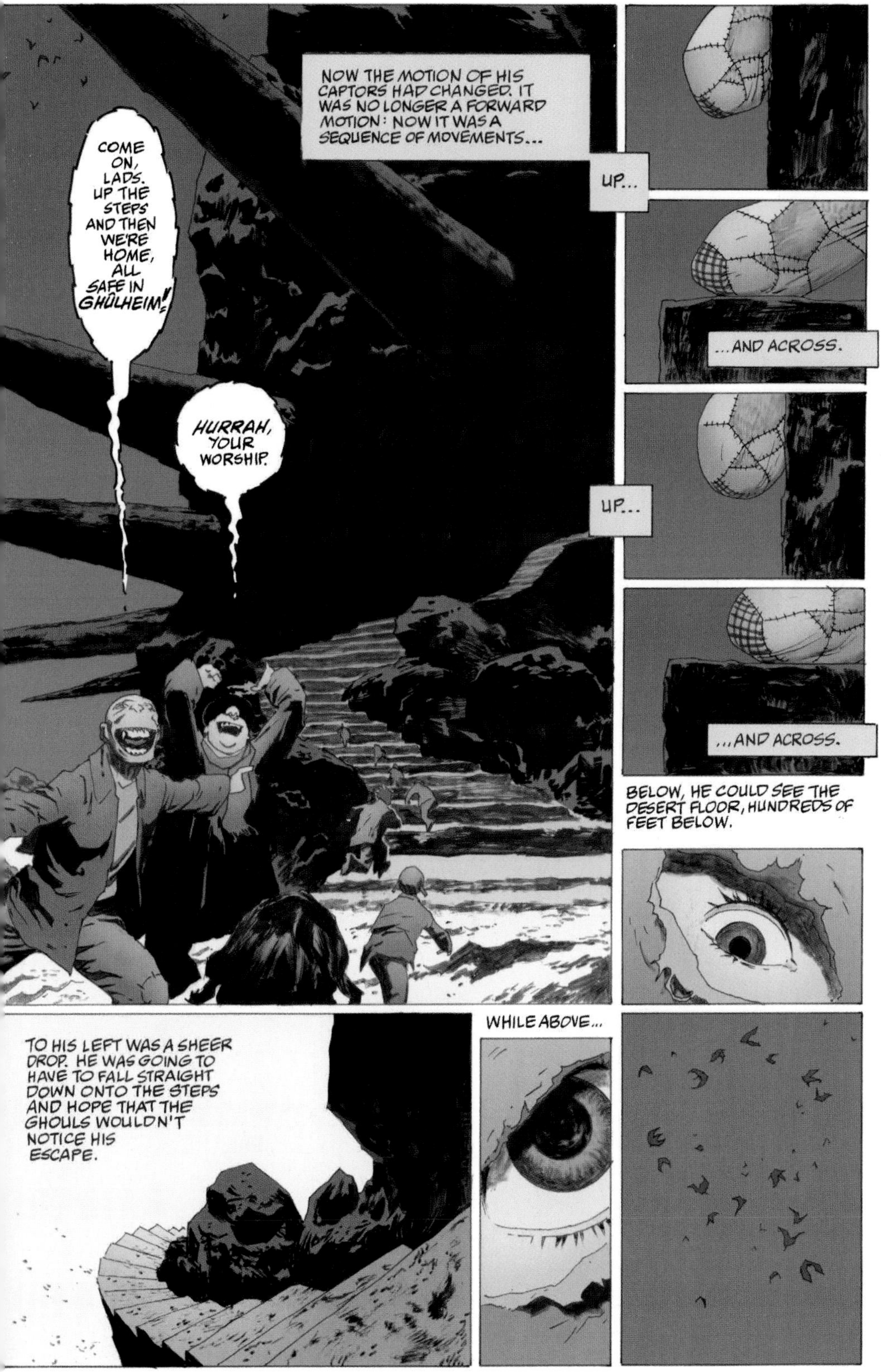
NOW THE MOTION OF HIS CAPTORS HAD CHANGED. IT WAS NO LONGER A FORWARD MOTION: NOW IT WAS A SEQUENCE OF MOVEMENTS...
COME ON, LADS. UP THE STEPS AND THEN WE'RE HOME, ALL SAFE IN GHÛLHEIM!
HURRAH, YOUR WORSHIP.
UP...
...AND ACROSS.
UP...
...AND ACROSS.
BELOW, HE COULD SEE THE DESERT FLOOR, HUNDREDS OF FEET BELOW.
TO HIS LEFT WAS A SHEER DROP. HE WAS GOING TO HAVE TO FALL STRAIGHT DOWN ONTO THE STEPS AND HOPE THAT THE GHOULS WOULDN'T NOTICE HIS ESCAPE.
WHILE ABOVE...

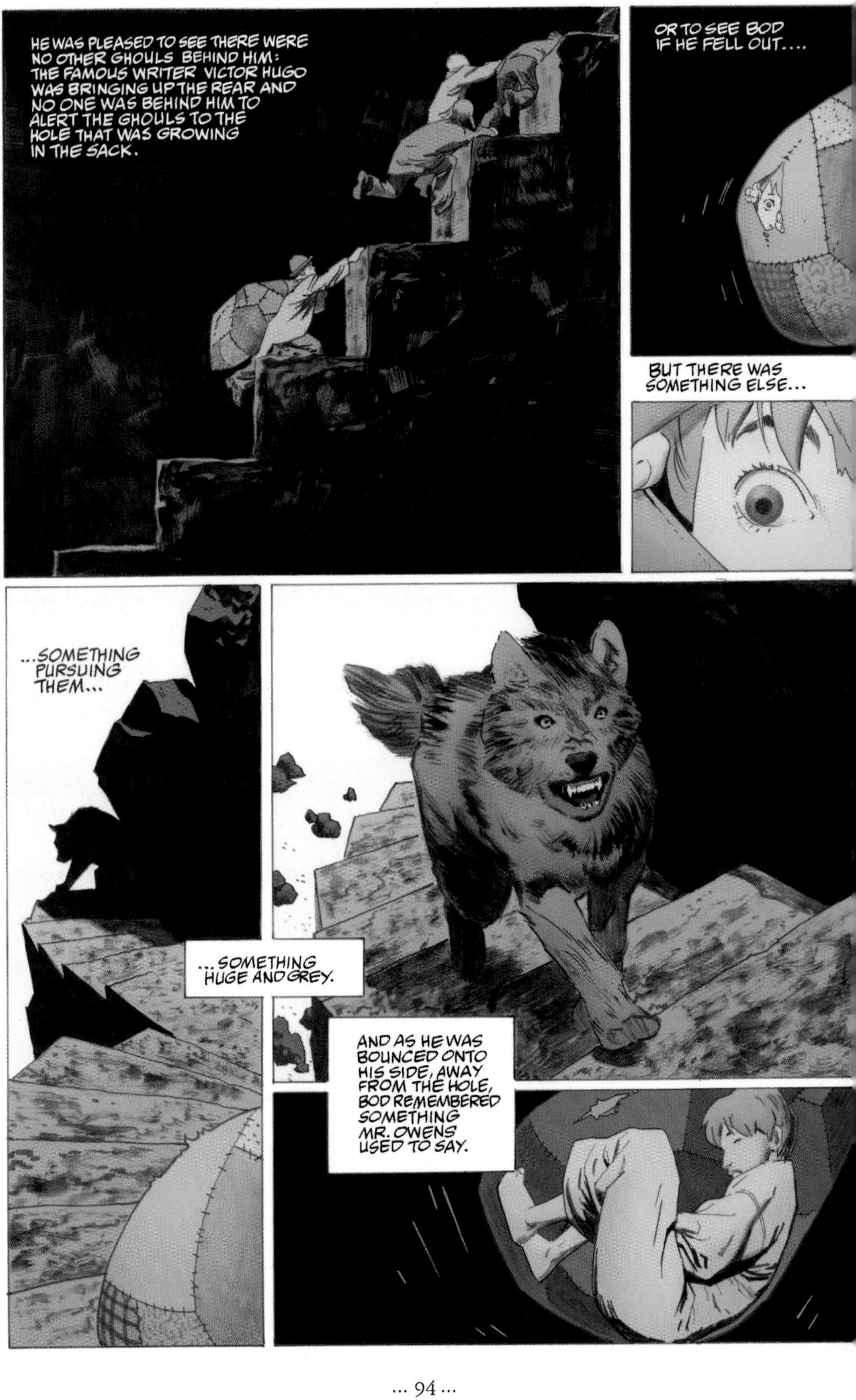
HE WAS PLEASED TO SEE THERE WERE NO OTHER GHOULS BEHIND HIM: THE FAMOUS WRITER VICTOR HUGO WAS BRINGING UP THE REAR AND NO ONE WAS BEHIND HIM TO ALERT THE GHOULS TO THE HOLE THAT WAS GROWING IN THE SACK.
OR TO SEE BOD IF HE FELL OUT....
BUT THERE WAS SOMETHING ELSE...
...SOMETHING PURSUING THEM...
...SOMETHING HUGE AND GREY.
AND AS HE WAS BOUNCED ONTO HIS SIDE, AWAY FROM THE HOLE, BOD REMEMBERED SOMETHING MR. OWENS USED TO SAY.

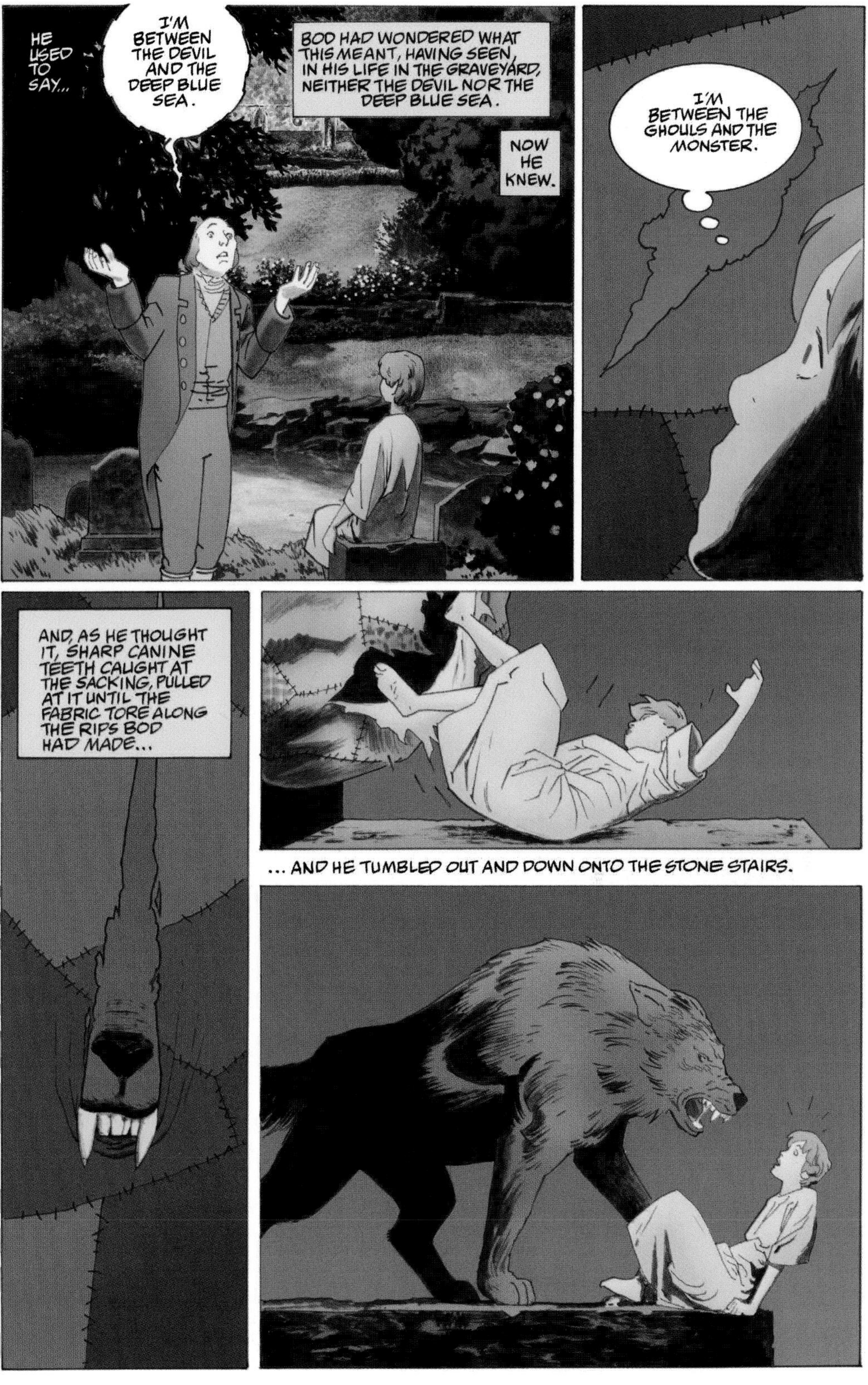
HE USED TO SAY...
I'M BETWEEN THE DEVIL AND THE DEEP BLUE SEA.
BOD HAD WONDERED WHAT THIS MEANT, HAVING SEEN, IN HIS LIFE IN THE GRAVEYARD, NEITHER THE DEVIL NOR THE DEEP BLUE SEA.
NOW HE KNEW.
I'M BETWEEN THE GHOULS AND THE MONSTER.
AND, AS HE THOUGHT IT, SHARP CANINE TEETH CAUGHT AT THE SACKING, PULLED AT IT UNTIL THE FABRIC TORE ALONG THE RIPS BOD HAD MADE...
... AND HE TUMBLED OUT AND DOWN ONTO THE STONE STAIRS.

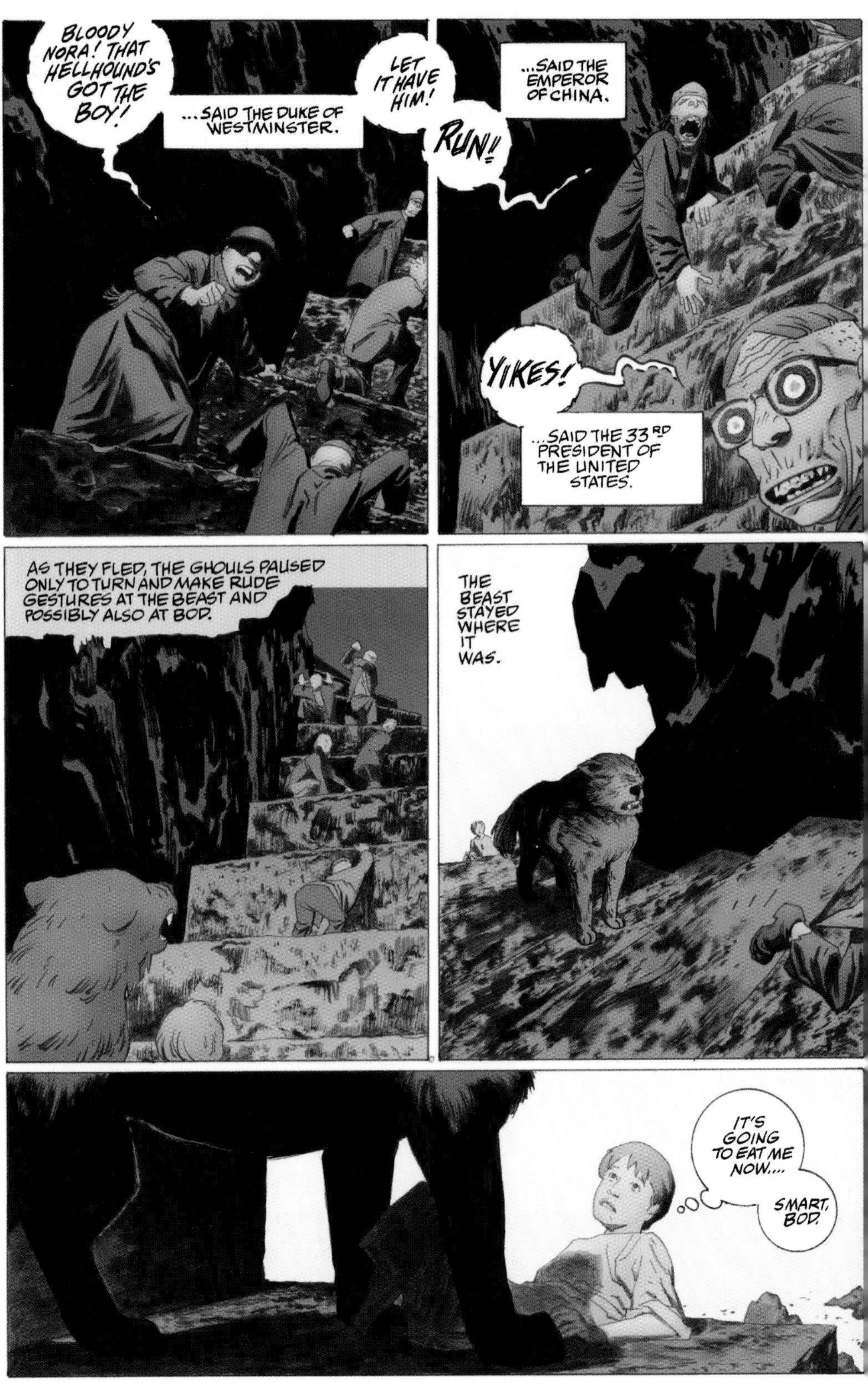
BLOODY NORA! THAT HELLHOUND'S GOT THE BOY!
...SAID THE DUKE OF WESTMINSTER.
LET IT HAVE HIM!
RUN!!
...SAID THE EMPEROR OF CHINA.
YIKES!
...SAID THE 33RD PRESIDENT OF THE UNITED STATES.
AS THEY FLED, THE GHOULS PAUSED ONLY TO TURN AND MAKE RUDE GESTURES AT THE BEAST AND POSSIBLY ALSO AT BOD.
THE BEAST STAYED WHERE IT WAS.
IT'S GOING TO EAT ME NOW.... SMART, BOD.

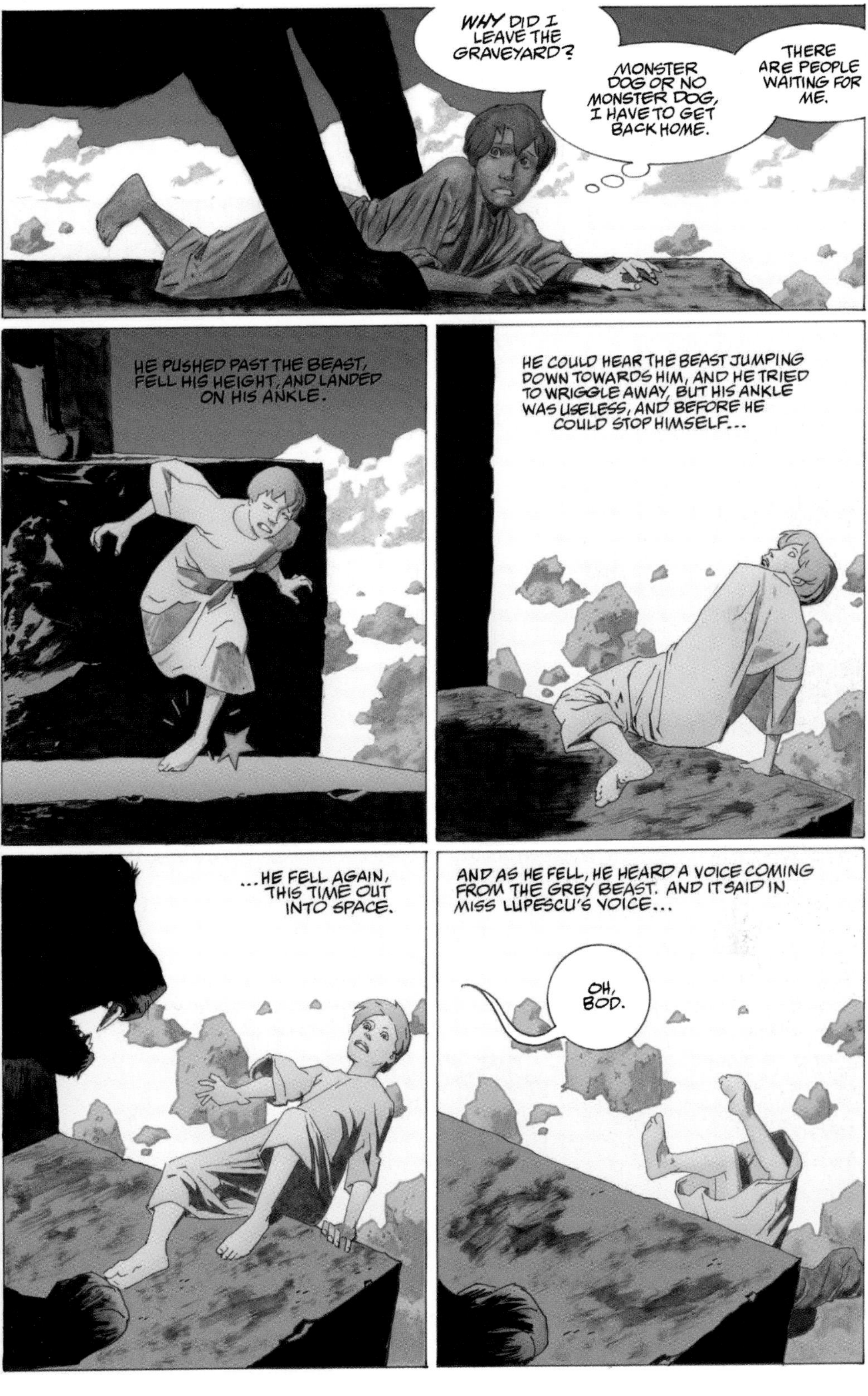
WHY DID I LEAVE THE GRAVEYARD?
MONSTER DOG OR NO MONSTER DOG, I HAVE TO GET BACK HOME.
THERE ARE PEOPLE WAITING FOR ME.
HE PUSHED PAST THE BEAST, FELL HIS HEIGHT, AND LANDED ON HIS ANKLE.
HE COULD HEAR THE BEAST JUMPING DOWN TOWARDS HIM, AND HE TRIED TO WRIGGLE AWAY, BUT HIS ANKLE WAS USELESS, AND BEFORE HE COULD STOP HIMSELF...
...HE FELL AGAIN, THIS TIME OUT INTO SPACE.
AND AS HE FELL, HE HEARD A VOICE COMING FROM THE GREY BEAST. AND IT SAID IN MISS LUPESCU'S VOICE...
OH, BOD.

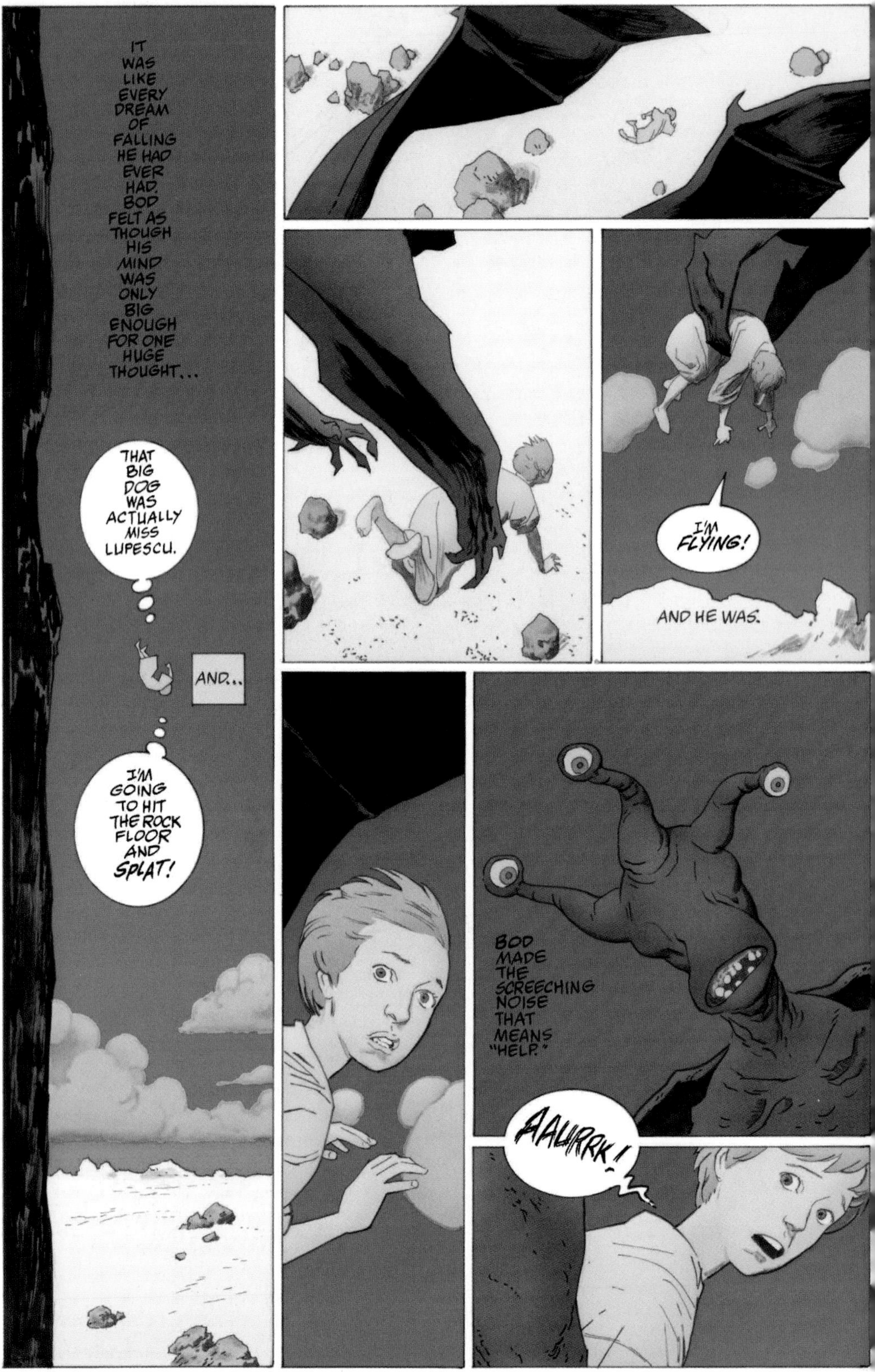
IT WAS LIKE EVERY DREAM OF FALLING HE HAD EVER HAD. BOD FELT AS THOUGH HIS MIND WAS ONLY BIG ENOUGH FOR ONE HUGE THOUGHT...
THAT BIG DOG WAS ACTUALLY MISS LUPESCU.
AND...
I'M GOING TO HIT THE ROCK FLOOR AND SPLAT!
I'M FLYING!
AND HE WAS.
BOD MADE THE SCREECHING NOISE THAT MEANS "HELP."
AAURRK!

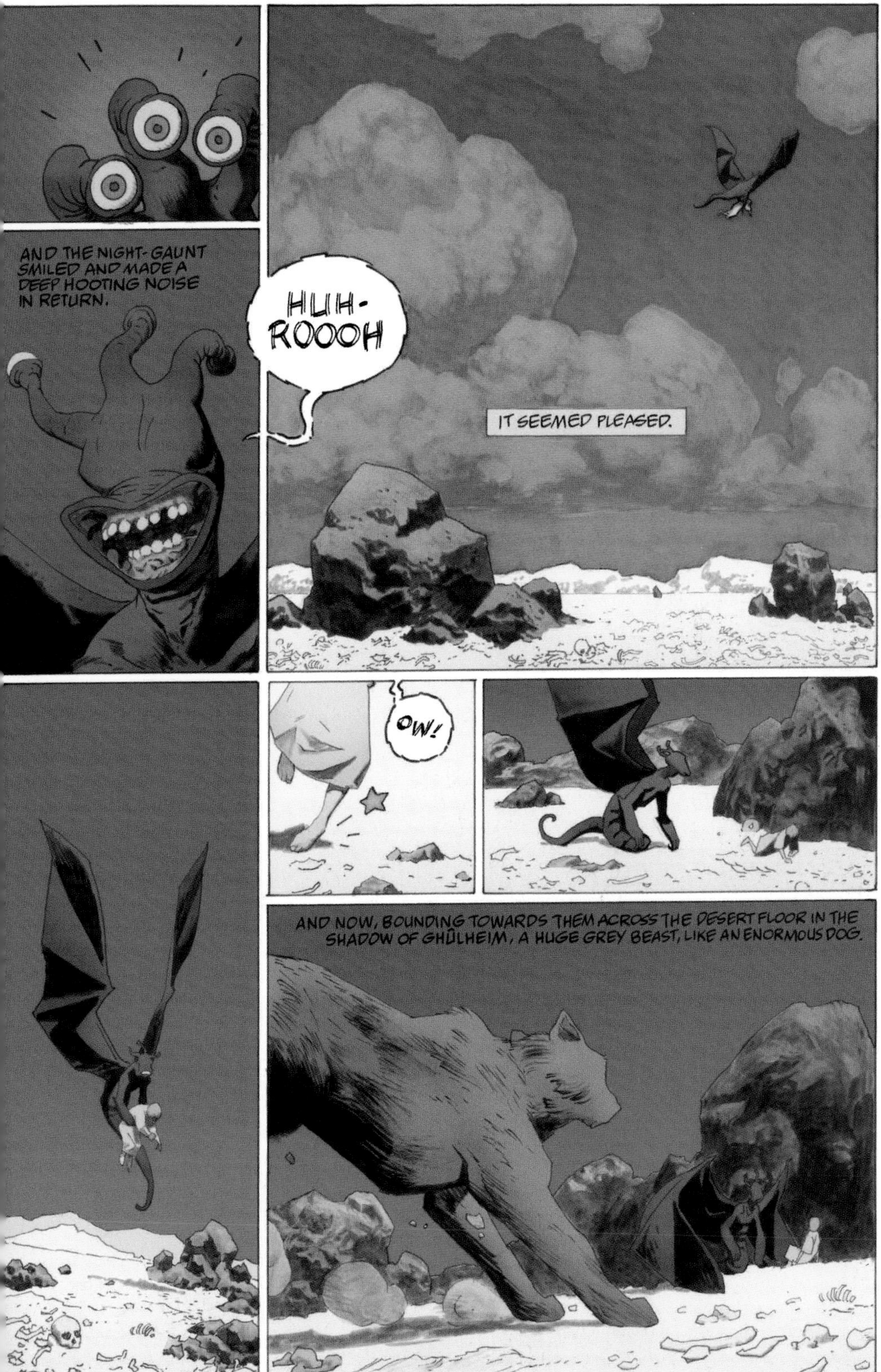
AND THE NIGHT-GAUNT SMILED AND MADE A DEEP HOOTING NOISE IN RETURN.
HUH-ROOOH
IT SEEMED PLEASED.
OW!
AND NOW, BOUNDING TOWARDS THEM ACROSS THE DESERT FLOOR IN THE SHADOW OF GHÛLHEIM, A HUGE GREY BEAST, LIKE AN ENORMOUS DOG.

THIS IS THE THIRD TIME THE NIGHT-GAUNTS HAVE SAVED YOUR LIFE, BOD.

" THE FIRST WAS WHEN YOU CALLED FOR HELP, AND THEY HEARD. THEY GOT THE MESSAGE TO ME, TELLING ME WHERE YOU WERE. "

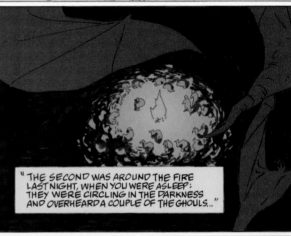

" THE SECOND WAS AROUND THE FIRE LAST NIGHT, WHEN YOU WERE ASLEEP: THEY WERE CIRCLING IN THE DARKNESS AND OVERHEARD A COUPLE OF THE GHOULS..."

HE'S ILL LUCK FOR US AND WE SHOULD BEAT HIS BRAINS IN WITH A ROCK AND PUT HIM SOMEWHERE WE CAN FIND HIM AGAIN.

AND WHEN HE'S PROPERLY ROTTED DOWN WE CAN EAT HIM.

"THE NIGHT-GAUNTS DEALT WITH THE MATTER SILENTLY."

AND NOW THIS.

MISS LUPESCU?

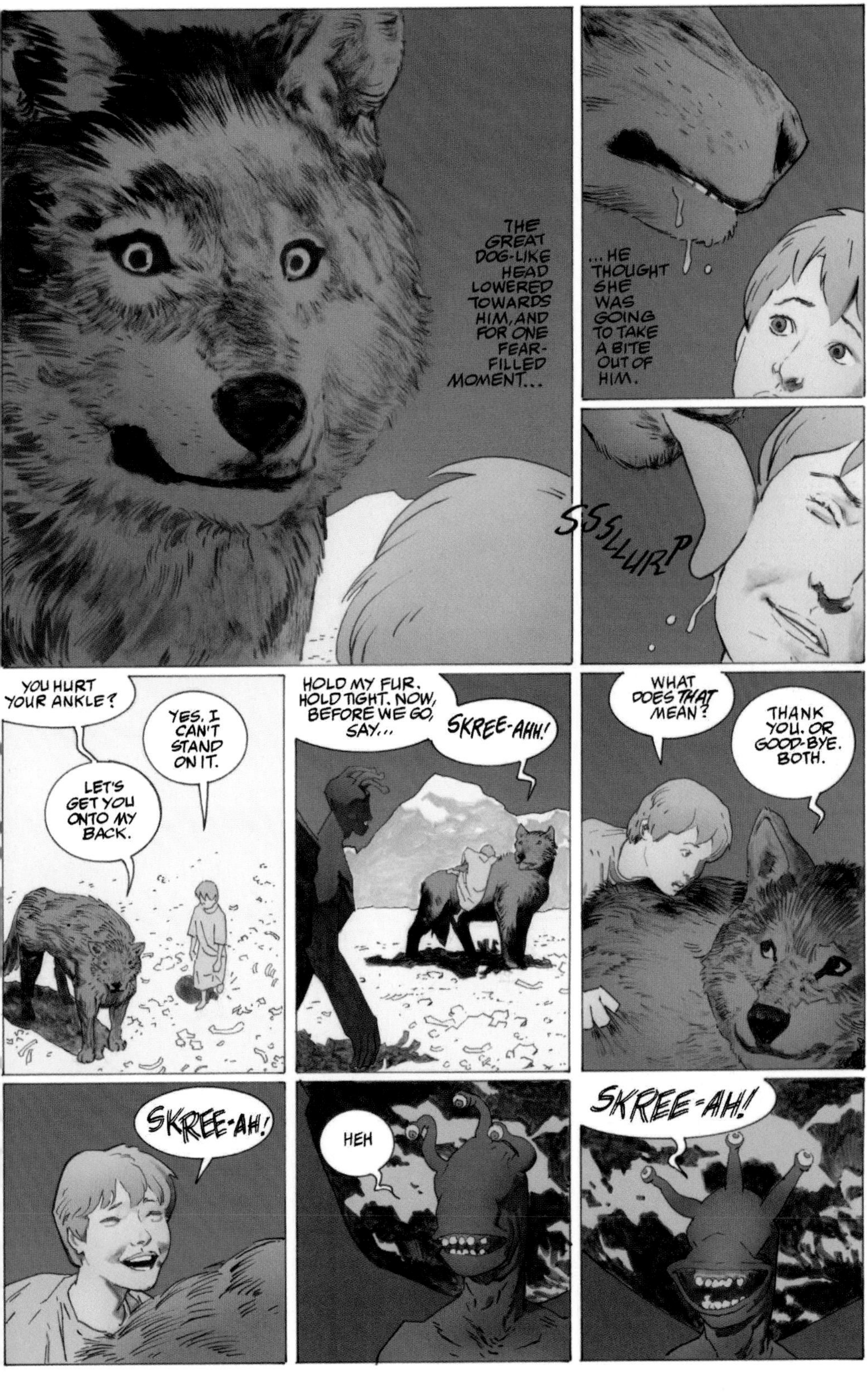
THE GREAT DOG-LIKE HEAD LOWERED TOWARDS HIM, AND FOR ONE FEAR-FILLED MOMENT...
...HE THOUGHT SHE WAS GOING TO TAKE A BITE OUT OF HIM.
SSSLLURP
YOU HURT YOUR ANKLE?
YES, I CAN'T STAND ON IT.
LET'S GET YOU ONTO MY BACK.
HOLD MY FUR. HOLD TIGHT. NOW, BEFORE WE GO, SAY...
SKREE-AHH!
WHAT DOES THAT MEAN?
THANK YOU. OR GOOD-BYE. BOTH.
SKREE-AH!
HEH
SKREE-AH!

THEN THE NIGHT-GAUNT SPREAD ITS GREAT LEATHERY WINGS AND THE WIND CAUGHT IT AND CARRIED IT ALOFT, LIKE A KITE THAT HAD BEGUN TO FLY.

HOLD ON TIGHTLY.

ARE WE GOING TO THE WALL OF GRAVES?

TO THE GHOUL-GATES? NO. THOSE ARE FOR GHOULS.

I AM A HOUND OF GOD. I TRAVEL MY OWN ROAD, INTO HELL AND OUT OF IT.

AND IT SEEMED TO BOD AS IF SHE RAN EVEN FASTER THEN.

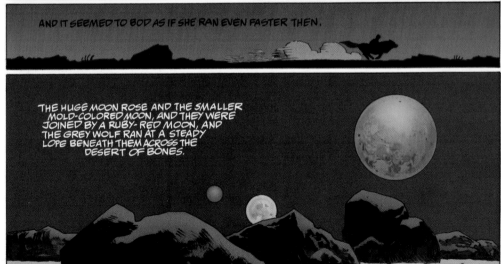

THE HUGE MOON ROSE AND THE SMALLER MOLD-COLORED MOON, AND THEY WERE JOINED BY A RUBY-RED MOON, AND THE GREY WOLF RAN AT A STEADY LOPE BENEATH THEM ACROSS THE DESERT OF BONES.

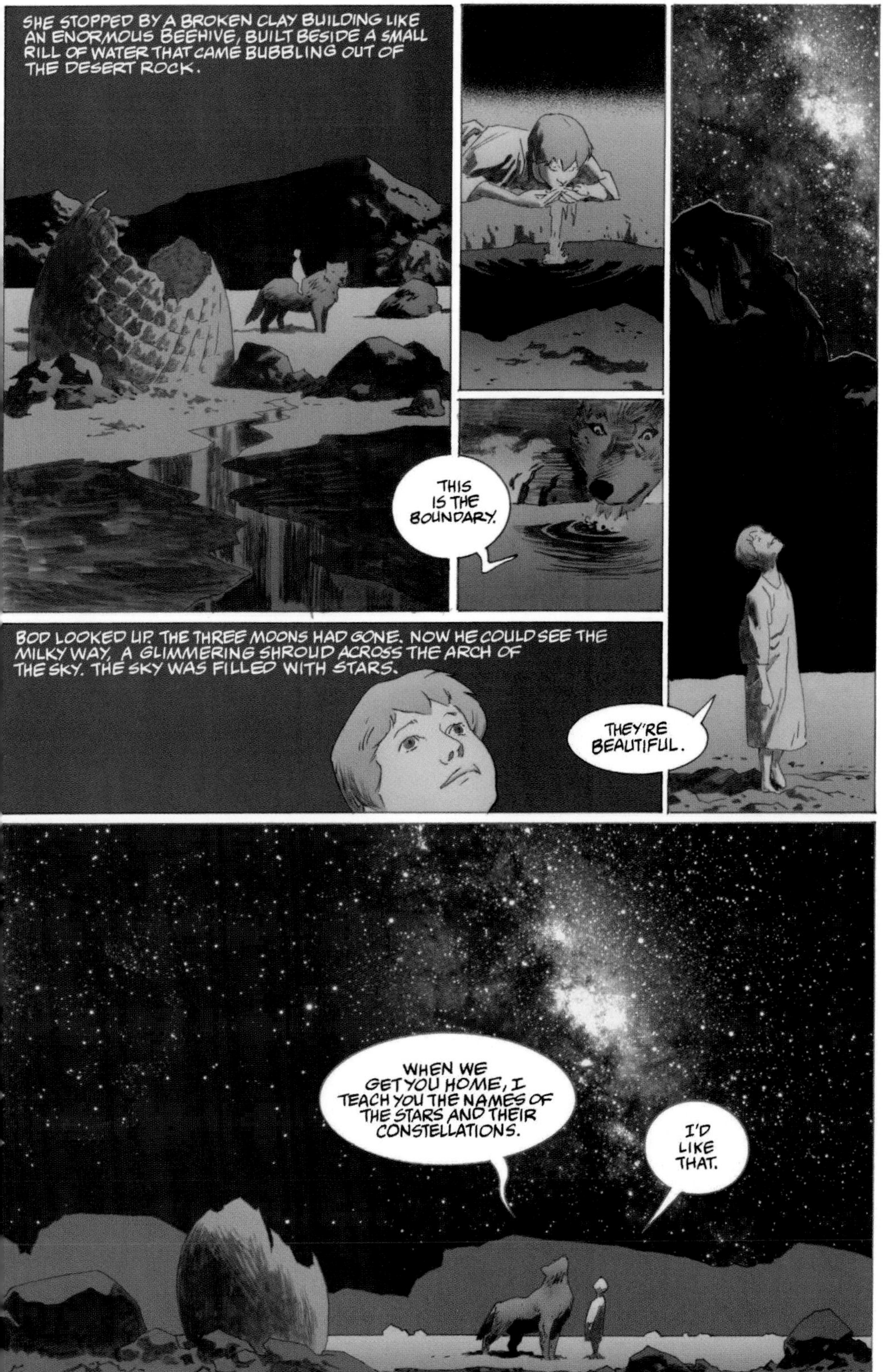
SHE STOPPED BY A BROKEN CLAY BUILDING LIKE AN ENORMOUS BEEHIVE, BUILT BESIDE A SMALL RILL OF WATER THAT CAME BUBBLING OUT OF THE DESERT ROCK.
THIS IS THE BOUNDARY.
BOD LOOKED UP. THE THREE MOONS HAD GONE. NOW HE COULD SEE THE MILKY WAY, A GLIMMERING SHROUD ACROSS THE ARCH OF THE SKY. THE SKY WAS FILLED WITH STARS.
THEY'RE BEAUTIFUL.
WHEN WE GET YOU HOME, I TEACH YOU THE NAMES OF THE STARS AND THEIR CONSTELLATIONS.
I'D LIKE THAT.

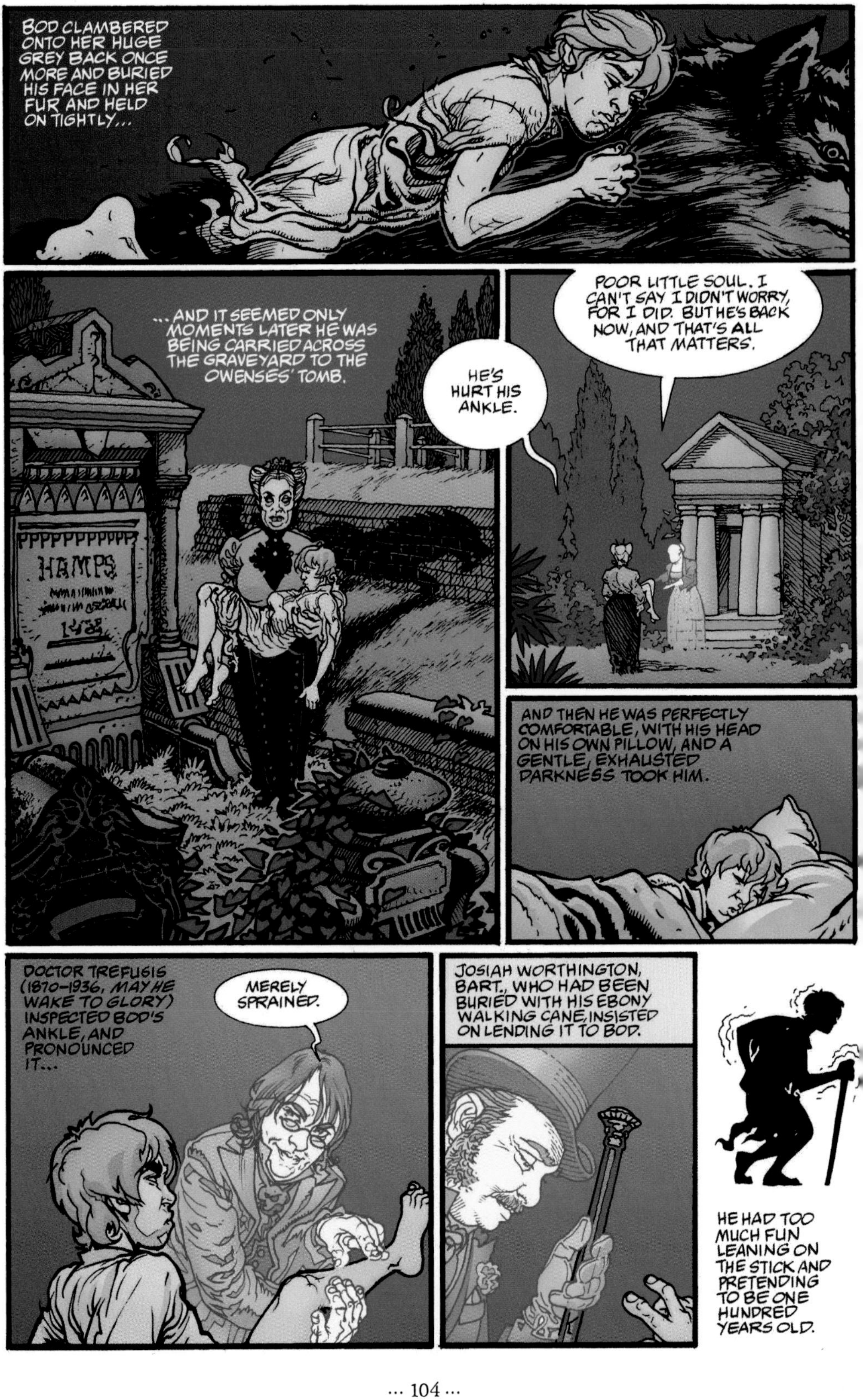
BOD CLAMBERED ONTO HER HUGE GREY BACK ONCE MORE AND BURIED HIS FACE IN HER FUR AND HELD ON TIGHTLY...
...AND IT SEEMED ONLY MOMENTS LATER HE WAS BEING CARRIED ACROSS THE GRAVEYARD TO THE OWENSES' TOMB.
HAMPS
HE'S HURT HIS ANKLE.
POOR LITTLE SOUL. I CAN'T SAY I DIDN'T WORRY, FOR I DID. BUT HE'S BACK NOW, AND THAT'S ALL THAT MATTERS.
AND THEN HE WAS PERFECTLY COMFORTABLE, WITH HIS HEAD ON HIS OWN PILLOW, AND A GENTLE, EXHAUSTED DARKNESS TOOK HIM.
DOCTOR TREFUSIS (1870–1936, MAY HE WAKE TO GLORY) INSPECTED BOD'S ANKLE, AND PRONOUNCED IT...
MERELY SPRAINED.
JOSIAH WORTHINGTON, BART., WHO HAD BEEN BURIED WITH HIS EBONY WALKING CANE, INSISTED ON LENDING IT TO BOD.
HE HAD TOO MUCH FUN LEANING ON THE STICK AND PRETENDING TO BE ONE HUNDRED YEARS OLD.

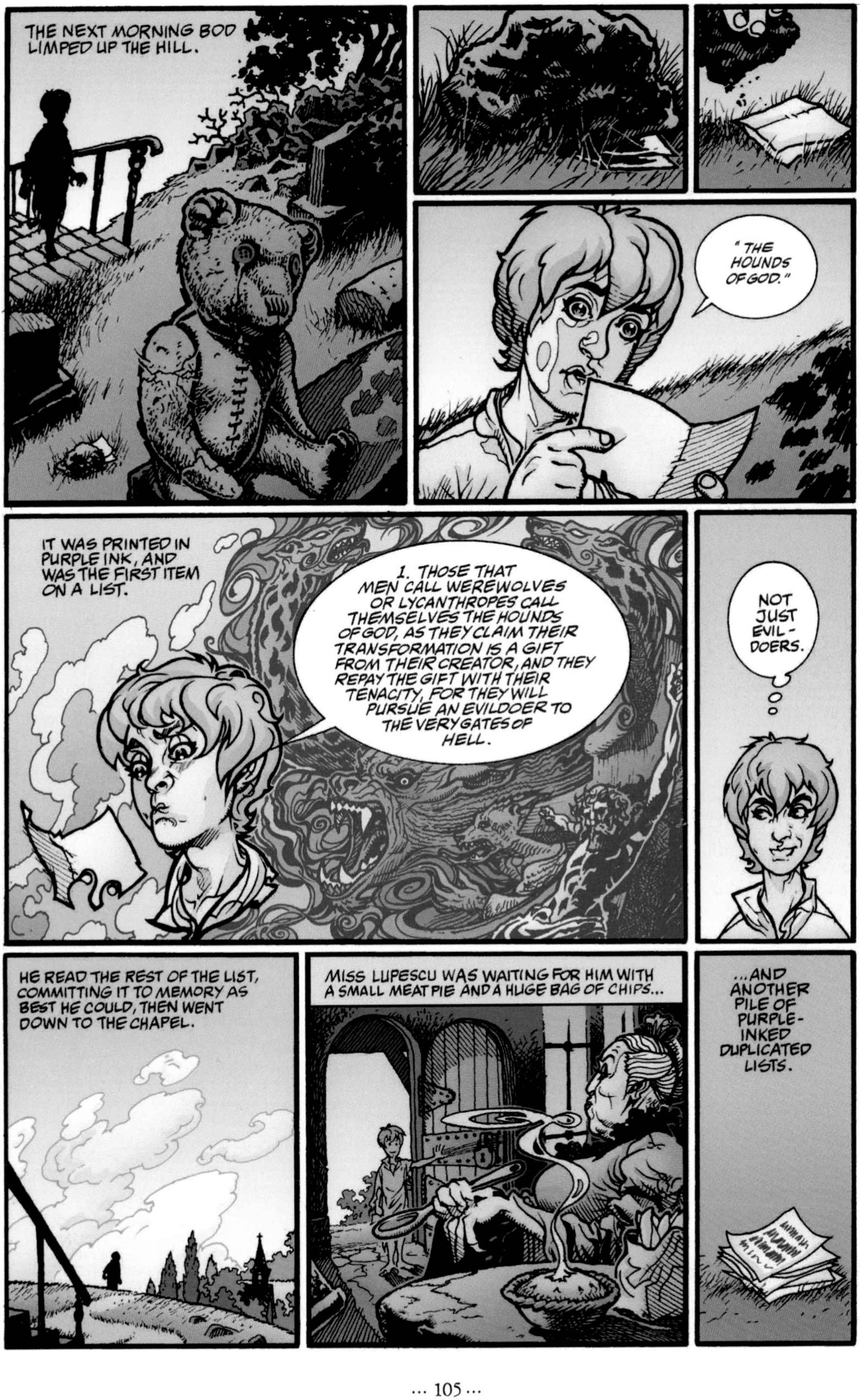
THE NEXT MORNING BOD LIMPED UP THE HILL.
"THE HOUNDS OF GOD."
IT WAS PRINTED IN PURPLE INK, AND WAS THE FIRST ITEM ON A LIST.
1. THOSE THAT MEN CALL WEREWOLVES OR LYCANTHROPES CALL THEMSELVES THE HOUNDS OF GOD, AS THEY CLAIM THEIR TRANSFORMATION IS A GIFT FROM THEIR CREATOR, AND THEY REPAY THE GIFT WITH THEIR TENACITY, FOR THEY WILL PURSUE AN EVILDOER TO THE VERY GATES OF HELL.
NOT JUST EVIL-DOERS.
HE READ THE REST OF THE LIST, COMMITTING IT TO MEMORY AS BEST HE COULD, THEN WENT DOWN TO THE CHAPEL.
MISS LUPESCU WAS WAITING FOR HIM WITH A SMALL MEAT PIE AND A HUGE BAG OF CHIPS...
...AND ANOTHER PILE OF PURPLE-INKED DUPLICATED LISTS.

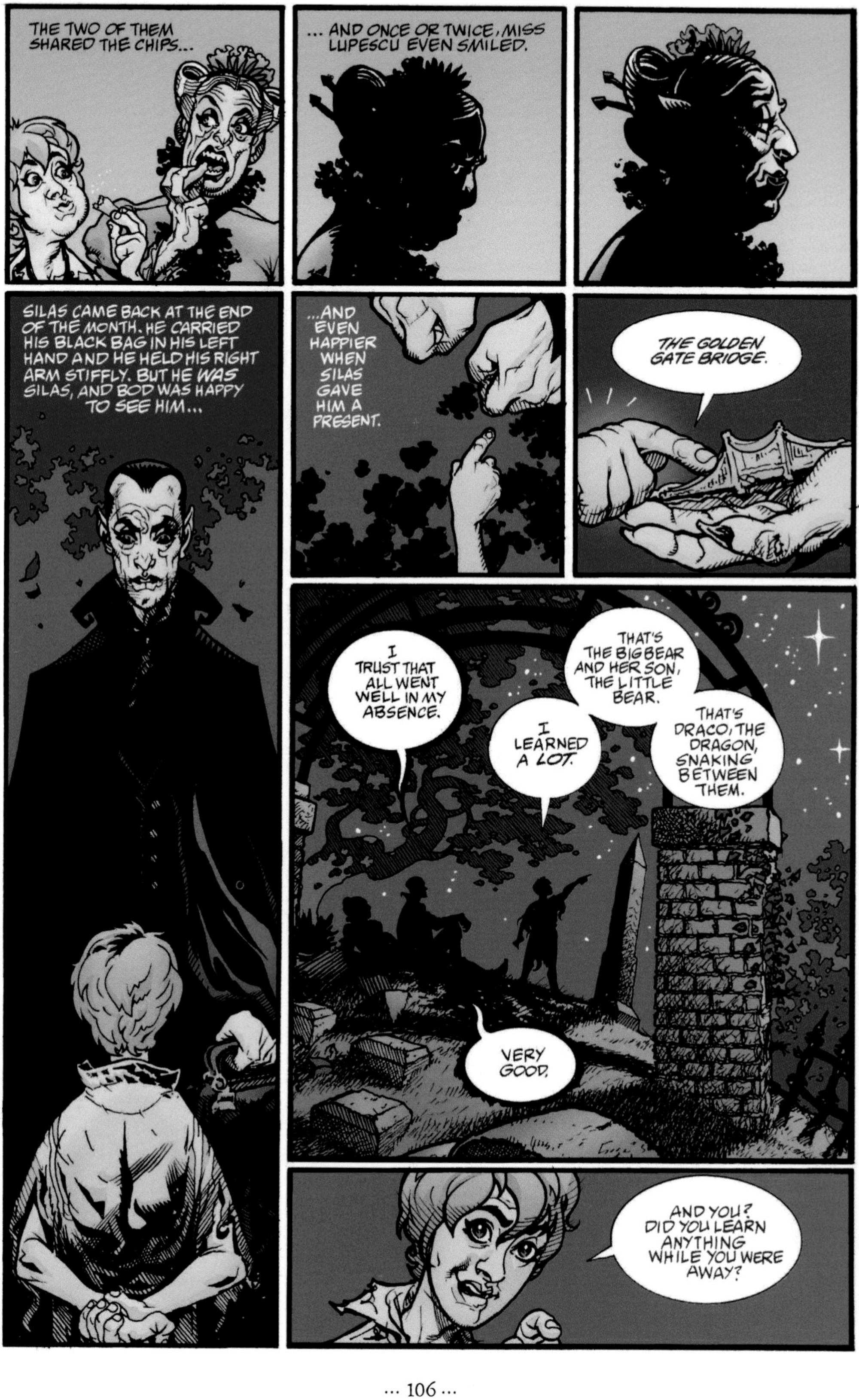
THE TWO OF THEM SHARED THE CHIPS...
... AND ONCE OR TWICE, MISS LUPESCU EVEN SMILED.
SILAS CAME BACK AT THE END OF THE MONTH. HE CARRIED HIS BLACK BAG IN HIS LEFT HAND AND HE HELD HIS RIGHT ARM STIFFLY. BUT HE WAS SILAS, AND BOD WAS HAPPY TO SEE HIM...
...AND EVEN HAPPIER WHEN SILAS GAVE HIM A PRESENT.
THE GOLDEN GATE BRIDGE.
I TRUST THAT ALL WENT WELL IN MY ABSENCE.
I LEARNED A LOT.
THAT'S THE BIG BEAR AND HER SON, THE LITTLE BEAR.
THAT'S DRACO, THE DRAGON, SNAKING BETWEEN THEM.
VERY GOOD.
AND YOU? DID YOU LEARN ANYTHING WHILE YOU WERE AWAY?

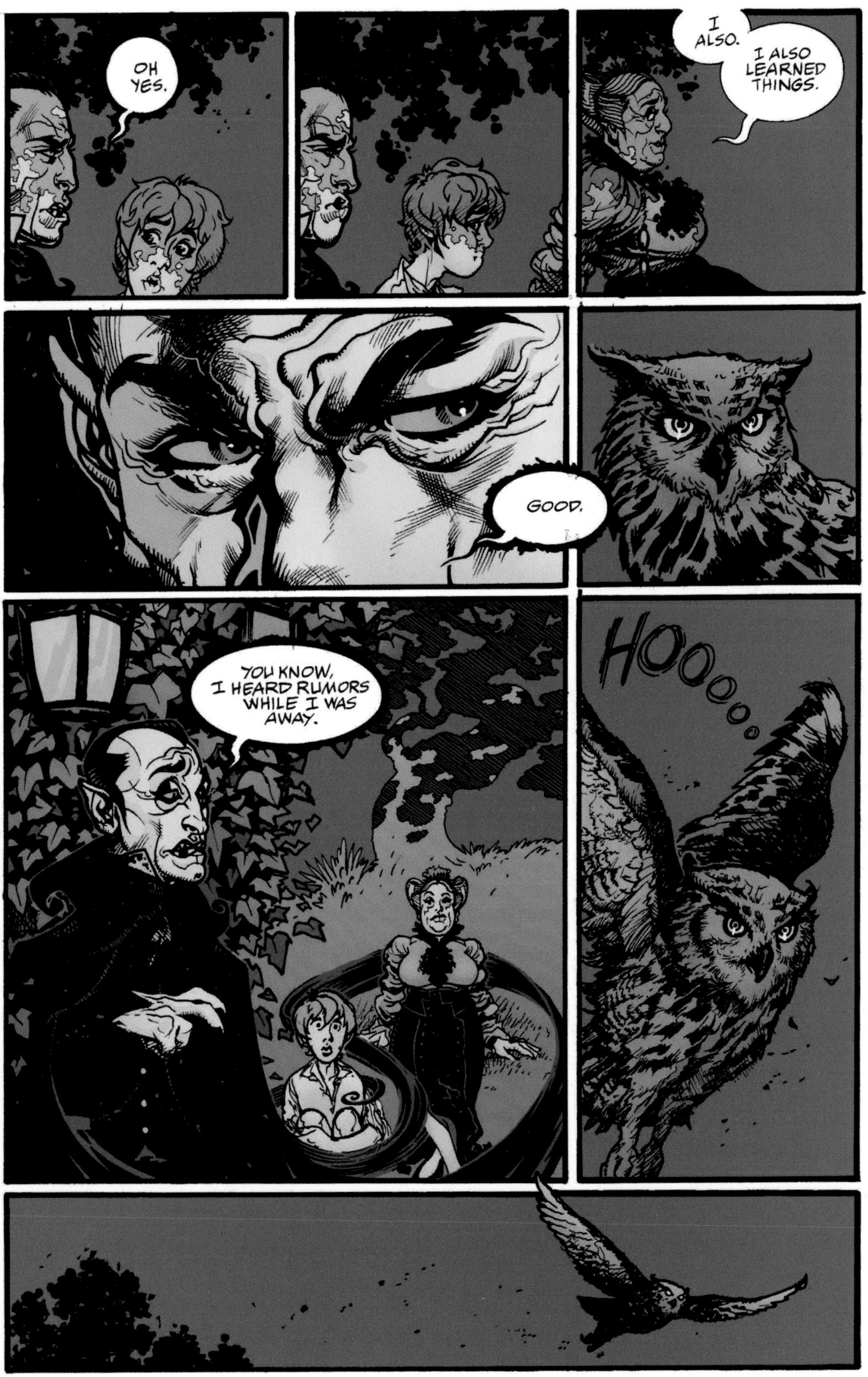
OH YES.
I ALSO.
I ALSO LEARNED THINGS.
GOOD.
YOU KNOW, I HEARD RUMORS WHILE I WAS AWAY.
HOOOOO...

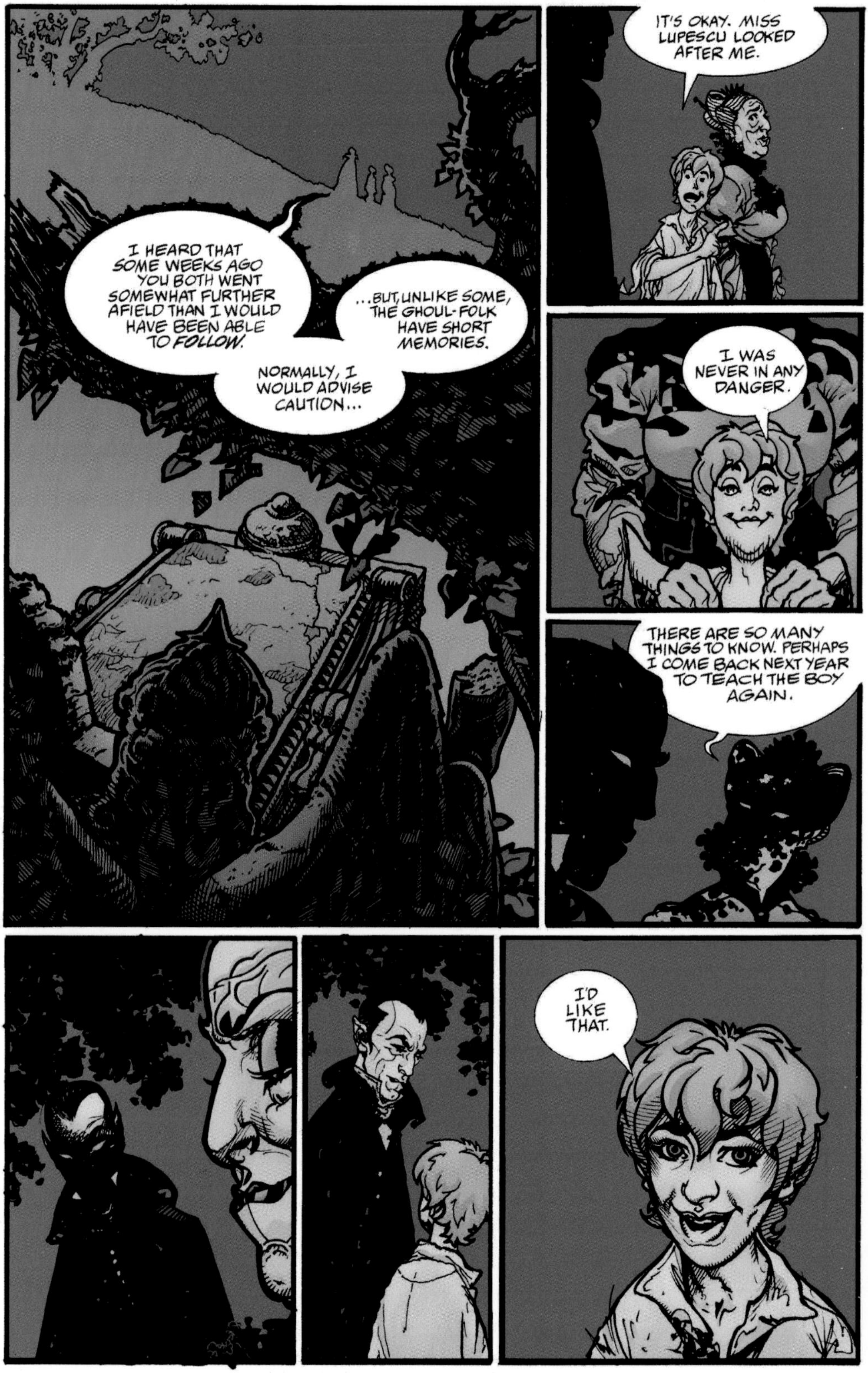
I HEARD THAT SOME WEEKS AGO YOU BOTH WENT SOMEWHAT FURTHER AFIELD THAN I WOULD HAVE BEEN ABLE TO FOLLOW.
...BUT, UNLIKE SOME, THE GHOUL-FOLK HAVE SHORT MEMORIES.
NORMALLY, I WOULD ADVISE CAUTION...
IT'S OKAY. MISS LUPESCU LOOKED AFTER ME.
I WAS NEVER IN ANY DANGER.
THERE ARE SO MANY THINGS TO KNOW. PERHAPS I COME BACK NEXT YEAR TO TEACH THE BOY AGAIN.
I'D LIKE THAT.

4
The Witch's Headstone

Illustrated by Galen Showman

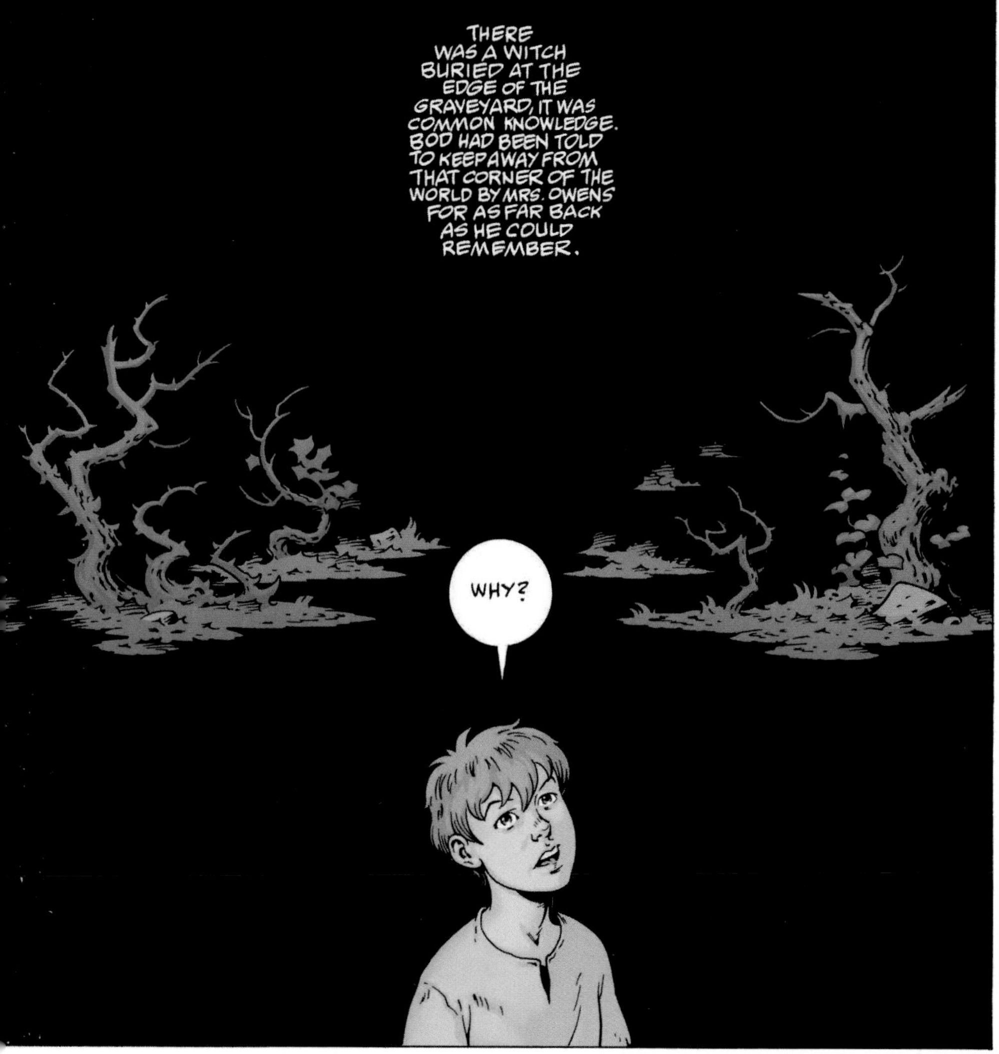
THERE WAS A WITCH BURIED AT THE EDGE OF THE GRAVEYARD, IT WAS COMMON KNOWLEDGE. BOD HAD BEEN TOLD TO KEEP AWAY FROM THAT CORNER OF THE WORLD BY MRS. OWENS FOR AS FAR BACK AS HE COULD REMEMBER.
WHY?

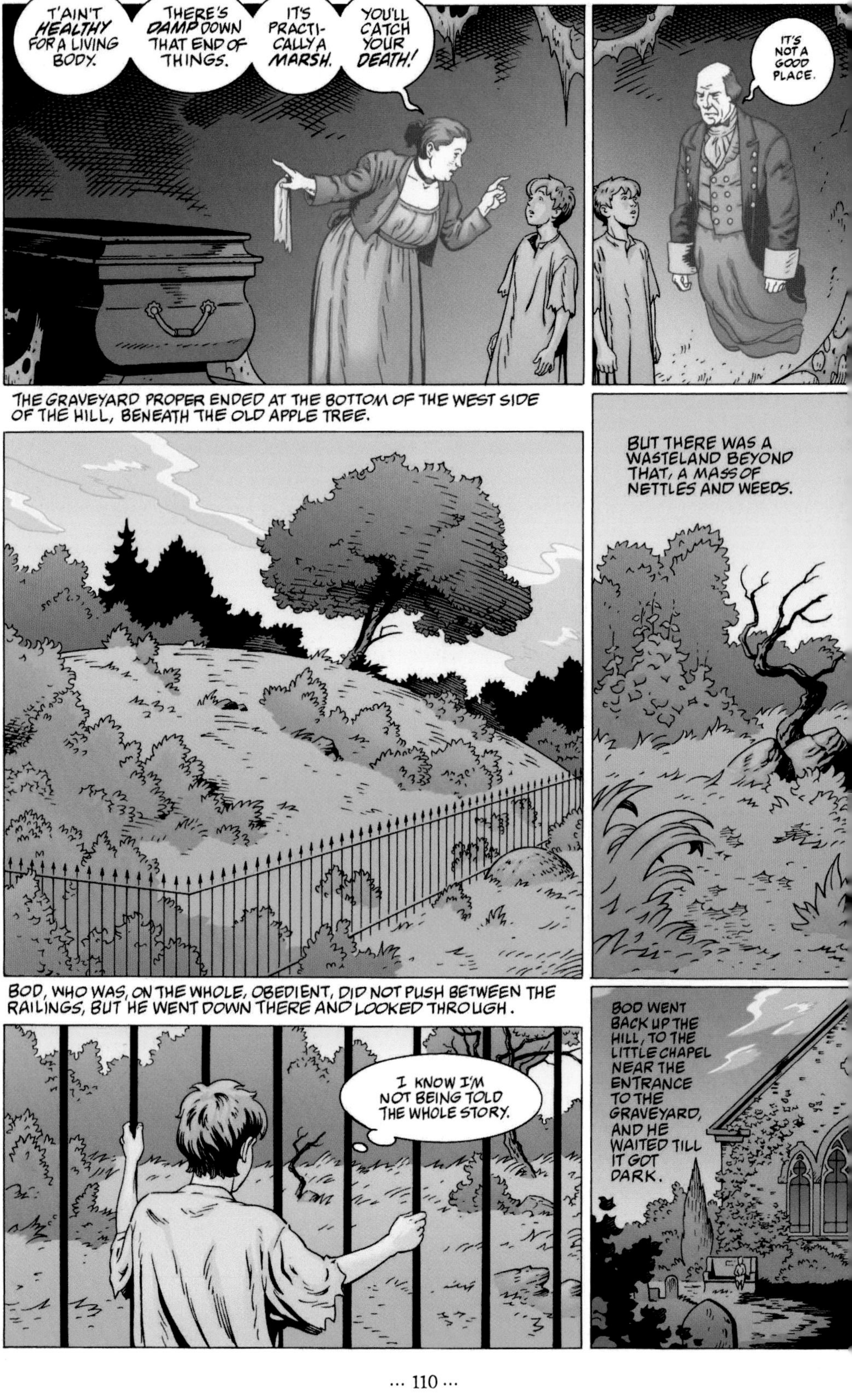
T'AIN'T HEALTHY FOR A LIVING BODY.
THERE'S DAMP DOWN THAT END OF THINGS.
IT'S PRACTI-CALLY A MARSH.
YOU'LL CATCH YOUR DEATH!
IT'S NOT A GOOD PLACE.
THE GRAVEYARD PROPER ENDED AT THE BOTTOM OF THE WEST SIDE OF THE HILL, BENEATH THE OLD APPLE TREE.
BUT THERE WAS A WASTELAND BEYOND THAT, A MASS OF NETTLES AND WEEDS.
BOD, WHO WAS, ON THE WHOLE, OBEDIENT, DID NOT PUSH BETWEEN THE RAILINGS, BUT HE WENT DOWN THERE AND LOOKED THROUGH.
I KNOW I'M NOT BEING TOLD THE WHOLE STORY.
BOD WENT BACK UP THE HILL, TO THE LITTLE CHAPEL NEAR THE ENTRANCE TO THE GRAVEYARD, AND HE WAITED TILL IT GOT DARK.

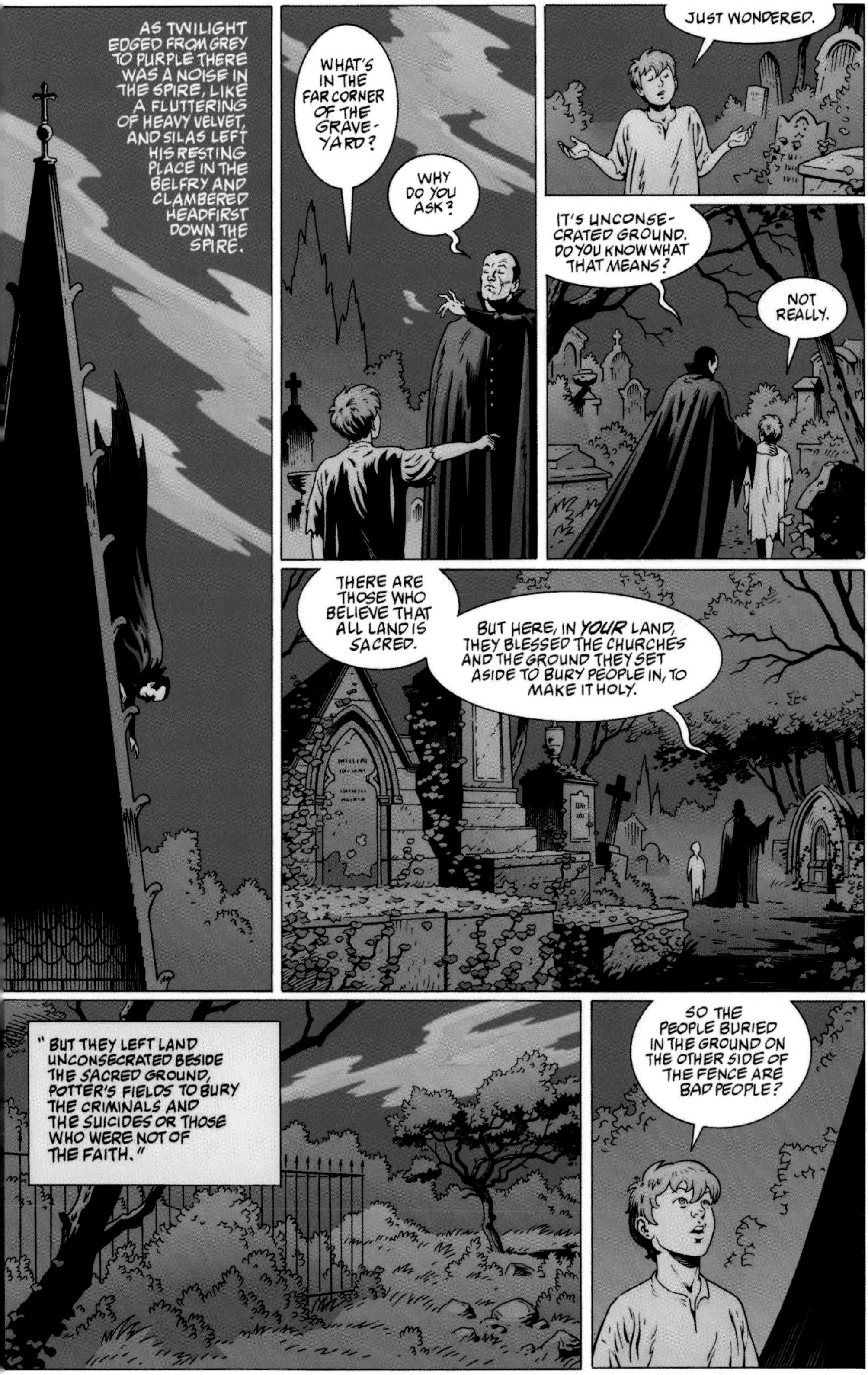
AS TWILIGHT EDGED FROM GREY TO PURPLE THERE WAS A NOISE IN THE SPIRE, LIKE A FLUTTERING OF HEAVY VELVET, AND SILAS LEFT HIS RESTING PLACE IN THE BELFRY AND CLAMBERED HEADFIRST DOWN THE SPIRE.
WHAT'S IN THE FAR CORNER OF THE GRAVE-YARD?
WHY DO YOU ASK?
JUST WONDERED.
IT'S UNCONSE-CRATED GROUND. DO YOU KNOW WHAT THAT MEANS?
NOT REALLY.
THERE ARE THOSE WHO BELIEVE THAT ALL LAND IS SACRED.
BUT HERE, IN *YOUR* LAND, THEY BLESSED THE CHURCHES AND THE GROUND THEY SET ASIDE TO BURY PEOPLE IN, TO MAKE IT HOLY.
" BUT THEY LEFT LAND UNCONSECRATED BESIDE THE *SACRED GROUND*, POTTER'S FIELDS TO BURY THE CRIMINALS AND THE SUICIDES OR THOSE WHO WERE NOT OF THE FAITH."
SO THE PEOPLE BURIED IN THE GROUND ON THE OTHER SIDE OF THE FENCE ARE BAD PEOPLE?

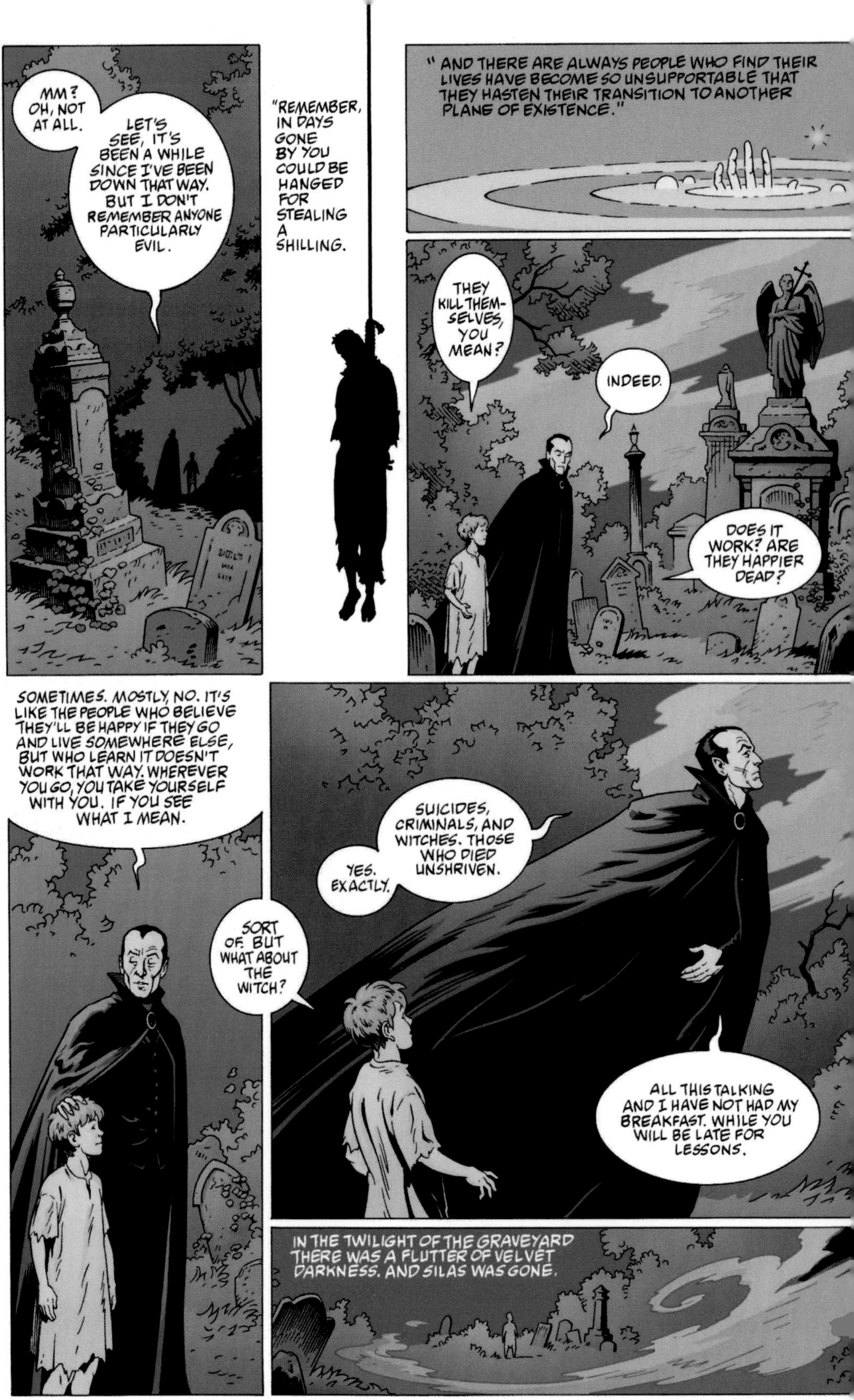
MM? OH, NOT AT ALL.
LET'S SEE, IT'S BEEN A WHILE SINCE I'VE BEEN DOWN THAT WAY. BUT I DON'T REMEMBER ANYONE PARTICULARLY EVIL.
"REMEMBER, IN DAYS GONE BY YOU COULD BE HANGED FOR STEALING A SHILLING.
" AND THERE ARE ALWAYS PEOPLE WHO FIND THEIR LIVES HAVE BECOME SO UNSUPPORTABLE THAT THEY HASTEN THEIR TRANSITION TO ANOTHER PLANE OF EXISTENCE."
THEY KILL THEM-SELVES, YOU MEAN?
INDEED.
DOES IT WORK? ARE THEY HAPPIER DEAD?
SOMETIMES. MOSTLY, NO. IT'S LIKE THE PEOPLE WHO BELIEVE THEY'LL BE HAPPY IF THEY GO AND LIVE SOMEWHERE ELSE, BUT WHO LEARN IT DOESN'T WORK THAT WAY. WHEREVER YOU GO, YOU TAKE YOURSELF WITH YOU. IF YOU SEE WHAT I MEAN.
SORT OF. BUT WHAT ABOUT THE WITCH?
SUICIDES, CRIMINALS, AND WITCHES. THOSE WHO DIED UNSHRIVEN.
YES. EXACTLY.
ALL THIS TALKING AND I HAVE NOT HAD MY BREAKFAST. WHILE YOU WILL BE LATE FOR LESSONS.
IN THE TWILIGHT OF THE GRAVEYARD THERE WAS A FLUTTER OF VELVET DARKNESS. AND SILAS WAS GONE.

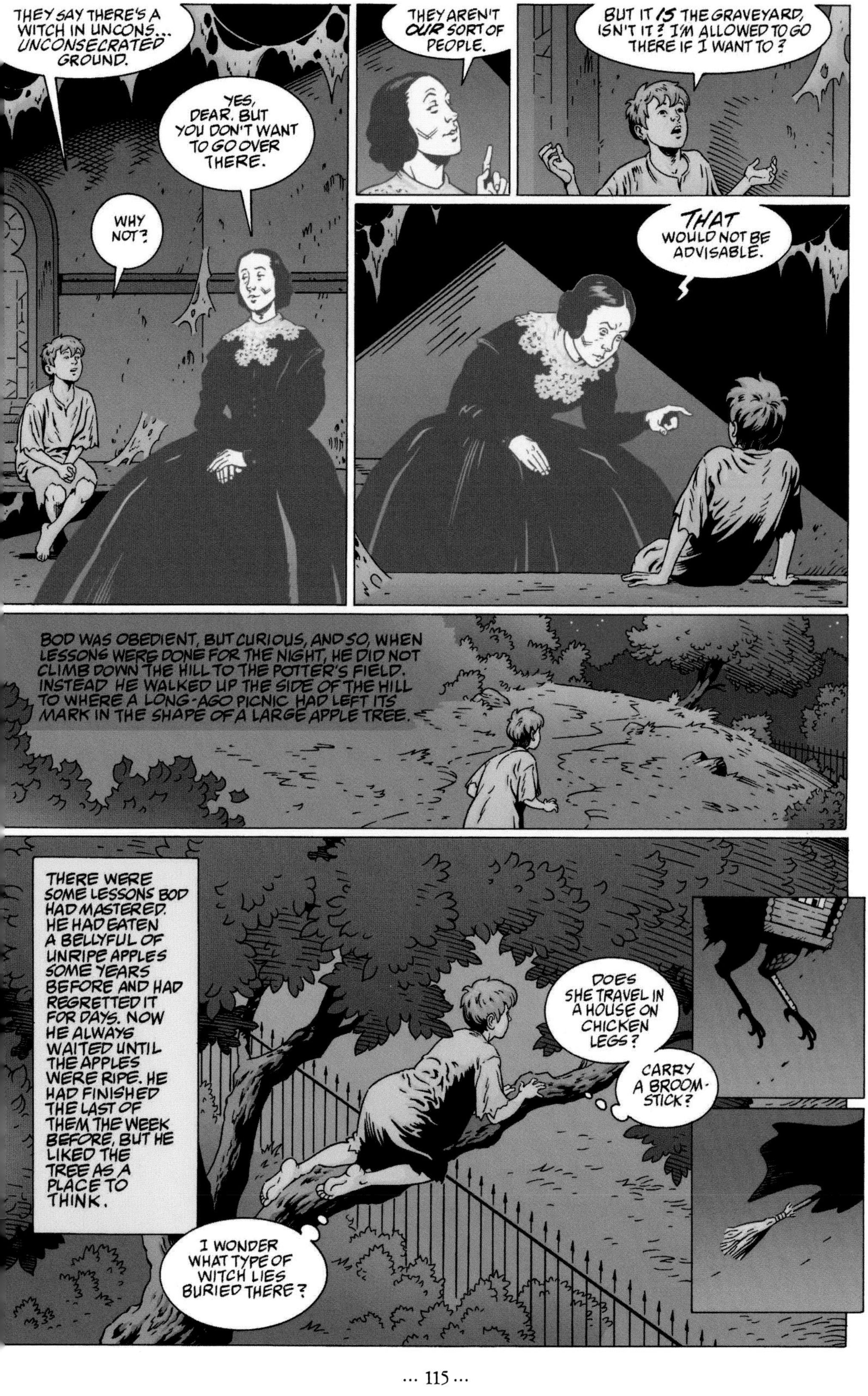
THEY SAY THERE'S A WITCH IN UNCONS... UNCONSECRATED GROUND.
YES, DEAR. BUT YOU DON'T WANT TO GO OVER THERE.
WHY NOT?
THEY AREN'T OUR SORT OF PEOPLE.
BUT IT IS THE GRAVEYARD, ISN'T IT? I'M ALLOWED TO GO THERE IF I WANT TO?
THAT WOULD NOT BE ADVISABLE.
BOD WAS OBEDIENT, BUT CURIOUS, AND SO, WHEN LESSONS WERE DONE FOR THE NIGHT, HE DID NOT CLIMB DOWN THE HILL TO THE POTTER'S FIELD. INSTEAD HE WALKED UP THE SIDE OF THE HILL TO WHERE A LONG-AGO PICNIC HAD LEFT ITS MARK IN THE SHAPE OF A LARGE APPLE TREE.
THERE WERE SOME LESSONS BOD HAD MASTERED. HE HAD EATEN A BELLYFUL OF UNRIPE APPLES SOME YEARS BEFORE AND HAD REGRETTED IT FOR DAYS. NOW HE ALWAYS WAITED UNTIL THE APPLES WERE RIPE. HE HAD FINISHED THE LAST OF THEM THE WEEK BEFORE, BUT HE LIKED THE TREE AS A PLACE TO THINK.
I WONDER WHAT TYPE OF WITCH LIES BURIED THERE?
DOES SHE TRAVEL IN A HOUSE ON CHICKEN LEGS?
CARRY A BROOM-STICK?

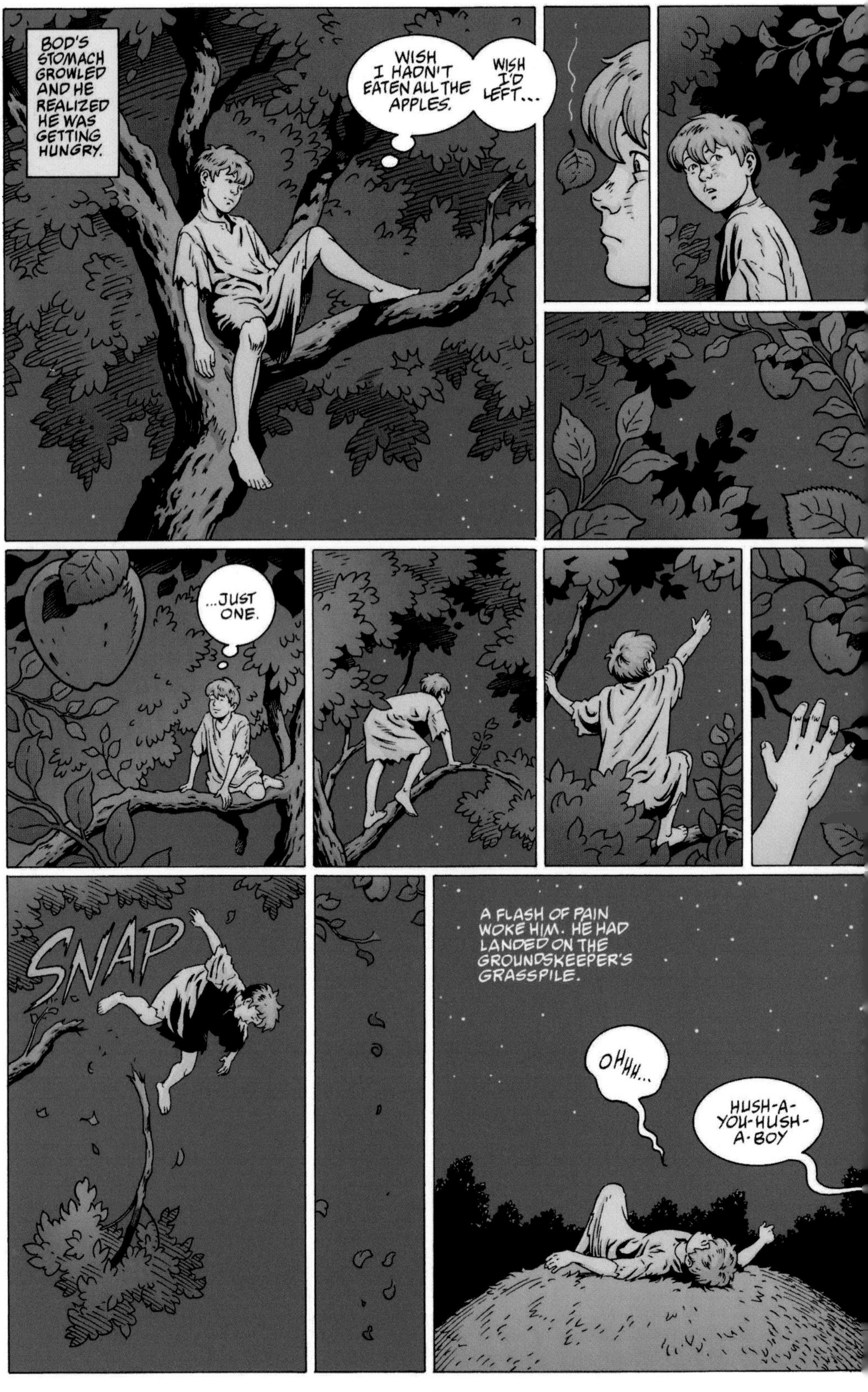
BOD'S STOMACH GROWLED AND HE REALIZED HE WAS GETTING HUNGRY.
WISH I HADN'T EATEN ALL THE APPLES.
WISH I'D LEFT...
...JUST ONE.
SNAP
A FLASH OF PAIN WOKE HIM. HE HAD LANDED ON THE GROUNDSKEEPER'S GRASSPILE.
OHHH...
HUSH-A-YOU-HUSH-A-BOY

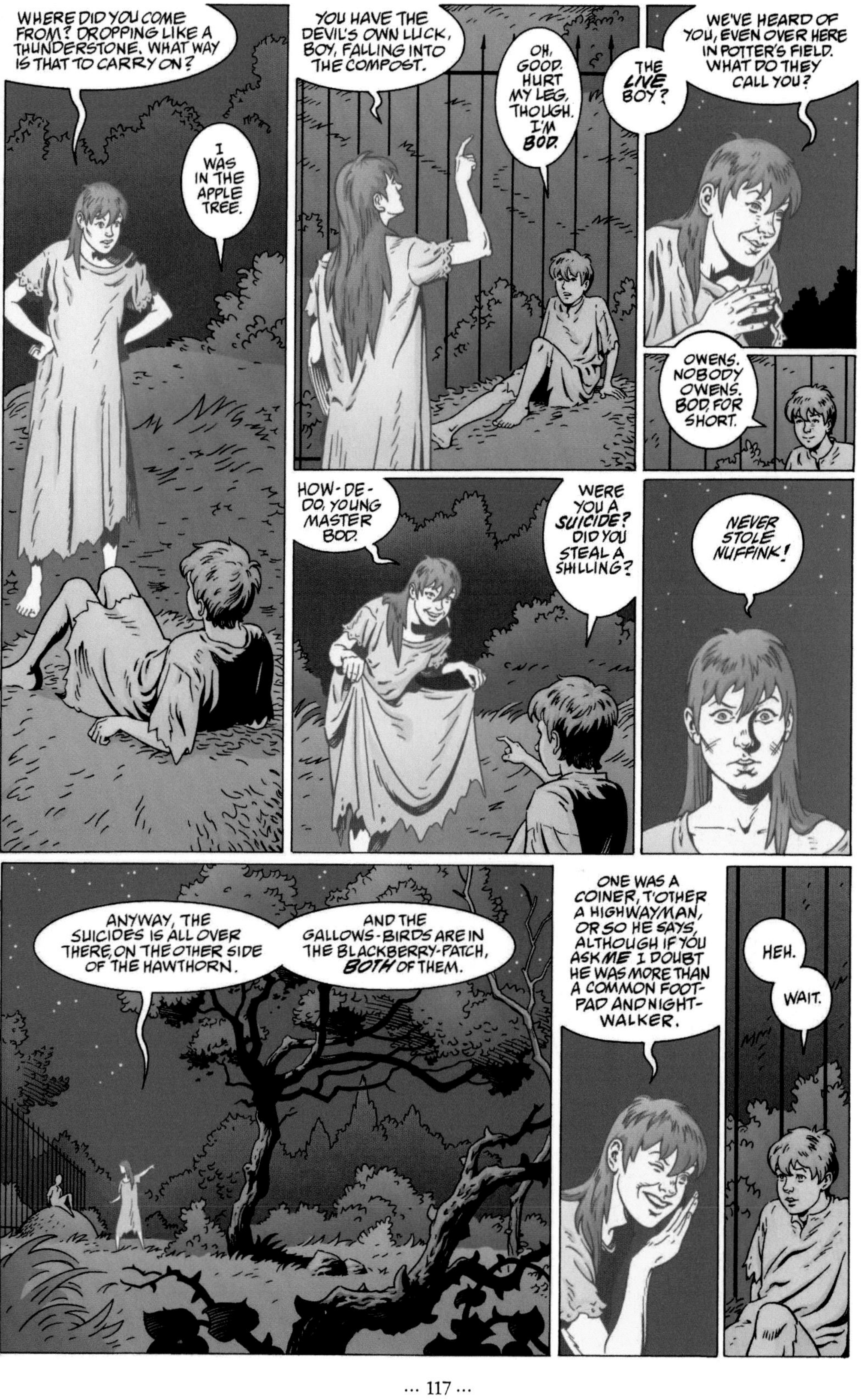
WHERE DID YOU COME FROM? DROPPING LIKE A THUNDERSTONE. WHAT WAY IS THAT TO CARRY ON?
I WAS IN THE APPLE TREE.
YOU HAVE THE DEVIL'S OWN LUCK, BOY, FALLING INTO THE COMPOST.
OH, GOOD. HURT MY LEG, THOUGH. I'M BOD.
THE LIVE BOY?
WE'VE HEARD OF YOU, EVEN OVER HERE IN POTTER'S FIELD. WHAT DO THEY CALL YOU?
OWENS. NOBODY OWENS. BOD, FOR SHORT.
HOW-DE-DO, YOUNG MASTER BOD.
WERE YOU A SUICIDE? DID YOU STEAL A SHILLING?
NEVER STOLE NUFFINK!
ANYWAY, THE SUICIDES IS ALL OVER THERE, ON THE OTHER SIDE OF THE HAWTHORN.
AND THE GALLOWS-BIRDS ARE IN THE BLACKBERRY-PATCH, BOTH OF THEM.
ONE WAS A COINER, T'OTHER A HIGHWAYMAN, OR SO HE SAYS, ALTHOUGH IF YOU ASK ME I DOUBT HE WAS MORE THAN A COMMON FOOT-PAD AND NIGHT-WALKER.
HEH.
WAIT.

THEY SAY A WITCH IS BURIED HERE.

DROWNDED AND BURNDED AND BURIED HERE WITHOUT AS MUCH AS A STONE TO MARK THE SPOT.

YOU WERE DROWNED *AND* BURNED?

WELL. LET ME TELL YOU.

THEY COME TO MY LITTLE COTTAGE AT DAWN, AND DRAGS ME OUT ONTO THE GREEN. "*YOU'RE A WITCH*," THEY SHOUTS, FAT AND FRESH-SCRUBBED ALL PINK IN THE MORNING, LIKE SO MANY *PIGWIGGINS*.

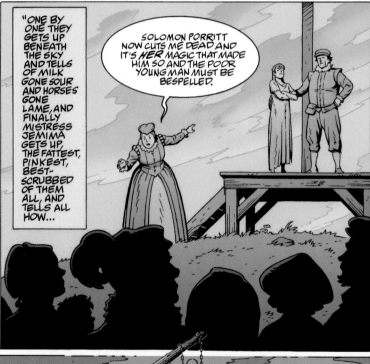

"ONE BY ONE THEY GETS UP BENEATH THE SKY AND TELLS OF MILK GONE SOUR AND HORSES GONE LAME, AND FINALLY MISTRESS JEMIMA GETS UP, THE FATTEST, PINKEST, BEST-SCRUBBED OF THEM ALL, AND TELLS ALL HOW...

SOLOMON PORRITT NOW CUTS ME DEAD AND IT'S *HER* MAGIC THAT MADE HIM SO AND THE POOR YOUNG MAN MUST BE BESPELLED.

"SO THEY STRAP ME TO THE CUCKING STOOL AND FORCES IT UNDER THE WATER OF THE DUCKPOND, SAYING IF I'M A WITCH I'LL NEITHER DROWN NOR CARE, BUT IF I AM NOT A WITCH, I'LL FEEL IT."

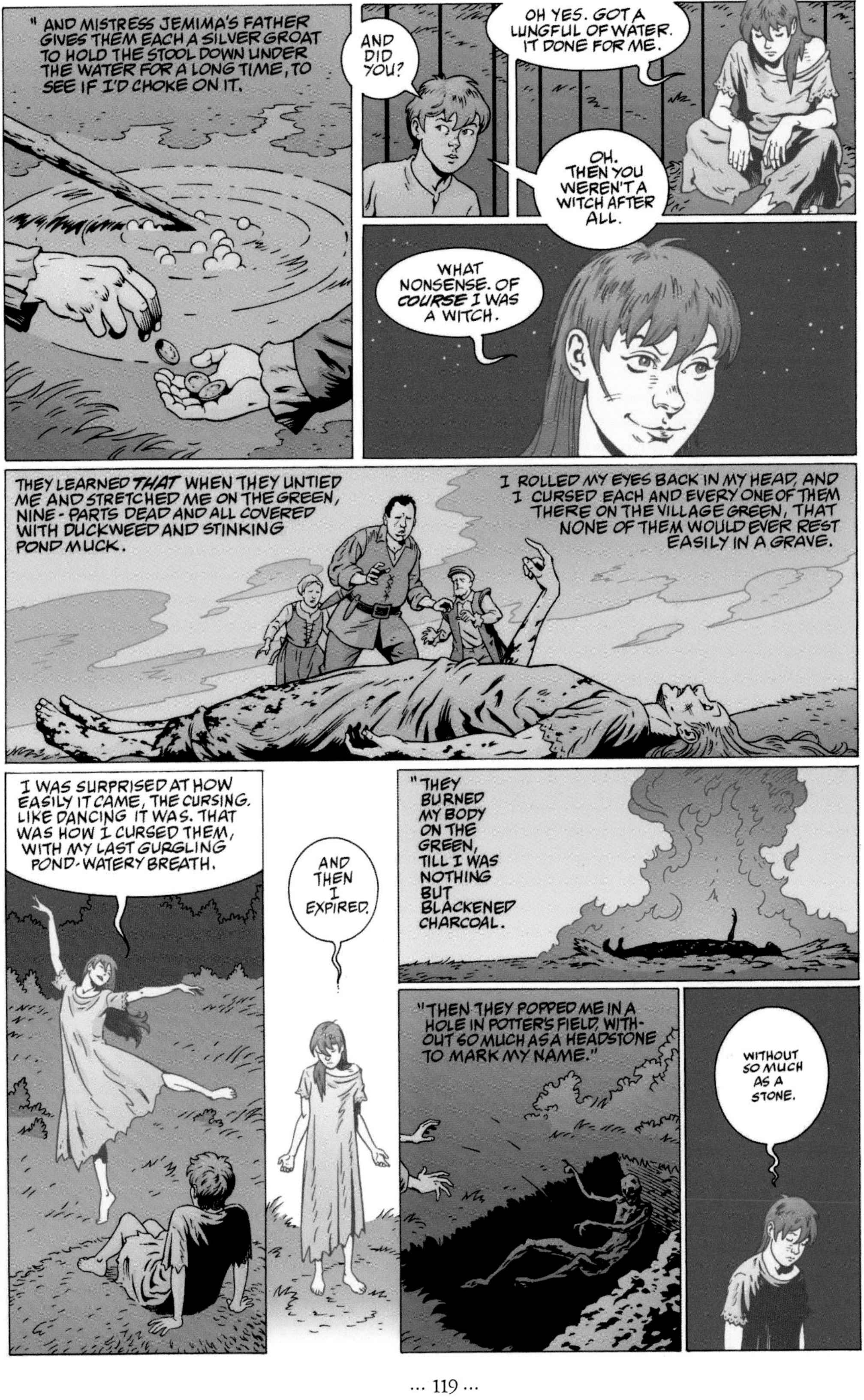
"AND MISTRESS JEMIMA'S FATHER GIVES THEM EACH A SILVER GROAT TO HOLD THE STOOL DOWN UNDER THE WATER FOR A LONG TIME, TO SEE IF I'D CHOKE ON IT.
AND DID YOU?
OH YES. GOT A LUNGFUL OF WATER. IT DONE FOR ME.
OH. THEN YOU WEREN'T A WITCH AFTER ALL.
WHAT NONSENSE. OF COURSE I WAS A WITCH.
THEY LEARNED THAT WHEN THEY UNTIED ME AND STRETCHED ME ON THE GREEN, NINE-PARTS DEAD AND ALL COVERED WITH DUCKWEED AND STINKING POND MUCK.
I ROLLED MY EYES BACK IN MY HEAD, AND I CURSED EACH AND EVERY ONE OF THEM THERE ON THE VILLAGE GREEN, THAT NONE OF THEM WOULD EVER REST EASILY IN A GRAVE.
I WAS SURPRISED AT HOW EASILY IT CAME, THE CURSING. LIKE DANCING IT WAS. THAT WAS HOW I CURSED THEM, WITH MY LAST GURGLING POND-WATERY BREATH.
AND THEN I EXPIRED.
"THEY BURNED MY BODY ON THE GREEN, TILL I WAS NOTHING BUT BLACKENED CHARCOAL.
"THEN THEY POPPED ME IN A HOLE IN POTTER'S FIELD, WITHOUT SO MUCH AS A HEADSTONE TO MARK MY NAME."
WITHOUT SO MUCH AS A STONE.

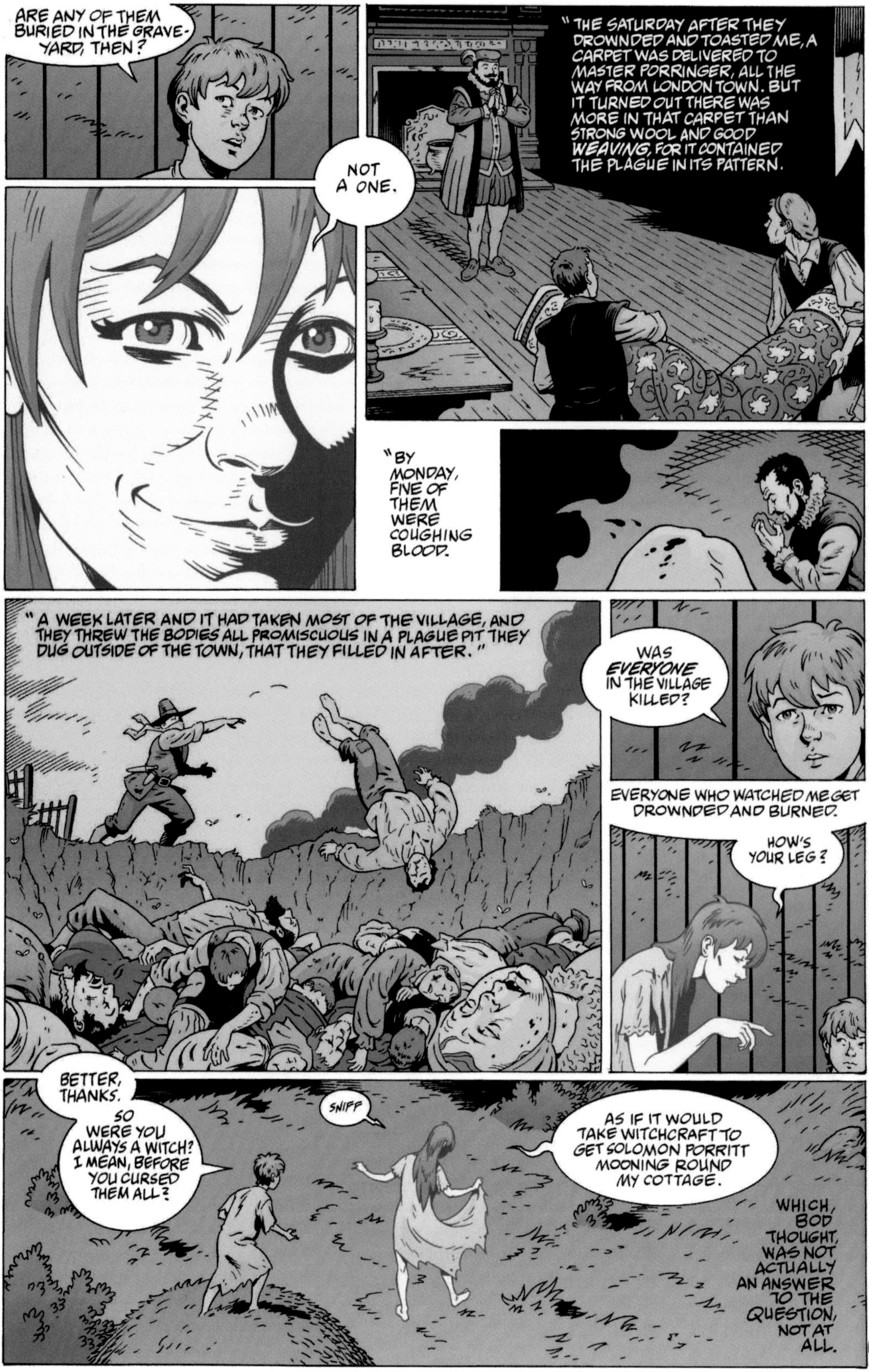
ARE ANY OF THEM BURIED IN THE GRAVEYARD, THEN?
"THE SATURDAY AFTER THEY DROWNED AND TOASTED ME, A CARPET WAS DELIVERED TO MASTER PORRINGER, ALL THE WAY FROM LONDON TOWN. BUT IT TURNED OUT THERE WAS MORE IN THAT CARPET THAN STRONG WOOL AND GOOD WEAVING, FOR IT CONTAINED THE PLAGUE IN ITS PATTERN.
NOT A ONE.
"BY MONDAY, FIVE OF THEM WERE COUGHING BLOOD.
"A WEEK LATER AND IT HAD TAKEN MOST OF THE VILLAGE, AND THEY THREW THE BODIES ALL PROMISCUOUS IN A PLAGUE PIT THEY DUG OUTSIDE OF THE TOWN, THAT THEY FILLED IN AFTER."
WAS EVERYONE IN THE VILLAGE KILLED?
EVERYONE WHO WATCHED ME GET DROWNDED AND BURNED.
HOW'S YOUR LEG?
BETTER, THANKS.
SO WERE YOU ALWAYS A WITCH? I MEAN, BEFORE YOU CURSED THEM ALL?
SNIFF
AS IF IT WOULD TAKE WITCHCRAFT TO GET SOLOMON PORRITT MOONING ROUND MY COTTAGE.
WHICH, BOD THOUGHT, WAS NOT ACTUALLY AN ANSWER TO THE QUESTION, NOT AT ALL.

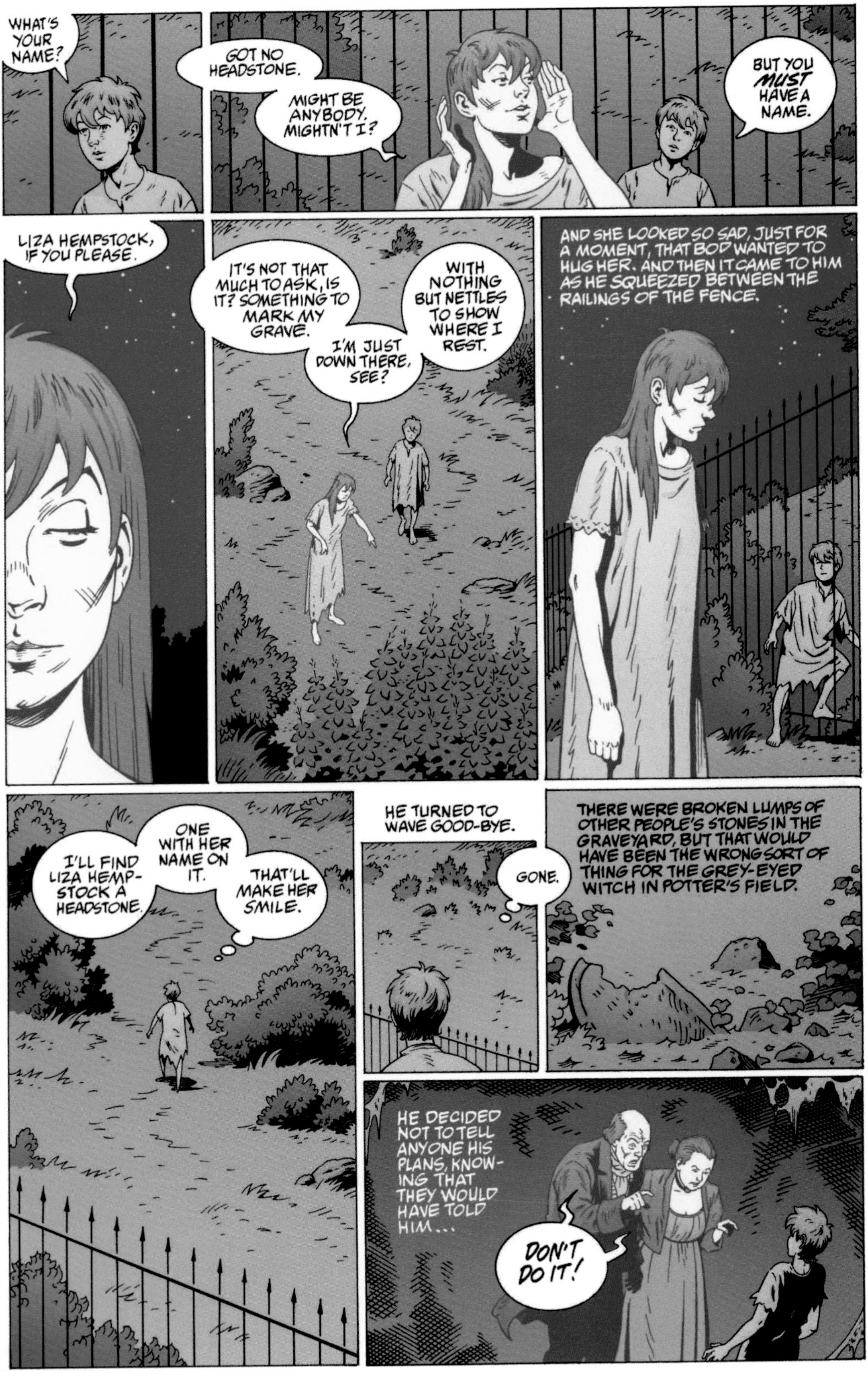
WHAT'S YOUR NAME?
GOT NO HEADSTONE.
MIGHT BE ANYBODY. MIGHTN'T I?
BUT YOU MUST HAVE A NAME.
LIZA HEMPSTOCK, IF YOU PLEASE.
IT'S NOT THAT MUCH TO ASK, IS IT? SOMETHING TO MARK MY GRAVE.
I'M JUST DOWN THERE, SEE?
WITH NOTHING BUT NETTLES TO SHOW WHERE I REST.
AND SHE LOOKED SO SAD, JUST FOR A MOMENT, THAT BOD WANTED TO HUG HER. AND THEN IT CAME TO HIM AS HE SQUEEZED BETWEEN THE RAILINGS OF THE FENCE.
I'LL FIND LIZA HEMPSTOCK A HEADSTONE.
ONE WITH HER NAME ON IT.
THAT'LL MAKE HER SMILE.
HE TURNED TO WAVE GOOD-BYE.
GONE.
THERE WERE BROKEN LUMPS OF OTHER PEOPLE'S STONES IN THE GRAVEYARD, BUT THAT WOULD HAVE BEEN THE WRONG SORT OF THING FOR THE GREY-EYED WITCH IN POTTER'S FIELD.
HE DECIDED NOT TO TELL ANYONE HIS PLANS, KNOWING THAT THEY WOULD HAVE TOLD HIM...
DON'T DO IT!

OVER THE NEXT FEW DAYS HIS MIND FILLED WITH PLANS, EACH MORE COMPLICATED AND EXTRAVAGANT THAN THE LAST. MR. PENNYWORTH DESPAIRED.

I DO BELIEVE THAT YOU ARE GETTING, IF ANYTHING, *WORSE.*

ARE THERE SPECIAL SHOPS WHERE THE LIVING PEOPLE GATHER THAT SELL ONLY HEADSTONES?

YOU ARE *OBVIOUS,* BOY.

HOW DO I GO ABOUT FINDING ONE? FADING IS THE *LEAST* OF MY PROBLEMS.

YOU ARE DIFFICULT TO *MISS.*

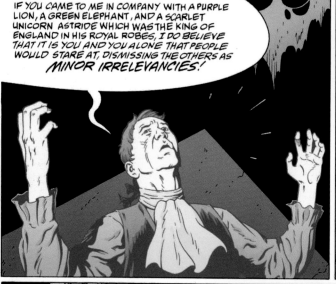

IF YOU CAME TO ME IN COMPANY WITH A PURPLE LION, A GREEN ELEPHANT, AND A SCARLET UNICORN ASTRIDE WHICH WAS THE KING OF ENGLAND IN HIS ROYAL ROBES, I DO BELIEVE THAT IT IS YOU AND YOU ALONE THAT PEOPLE WOULD STARE AT, DISMISSING THE OTHERS AS *MINOR IRRELEVANCIES!*

WHAT?

HE TOOK ADVANTAGE OF MISS BORROWS'S WILLINGNESS TO BE DIVERTED FROM THE SUBJECTS OF GRAMMAR AND COMPOSITION TO ASK HER ABOUT...

HOW EXACTLY DOES IT WORK?

MONEY.

HOW DO YOU USE IT TO GET THE THINGS YOU WANT?

BOD HAD A NUMBER OF COINS HE HAD FOUND OVER THE YEARS, AND HE THOUGHT HE COULD FINALLY GET SOME USE FROM THEM.

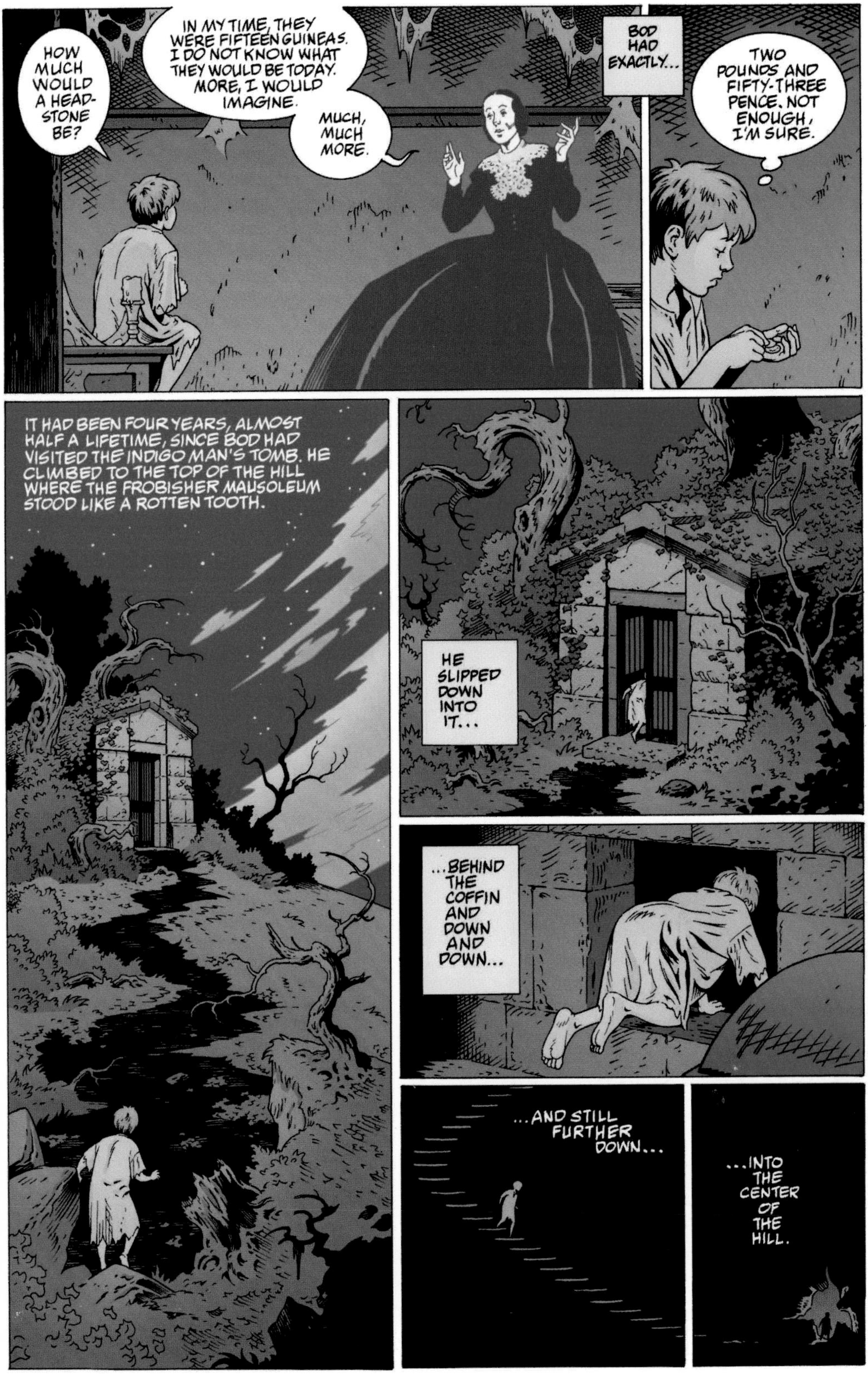
HOW MUCH WOULD A HEAD-STONE BE?
IN MY TIME, THEY WERE FIFTEEN GUINEAS. I DO NOT KNOW WHAT THEY WOULD BE TODAY. MORE, I WOULD IMAGINE.
MUCH, MUCH MORE.
BOD HAD EXACTLY...
TWO POUNDS AND FIFTY-THREE PENCE. NOT ENOUGH, I'M SURE.
IT HAD BEEN FOUR YEARS, ALMOST HALF A LIFETIME, SINCE BOD HAD VISITED THE INDIGO MAN'S TOMB. HE CLIMBED TO THE TOP OF THE HILL WHERE THE FROBISHER MAUSOLEUM STOOD LIKE A ROTTEN TOOTH.
HE SLIPPED DOWN INTO IT...
...BEHIND THE COFFIN AND DOWN AND DOWN...
...AND STILL FURTHER DOWN...
...INTO THE CENTER OF THE HILL.

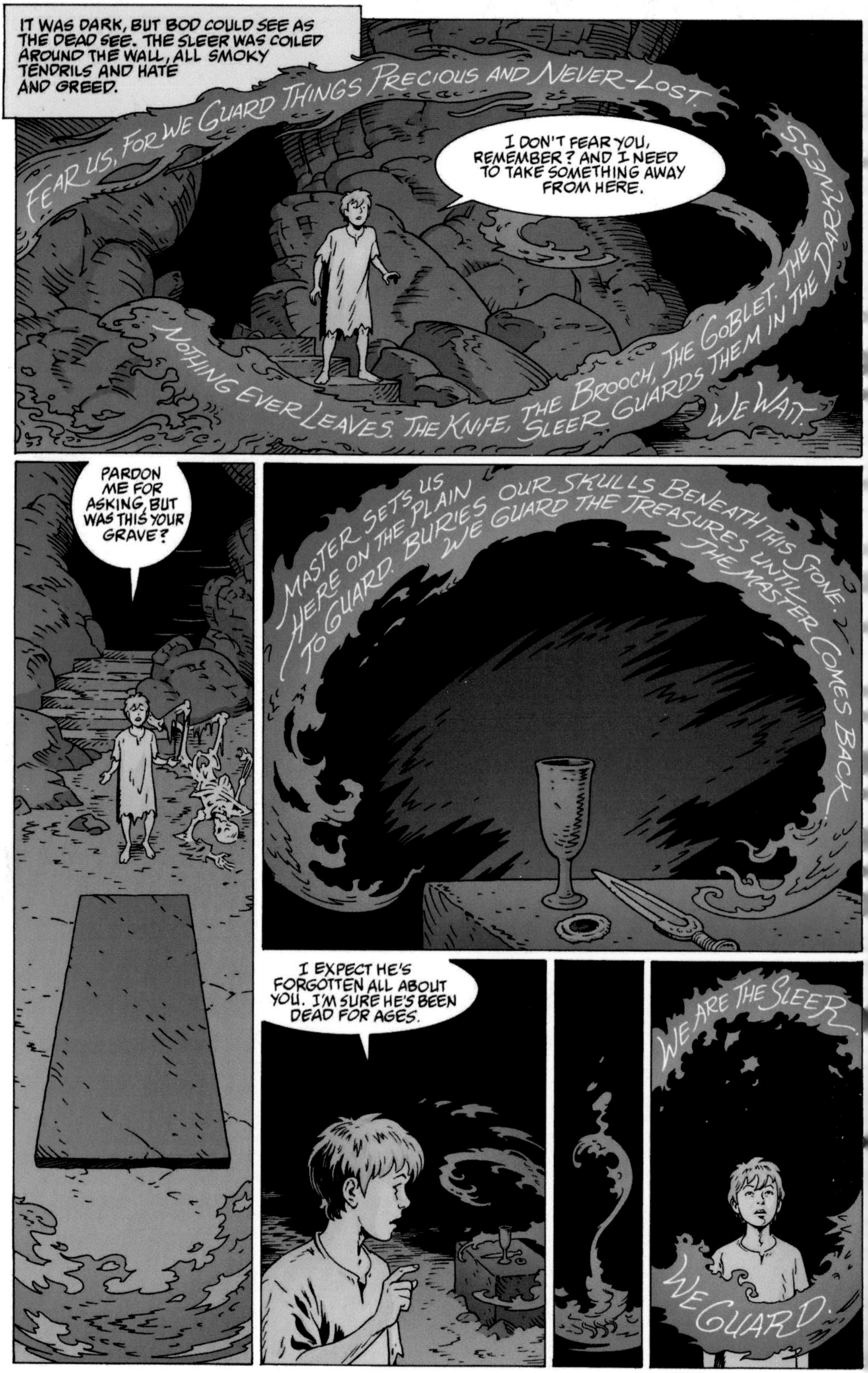
IT WAS DARK, BUT BOD COULD SEE AS THE DEAD SEE. THE SLEER WAS COILED AROUND THE WALL, ALL SMOKY TENDRILS AND HATE AND GREED.
FEAR US, FOR WE GUARD THINGS PRECIOUS AND NEVER-LOST.
I DON'T FEAR YOU, REMEMBER? AND I NEED TO TAKE SOMETHING AWAY FROM HERE.
NOTHING EVER LEAVES. THE KNIFE, THE BROOCH, THE GOBLET. THE SLEER GUARDS THEM IN THE DARKNESS.
WE WAIT.
PARDON ME FOR ASKING, BUT WAS THIS YOUR GRAVE?
MASTER SETS US HERE ON THE PLAIN TO GUARD. BURIES OUR SKULLS BENEATH THIS STONE. WE GUARD THE TREASURES UNTIL THE MASTER COMES BACK.
I EXPECT HE'S FORGOTTEN ALL ABOUT YOU. I'M SURE HE'S BEEN DEAD FOR AGES.
WE ARE THE SLEER.
WE GUARD.

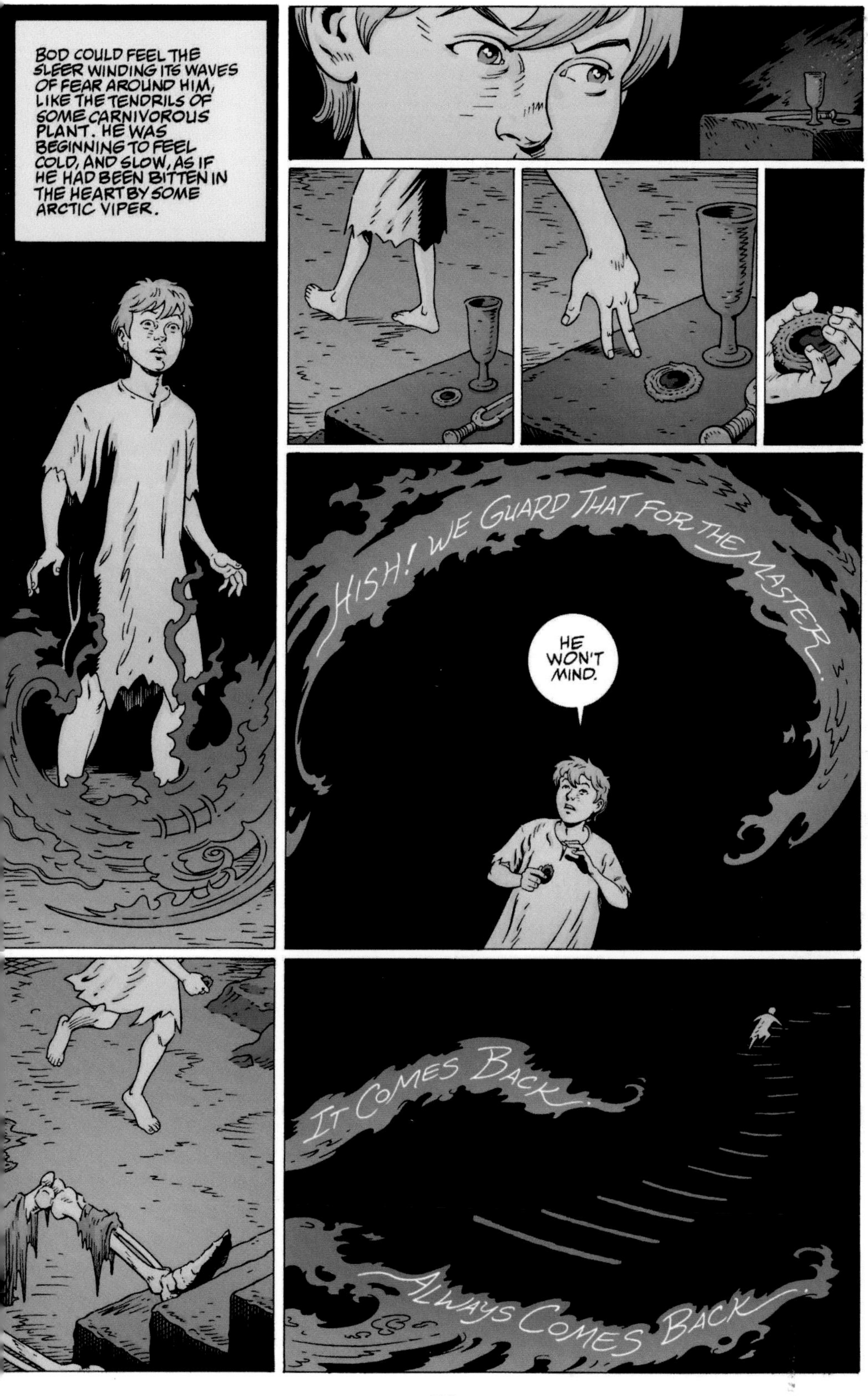
BOD COULD FEEL THE SLEER WINDING ITS WAVES OF FEAR AROUND HIM, LIKE THE TENDRILS OF SOME CARNIVOROUS PLANT. HE WAS BEGINNING TO FEEL COLD, AND SLOW, AS IF HE HAD BEEN BITTEN IN THE HEART BY SOME ARCTIC VIPER.
HISH! WE GUARD THAT FOR THE MASTER.
HE WON'T MIND.
IT COMES BACK.
ALWAYS COMES BACK.

BOD WENT UP THE STONE STEPS AS FAST AS HE COULD.

AT ONE POINT HE IMAGINED THAT THERE WAS SOMETHING COMING AFTER HIM.

BUT WHEN HE BROKE OUT OF THE TOP NOTHING MOVED OR FOLLOWED.

BOD SAT IN THE OPEN AIR AND HELD THE BROOCH. HE THOUGHT IT WAS ALL BLACK, AT FIRST, BUT THEN THE SUN ROSE, AND HE COULD SEE THAT THE STONE IN THE CENTER OF THE BLACK METAL WAS A SWIRLING RED.

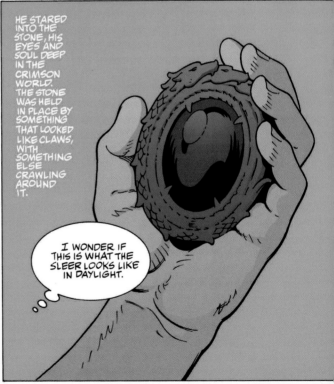

HE STARED INTO THE STONE, HIS EYES AND SOUL DEEP IN THE CRIMSON WORLD. THE STONE WAS HELD IN PLACE BY SOMETHING THAT LOOKED LIKE CLAWS, WITH SOMETHING ELSE CRAWLING AROUND IT.

I WONDER IF THIS IS WHAT THE SLEER LOOKS LIKE IN DAYLIGHT.

HE WANDERED DOWN THE HILL, TAKING ALL THE SHORTCUTS HE KNEW, THROUGH THE IVY TANGLE AND ON AND OVER AND INTO THE POTTER'S FIELD.

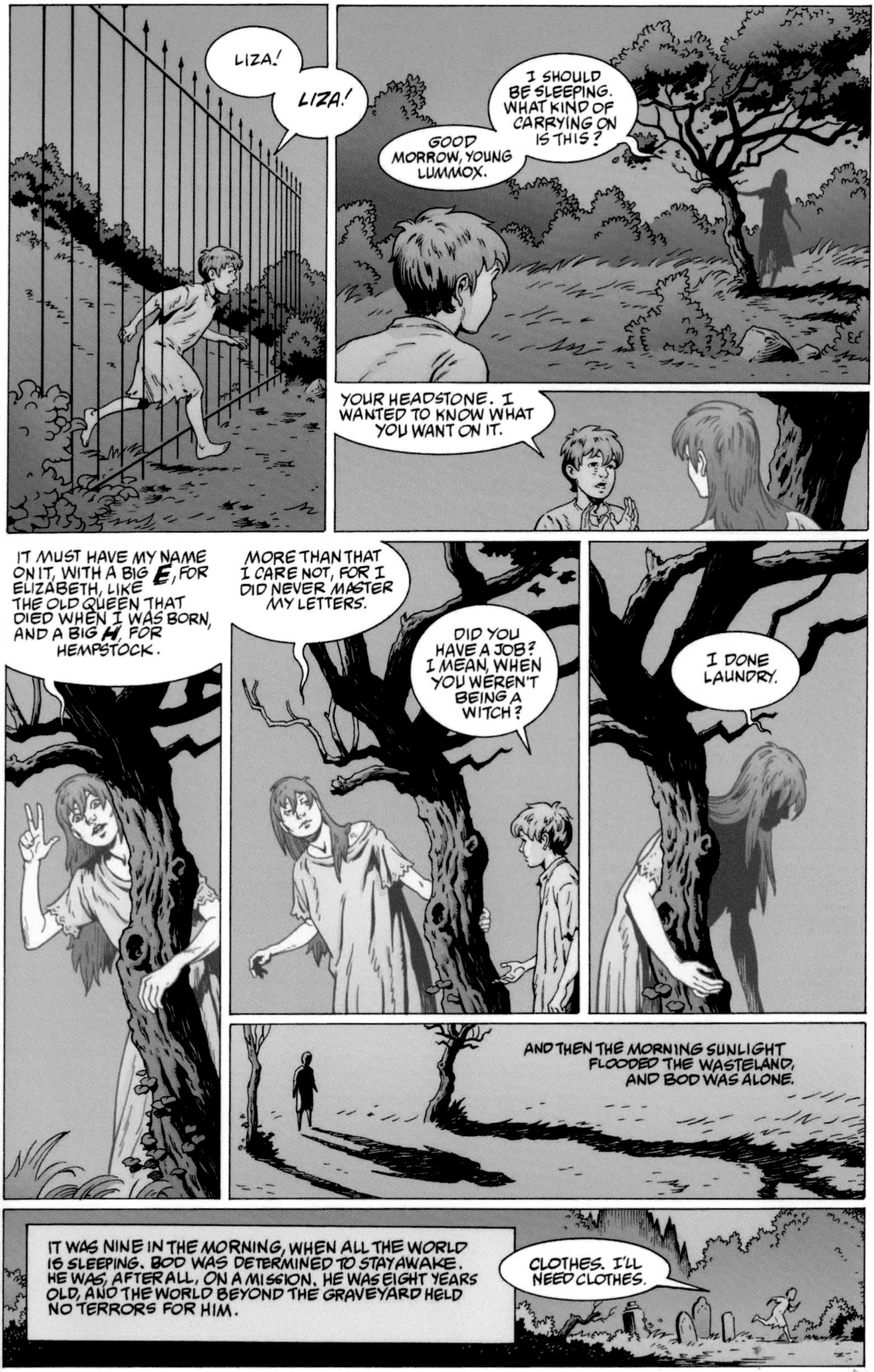
LIZA!
LIZA!
GOOD MORROW, YOUNG LUMMOX.
I SHOULD BE SLEEPING. WHAT KIND OF CARRYING ON IS THIS?
YOUR HEADSTONE. I WANTED TO KNOW WHAT YOU WANT ON IT.
IT MUST HAVE MY NAME ON IT, WITH A BIG E, FOR ELIZABETH, LIKE THE OLD QUEEN THAT DIED WHEN I WAS BORN, AND A BIG H, FOR HEMPSTOCK.
MORE THAN THAT I CARE NOT, FOR I DID NEVER MASTER MY LETTERS.
DID YOU HAVE A JOB? I MEAN, WHEN YOU WEREN'T BEING A WITCH?
I DONE LAUNDRY.
AND THEN THE MORNING SUNLIGHT FLOODED THE WASTELAND, AND BOD WAS ALONE.
IT WAS NINE IN THE MORNING, WHEN ALL THE WORLD IS SLEEPING. BOD WAS DETERMINED TO STAY AWAKE. HE WAS, AFTER ALL, ON A MISSION. HE WAS EIGHT YEARS OLD, AND THE WORLD BEYOND THE GRAVEYARD HELD NO TERRORS FOR HIM.
CLOTHES. I'LL NEED CLOTHES.

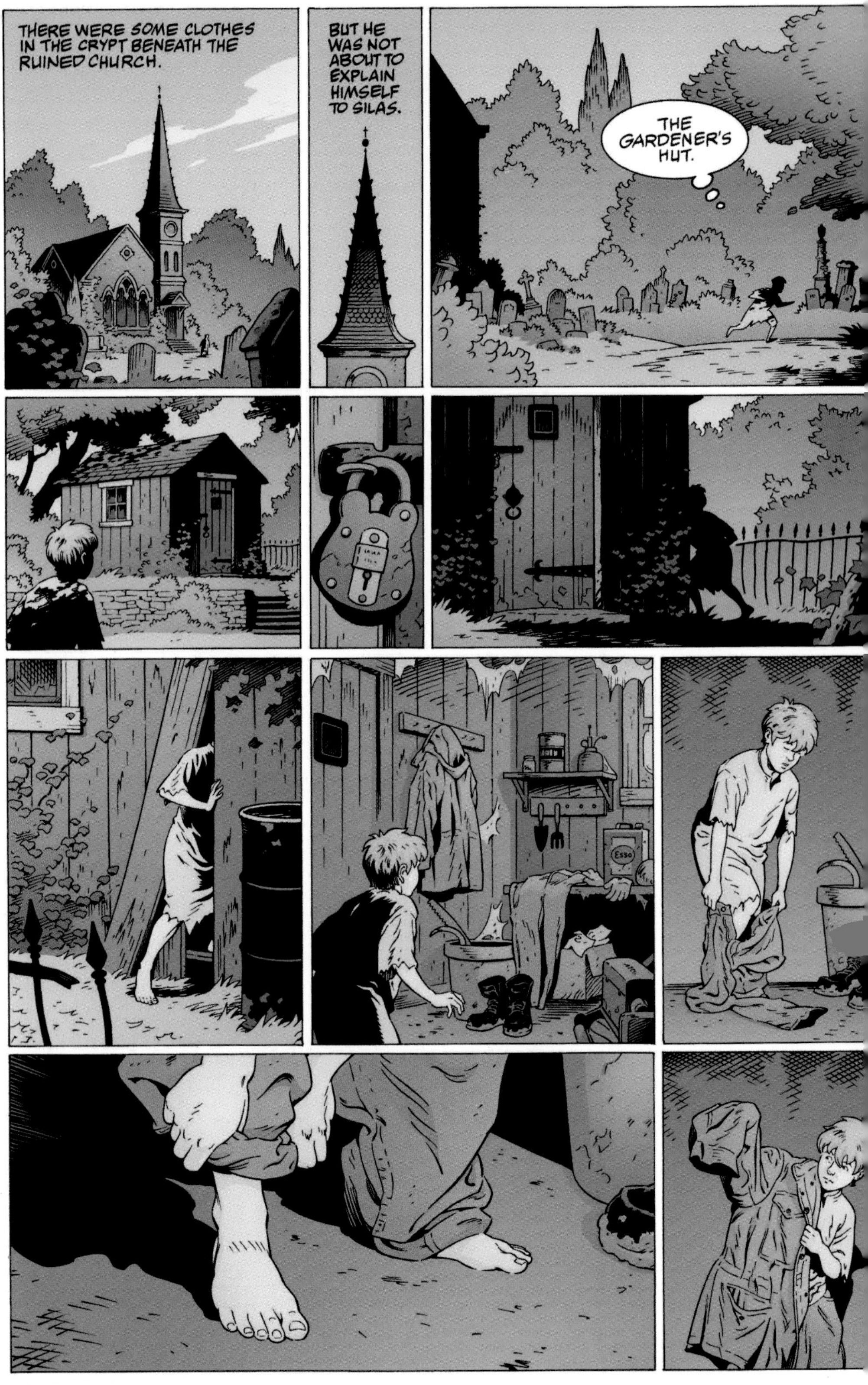
THERE WERE SOME CLOTHES IN THE CRYPT BENEATH THE RUINED CHURCH.
BUT HE WAS NOT ABOUT TO EXPLAIN HIMSELF TO SILAS.
THE GARDENER'S HUT.
ESSO

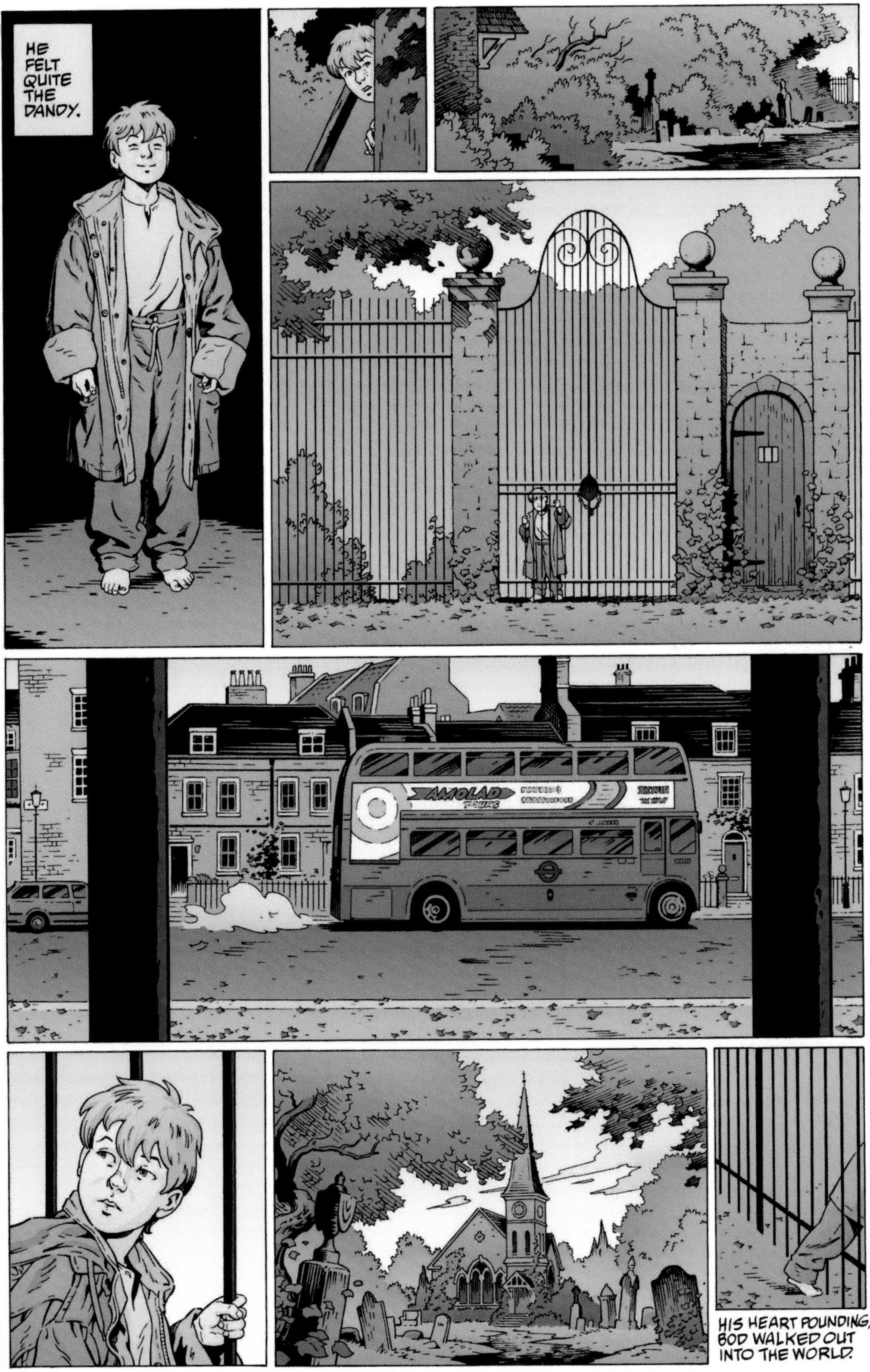
HE FELT QUITE THE DANDY.
HIS HEART POUNDING, BOD WALKED OUT INTO THE WORLD.

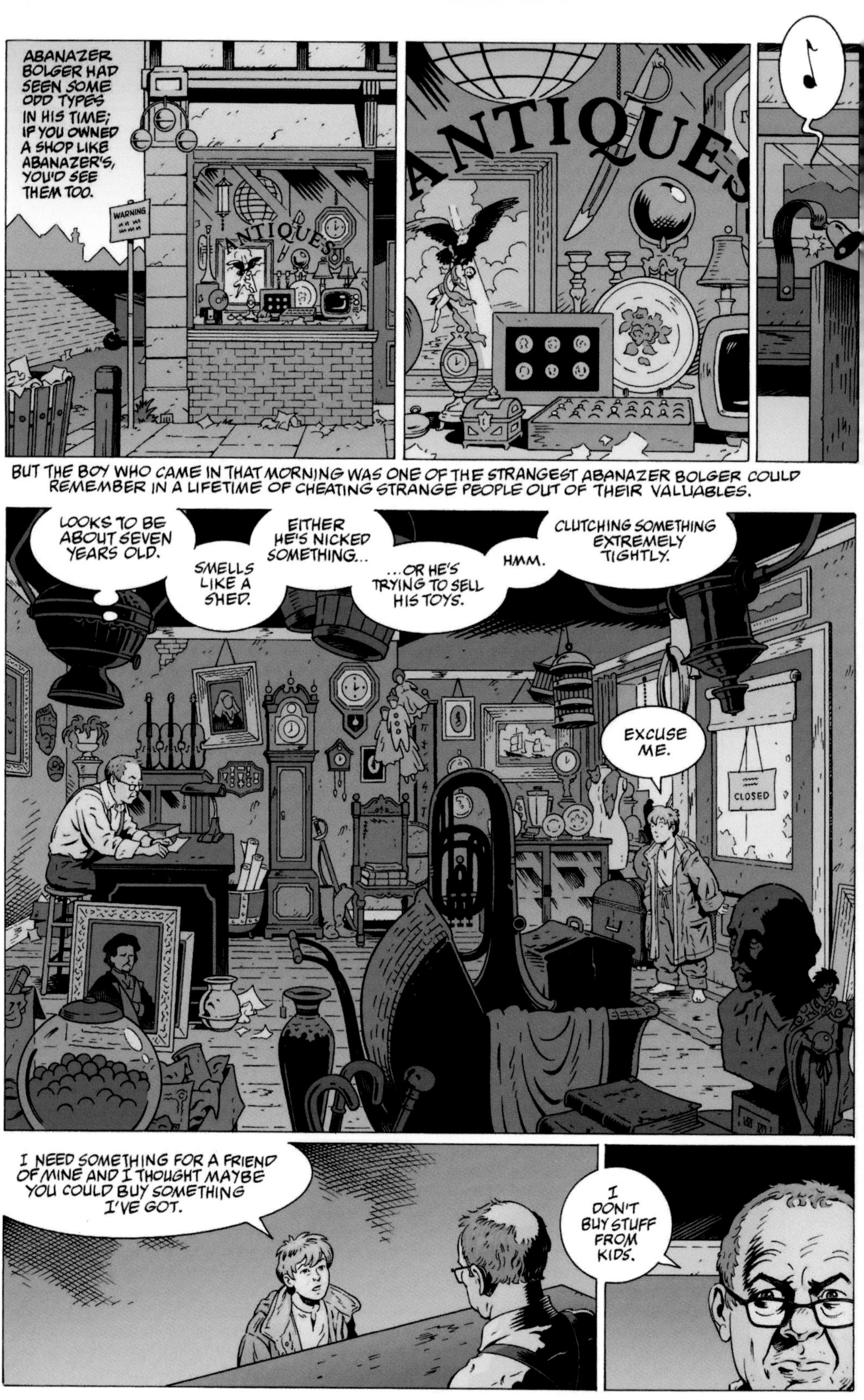
ABANAZER BOLGER HAD SEEN SOME ODD TYPES IN HIS TIME; IF YOU OWNED A SHOP LIKE ABANAZER'S, YOU'D SEE THEM TOO.
WARNING
ANTIQUES
ANTIQUES
♪
BUT THE BOY WHO CAME IN THAT MORNING WAS ONE OF THE STRANGEST ABANAZER BOLGER COULD REMEMBER IN A LIFETIME OF CHEATING STRANGE PEOPLE OUT OF THEIR VALUABLES.
LOOKS TO BE ABOUT SEVEN YEARS OLD.
SMELLS LIKE A SHED.
EITHER HE'S NICKED SOMETHING...
...OR HE'S TRYING TO SELL HIS TOYS.
HMM.
CLUTCHING SOMETHING EXTREMELY TIGHTLY.
EXCUSE ME.
CLOSED
I NEED SOMETHING FOR A FRIEND OF MINE AND I THOUGHT MAYBE YOU COULD BUY SOMETHING I'VE GOT.
I DON'T BUY STUFF FROM KIDS.

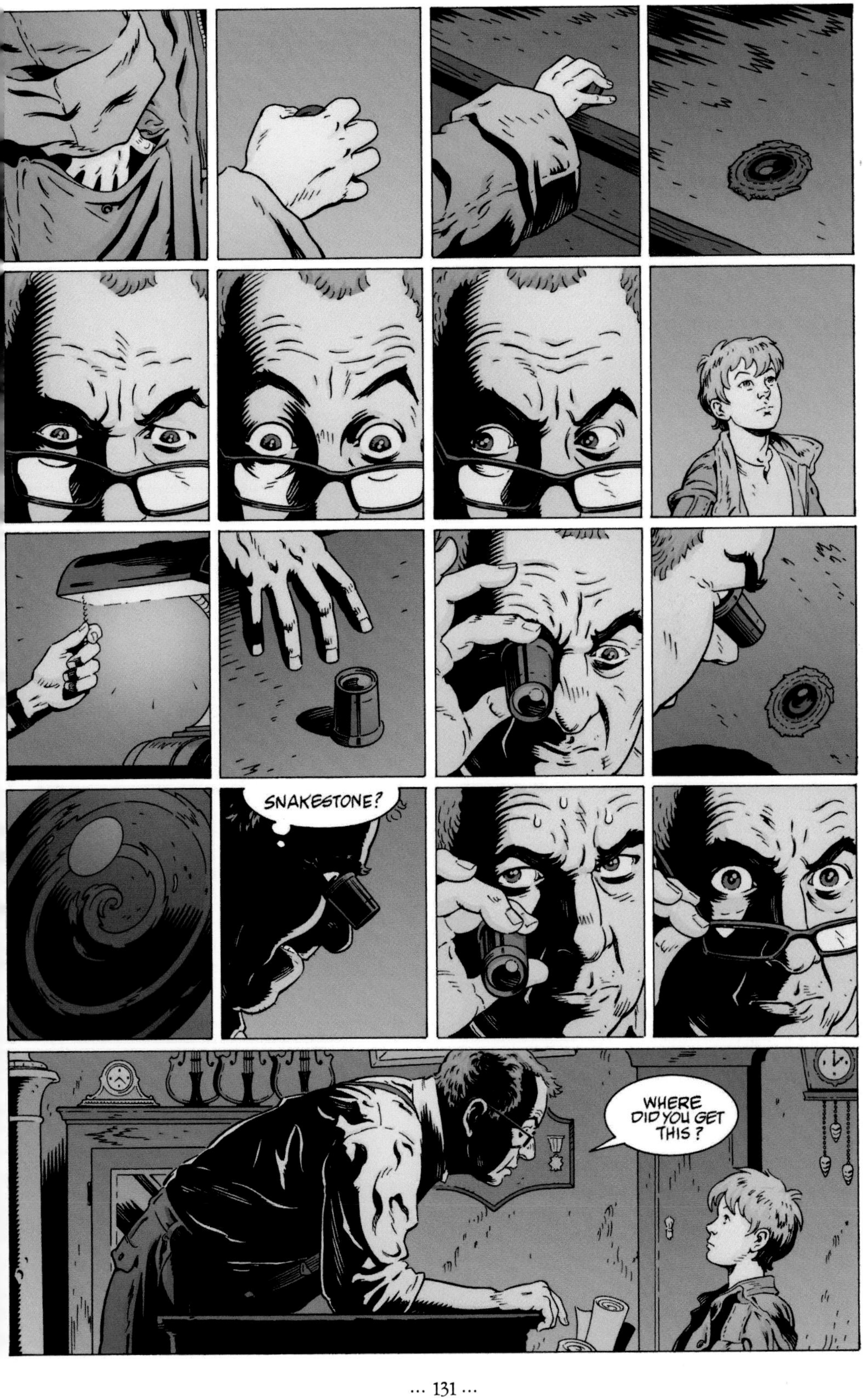
SNAKESTONE?
WHERE DID YOU GET THIS?

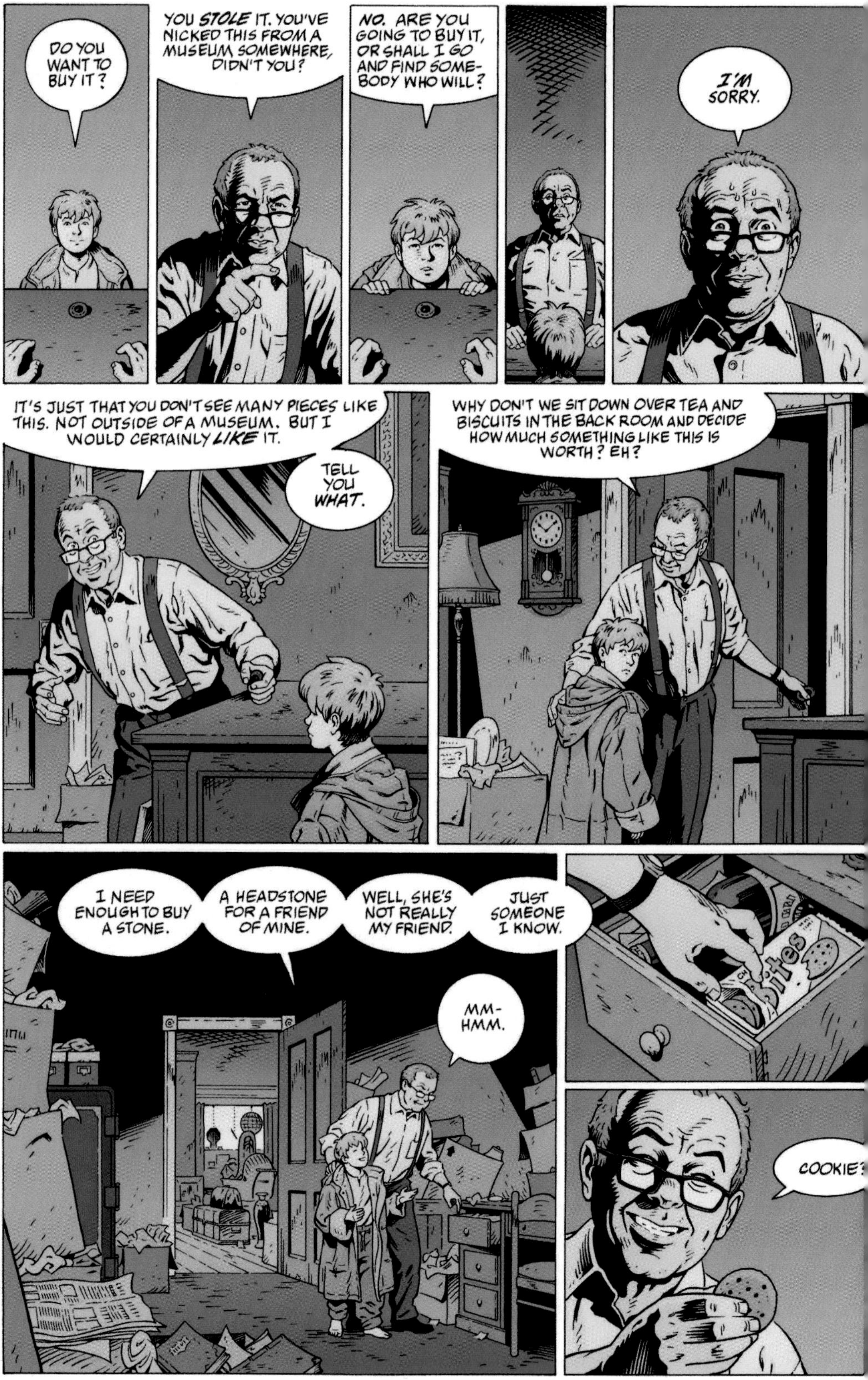
DO YOU WANT TO BUY IT?
YOU STOLE IT. YOU'VE NICKED THIS FROM A MUSEUM SOMEWHERE, DIDN'T YOU?
NO. ARE YOU GOING TO BUY IT, OR SHALL I GO AND FIND SOMEBODY WHO WILL?
I'M SORRY.
IT'S JUST THAT YOU DON'T SEE MANY PIECES LIKE THIS. NOT OUTSIDE OF A MUSEUM. BUT I WOULD CERTAINLY LIKE IT.
TELL YOU WHAT.
WHY DON'T WE SIT DOWN OVER TEA AND BISCUITS IN THE BACK ROOM AND DECIDE HOW MUCH SOMETHING LIKE THIS IS WORTH? EH?
I NEED ENOUGH TO BUY A STONE.
A HEADSTONE FOR A FRIEND OF MINE.
WELL, SHE'S NOT REALLY MY FRIEND.
JUST SOMEONE I KNOW.
MM-HMM.
Bites
COOKIE?

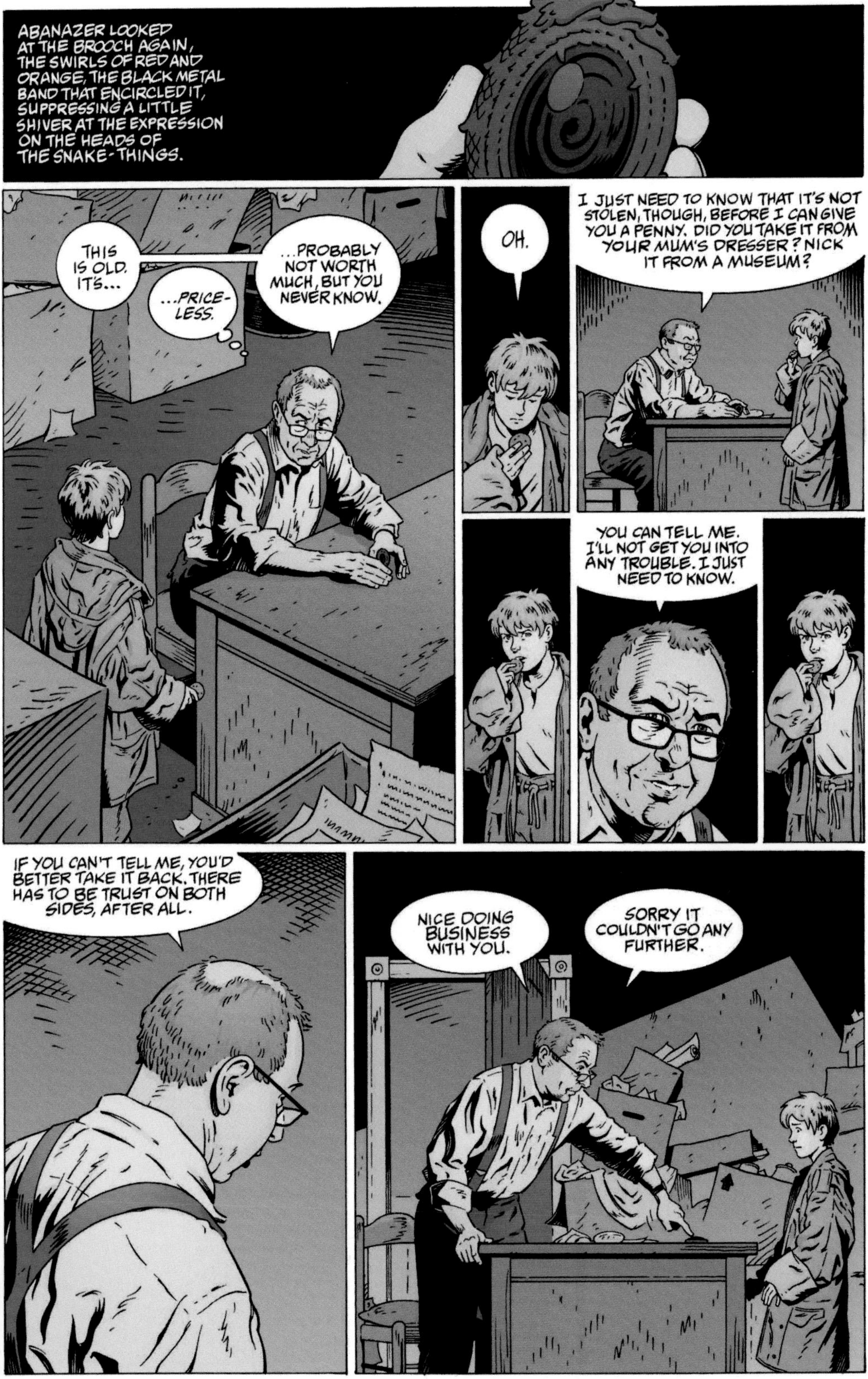
ABANAZER LOOKED AT THE BROOCH AGAIN, THE SWIRLS OF RED AND ORANGE, THE BLACK METAL BAND THAT ENCIRCLED IT, SUPPRESSING A LITTLE SHIVER AT THE EXPRESSION ON THE HEADS OF THE SNAKE-THINGS.
THIS IS OLD. IT'S...
...PRICE-LESS.
...PROBABLY NOT WORTH MUCH, BUT YOU NEVER KNOW.
OH.
I JUST NEED TO KNOW THAT IT'S NOT STOLEN, THOUGH, BEFORE I CAN GIVE YOU A PENNY. DID YOU TAKE IT FROM YOUR MUM'S DRESSER? NICK IT FROM A MUSEUM?
YOU CAN TELL ME. I'LL NOT GET YOU INTO ANY TROUBLE. I JUST NEED TO KNOW.
IF YOU CAN'T TELL ME, YOU'D BETTER TAKE IT BACK. THERE HAS TO BE TRUST ON BOTH SIDES, AFTER ALL.
NICE DOING BUSINESS WITH YOU.
SORRY IT COULDN'T GO ANY FURTHER.

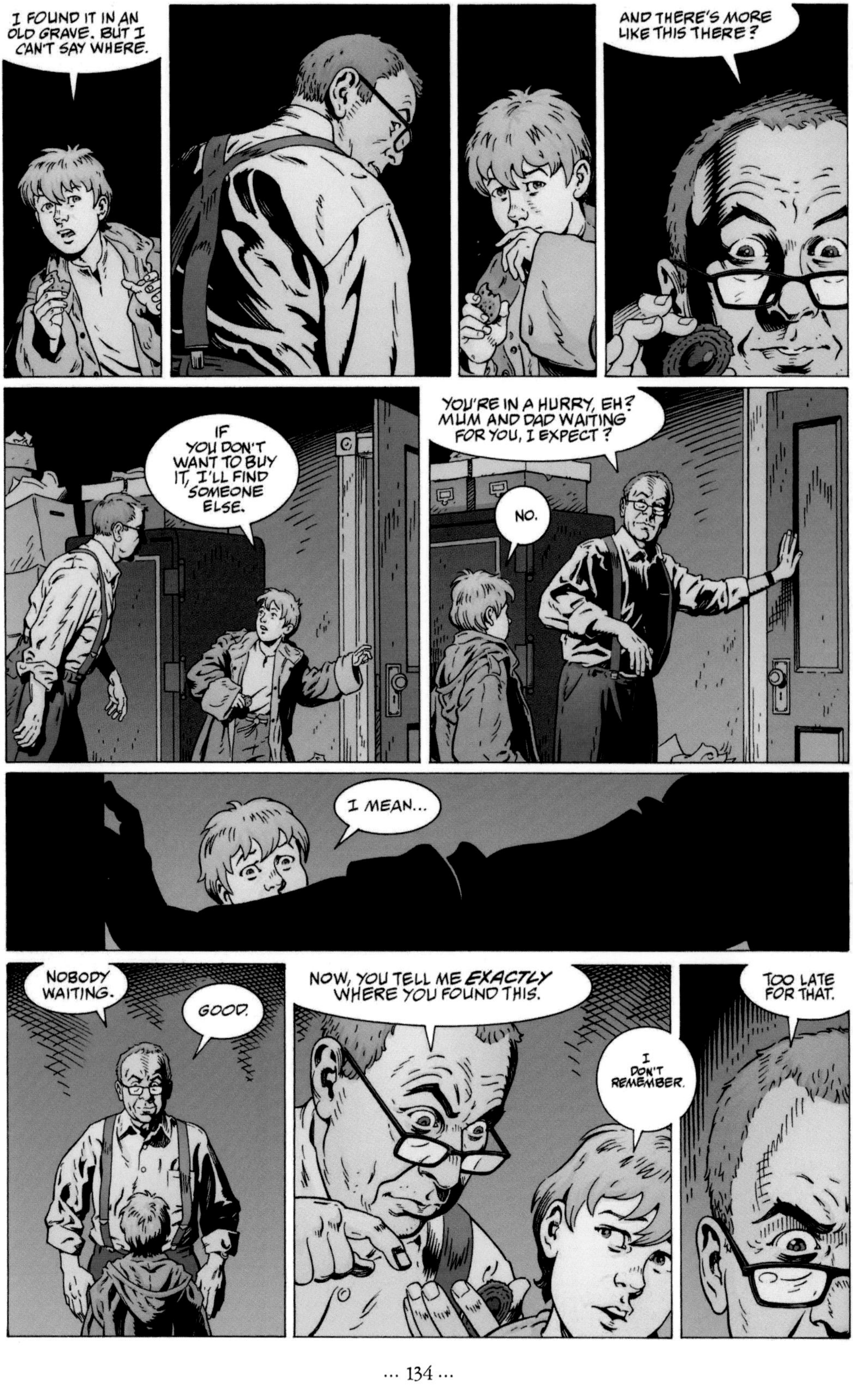
I FOUND IT IN AN OLD GRAVE. BUT I CAN'T SAY WHERE.
AND THERE'S MORE LIKE THIS THERE?
IF YOU DON'T WANT TO BUY IT, I'LL FIND SOMEONE ELSE.
YOU'RE IN A HURRY, EH? MUM AND DAD WAITING FOR YOU, I EXPECT?
NO.
I MEAN...
NOBODY WAITING.
GOOD.
NOW, YOU TELL ME *EXACTLY* WHERE YOU FOUND THIS.
I DON'T REMEMBER.
TOO LATE FOR THAT.

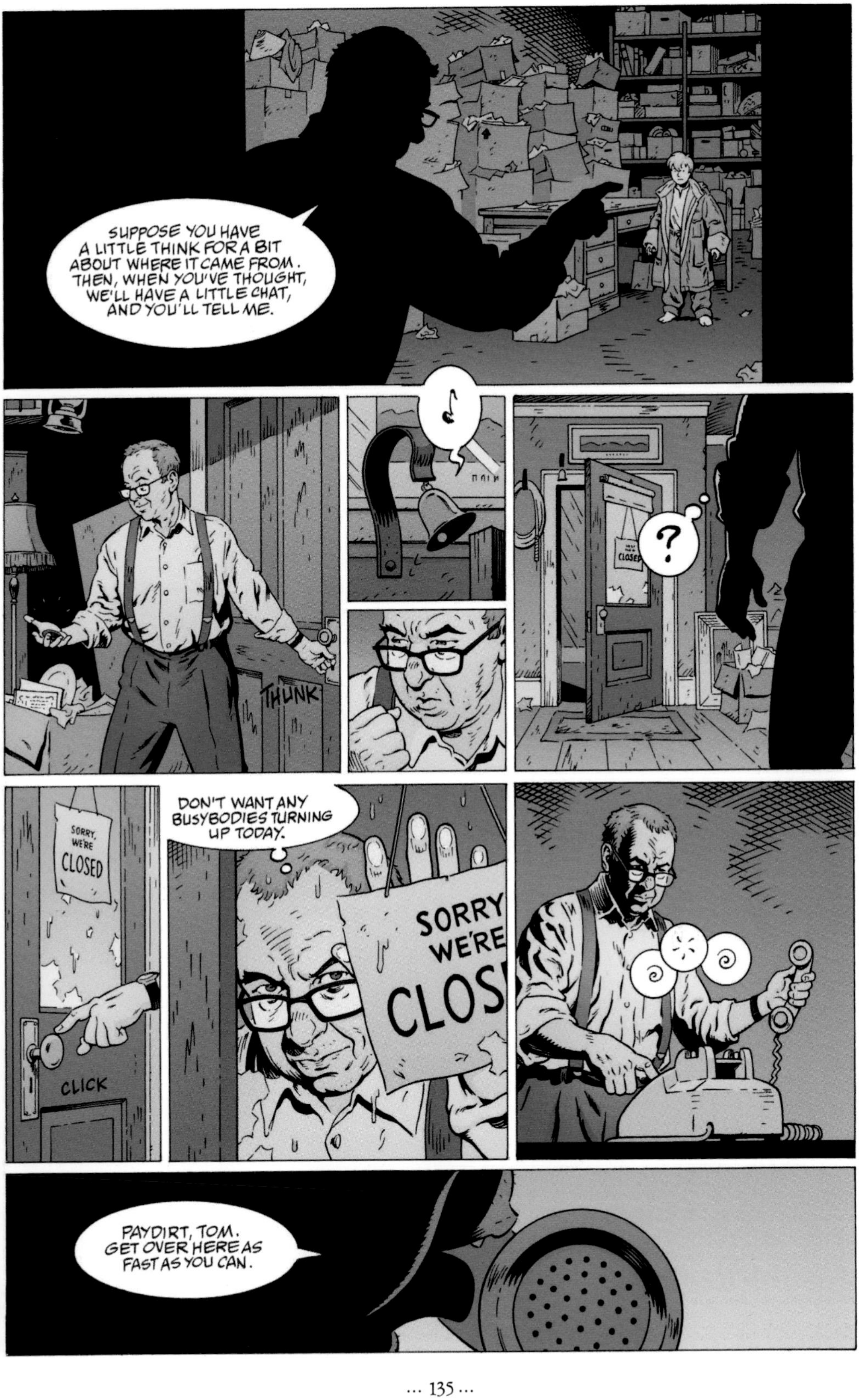

SUPPOSE YOU HAVE A LITTLE THINK FOR A BIT ABOUT WHERE IT CAME FROM. THEN, WHEN YOU'VE THOUGHT, WE'LL HAVE A LITTLE CHAT, AND YOU'LL TELL ME.
THUNK
?
SORRY, WE'RE CLOSED
DON'T WANT ANY BUSYBODIES TURNING UP TODAY.
CLICK
SORRY WE'RE CLOS
PAYDIRT, TOM. GET OVER HERE AS FAST AS YOU CAN.

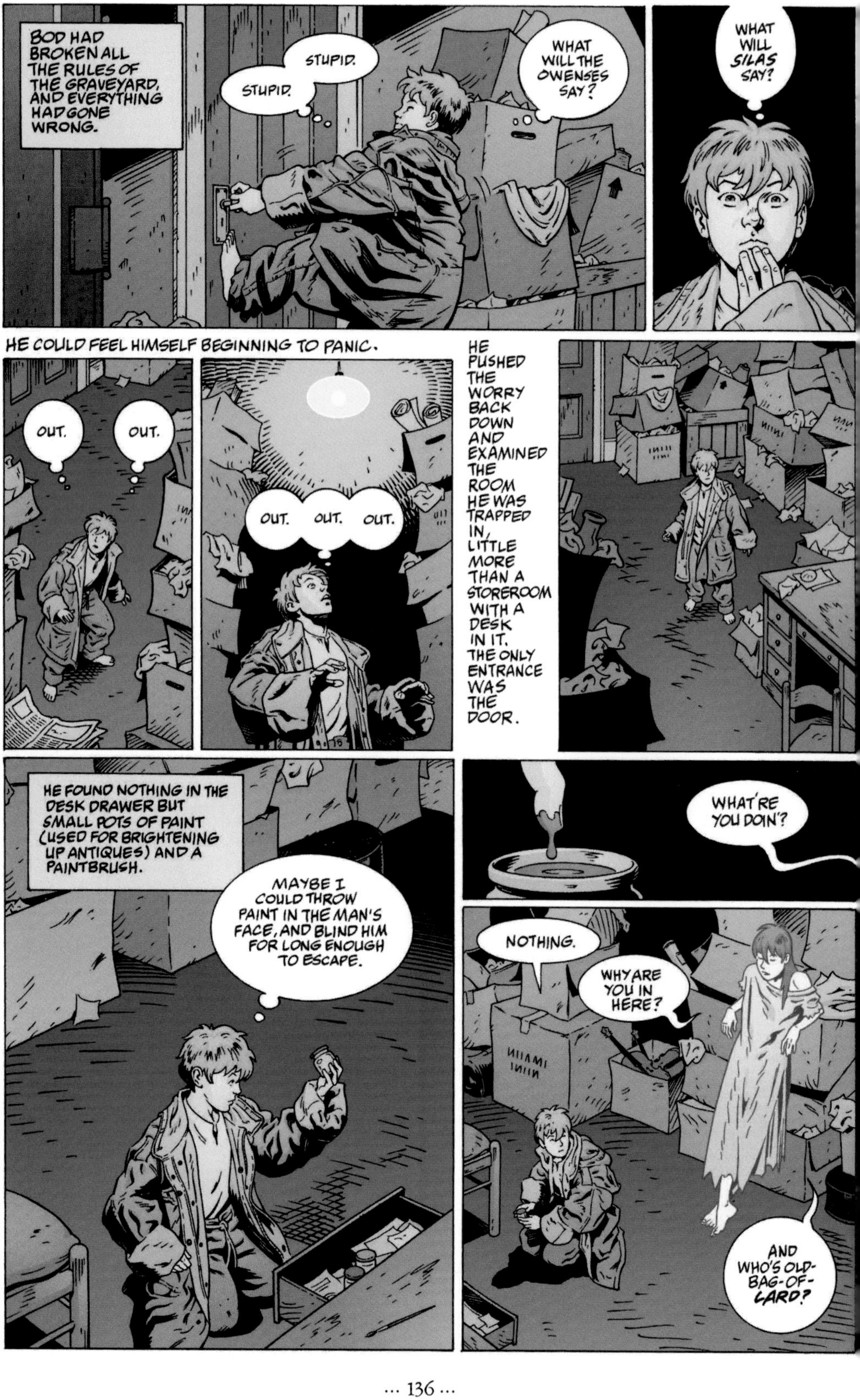
BOD HAD BROKEN ALL THE RULES OF THE GRAVEYARD, AND EVERYTHING HAD GONE WRONG.
STUPID.
STUPID.
WHAT WILL THE OWENSES SAY?
WHAT WILL SILAS SAY?
HE COULD FEEL HIMSELF BEGINNING TO PANIC.
OUT.
OUT.
OUT. OUT. OUT.
HE PUSHED THE WORRY BACK DOWN AND EXAMINED THE ROOM HE WAS TRAPPED IN, LITTLE MORE THAN A STOREROOM WITH A DESK IN IT. THE ONLY ENTRANCE WAS THE DOOR.
HE FOUND NOTHING IN THE DESK DRAWER BUT SMALL POTS OF PAINT (USED FOR BRIGHTENING UP ANTIQUES) AND A PAINTBRUSH.
MAYBE I COULD THROW PAINT IN THE MAN'S FACE, AND BLIND HIM FOR LONG ENOUGH TO ESCAPE.
WHAT'RE YOU DOIN'?
NOTHING.
WHY ARE YOU IN HERE?
AND WHO'S OLD-BAG-OF-LARD?

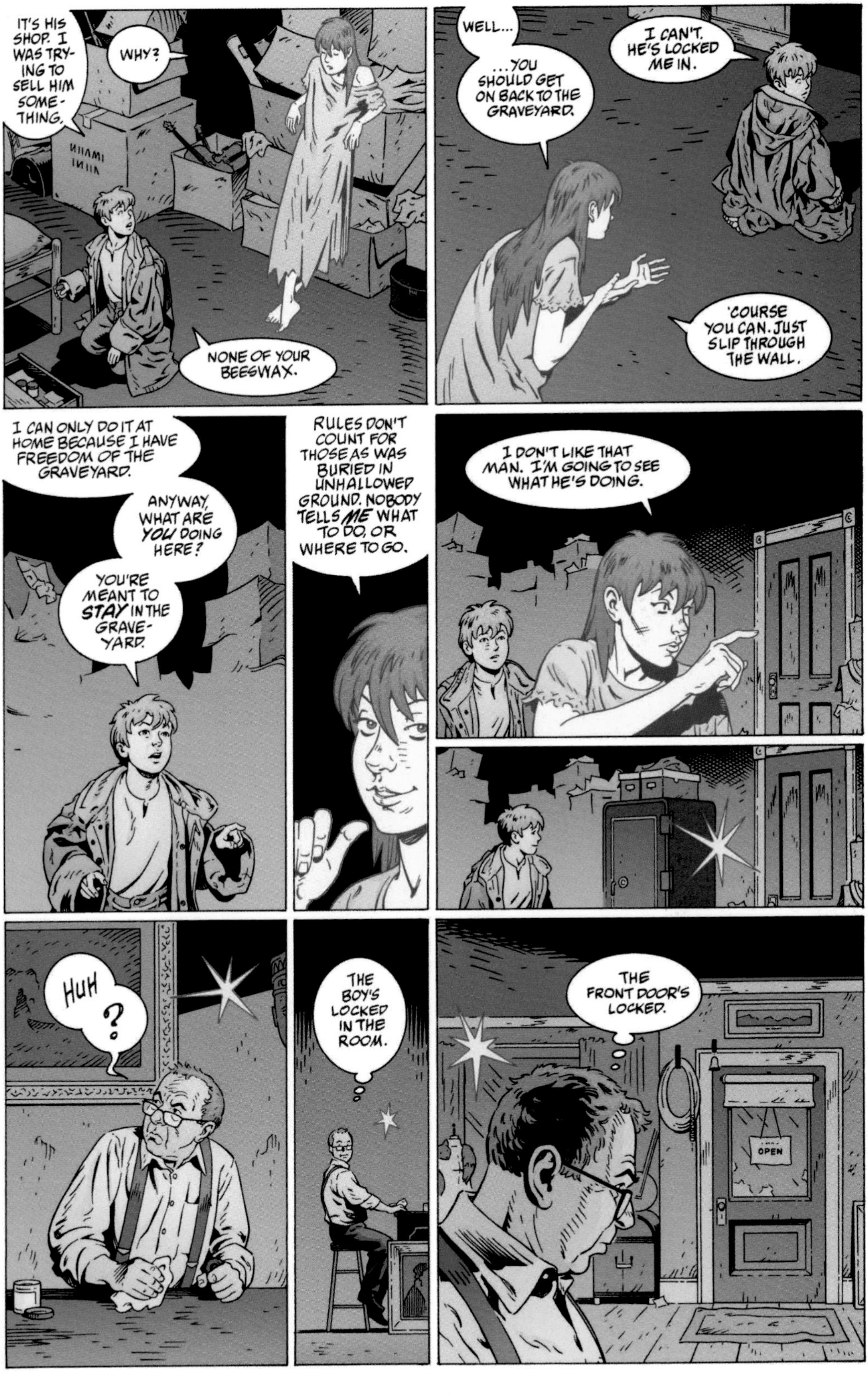
IT'S HIS SHOP. I WAS TRYING TO SELL HIM SOMETHING.
WHY?
NONE OF YOUR BEESWAX.
WELL...
...YOU SHOULD GET ON BACK TO THE GRAVEYARD.
I CAN'T. HE'S LOCKED ME IN.
'COURSE YOU CAN. JUST SLIP THROUGH THE WALL.
I CAN ONLY DO IT AT HOME BECAUSE I HAVE FREEDOM OF THE GRAVEYARD.
ANYWAY, WHAT ARE YOU DOING HERE?
YOU'RE MEANT TO STAY IN THE GRAVEYARD.
RULES DON'T COUNT FOR THOSE AS WAS BURIED IN UNHALLOWED GROUND. NOBODY TELLS ME WHAT TO DO, OR WHERE TO GO.
I DON'T LIKE THAT MAN. I'M GOING TO SEE WHAT HE'S DOING.
HUH?
THE BOY'S LOCKED IN THE ROOM.
THE FRONT DOOR'S LOCKED.
OPEN

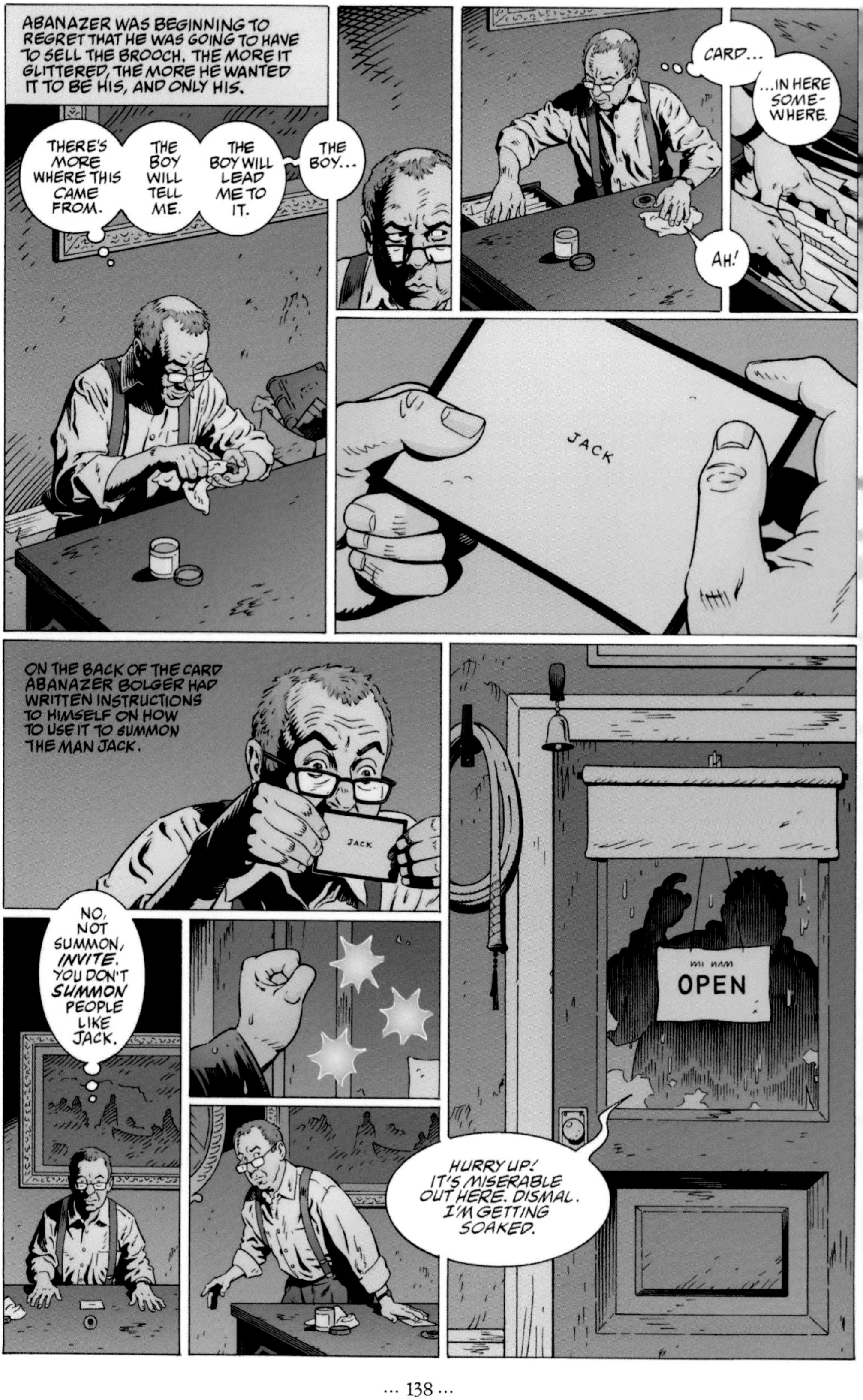
ABANAZER WAS BEGINNING TO REGRET THAT HE WAS GOING TO HAVE TO SELL THE BROOCH. THE MORE IT GLITTERED, THE MORE HE WANTED IT TO BE HIS, AND ONLY HIS.
THERE'S MORE WHERE THIS CAME FROM.
THE BOY WILL TELL ME.
THE BOY WILL LEAD ME TO IT.
THE BOY...
CARD...
...IN HERE SOMEWHERE.
AH!
JACK
ON THE BACK OF THE CARD ABANAZER BOLGER HAD WRITTEN INSTRUCTIONS TO HIMSELF ON HOW TO USE IT TO SUMMON THE MAN JACK.
JACK
NO, NOT SUMMON, *INVITE*. YOU DON'T *SUMMON* PEOPLE LIKE JACK.
OPEN
HURRY UP! IT'S MISERABLE OUT HERE. DISMAL. I'M GETTING SOAKED.

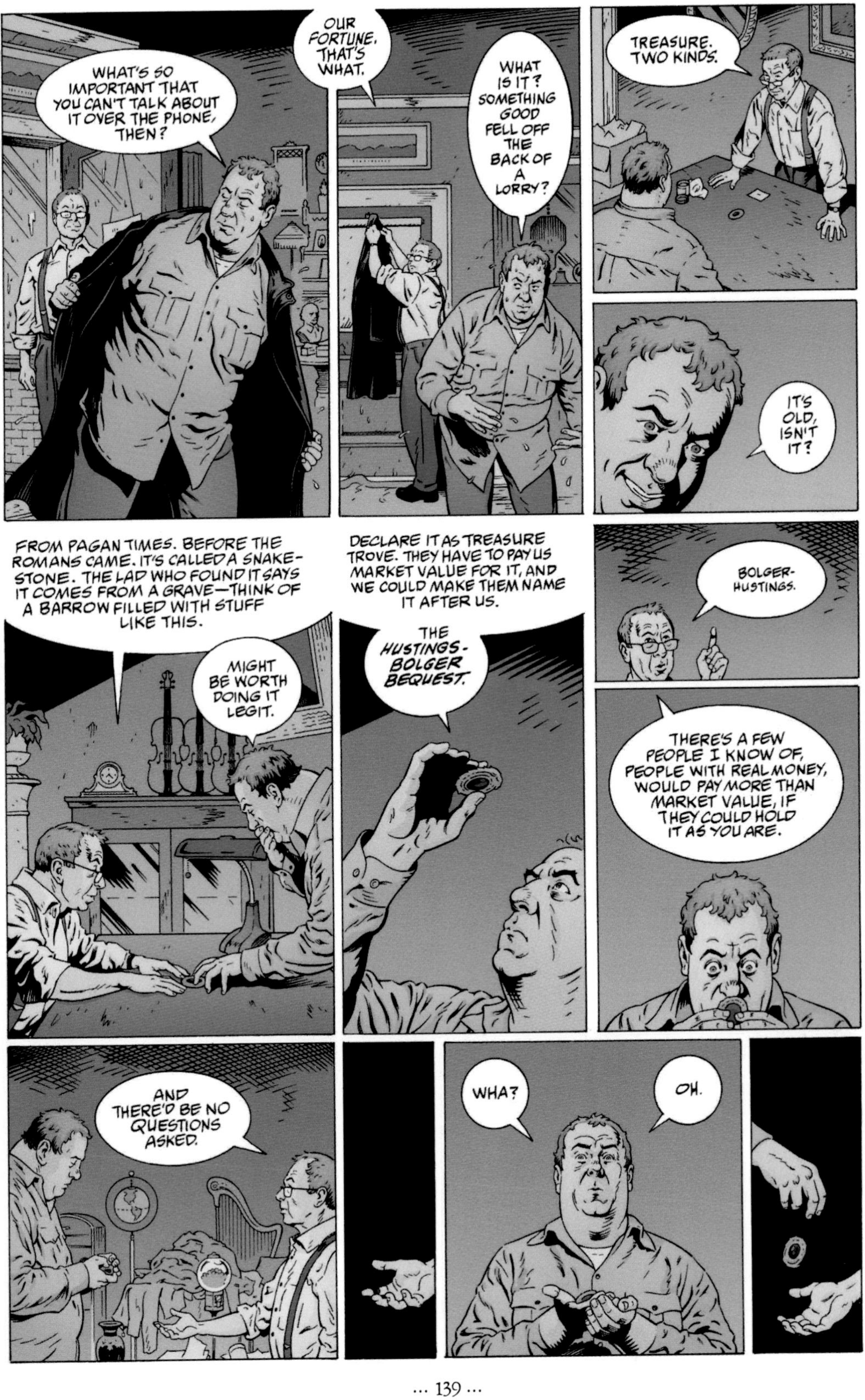
WHAT'S SO IMPORTANT THAT YOU CAN'T TALK ABOUT IT OVER THE PHONE, THEN?
OUR FORTUNE. THAT'S WHAT.
WHAT IS IT? SOMETHING GOOD FELL OFF THE BACK OF A LORRY?
TREASURE. TWO KINDS.
IT'S OLD, ISN'T IT?
FROM PAGAN TIMES. BEFORE THE ROMANS CAME. IT'S CALLED A SNAKE-STONE. THE LAD WHO FOUND IT SAYS IT COMES FROM A GRAVE—THINK OF A BARROW FILLED WITH STUFF LIKE THIS.
MIGHT BE WORTH DOING IT LEGIT.
DECLARE IT AS TREASURE TROVE. THEY HAVE TO PAY US MARKET VALUE FOR IT, AND WE COULD MAKE THEM NAME IT AFTER US.
THE HUSTINGS-BOLGER BEQUEST.
BOLGER-HUSTINGS.
THERE'S A FEW PEOPLE I KNOW OF, PEOPLE WITH REAL MONEY, WOULD PAY MORE THAN MARKET VALUE, IF THEY COULD HOLD IT AS YOU ARE.
AND THERE'D BE NO QUESTIONS ASKED.
WHA?
OH.

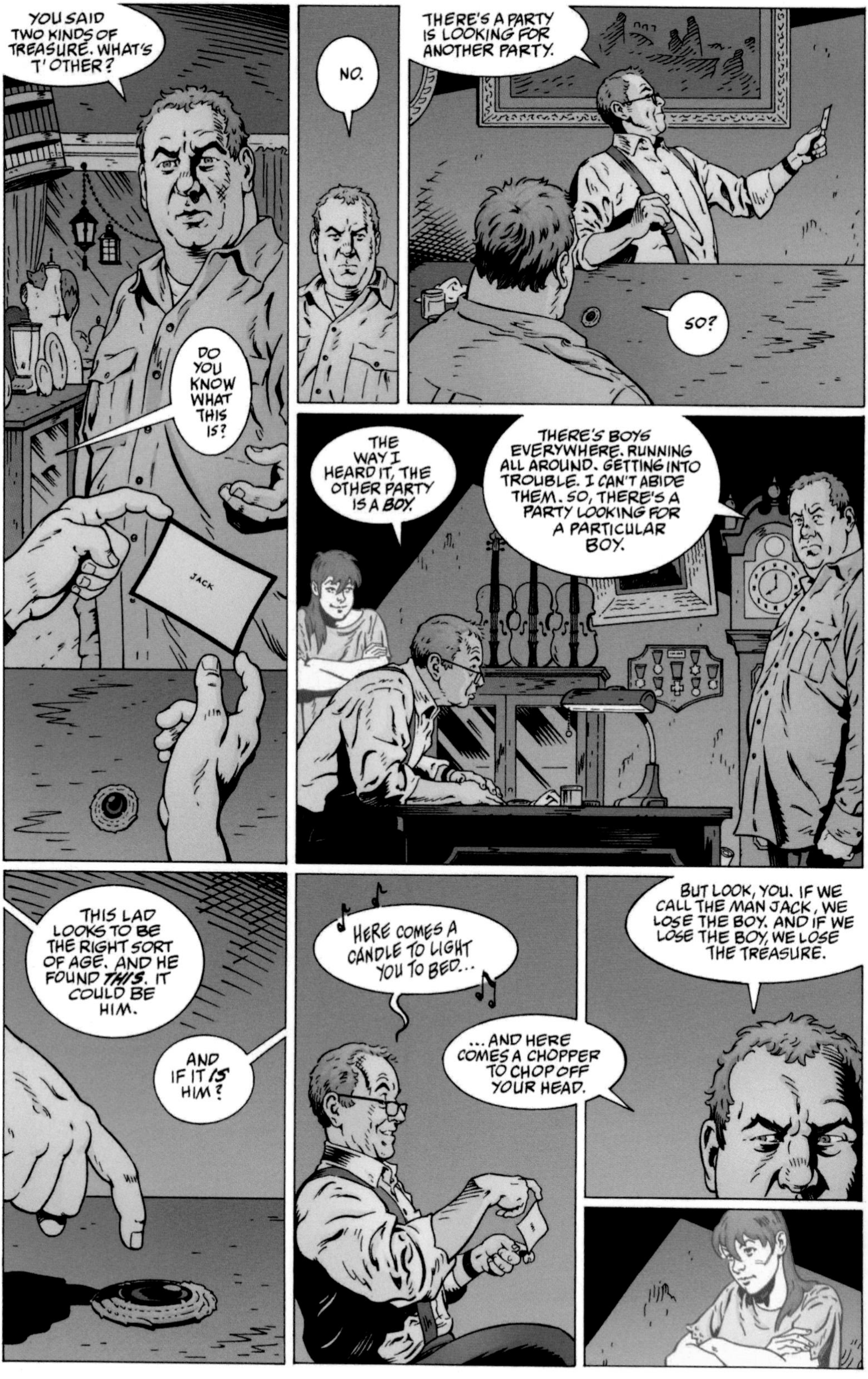
YOU SAID TWO KINDS OF TREASURE. WHAT'S T' OTHER?
DO YOU KNOW WHAT THIS IS?
JACK
NO.
THERE'S A PARTY IS LOOKING FOR ANOTHER PARTY.
SO?
THE WAY I HEARD IT, THE OTHER PARTY IS A BOY.
THERE'S BOYS EVERYWHERE. RUNNING ALL AROUND. GETTING INTO TROUBLE. I CAN'T ABIDE THEM. SO, THERE'S A PARTY LOOKING FOR A PARTICULAR BOY.
THIS LAD LOOKS TO BE THE RIGHT SORT OF AGE. AND HE FOUND THIS. IT COULD BE HIM.
AND IF IT IS HIM?
HERE COMES A CANDLE TO LIGHT YOU TO BED...
...AND HERE COMES A CHOPPER TO CHOP OFF YOUR HEAD.
BUT LOOK, YOU. IF WE CALL THE MAN JACK, WE LOSE THE BOY. AND IF WE LOSE THE BOY, WE LOSE THE TREASURE.

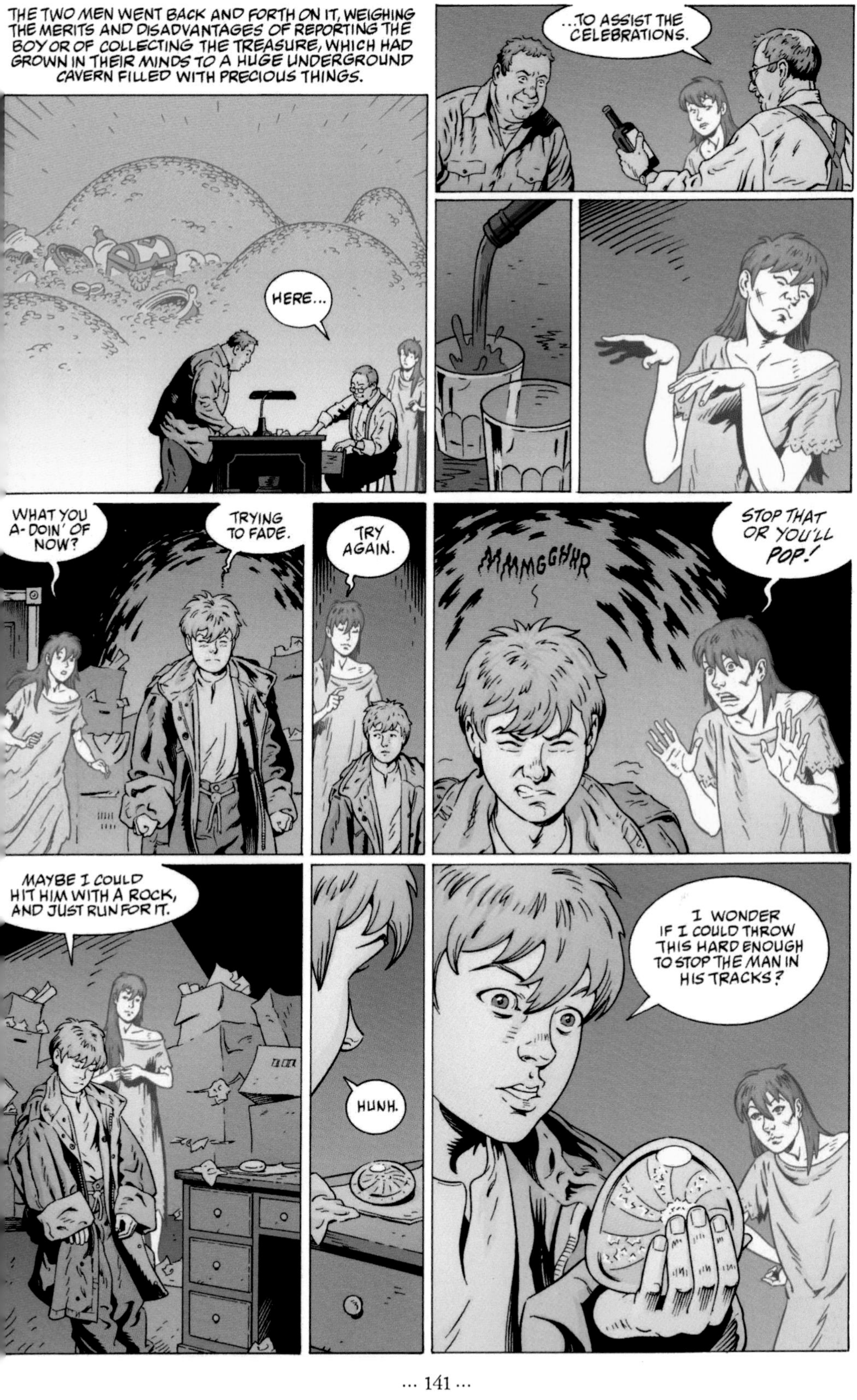
THE TWO MEN WENT BACK AND FORTH ON IT, WEIGHING THE MERITS AND DISADVANTAGES OF REPORTING THE BOY OR OF COLLECTING THE TREASURE, WHICH HAD GROWN IN THEIR MINDS TO A HUGE UNDERGROUND CAVERN FILLED WITH PRECIOUS THINGS.
HERE...
...TO ASSIST THE CELEBRATIONS.
WHAT YOU A-DOIN' OF NOW?
TRYING TO FADE.
TRY AGAIN.
MMMGGHHR
STOP THAT OR YOU'LL POP!
MAYBE I COULD HIT HIM WITH A ROCK, AND JUST RUN FOR IT.
HUNH.
I WONDER IF I COULD THROW THIS HARD ENOUGH TO STOP THE MAN IN HIS TRACKS?

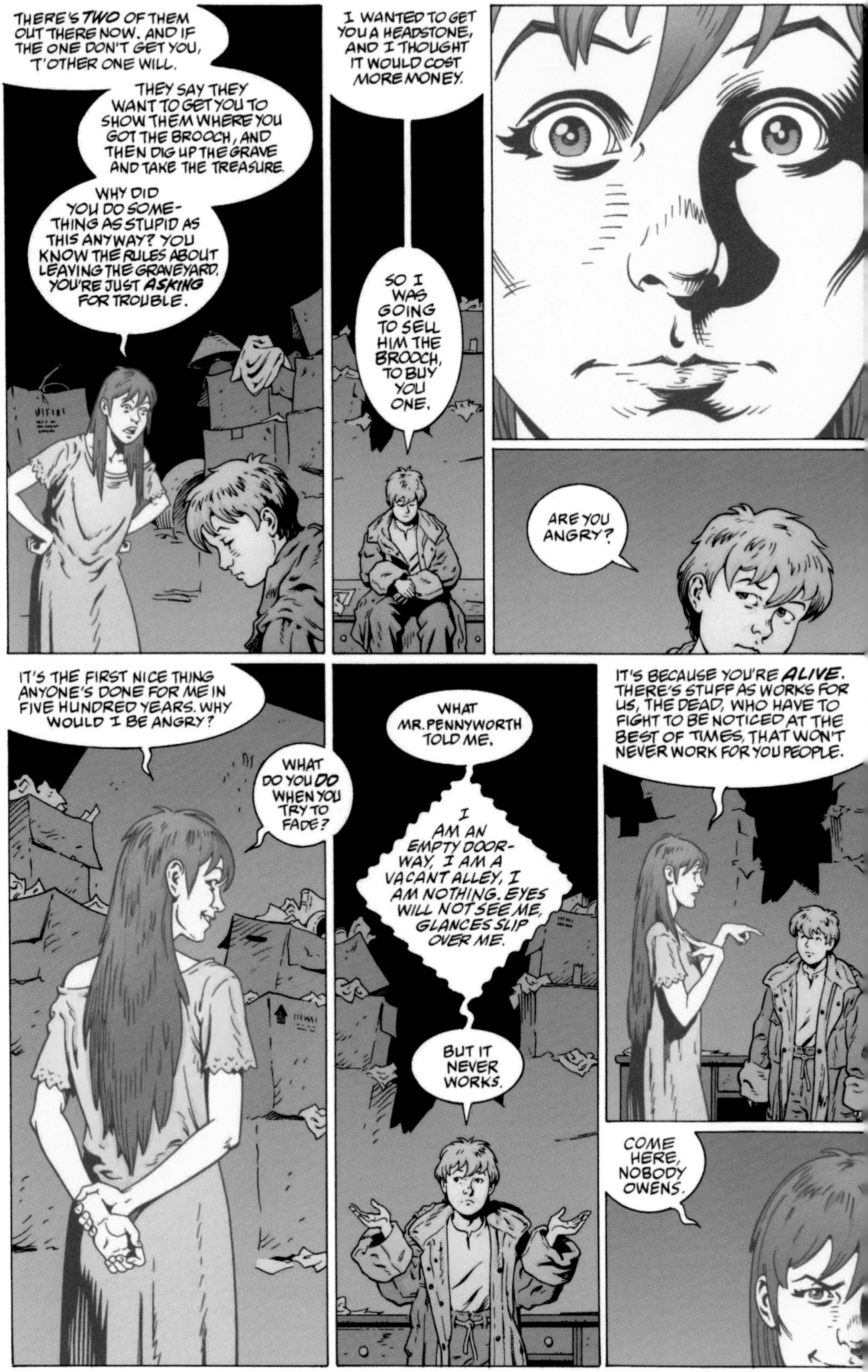
THERE'S TWO OF THEM OUT THERE NOW. AND IF THE ONE DON'T GET YOU, T'OTHER ONE WILL.
THEY SAY THEY WANT TO GET YOU TO SHOW THEM WHERE YOU GOT THE BROOCH, AND THEN DIG UP THE GRAVE AND TAKE THE TREASURE.
WHY DID YOU DO SOMETHING AS STUPID AS THIS ANYWAY? YOU KNOW THE RULES ABOUT LEAVING THE GRAVEYARD. YOU'RE JUST ASKING FOR TROUBLE.
I WANTED TO GET YOU A HEADSTONE, AND I THOUGHT IT WOULD COST MORE MONEY.
SO I WAS GOING TO SELL HIM THE BROOCH, TO BUY YOU ONE.
ARE YOU ANGRY?
IT'S THE FIRST NICE THING ANYONE'S DONE FOR ME IN FIVE HUNDRED YEARS. WHY WOULD I BE ANGRY?
WHAT DO YOU DO WHEN YOU TRY TO FADE?
WHAT MR. PENNYWORTH TOLD ME.
I AM AN EMPTY DOORWAY, I AM A VACANT ALLEY, I AM NOTHING. EYES WILL NOT SEE ME, GLANCES SLIP OVER ME.
BUT IT NEVER WORKS.
IT'S BECAUSE YOU'RE ALIVE. THERE'S STUFF AS WORKS FOR US, THE DEAD, WHO HAVE TO FIGHT TO BE NOTICED AT THE BEST OF TIMES, THAT WON'T NEVER WORK FOR YOU PEOPLE.
COME HERE, NOBODY OWENS.

IT'S BECAUSE OF ME YOU GOT INTO THIS. NOW, PERHAPS I CAN DO A GOOD TURN FOR YOU.

HER COLD HAND FELT LIKE A WET SILK SCARF AGAINST HIS SKIN.

Be Hole, Be Dust, Be Dream, Be Wind
Be Night, Be Dark, Be Wish, Be Mind,
Now Slip, Now Slide, Now Move UnSeen,
Above, Beneath, Betwixt, Between.

SOMETHING HUGE TOUCHED HIM, BRUSHED HIM FROM HEAD TO FEET, AND HE SHIVERED. HIS HAIR PRICKLED, AND HIS SKIN WAS ALL GOOSEFLESH.

SOMETHING HAD CHANGED.

JUST GIVED YOU A HELPING HAND. I MAY BE DEAD, BUT I'M A DEAD WITCH, REMEMBER?

WHAT DID YOU DO?

WE DON'T FORGET.

BUT—

HUSH UP. THEY'RE COMING BACK.

NOW THEN, CHUMMY.

I'M SURE WE'RE ALL GOING TO BE GOOD FRIENDS.

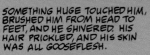

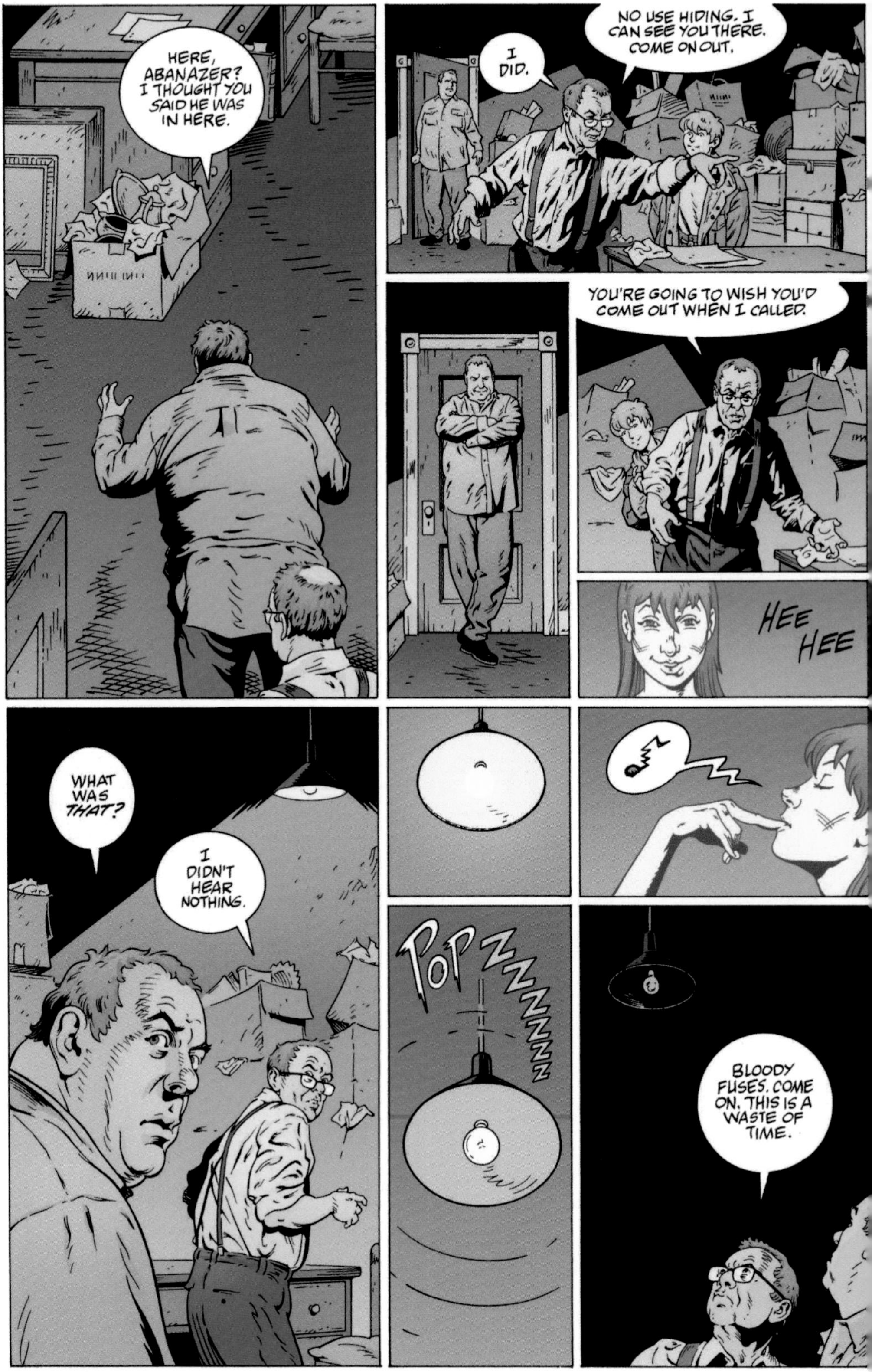
HERE, ABANAZER? I THOUGHT YOU SAID HE WAS IN HERE.
I DID.
NO USE HIDING. I CAN SEE YOU THERE. COME ON OUT.
YOU'RE GOING TO WISH YOU'D COME OUT WHEN I CALLED.
HEE HEE
WHAT WAS *THAT*?
I DIDN'T HEAR NOTHING.
POPZZZZZ
BLOODY FUSES. COME ON. THIS IS A WASTE OF TIME.

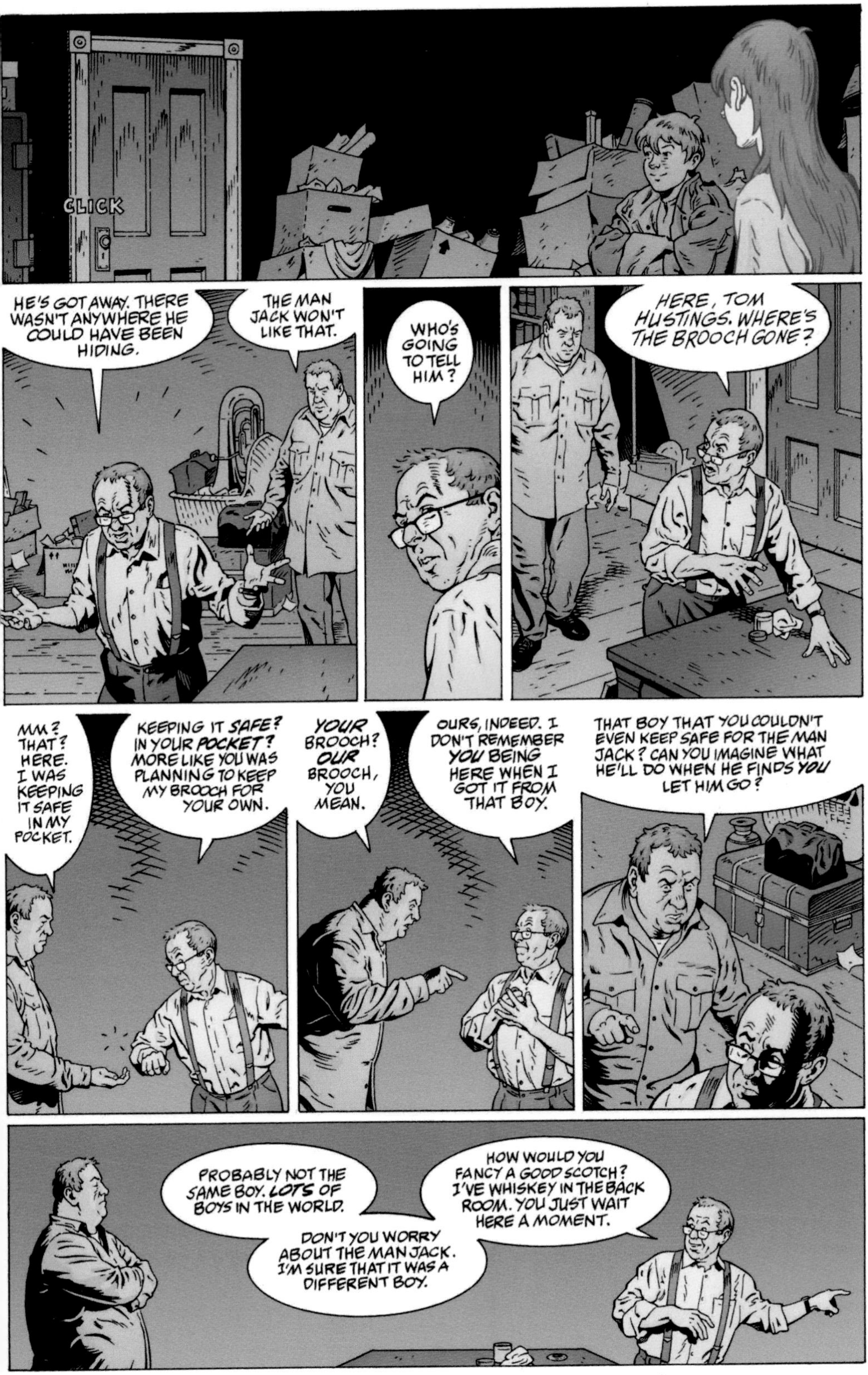
CLICK
HE'S GOT AWAY. THERE WASN'T ANYWHERE HE COULD HAVE BEEN HIDING.
THE MAN JACK WON'T LIKE THAT.
WHO'S GOING TO TELL HIM?
HERE, TOM HUSTINGS. WHERE'S THE BROOCH GONE?
MM? THAT? HERE. I WAS KEEPING IT SAFE IN MY POCKET.
KEEPING IT SAFE? IN YOUR POCKET? MORE LIKE YOU WAS PLANNING TO KEEP MY BROOCH FOR YOUR OWN.
YOUR BROOCH? OUR BROOCH, YOU MEAN.
OURS, INDEED. I DON'T REMEMBER YOU BEING HERE WHEN I GOT IT FROM THAT BOY.
THAT BOY THAT YOU COULDN'T EVEN KEEP SAFE FOR THE MAN JACK? CAN YOU IMAGINE WHAT HE'LL DO WHEN HE FINDS YOU LET HIM GO?
PROBABLY NOT THE SAME BOY. LOTS OF BOYS IN THE WORLD.
DON'T YOU WORRY ABOUT THE MAN JACK. I'M SURE THAT IT WAS A DIFFERENT BOY.
HOW WOULD YOU FANCY A GOOD SCOTCH? I'VE WHISKEY IN THE BACK ROOM. YOU JUST WAIT HERE A MOMENT.

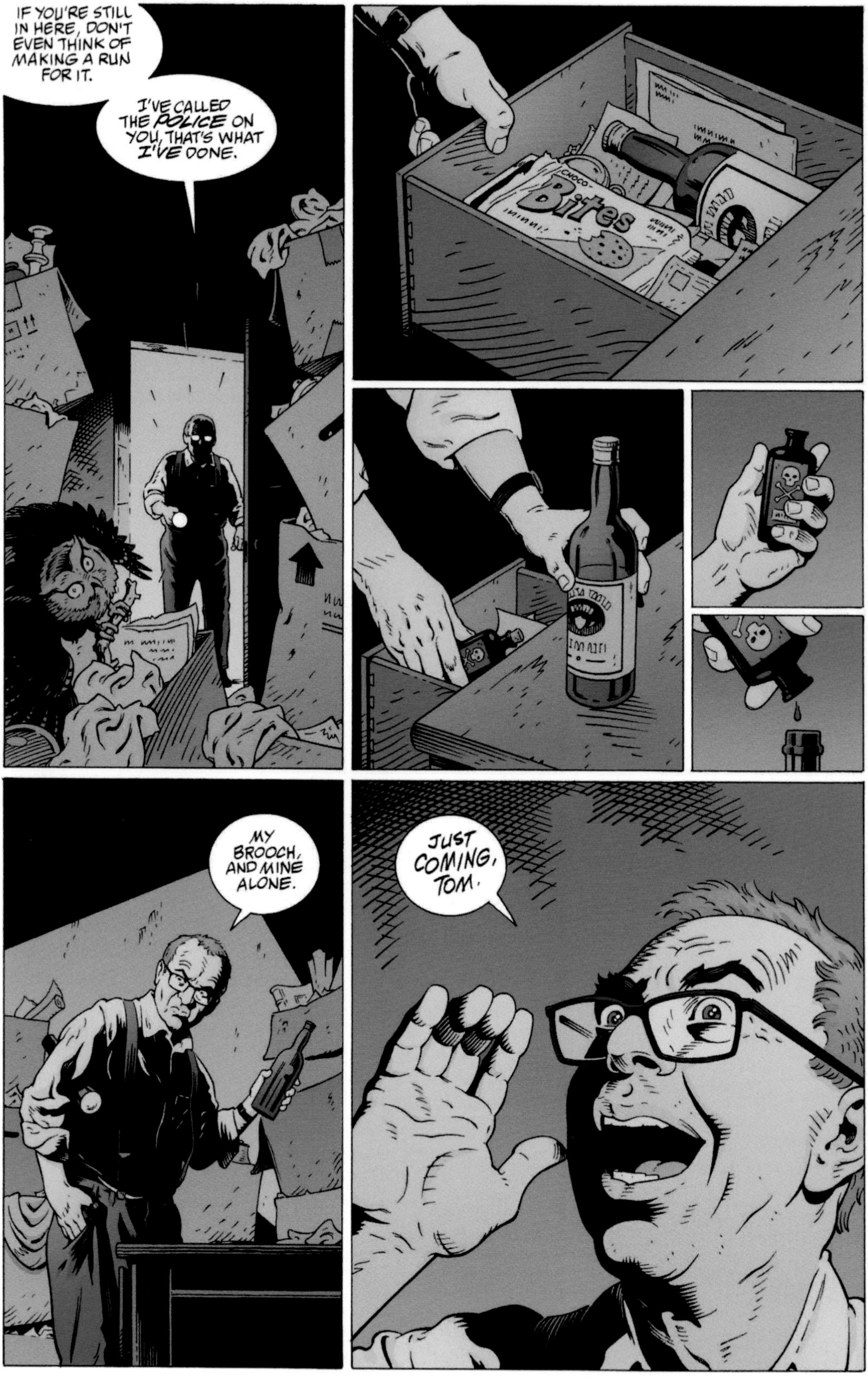
IF YOU'RE STILL IN HERE, DON'T EVEN THINK OF MAKING A RUN FOR IT.
I'VE CALLED THE POLICE ON YOU, THAT'S WHAT I'VE DONE.
CHOCO Bites
MY BROOCH, AND MINE ALONE.
JUST COMING, TOM.

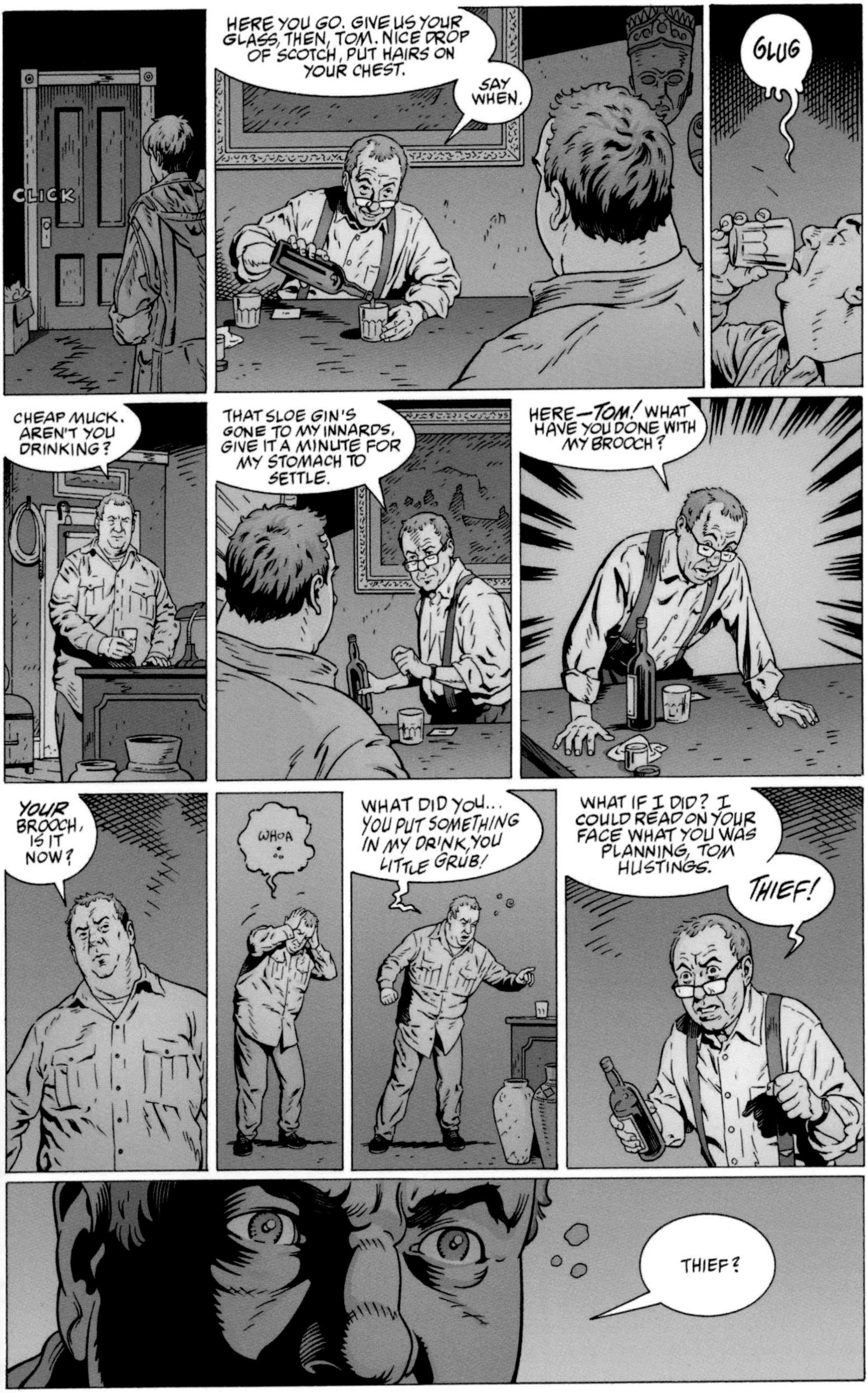
CLICK
HERE YOU GO. GIVE US YOUR GLASS, THEN, TOM. NICE DROP OF SCOTCH, PUT HAIRS ON YOUR CHEST.
SAY WHEN.
GLUG
CHEAP MUCK. AREN'T YOU DRINKING?
THAT SLOE GIN'S GONE TO MY INNARDS, GIVE IT A MINUTE FOR MY STOMACH TO SETTLE.
HERE—TOM! WHAT HAVE YOU DONE WITH MY BROOCH?
YOUR BROOCH, IS IT NOW?
WHOA
WHAT DID YOU... YOU PUT SOMETHING IN MY DRINK, YOU LITTLE GRUB!
WHAT IF I DID? I COULD READ ON YOUR FACE WHAT YOU WAS PLANNING, TOM HUSTINGS.
THIEF!
THIEF?

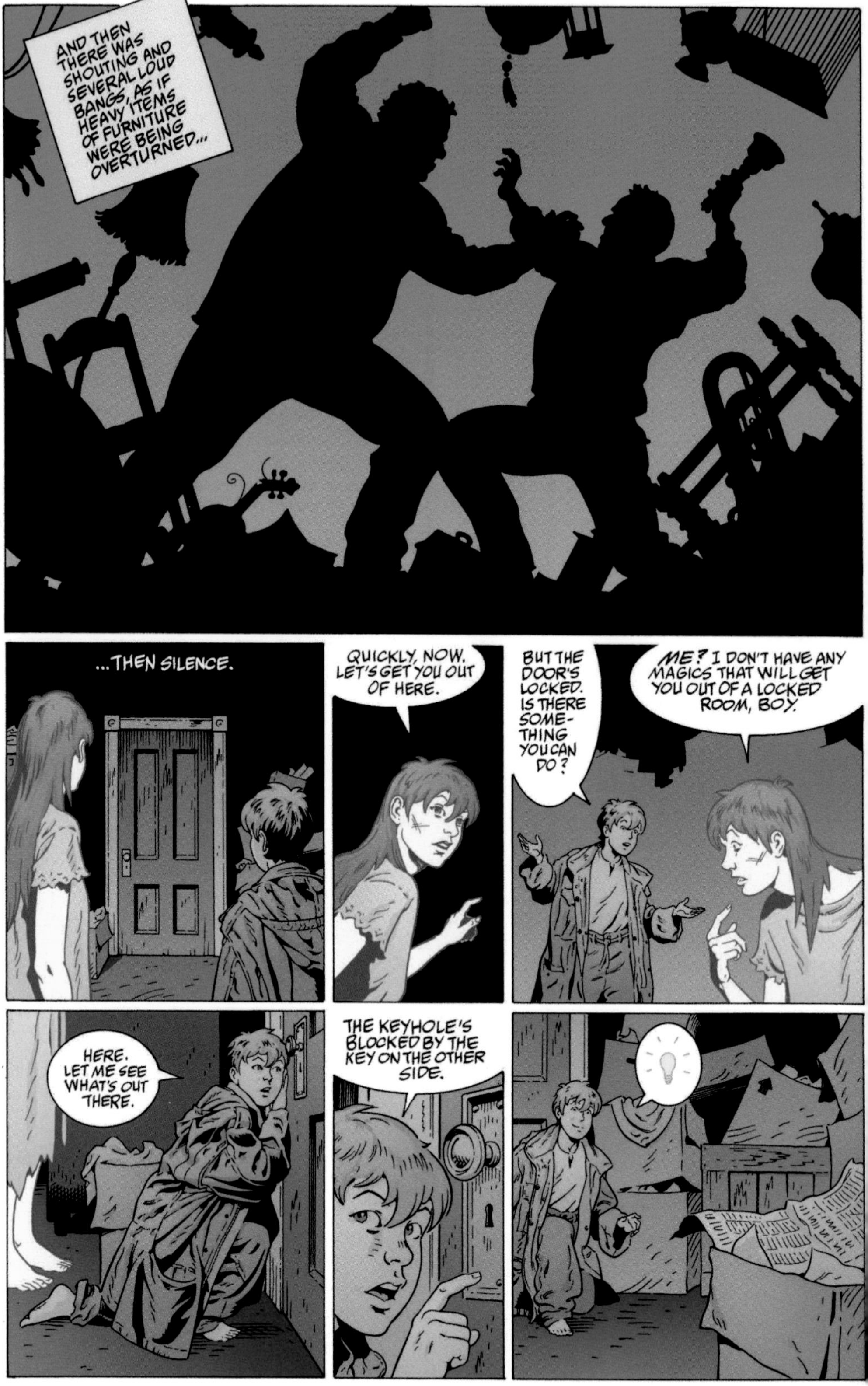
AND THEN THERE WAS SHOUTING AND SEVERAL LOUD BANGS, AS IF HEAVY ITEMS OF FURNITURE WERE BEING OVERTURNED...
...THEN SILENCE.
QUICKLY, NOW. LET'S GET YOU OUT OF HERE.
BUT THE DOOR'S LOCKED. IS THERE SOMETHING YOU CAN DO?
ME? I DON'T HAVE ANY MAGICS THAT WILL GET YOU OUT OF A LOCKED ROOM, BOY.
HERE. LET ME SEE WHAT'S OUT THERE.
THE KEYHOLE'S BLOCKED BY THE KEY ON THE OTHER SIDE.

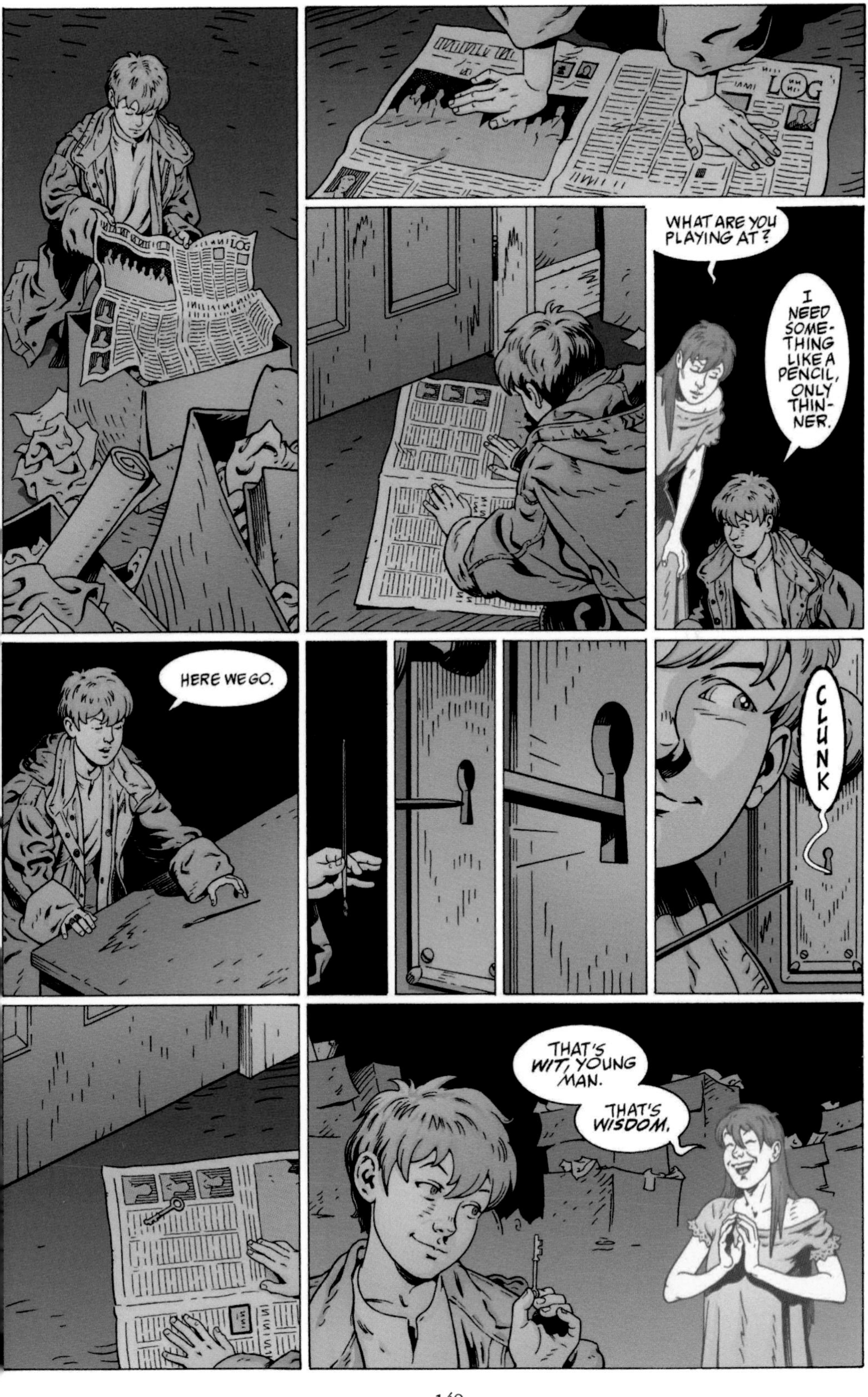
WHAT ARE YOU PLAYING AT?
I NEED SOMETHING LIKE A PENCIL, ONLY THINNER.
HERE WE GO.
CLUNK
THAT'S *WIT*, YOUNG MAN.
THAT'S *WISDOM*.

THE PLACE WAS A CHAOS OF WRECKED CLOCKS AND CHAIRS. AND IN THE MIDST OF IT THE BULK OF TOM HUSTINGS LAY, FALLEN ON THE SMALLER FIGURE OF ABANAZER BOLGER.

CLICK

ARE THEY DEAD?

NO SUCH LUCK.

ON THE FLOOR BESIDE THE MEN WAS A BROOCH OF GLITTERING SILVER; A CRIMSON-ORANGE-BANDED STONE, HELD IN PLACE WITH CLAWS AND SNAKE-HEADS.

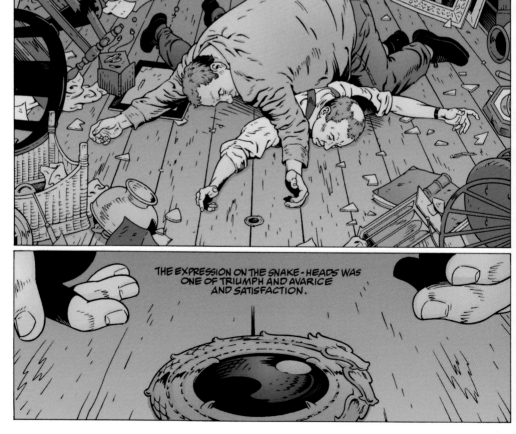

THE EXPRESSION ON THE SNAKE-HEADS WAS ONE OF TRIUMPH AND AVARICE AND SATISFACTION.

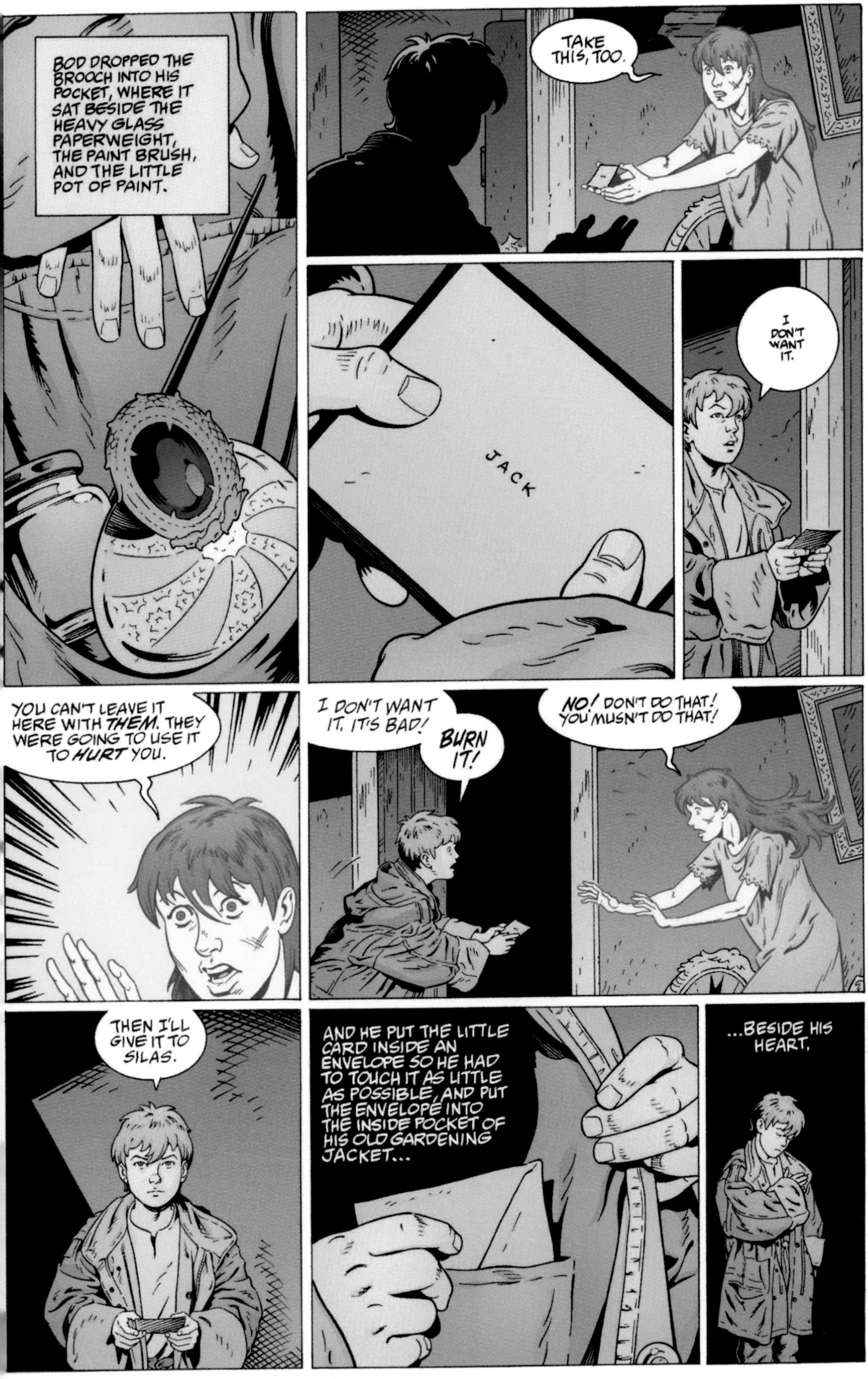
BOD DROPPED THE BROOCH INTO HIS POCKET, WHERE IT SAT BESIDE THE HEAVY GLASS PAPERWEIGHT, THE PAINT BRUSH, AND THE LITTLE POT OF PAINT.
TAKE THIS, TOO.
JACK
I DON'T WANT IT.
YOU CAN'T LEAVE IT HERE WITH THEM. THEY WERE GOING TO USE IT TO HURT YOU.
I DON'T WANT IT. IT'S BAD!
BURN IT!
NO! DON'T DO THAT! YOU MUSN'T DO THAT!
THEN I'LL GIVE IT TO SILAS.
AND HE PUT THE LITTLE CARD INSIDE AN ENVELOPE SO HE HAD TO TOUCH IT AS LITTLE AS POSSIBLE, AND PUT THE ENVELOPE INTO THE INSIDE POCKET OF HIS OLD GARDENING JACKET...
...BESIDE HIS HEART.

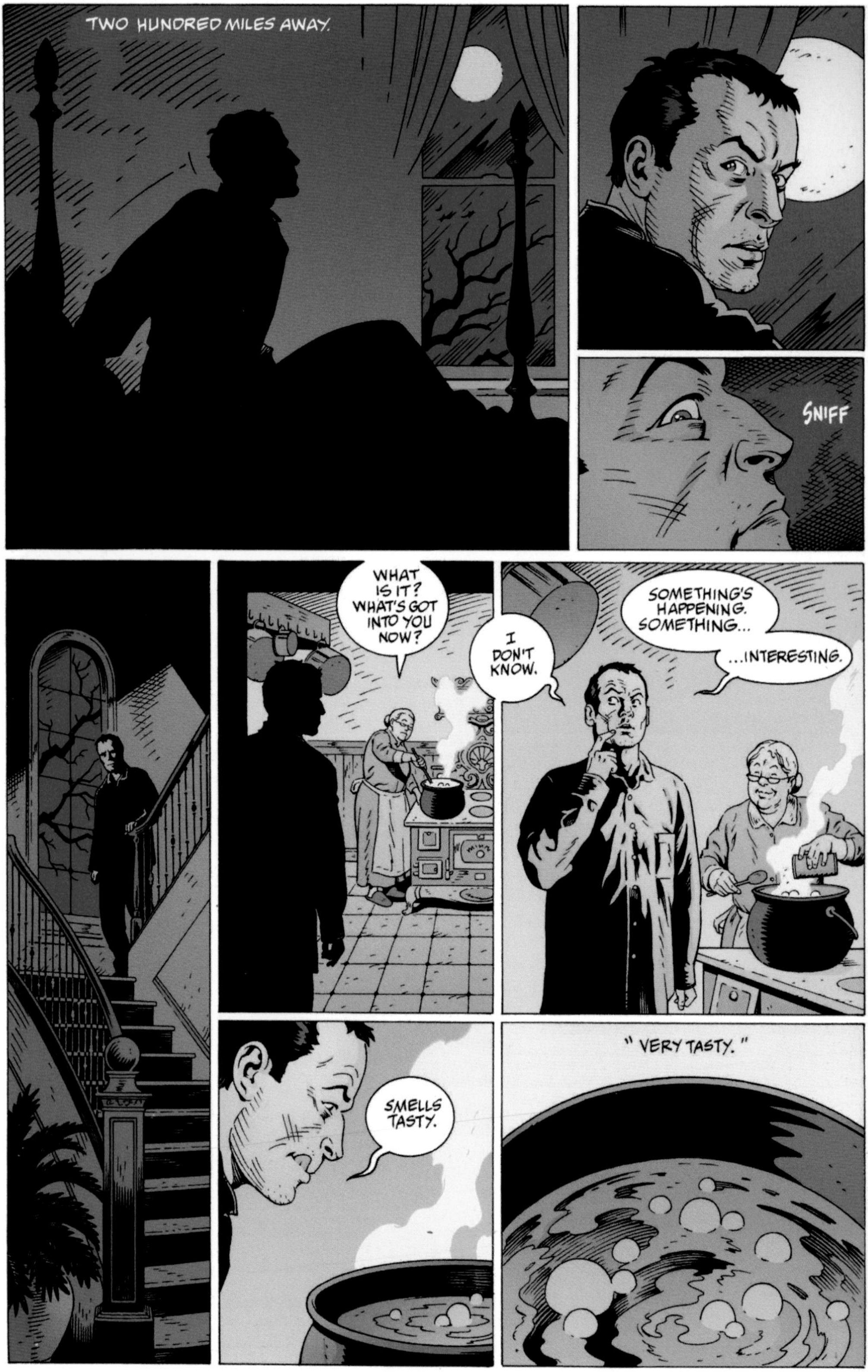
TWO HUNDRED MILES AWAY.
SNIFF
WHAT IS IT? WHAT'S GOT INTO YOU NOW?
I DON'T KNOW.
SOMETHING'S HAPPENING. SOMETHING...
...INTERESTING.
SMELLS TASTY.
" VERY TASTY. "

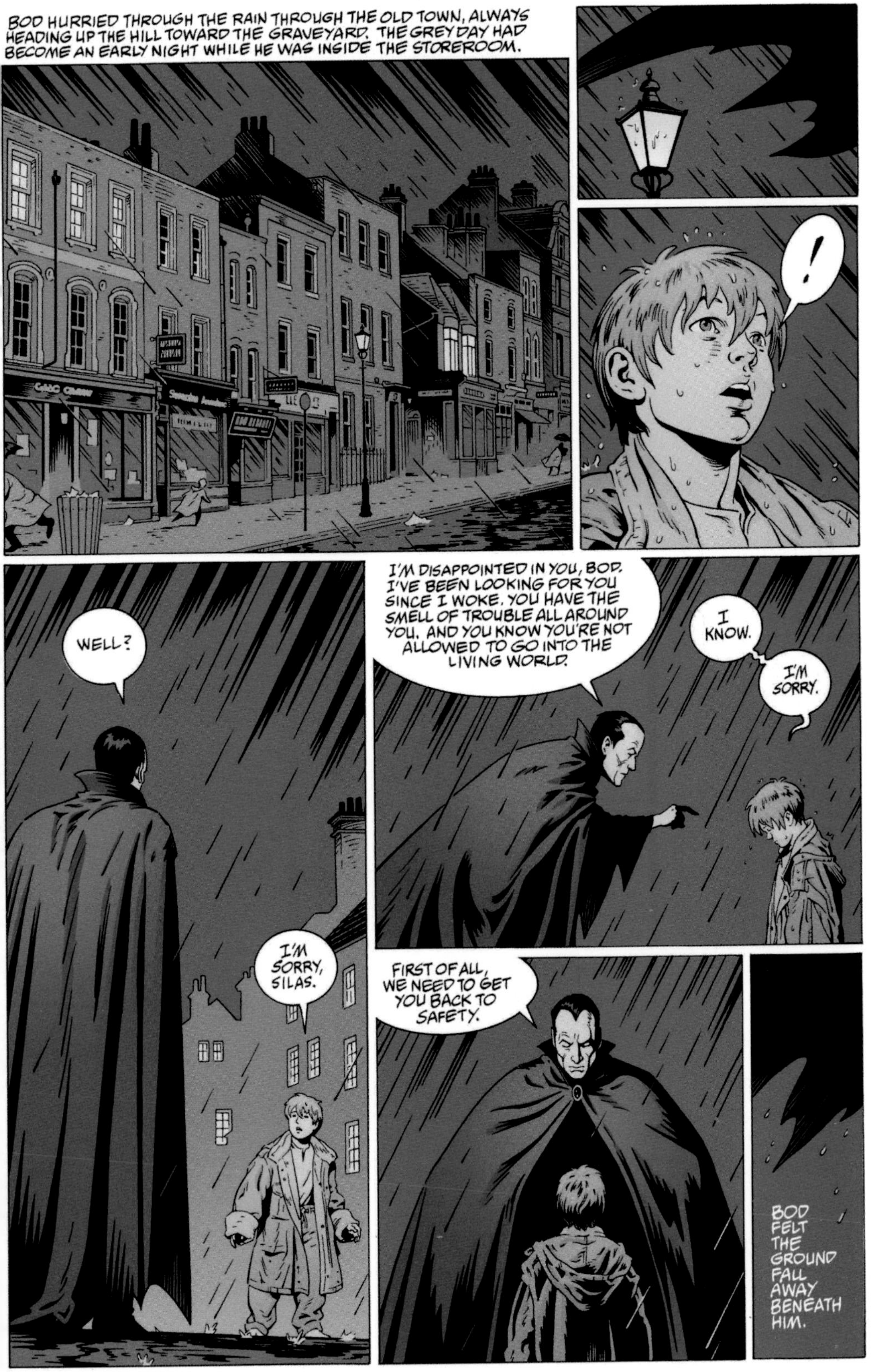
BOD HURRIED THROUGH THE RAIN THROUGH THE OLD TOWN, ALWAYS HEADING UP THE HILL TOWARD THE GRAVEYARD. THE GREY DAY HAD BECOME AN EARLY NIGHT WHILE HE WAS INSIDE THE STOREROOM.
!
WELL?
I'M SORRY, SILAS.
I'M DISAPPOINTED IN YOU, BOD. I'VE BEEN LOOKING FOR YOU SINCE I WOKE. YOU HAVE THE SMELL OF TROUBLE ALL AROUND YOU. AND YOU KNOW YOU'RE NOT ALLOWED TO GO INTO THE LIVING WORLD.
I KNOW.
I'M SORRY.
FIRST OF ALL, WE NEED TO GET YOU BACK TO SAFETY.
BOD FELT THE GROUND FALL AWAY BENEATH HIM.

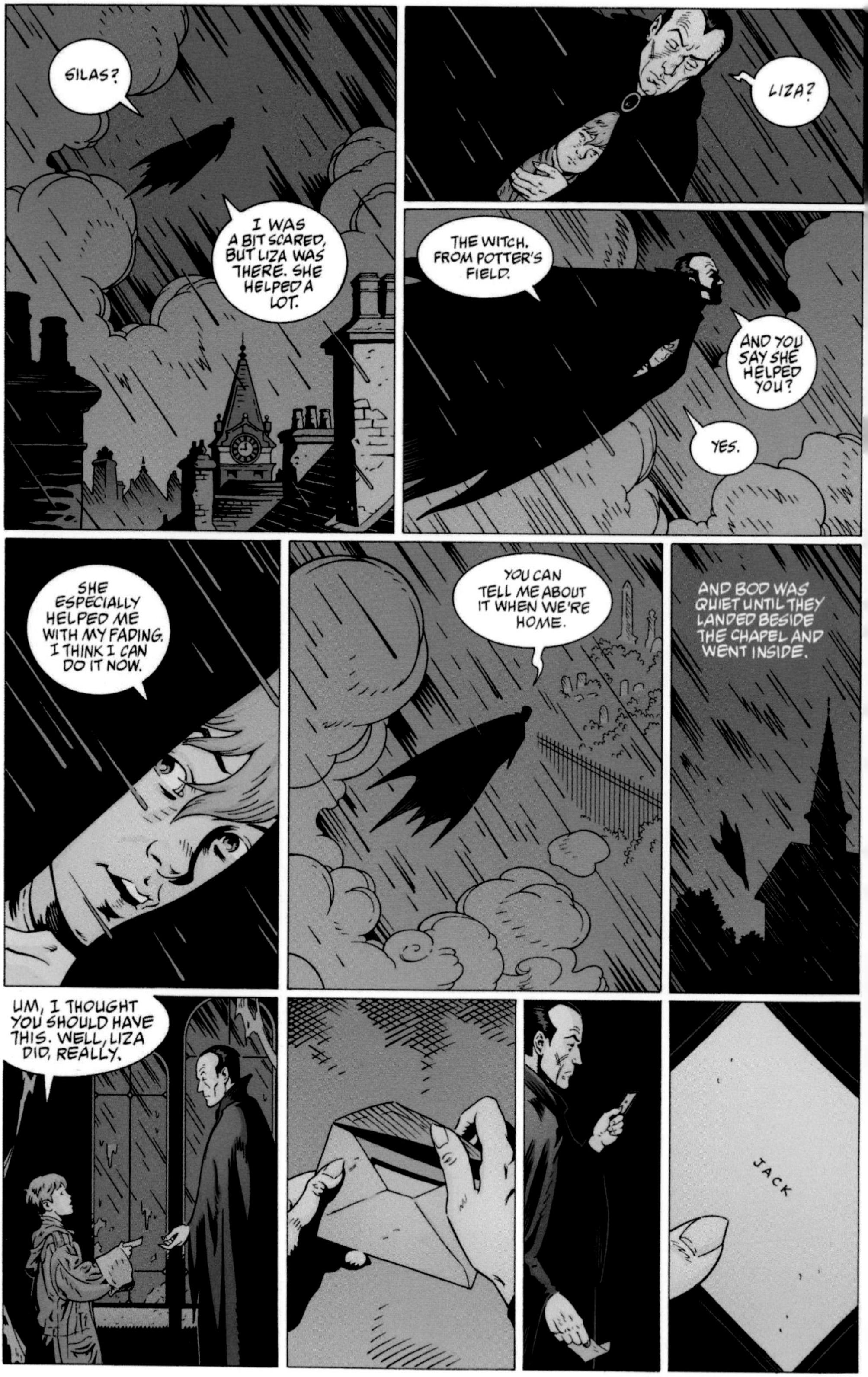
SILAS?
I WAS A BIT SCARED, BUT LIZA WAS THERE. SHE HELPED A LOT.
LIZA?
THE WITCH. FROM POTTER'S FIELD.
AND YOU SAY SHE HELPED YOU?
YES.
SHE ESPECIALLY HELPED ME WITH MY FADING. I THINK I CAN DO IT NOW.
YOU CAN TELL ME ABOUT IT WHEN WE'RE HOME.
AND BOD WAS QUIET UNTIL THEY LANDED BESIDE THE CHAPEL AND WENT INSIDE.
UM, I THOUGHT YOU SHOULD HAVE THIS. WELL, LIZA DID, REALLY.
JACK

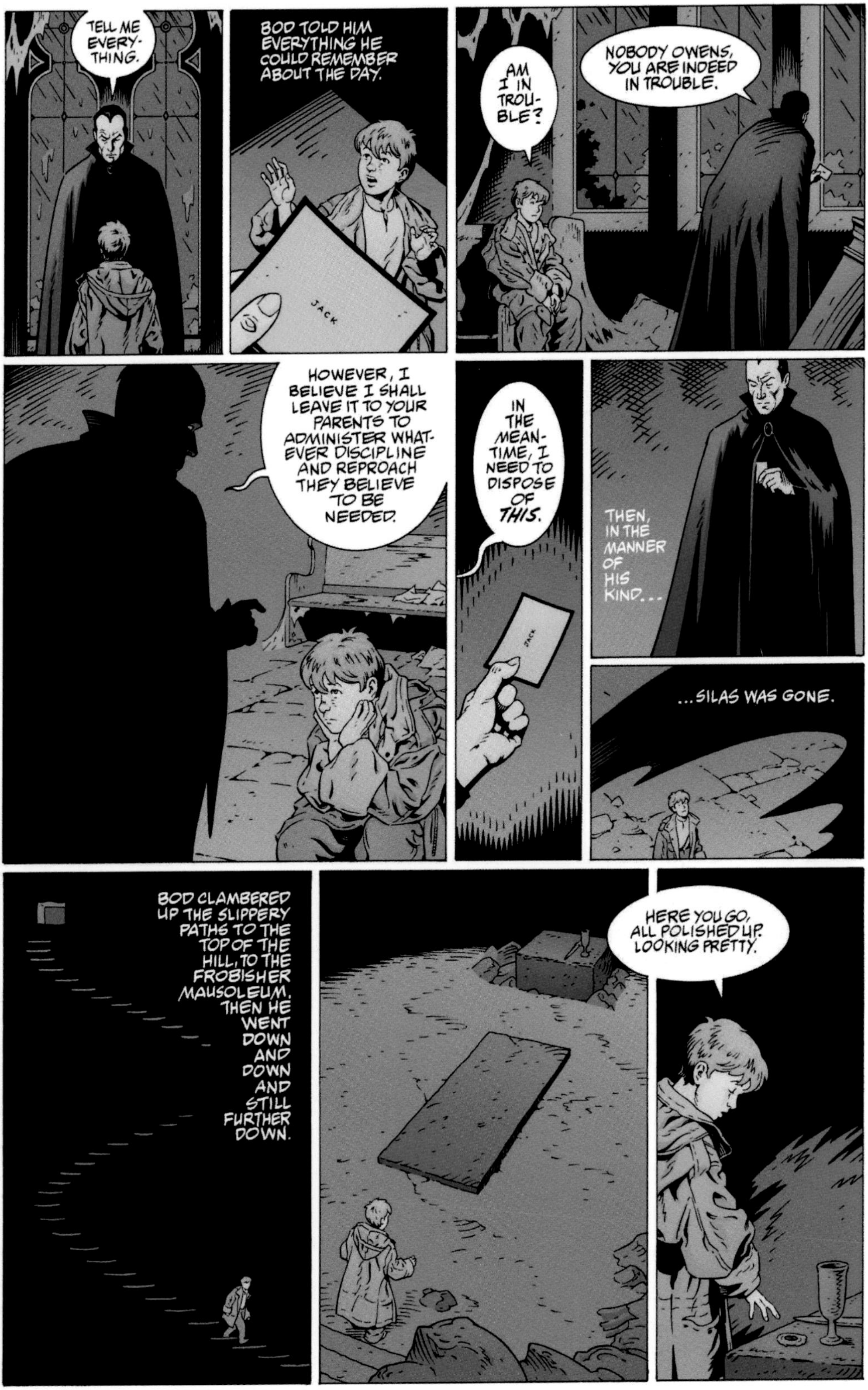
TELL ME EVERYTHING.
BOD TOLD HIM EVERYTHING HE COULD REMEMBER ABOUT THE DAY.
JACK
AM I IN TROUBLE?
NOBODY OWENS, YOU ARE INDEED IN TROUBLE.
HOWEVER, I BELIEVE I SHALL LEAVE IT TO YOUR PARENTS TO ADMINISTER WHATEVER DISCIPLINE AND REPROACH THEY BELIEVE TO BE NEEDED.
IN THE MEANTIME, I NEED TO DISPOSE OF THIS.
JACK
THEN, IN THE MANNER OF HIS KIND...
...SILAS WAS GONE.
BOD CLAMBERED UP THE SLIPPERY PATHS TO THE TOP OF THE HILL, TO THE FROBISHER MAUSOLEUM, THEN HE WENT DOWN AND DOWN AND STILL FURTHER DOWN.
HERE YOU GO, ALL POLISHED UP. LOOKING PRETTY.

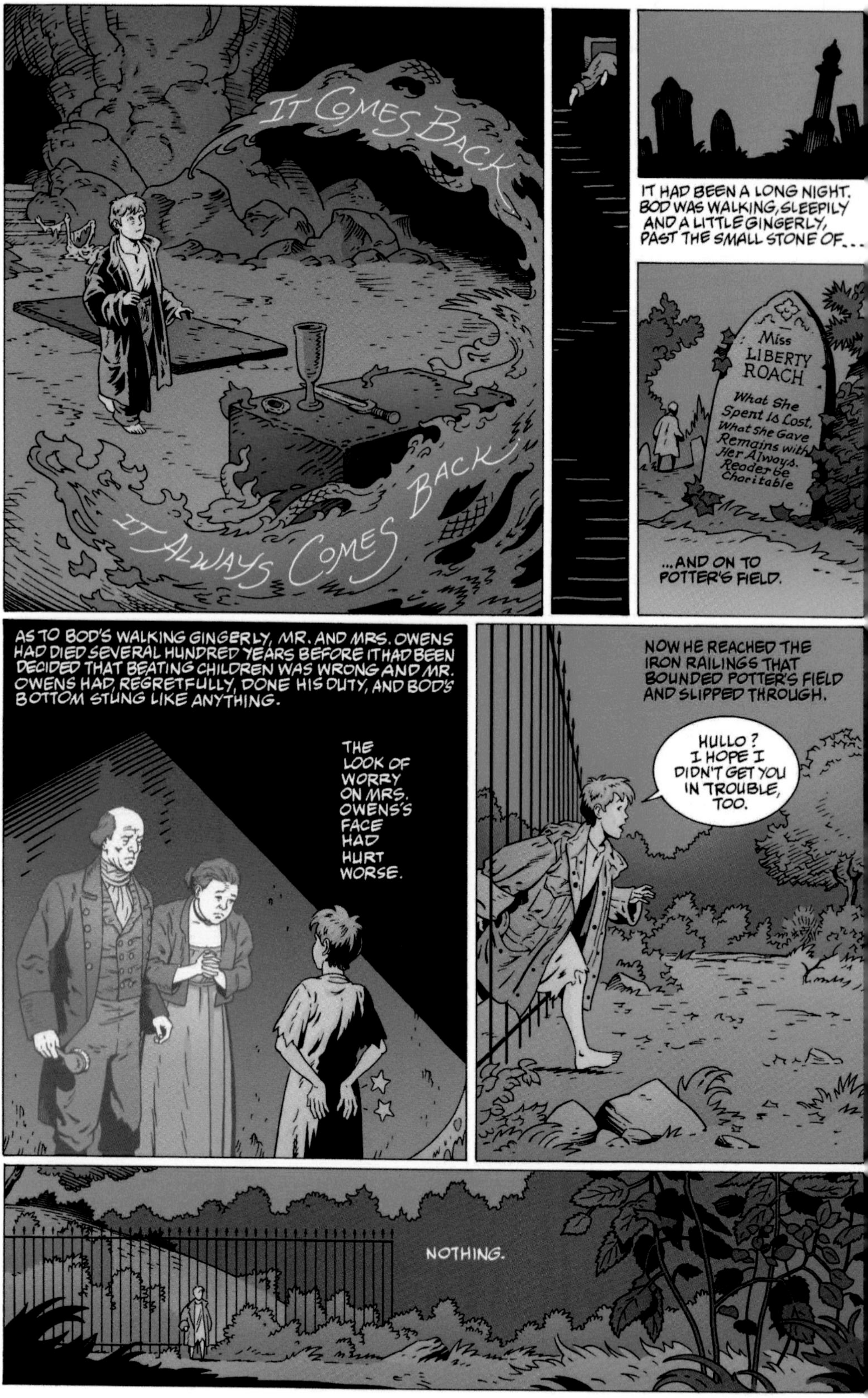
IT COMES BACK
IT ALWAYS COMES BACK
IT HAD BEEN A LONG NIGHT. BOD WAS WALKING, SLEEPILY AND A LITTLE GINGERLY, PAST THE SMALL STONE OF...
Miss LIBERTY ROACH What She Spent is Lost, What She Gave Remains with Her Always. Reader be Charitable
...AND ON TO POTTER'S FIELD.
AS TO BOD'S WALKING GINGERLY, MR. AND MRS. OWENS HAD DIED SEVERAL HUNDRED YEARS BEFORE IT HAD BEEN DECIDED THAT BEATING CHILDREN WAS WRONG AND MR. OWENS HAD, REGRETFULLY, DONE HIS DUTY, AND BOD'S BOTTOM STUNG LIKE ANYTHING.
THE LOOK OF WORRY ON MRS. OWENS'S FACE HAD HURT WORSE.
NOW HE REACHED THE IRON RAILINGS THAT BOUNDED POTTER'S FIELD AND SLIPPED THROUGH.
HULLO? I HOPE I DIDN'T GET YOU IN TROUBLE, TOO.
NOTHING.

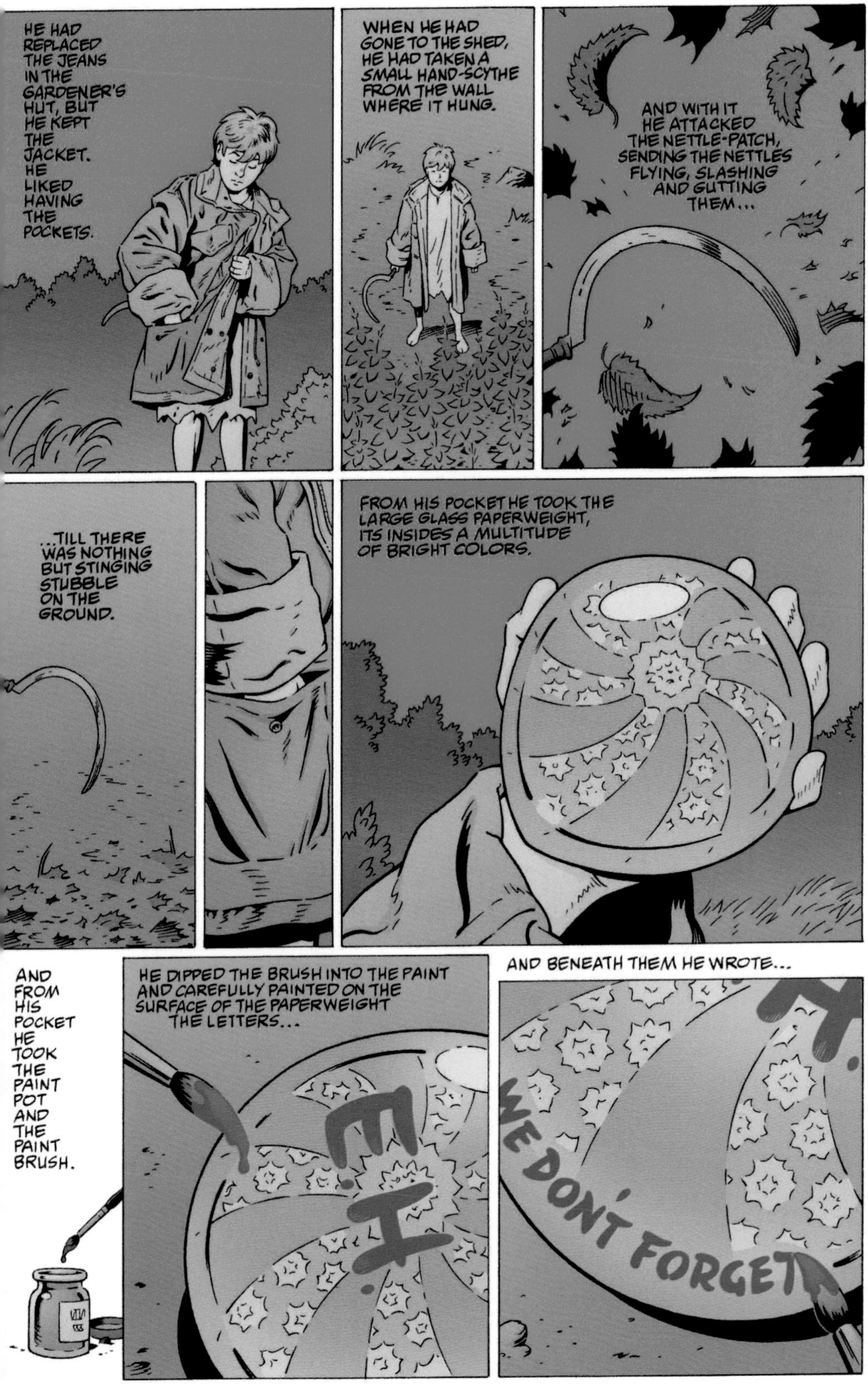
HE HAD REPLACED THE JEANS IN THE GARDENER'S HUT, BUT HE KEPT THE JACKET. HE LIKED HAVING THE POCKETS.
WHEN HE HAD GONE TO THE SHED, HE HAD TAKEN A SMALL HAND-SCYTHE FROM THE WALL WHERE IT HUNG.
AND WITH IT HE ATTACKED THE NETTLE-PATCH, SENDING THE NETTLES FLYING, SLASHING AND GUTTING THEM...
...TILL THERE WAS NOTHING BUT STINGING STUBBLE ON THE GROUND.
FROM HIS POCKET HE TOOK THE LARGE GLASS PAPERWEIGHT, ITS INSIDES A MULTITUDE OF BRIGHT COLORS.
AND FROM HIS POCKET HE TOOK THE PAINT POT AND THE PAINT BRUSH.
HE DIPPED THE BRUSH INTO THE PAINT AND CAREFULLY PAINTED ON THE SURFACE OF THE PAPERWEIGHT THE LETTERS...
E.I.
AND BENEATH THEM HE WROTE...
WE DON'T FORGET

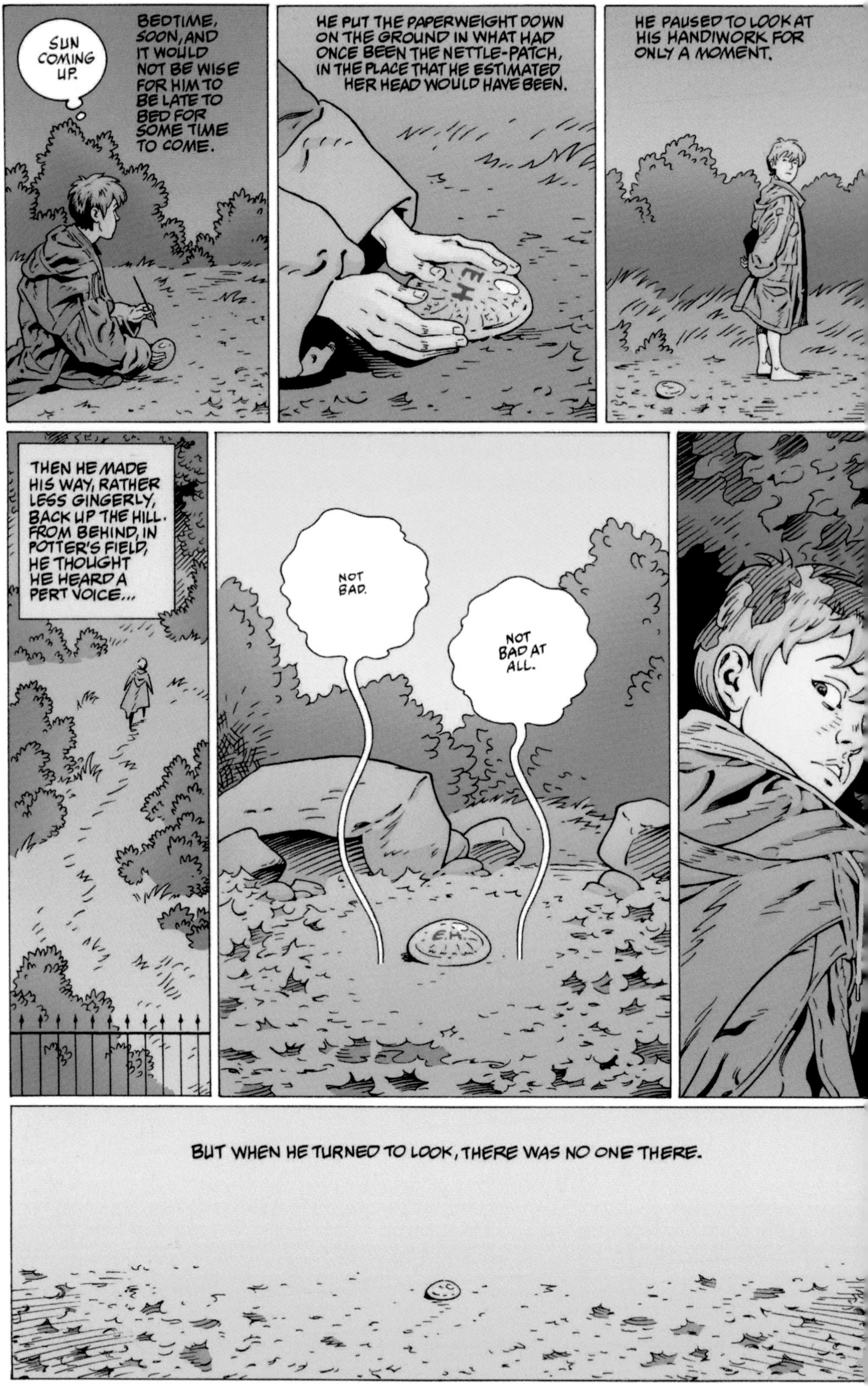
SUN COMING UP.
BEDTIME, SOON, AND IT WOULD NOT BE WISE FOR HIM TO BE LATE TO BED FOR SOME TIME TO COME.
HE PUT THE PAPERWEIGHT DOWN ON THE GROUND IN WHAT HAD ONCE BEEN THE NETTLE-PATCH, IN THE PLACE THAT HE ESTIMATED HER HEAD WOULD HAVE BEEN.
E.H.
HE PAUSED TO LOOK AT HIS HANDIWORK FOR ONLY A MOMENT.
THEN HE MADE HIS WAY, RATHER LESS GINGERLY, BACK UP THE HILL. FROM BEHIND, IN POTTER'S FIELD, HE THOUGHT HE HEARD A PERT VOICE...
NOT BAD.
NOT BAD AT ALL.
E.H.
BUT WHEN HE TURNED TO LOOK, THERE WAS NO ONE THERE.

5

Danse Macabre

Illustrated by Jill Thompson

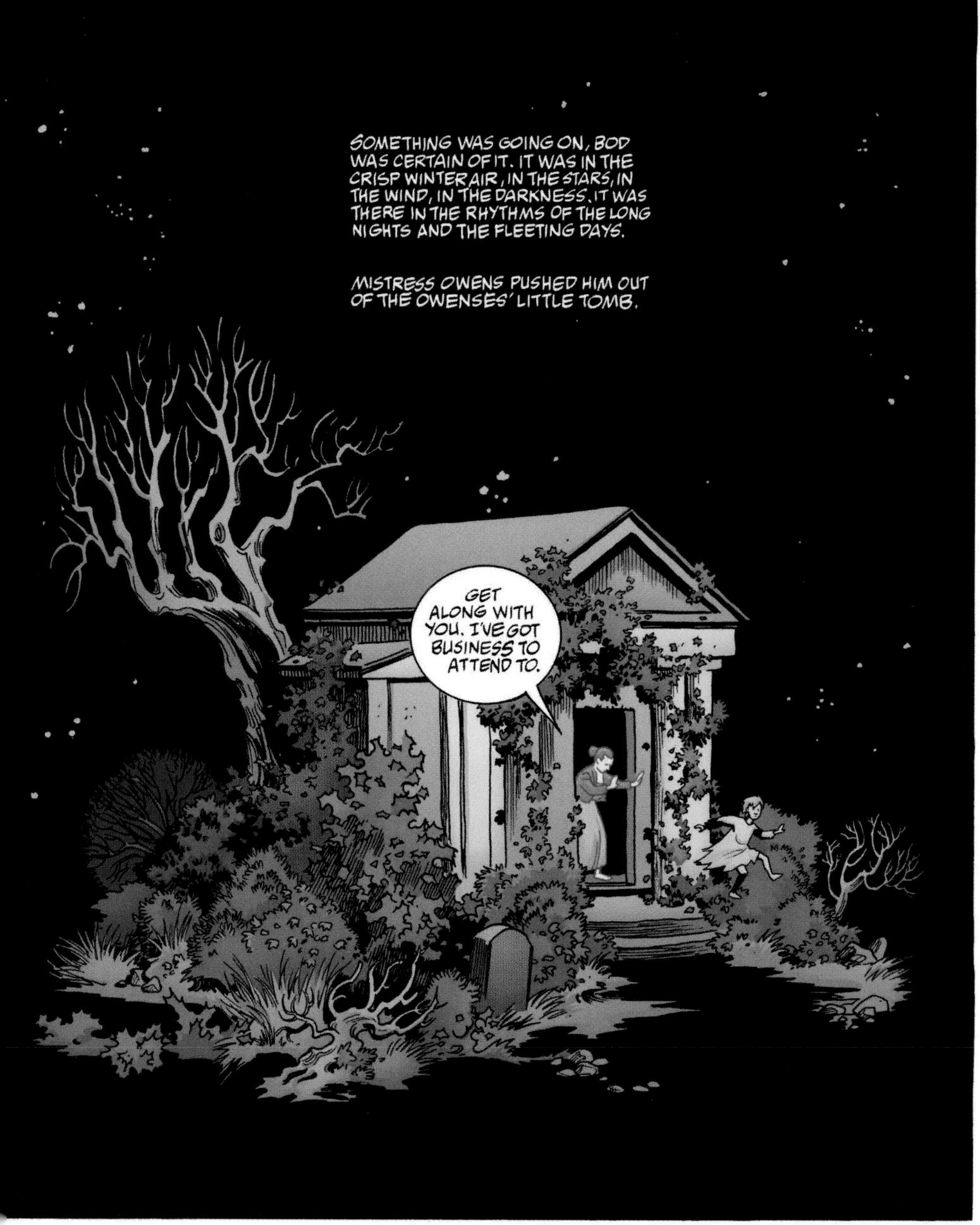
SOMETHING WAS GOING ON, BOD WAS CERTAIN OF IT. IT WAS IN THE CRISP WINTER AIR, IN THE STARS, IN THE WIND, IN THE DARKNESS. IT WAS THERE IN THE RHYTHMS OF THE LONG NIGHTS AND THE FLEETING DAYS.
MISTRESS OWENS PUSHED HIM OUT OF THE OWENSES' LITTLE TOMB.
GET ALONG WITH YOU. I'VE GOT BUSINESS TO ATTEND TO.

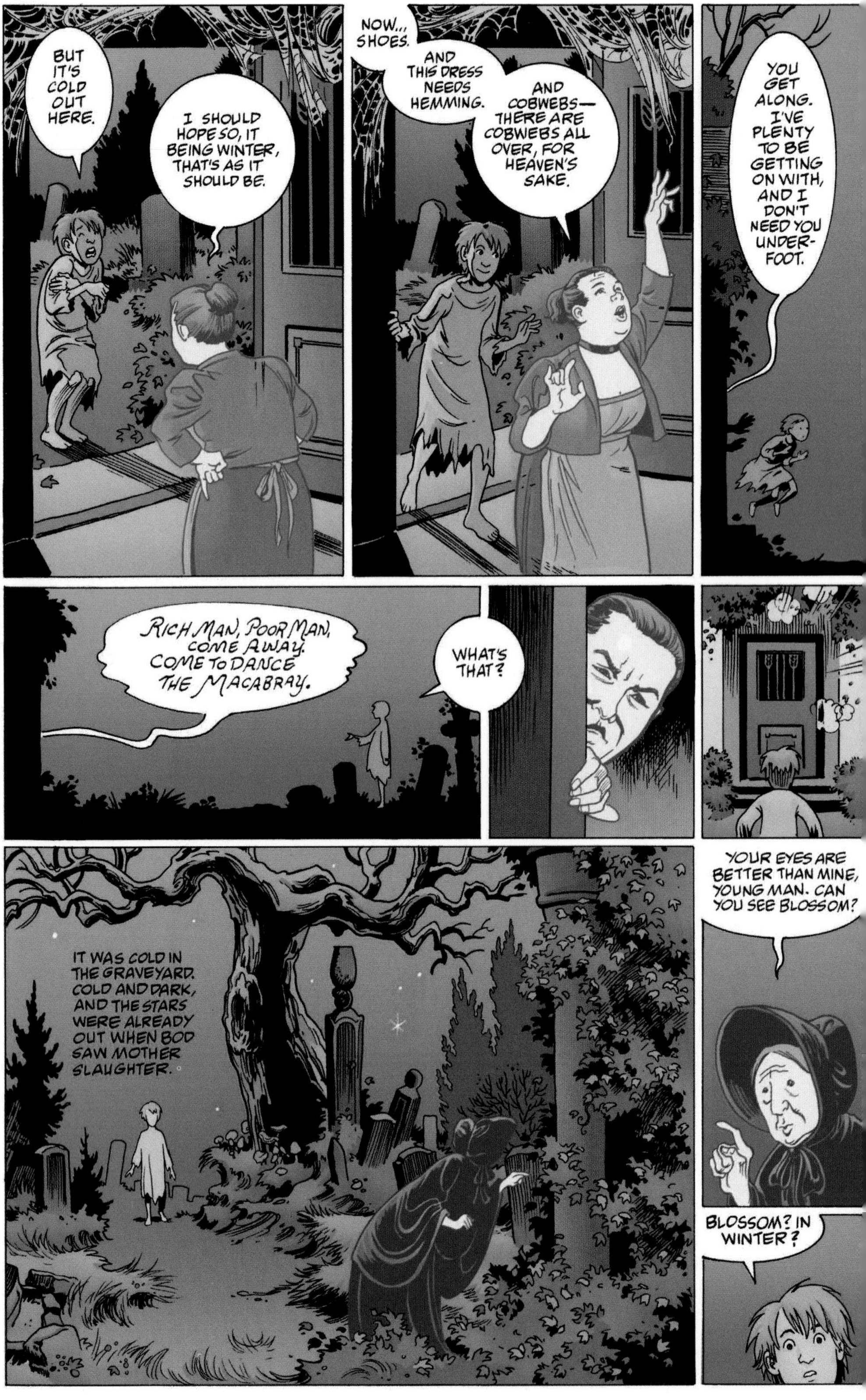
BUT IT'S COLD OUT HERE.
I SHOULD HOPE SO, IT BEING WINTER, THAT'S AS IT SHOULD BE.
NOW... SHOES.
AND THIS DRESS NEEDS HEMMING.
AND COBWEBS— THERE ARE COBWEBS ALL OVER, FOR HEAVEN'S SAKE.
YOU GET ALONG. I'VE PLENTY TO BE GETTING ON WITH, AND I DON'T NEED YOU UNDER-FOOT.
RICH MAN, POOR MAN, COME AWAY. COME TO DANCE THE MACABRAY.
WHAT'S THAT?
IT WAS COLD IN THE GRAVEYARD. COLD AND DARK, AND THE STARS WERE ALREADY OUT WHEN BOD SAW MOTHER SLAUGHTER.
YOUR EYES ARE BETTER THAN MINE, YOUNG MAN. CAN YOU SEE BLOSSOM?
BLOSSOM? IN WINTER?

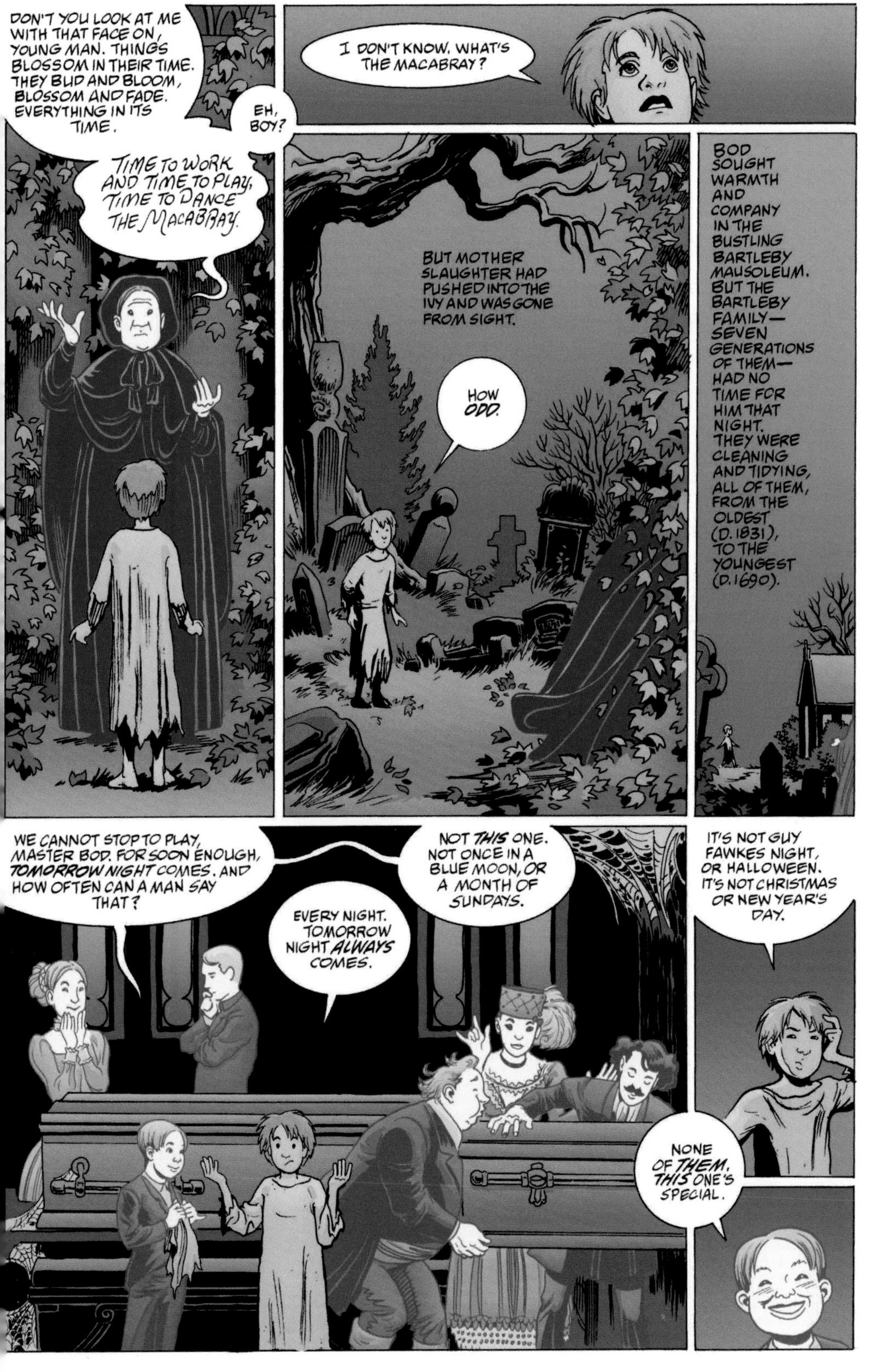
DON'T YOU LOOK AT ME WITH THAT FACE ON, YOUNG MAN. THINGS BLOSSOM IN THEIR TIME. THEY BUD AND BLOOM, BLOSSOM AND FADE. EVERYTHING IN ITS TIME.
EH, BOY?
I DON'T KNOW. WHAT'S THE MACABRAY?
TIME TO WORK AND TIME TO PLAY, TIME TO DANCE THE MACABRAY.
BUT MOTHER SLAUGHTER HAD PUSHED INTO THE IVY AND WAS GONE FROM SIGHT.
HOW ODD.
BOD SOUGHT WARMTH AND COMPANY IN THE BUSTLING BARTLEBY MAUSOLEUM. BUT THE BARTLEBY FAMILY—SEVEN GENERATIONS OF THEM—HAD NO TIME FOR HIM THAT NIGHT. THEY WERE CLEANING AND TIDYING, ALL OF THEM, FROM THE OLDEST (D.1831), TO THE YOUNGEST (D.1690).
WE CANNOT STOP TO PLAY, MASTER BOD. FOR SOON ENOUGH, TOMORROW NIGHT COMES. AND HOW OFTEN CAN A MAN SAY THAT?
EVERY NIGHT. TOMORROW NIGHT ALWAYS COMES.
NOT THIS ONE. NOT ONCE IN A BLUE MOON, OR A MONTH OF SUNDAYS.
IT'S NOT GUY FAWKES NIGHT, OR HALLOWEEN. IT'S NOT CHRISTMAS OR NEW YEAR'S DAY.
NONE OF THEM. THIS ONE'S SPECIAL.

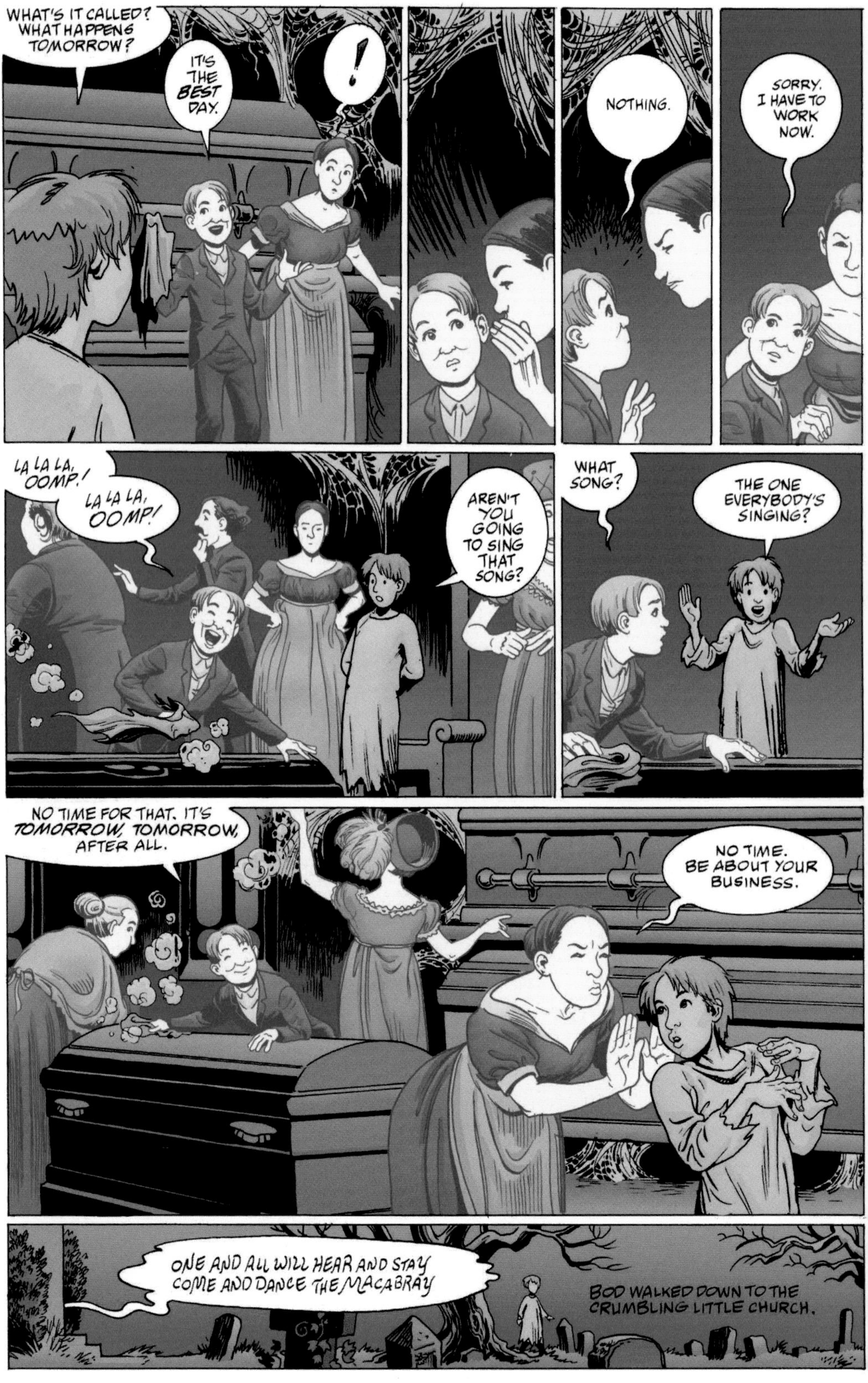
WHAT'S IT CALLED? WHAT HAPPENS TOMORROW?
IT'S THE BEST DAY.
!
NOTHING.
SORRY. I HAVE TO WORK NOW.
LA LA LA, OOMP!
LA LA LA, OOMP!
AREN'T YOU GOING TO SING THAT SONG?
WHAT SONG?
THE ONE EVERYBODY'S SINGING?
NO TIME FOR THAT. IT'S TOMORROW, TOMORROW, AFTER ALL.
NO TIME. BE ABOUT YOUR BUSINESS.
ONE AND ALL WILL HEAR AND STAY
COME AND DANCE THE MACABRAY
BOD WALKED DOWN TO THE CRUMBLING LITTLE CHURCH.

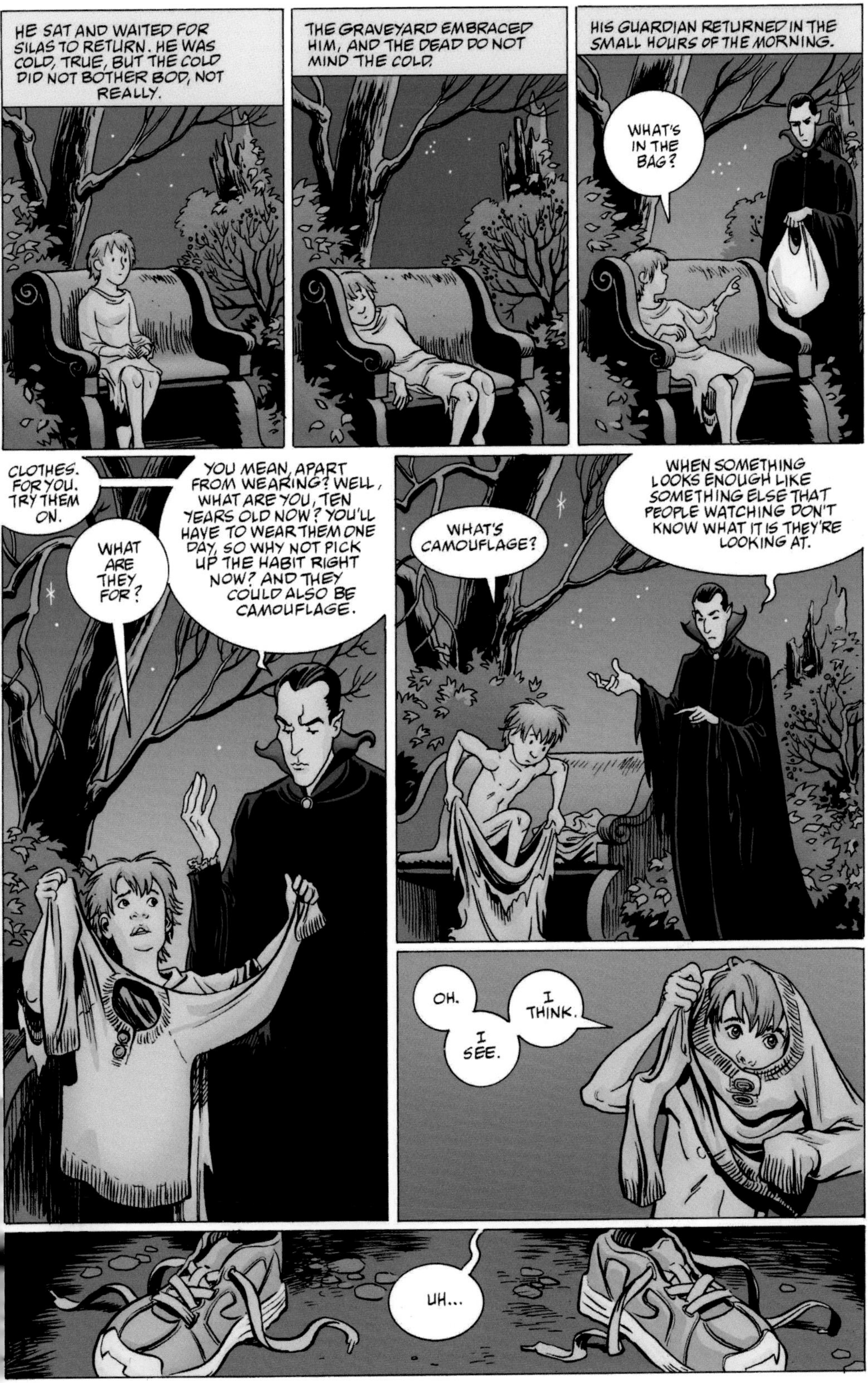
HE SAT AND WAITED FOR SILAS TO RETURN. HE WAS COLD, TRUE, BUT THE COLD DID NOT BOTHER BOD, NOT REALLY.
THE GRAVEYARD EMBRACED HIM, AND THE DEAD DO NOT MIND THE COLD.
HIS GUARDIAN RETURNED IN THE SMALL HOURS OF THE MORNING.
WHAT'S IN THE BAG?
CLOTHES. FOR YOU. TRY THEM ON.
WHAT ARE THEY FOR?
YOU MEAN, APART FROM WEARING? WELL, WHAT ARE YOU, TEN YEARS OLD NOW? YOU'LL HAVE TO WEAR THEM ONE DAY, SO WHY NOT PICK UP THE HABIT RIGHT NOW? AND THEY COULD ALSO BE CAMOUFLAGE.
WHAT'S CAMOUFLAGE?
WHEN SOMETHING LOOKS ENOUGH LIKE SOMETHING ELSE THAT PEOPLE WATCHING DON'T KNOW WHAT IT IS THEY'RE LOOKING AT.
OH.
I SEE.
I THINK.
UH...

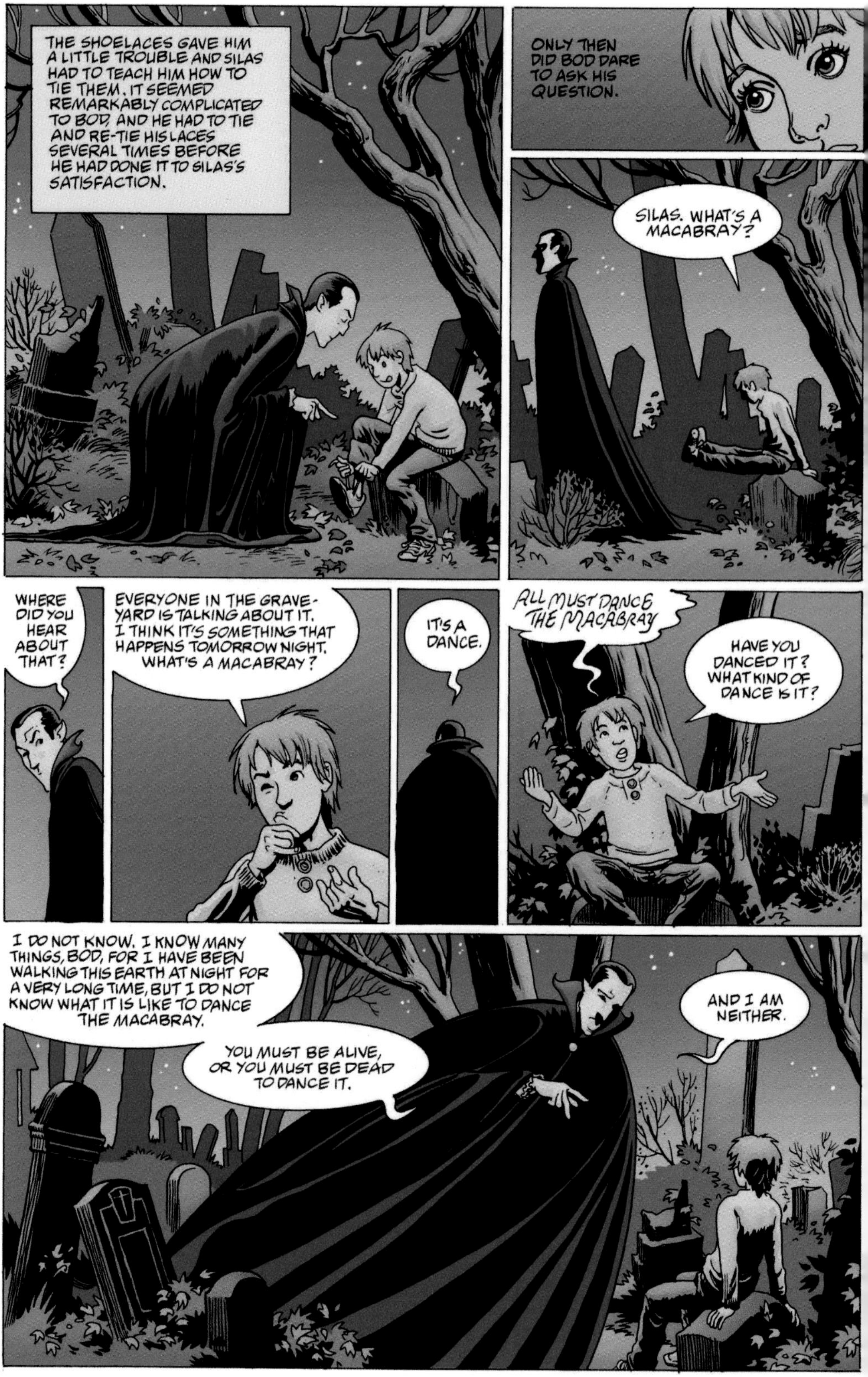
THE SHOELACES GAVE HIM A LITTLE TROUBLE AND SILAS HAD TO TEACH HIM HOW TO TIE THEM. IT SEEMED REMARKABLY COMPLICATED TO BOD, AND HE HAD TO TIE AND RE-TIE HIS LACES SEVERAL TIMES BEFORE HE HAD DONE IT TO SILAS'S SATISFACTION.
ONLY THEN DID BOD DARE TO ASK HIS QUESTION.
SILAS. WHAT'S A MACABRAY?
WHERE DID YOU HEAR ABOUT THAT?
EVERYONE IN THE GRAVE-YARD IS TALKING ABOUT IT. I THINK IT'S SOMETHING THAT HAPPENS TOMORROW NIGHT. WHAT'S A MACABRAY?
IT'S A DANCE.
ALL MUST DANCE THE MACABRAY
HAVE YOU DANCED IT? WHAT KIND OF DANCE IS IT?
I DO NOT KNOW. I KNOW MANY THINGS, BOD, FOR I HAVE BEEN WALKING THIS EARTH AT NIGHT FOR A VERY LONG TIME, BUT I DO NOT KNOW WHAT IT IS LIKE TO DANCE THE MACABRAY.
YOU MUST BE ALIVE, OR YOU MUST BE DEAD TO DANCE IT.
AND I AM NEITHER.

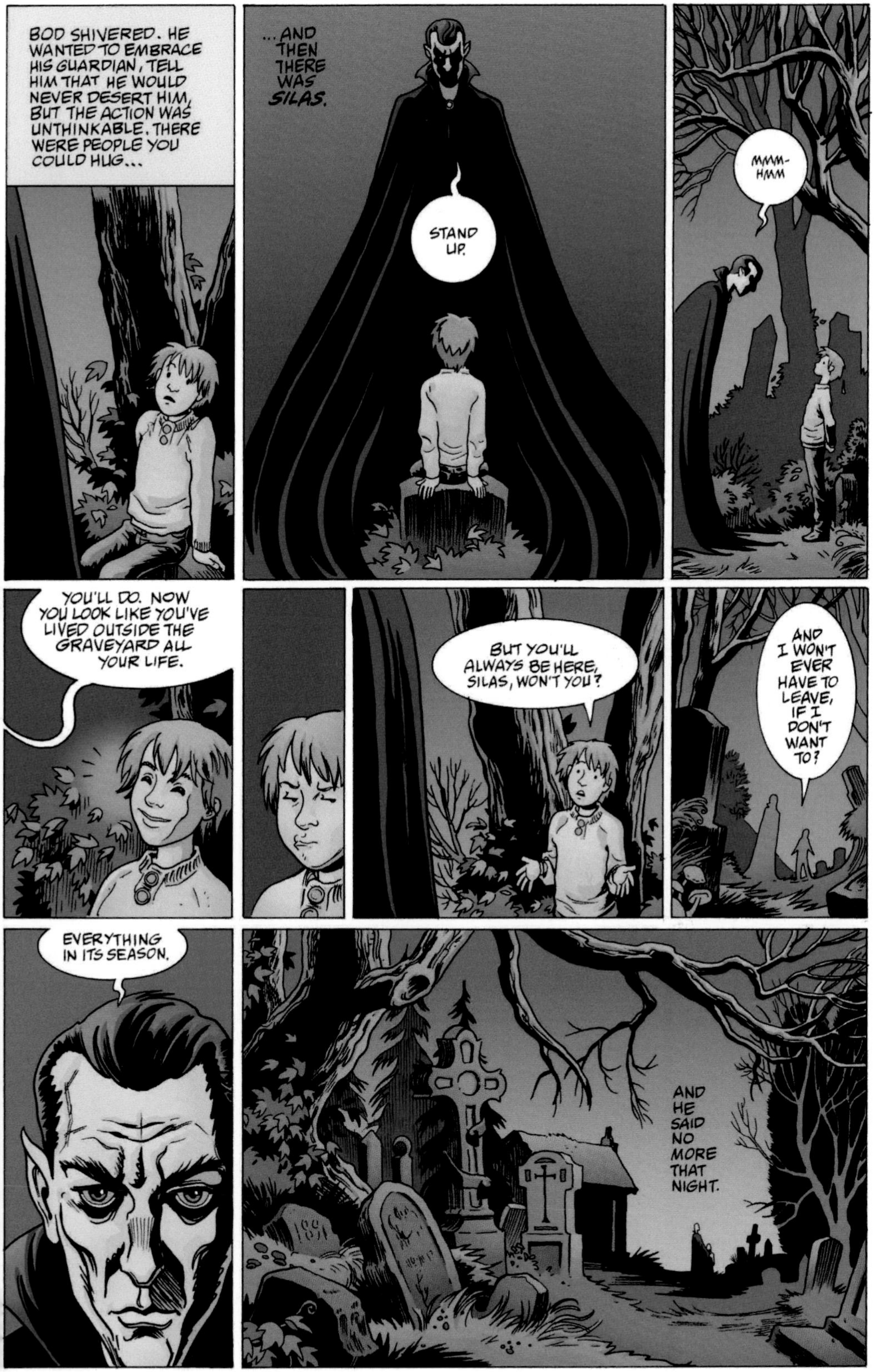
BOD SHIVERED. HE WANTED TO EMBRACE HIS GUARDIAN, TELL HIM THAT HE WOULD NEVER DESERT HIM, BUT THE ACTION WAS UNTHINKABLE. THERE WERE PEOPLE YOU COULD HUG...
...AND THEN THERE WAS SILAS.
STAND UP.
MMM-HMM
YOU'LL DO. NOW YOU LOOK LIKE YOU'VE LIVED OUTSIDE THE GRAVEYARD ALL YOUR LIFE.
BUT YOU'LL ALWAYS BE HERE, SILAS, WON'T YOU?
AND I WON'T EVER HAVE TO LEAVE, IF I DON'T WANT TO?
EVERYTHING IN ITS SEASON.
AND HE SAID NO MORE THAT NIGHT.

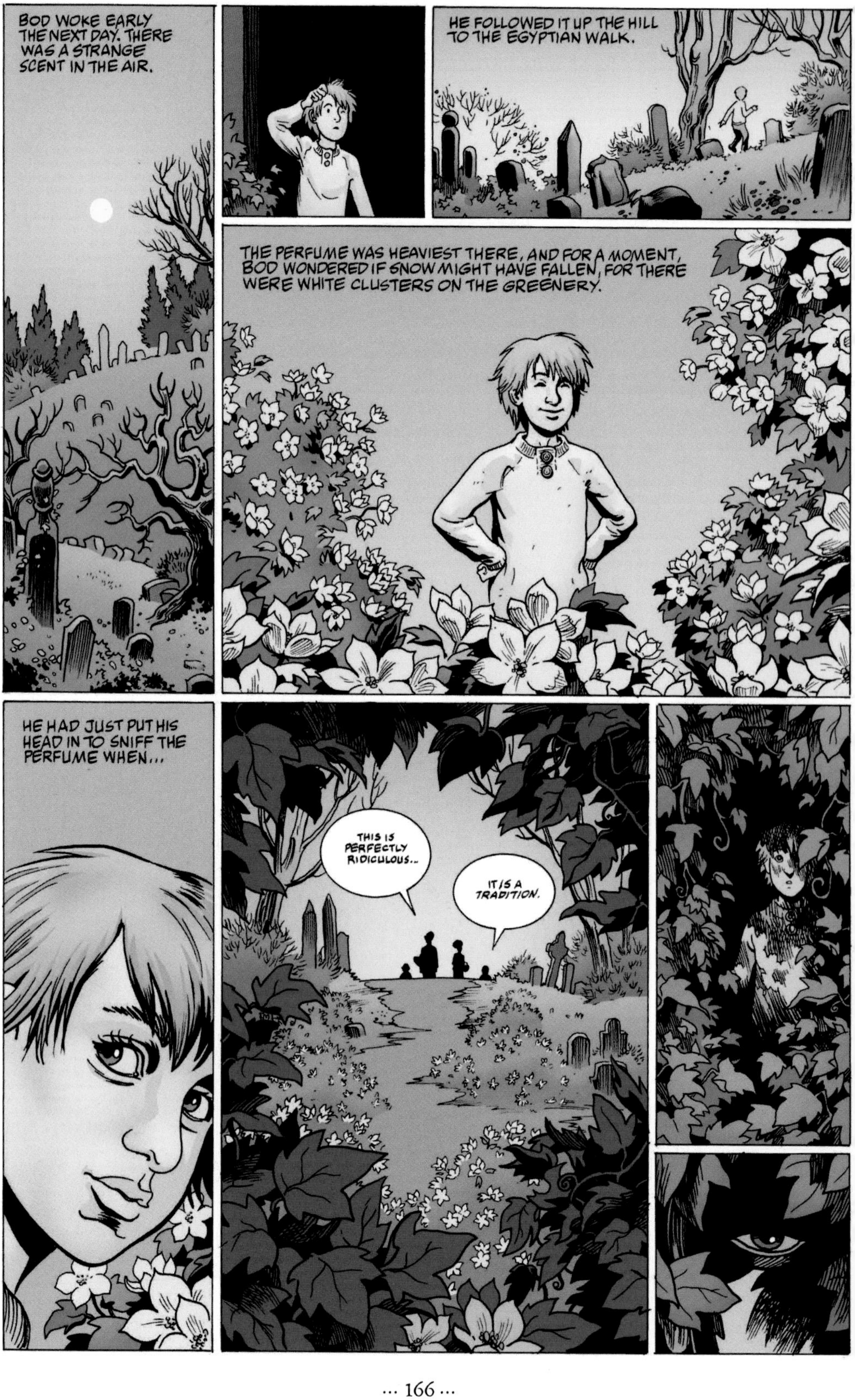
BOD WOKE EARLY THE NEXT DAY. THERE WAS A STRANGE SCENT IN THE AIR.
HE FOLLOWED IT UP THE HILL TO THE EGYPTIAN WALK.
THE PERFUME WAS HEAVIEST THERE, AND FOR A MOMENT, BOD WONDERED IF SNOW MIGHT HAVE FALLEN, FOR THERE WERE WHITE CLUSTERS ON THE GREENERY.
HE HAD JUST PUT HIS HEAD IN TO SNIFF THE PERFUME WHEN...
THIS IS PERFECTLY RIDICULOUS...
IT IS A TRADITION.

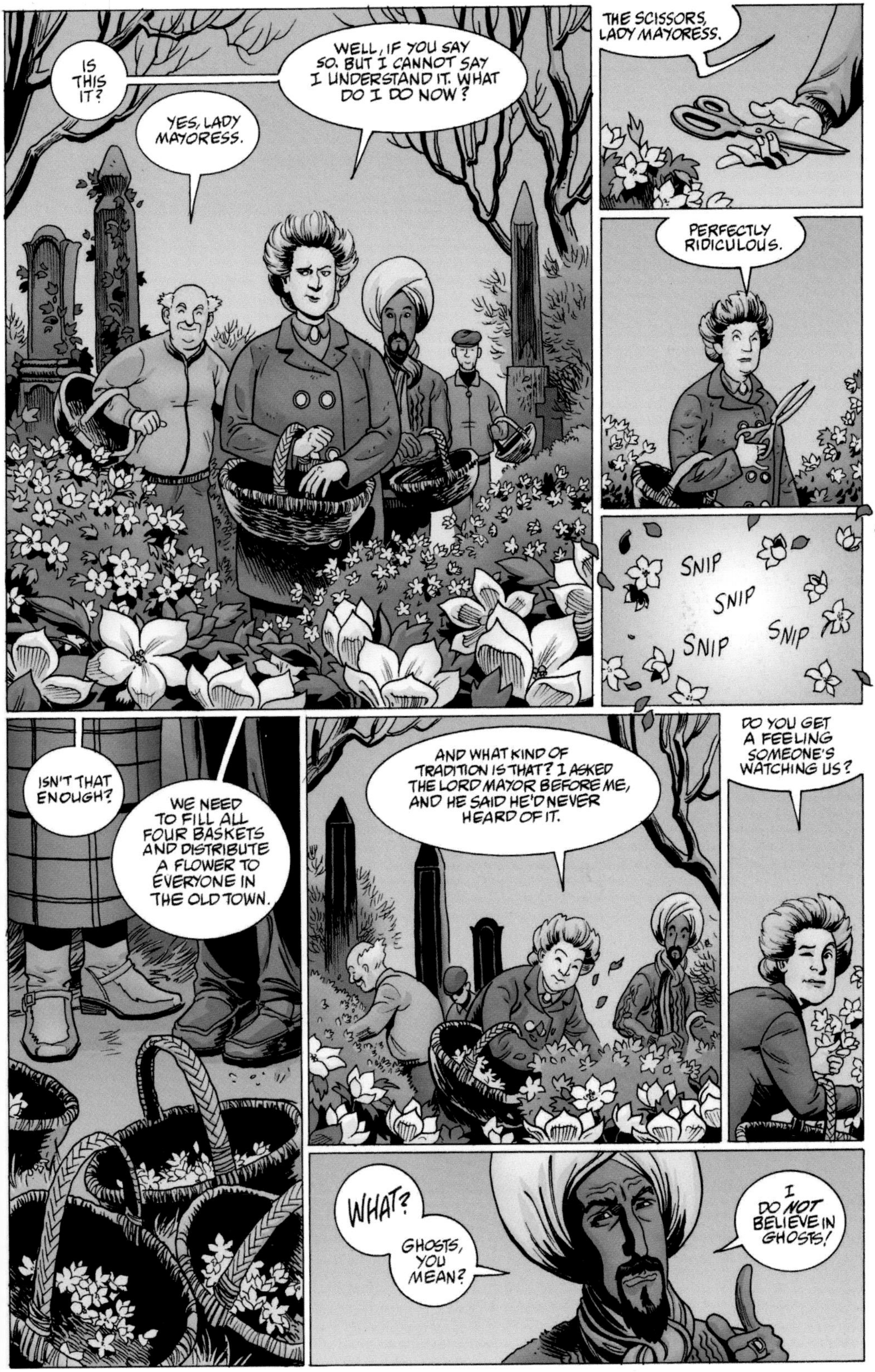
IS THIS IT?
WELL, IF YOU SAY SO. BUT I CANNOT SAY I UNDERSTAND IT. WHAT DO I DO NOW?
YES, LADY MAYORESS.
THE SCISSORS, LADY MAYORESS.
PERFECTLY RIDICULOUS.
SNIP
SNIP
SNIP
SNIP
ISN'T THAT ENOUGH?
WE NEED TO FILL ALL FOUR BASKETS AND DISTRIBUTE A FLOWER TO EVERYONE IN THE OLD TOWN.
AND WHAT KIND OF TRADITION IS THAT? I ASKED THE LORD MAYOR BEFORE ME, AND HE SAID HE'D NEVER HEARD OF IT.
DO YOU GET A FEELING SOMEONE'S WATCHING US?
WHAT?
GHOSTS, YOU MEAN?
I DO NOT BELIEVE IN GHOSTS!

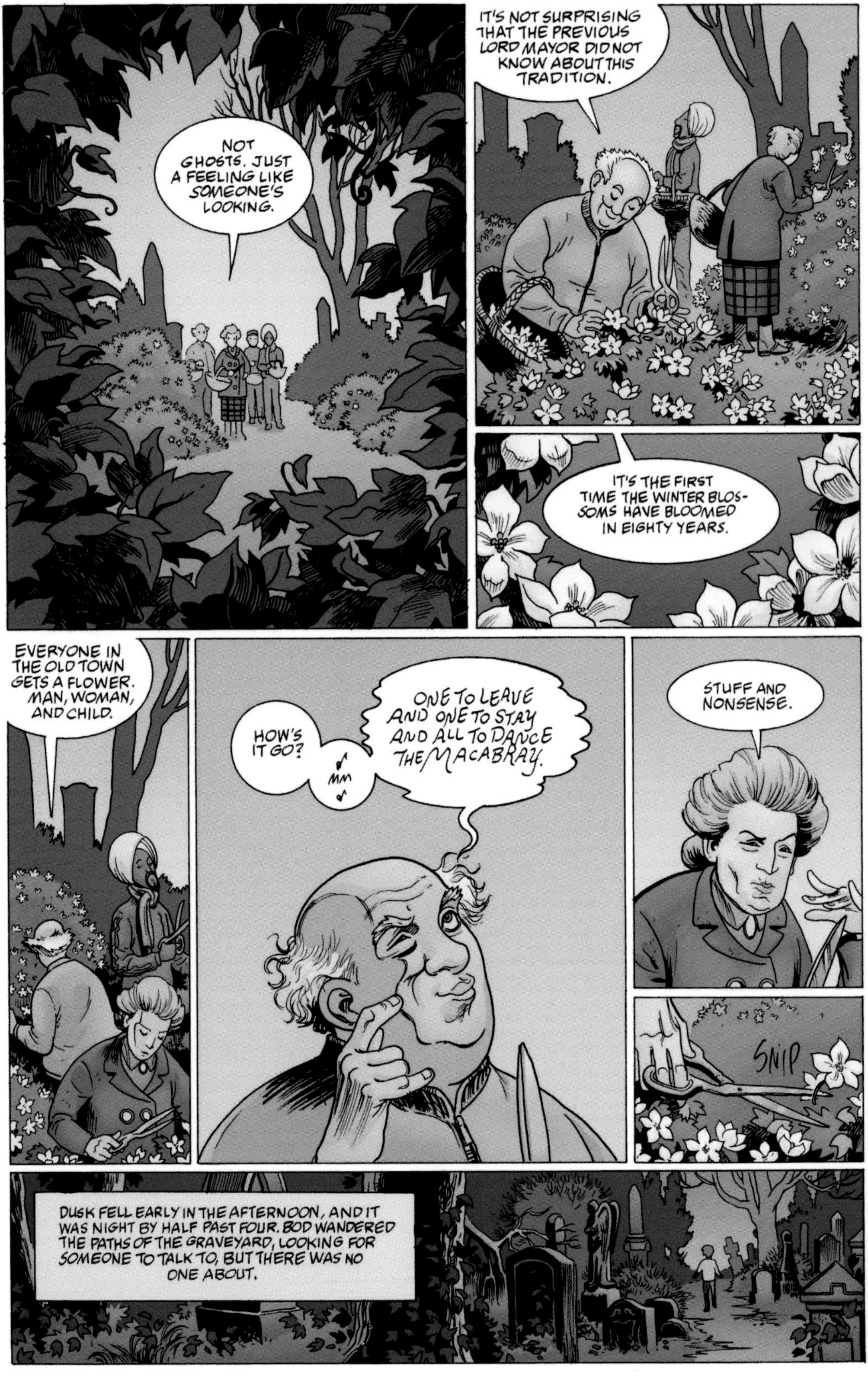
NOT GHOSTS. JUST A FEELING LIKE SOMEONE'S LOOKING.
IT'S NOT SURPRISING THAT THE PREVIOUS LORD MAYOR DID NOT KNOW ABOUT THIS TRADITION.
IT'S THE FIRST TIME THE WINTER BLOSSOMS HAVE BLOOMED IN EIGHTY YEARS.
EVERYONE IN THE OLD TOWN GETS A FLOWER. MAN, WOMAN, AND CHILD.
HOW'S IT GO?
MM
ONE TO LEAVE AND ONE TO STAY AND ALL TO DANCE THE MACABRAY.
STUFF AND NONSENSE.
SNIP
DUSK FELL EARLY IN THE AFTERNOON, AND IT WAS NIGHT BY HALF PAST FOUR. BOD WANDERED THE PATHS OF THE GRAVEYARD, LOOKING FOR SOMEONE TO TALK TO, BUT THERE WAS NO ONE ABOUT.

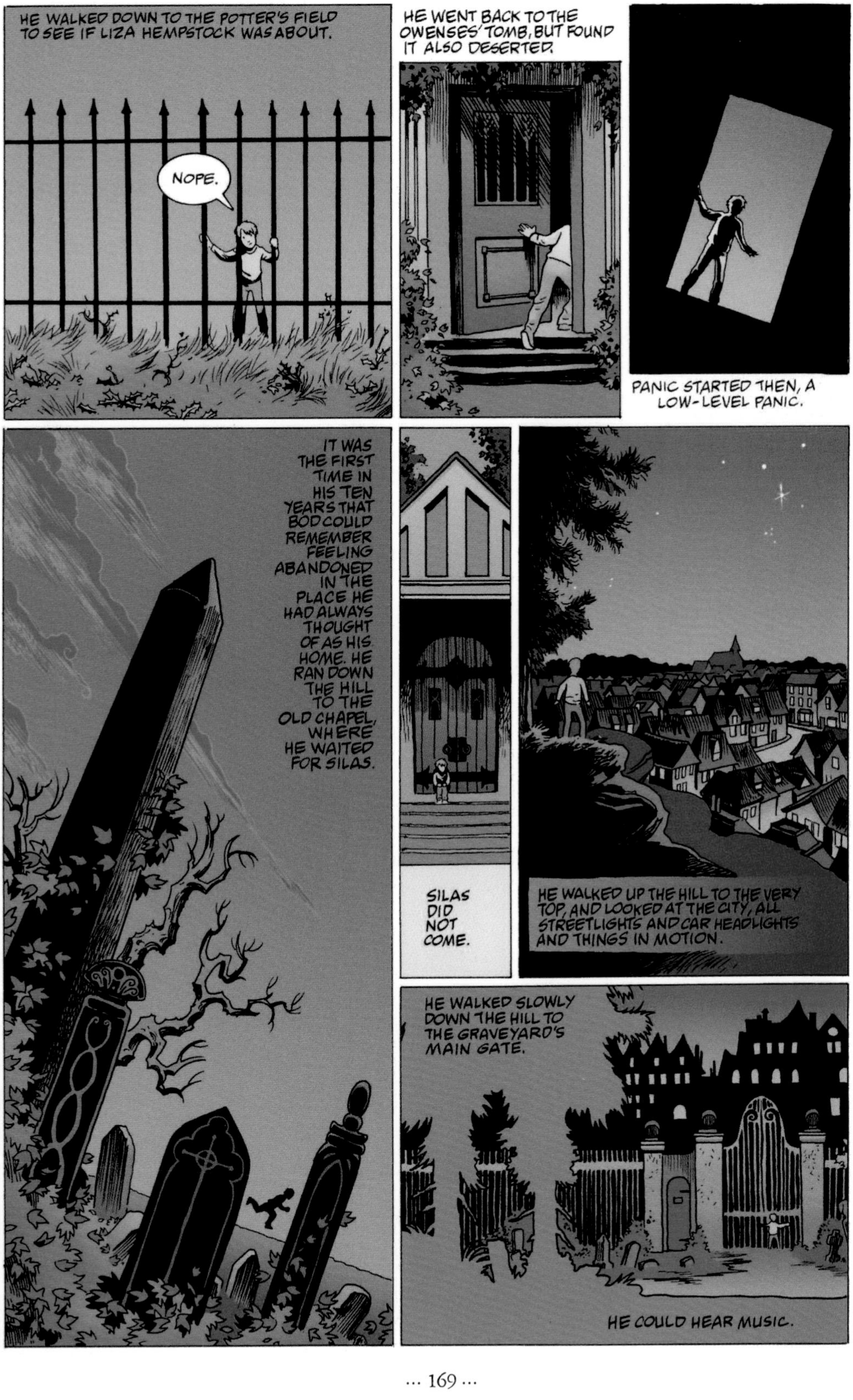
HE WALKED DOWN TO THE POTTER'S FIELD TO SEE IF LIZA HEMPSTOCK WAS ABOUT.
NOPE.
HE WENT BACK TO THE OWENSES' TOMB, BUT FOUND IT ALSO DESERTED.
PANIC STARTED THEN, A LOW-LEVEL PANIC.
IT WAS THE FIRST TIME IN HIS TEN YEARS THAT BOD COULD REMEMBER FEELING ABANDONED IN THE PLACE HE HAD ALWAYS THOUGHT OF AS HIS HOME. HE RAN DOWN THE HILL TO THE OLD CHAPEL, WHERE HE WAITED FOR SILAS.
SILAS DID NOT COME.
HE WALKED UP THE HILL TO THE VERY TOP, AND LOOKED AT THE CITY, ALL STREETLIGHTS AND CAR HEADLIGHTS AND THINGS IN MOTION.
HE WALKED SLOWLY DOWN THE HILL TO THE GRAVEYARD'S MAIN GATE.
HE COULD HEAR MUSIC.

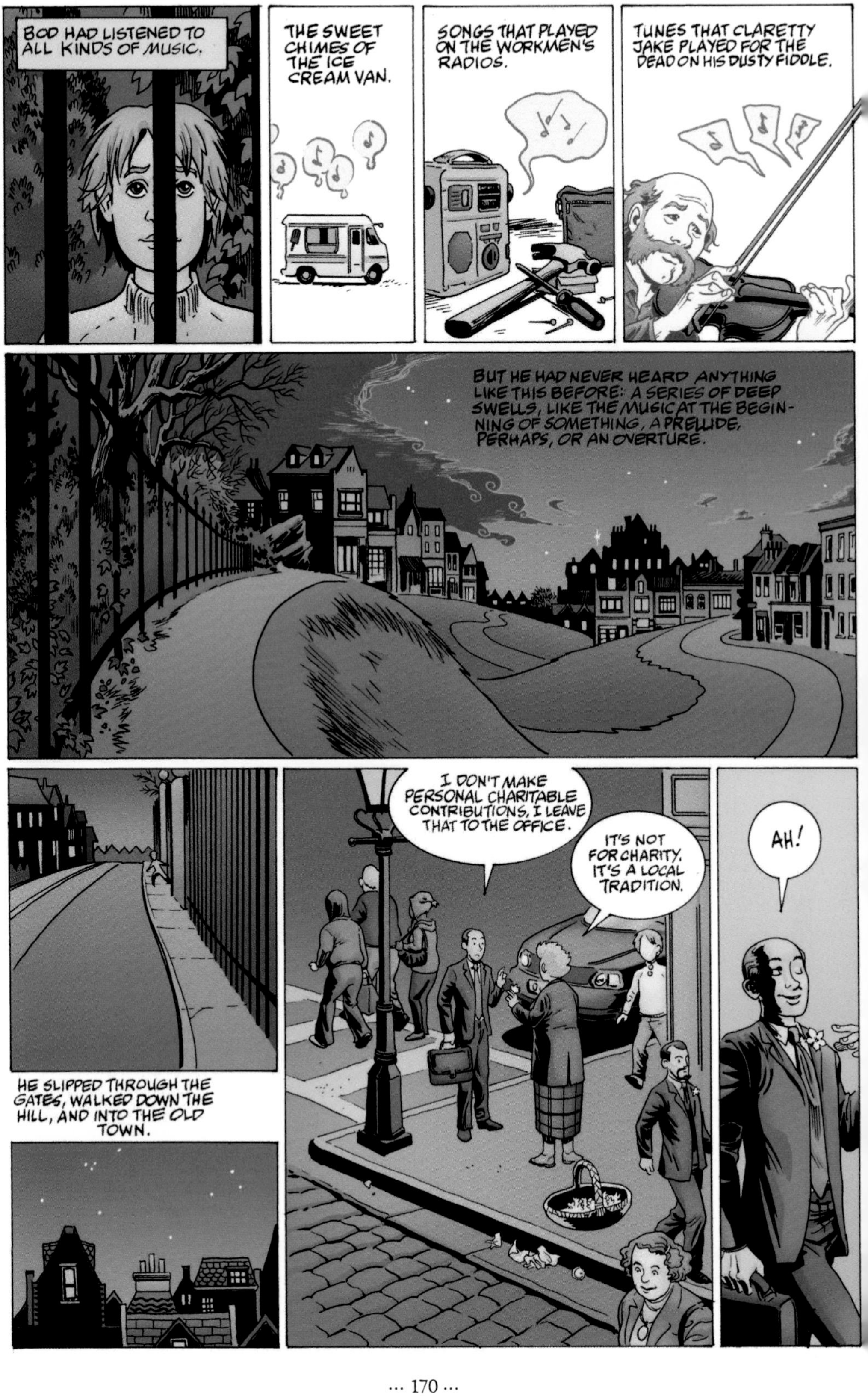
BOD HAD LISTENED TO ALL KINDS OF MUSIC.
THE SWEET CHIMES OF THE ICE CREAM VAN.
SONGS THAT PLAYED ON THE WORKMEN'S RADIOS.
TUNES THAT CLARETTY JAKE PLAYED FOR THE DEAD ON HIS DUSTY FIDDLE.
BUT HE HAD NEVER HEARD ANYTHING LIKE THIS BEFORE: A SERIES OF DEEP SWELLS, LIKE THE MUSIC AT THE BEGINNING OF SOMETHING, A PRELUDE, PERHAPS, OR AN OVERTURE.
HE SLIPPED THROUGH THE GATES, WALKED DOWN THE HILL, AND INTO THE OLD TOWN.
I DON'T MAKE PERSONAL CHARITABLE CONTRIBUTIONS, I LEAVE THAT TO THE OFFICE.
IT'S NOT FOR CHARITY. IT'S A LOCAL TRADITION.
AH!

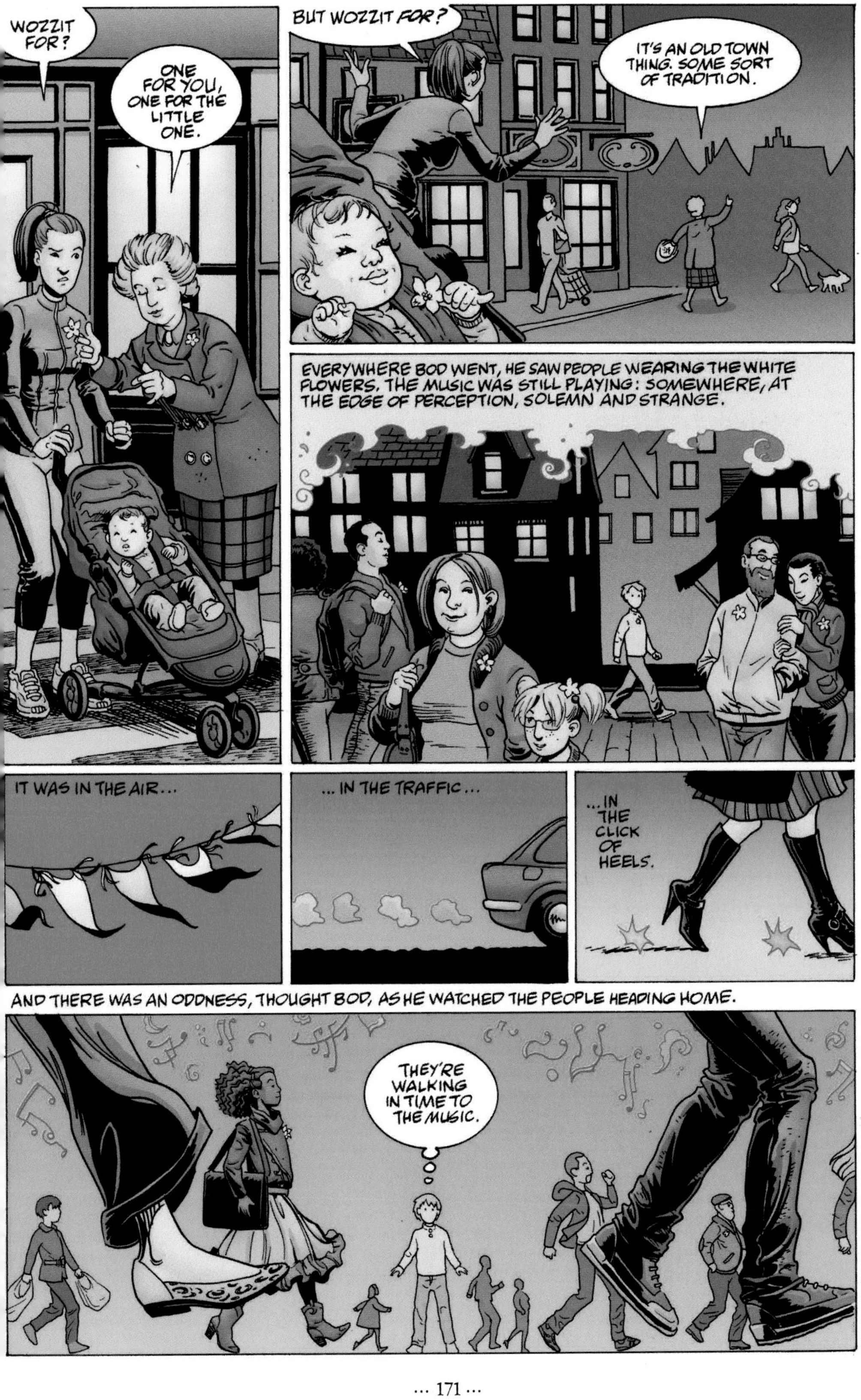
WOZZIT FOR?
ONE FOR YOU, ONE FOR THE LITTLE ONE.
BUT WOZZIT FOR?
IT'S AN OLD TOWN THING. SOME SORT OF TRADITION.
EVERYWHERE BOD WENT, HE SAW PEOPLE WEARING THE WHITE FLOWERS. THE MUSIC WAS STILL PLAYING: SOMEWHERE, AT THE EDGE OF PERCEPTION, SOLEMN AND STRANGE.
IT WAS IN THE AIR...
... IN THE TRAFFIC...
...IN THE CLICK OF HEELS.
AND THERE WAS AN ODDNESS, THOUGHT BOD, AS HE WATCHED THE PEOPLE HEADING HOME.
THEY'RE WALKING IN TIME TO THE MUSIC.

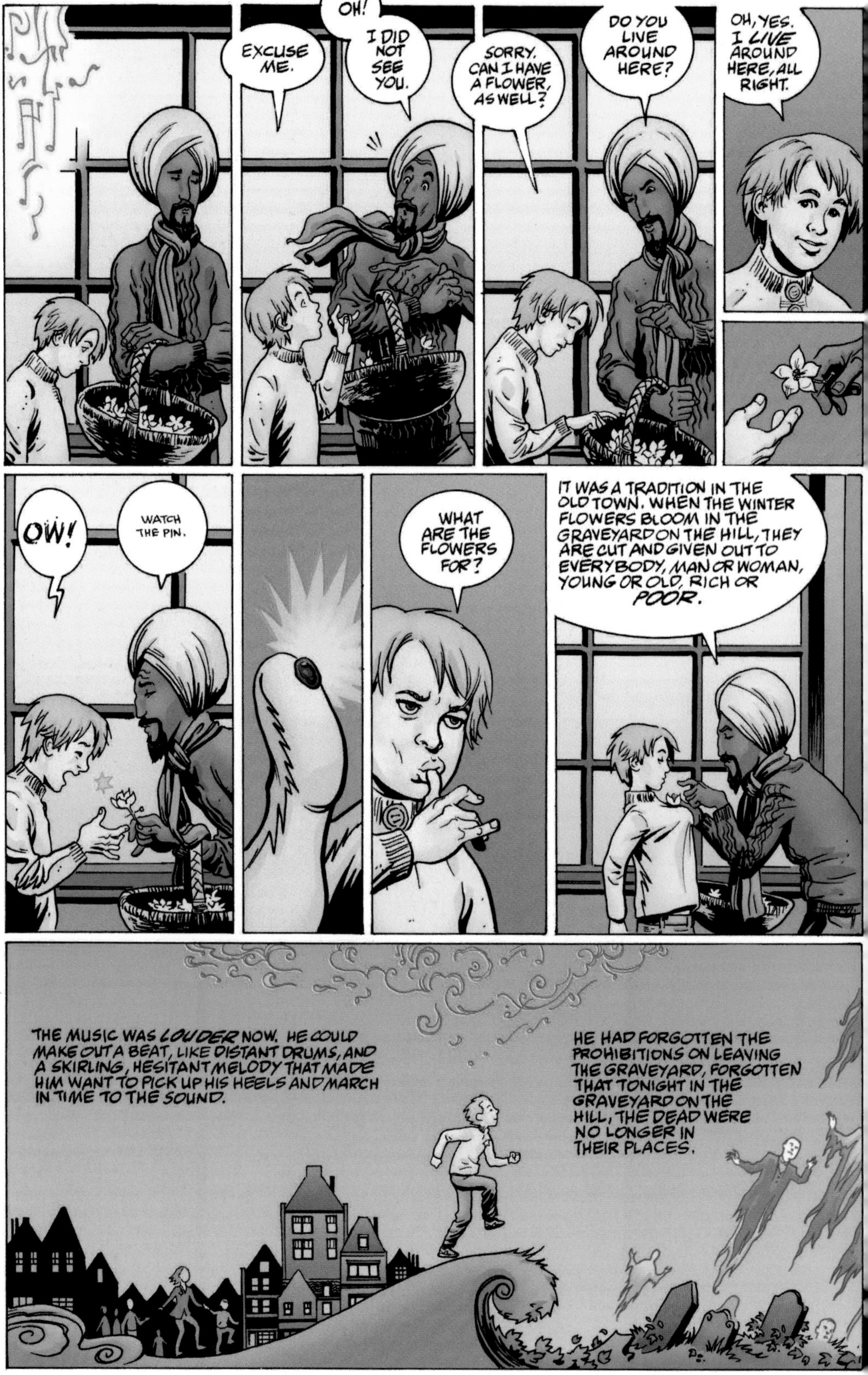
EXCUSE ME.
OH!
I DID NOT SEE YOU.
SORRY. CAN I HAVE A FLOWER, AS WELL?
DO YOU LIVE AROUND HERE?
OH, YES. I LIVE AROUND HERE, ALL RIGHT.
OW!
WATCH THE PIN.
WHAT ARE THE FLOWERS FOR?
IT WAS A TRADITION IN THE OLD TOWN. WHEN THE WINTER FLOWERS BLOOM IN THE GRAVEYARD ON THE HILL, THEY ARE CUT AND GIVEN OUT TO EVERYBODY, MAN OR WOMAN, YOUNG OR OLD, RICH OR POOR.
THE MUSIC WAS LOUDER NOW. HE COULD MAKE OUT A BEAT, LIKE DISTANT DRUMS, AND A SKIRLING, HESITANT MELODY THAT MADE HIM WANT TO PICK UP HIS HEELS AND MARCH IN TIME TO THE SOUND.
HE HAD FORGOTTEN THE PROHIBITIONS ON LEAVING THE GRAVEYARD, FORGOTTEN THAT TONIGHT IN THE GRAVEYARD ON THE HILL, THE DEAD WERE NO LONGER IN THEIR PLACES.

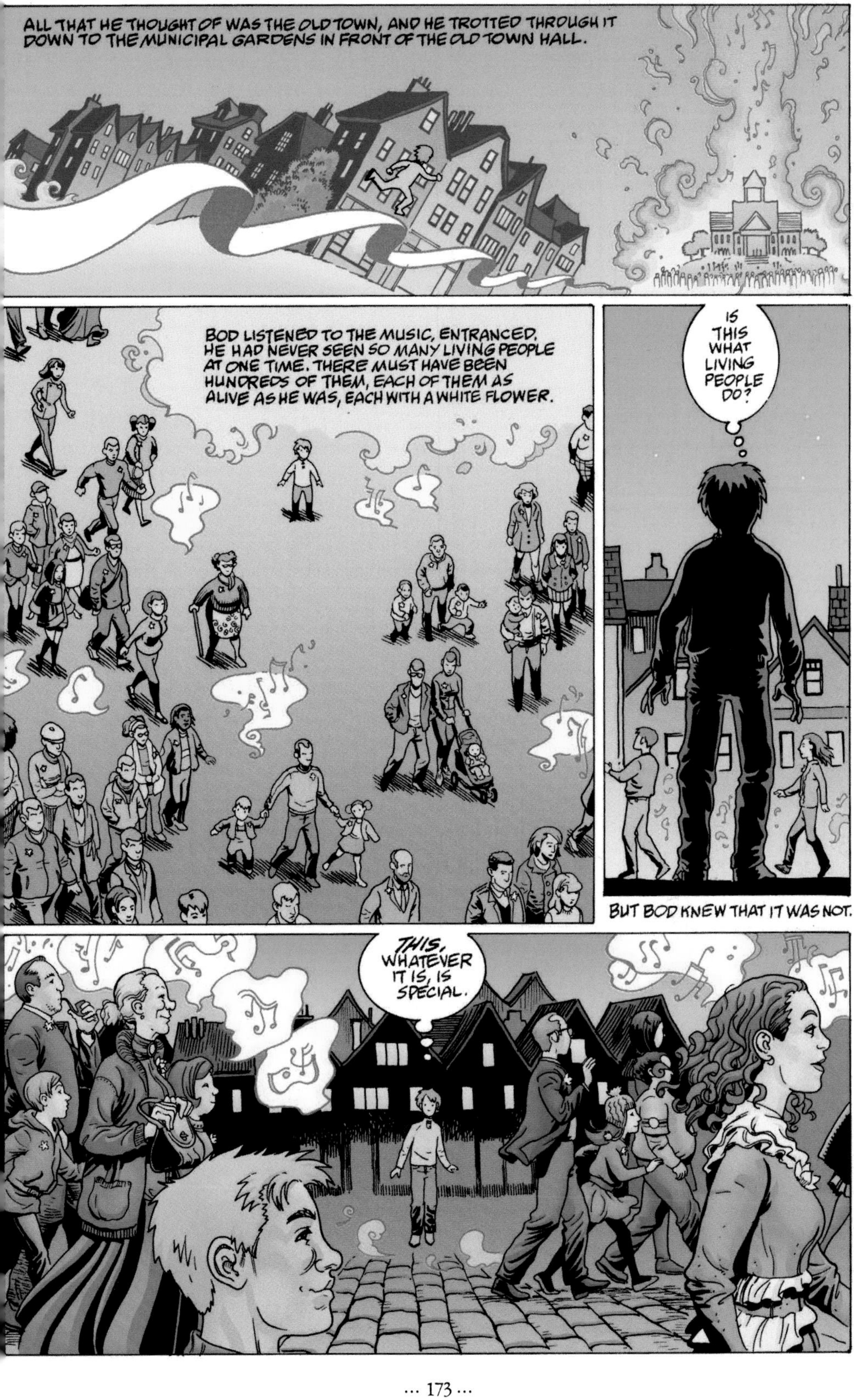
ALL THAT HE THOUGHT OF WAS THE OLD TOWN, AND HE TROTTED THROUGH IT DOWN TO THE MUNICIPAL GARDENS IN FRONT OF THE OLD TOWN HALL.
BOD LISTENED TO THE MUSIC, ENTRANCED. HE HAD NEVER SEEN SO MANY LIVING PEOPLE AT ONE TIME. THERE MUST HAVE BEEN HUNDREDS OF THEM, EACH OF THEM AS ALIVE AS HE WAS, EACH WITH A WHITE FLOWER.
IS THIS WHAT LIVING PEOPLE DO?
BUT BOD KNEW THAT IT WAS NOT.
THIS, WHATEVER IT IS, IS SPECIAL.

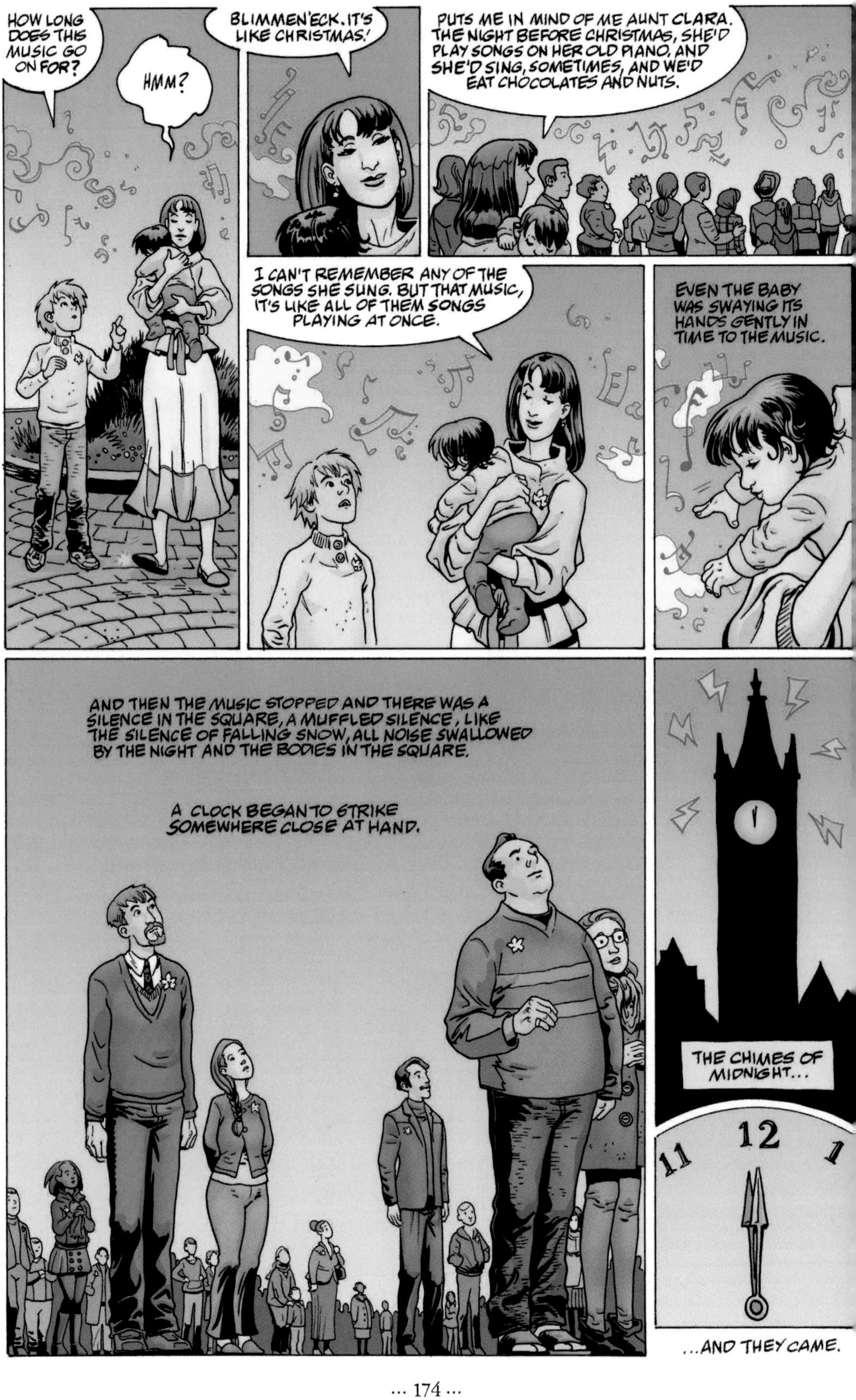
HOW LONG DOES THIS MUSIC GO ON FOR?
HMM?
BLIMMEN'ECK. IT'S LIKE CHRISTMAS!
PUTS ME IN MIND OF ME AUNT CLARA. THE NIGHT BEFORE CHRISTMAS, SHE'D PLAY SONGS ON HER OLD PIANO, AND SHE'D SING, SOMETIMES, AND WE'D EAT CHOCOLATES AND NUTS.
I CAN'T REMEMBER ANY OF THE SONGS SHE SUNG. BUT THAT MUSIC, IT'S LIKE ALL OF THEM SONGS PLAYING AT ONCE.
EVEN THE BABY WAS SWAYING ITS HANDS GENTLY IN TIME TO THE MUSIC.
AND THEN THE MUSIC STOPPED AND THERE WAS A SILENCE IN THE SQUARE, A MUFFLED SILENCE, LIKE THE SILENCE OF FALLING SNOW, ALL NOISE SWALLOWED BY THE NIGHT AND THE BODIES IN THE SQUARE.
A CLOCK BEGAN TO STRIKE SOMEWHERE CLOSE AT HAND.
THE CHIMES OF MIDNIGHT...
11
12
1
...AND THEY CAME.

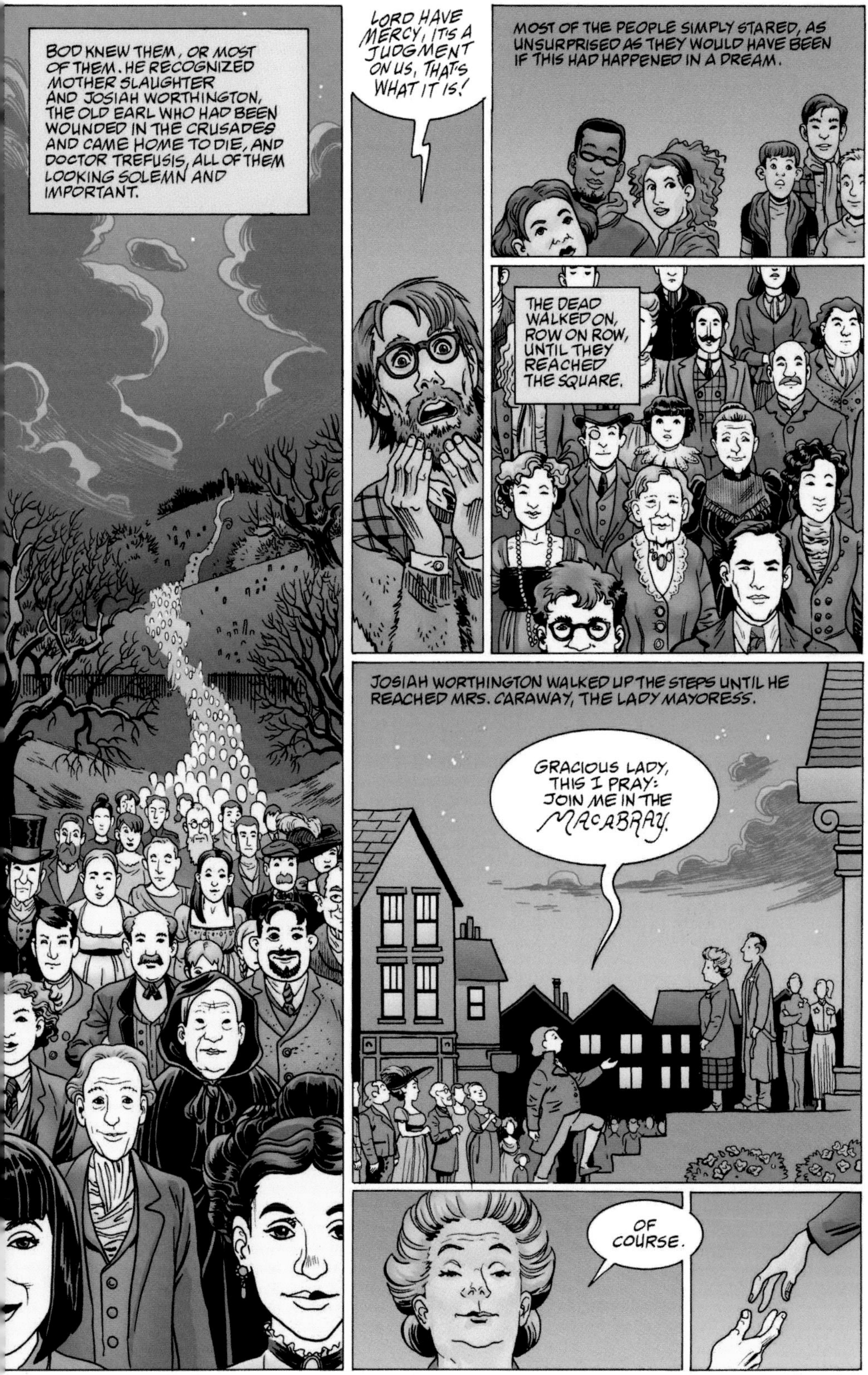
BOD KNEW THEM, OR MOST OF THEM. HE RECOGNIZED MOTHER SLAUGHTER AND JOSIAH WORTHINGTON, THE OLD EARL WHO HAD BEEN WOUNDED IN THE CRUSADES AND CAME HOME TO DIE, AND DOCTOR TREFUSIS, ALL OF THEM LOOKING SOLEMN AND IMPORTANT.
LORD HAVE MERCY, IT'S A JUDGMENT ON US, THAT'S WHAT IT IS!
MOST OF THE PEOPLE SIMPLY STARED, AS UNSURPRISED AS THEY WOULD HAVE BEEN IF THIS HAD HAPPENED IN A DREAM.
THE DEAD WALKED ON, ROW ON ROW, UNTIL THEY REACHED THE SQUARE.
JOSIAH WORTHINGTON WALKED UP THE STEPS UNTIL HE REACHED MRS. CARAWAY, THE LADY MAYORESS.
GRACIOUS LADY, THIS I PRAY: JOIN ME IN THE MACABRAY.
OF COURSE.

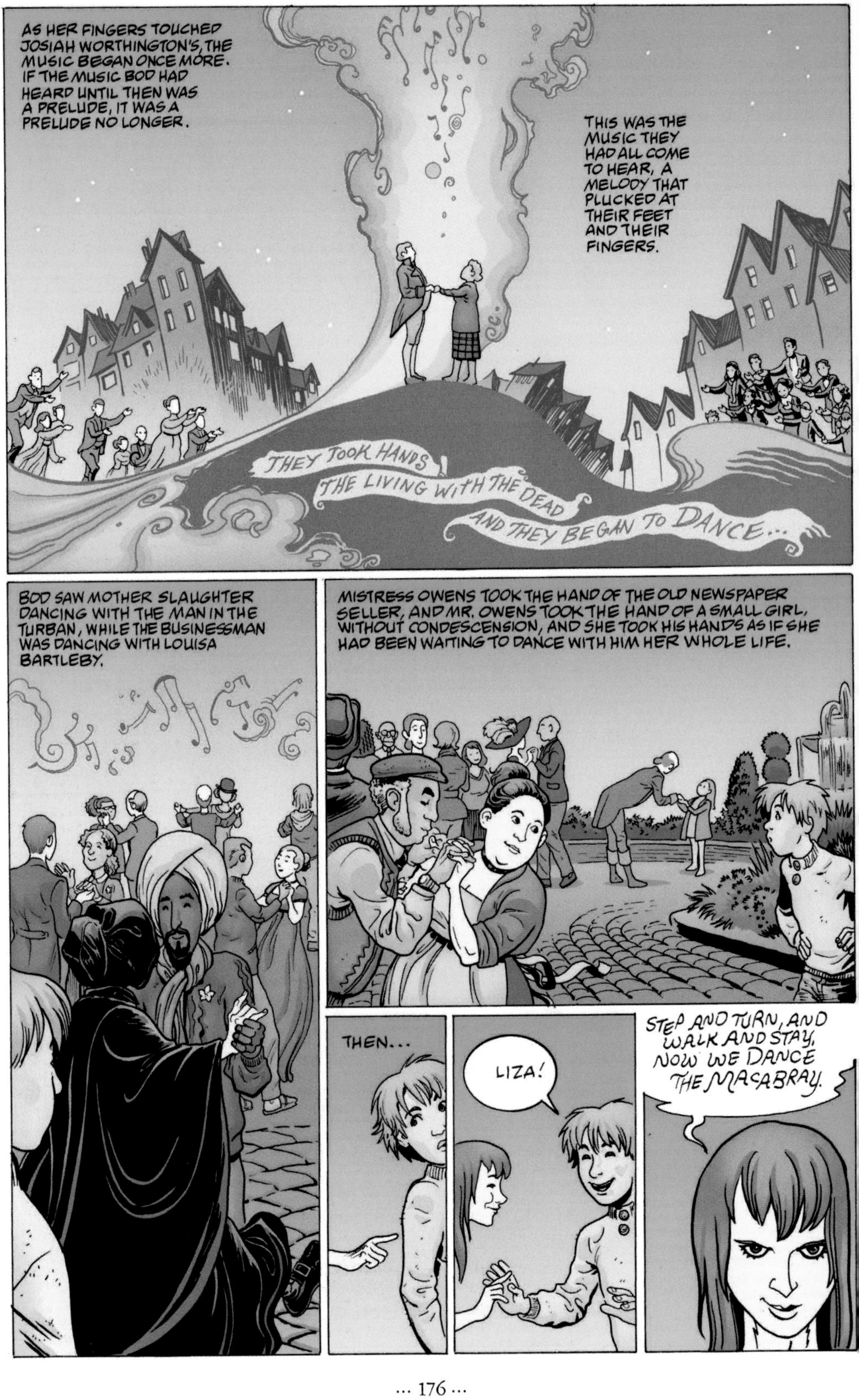
AS HER FINGERS TOUCHED JOSIAH WORTHINGTON'S, THE MUSIC BEGAN ONCE MORE. IF THE MUSIC BOD HAD HEARD UNTIL THEN WAS A PRELUDE, IT WAS A PRELUDE NO LONGER.
THIS WAS THE MUSIC THEY HAD ALL COME TO HEAR, A MELODY THAT PLUCKED AT THEIR FEET AND THEIR FINGERS.
THEY TOOK HANDS,
THE LIVING WITH THE DEAD
AND THEY BEGAN TO DANCE...
BOD SAW MOTHER SLAUGHTER DANCING WITH THE MAN IN THE TURBAN, WHILE THE BUSINESSMAN WAS DANCING WITH LOUISA BARTLEBY.
MISTRESS OWENS TOOK THE HAND OF THE OLD NEWSPAPER SELLER, AND MR. OWENS TOOK THE HAND OF A SMALL GIRL, WITHOUT CONDESCENSION, AND SHE TOOK HIS HANDS AS IF SHE HAD BEEN WAITING TO DANCE WITH HIM HER WHOLE LIFE.
THEN...
LIZA!
STEP AND TURN, AND WALK AND STAY, NOW WE DANCE THE MACABRAY.

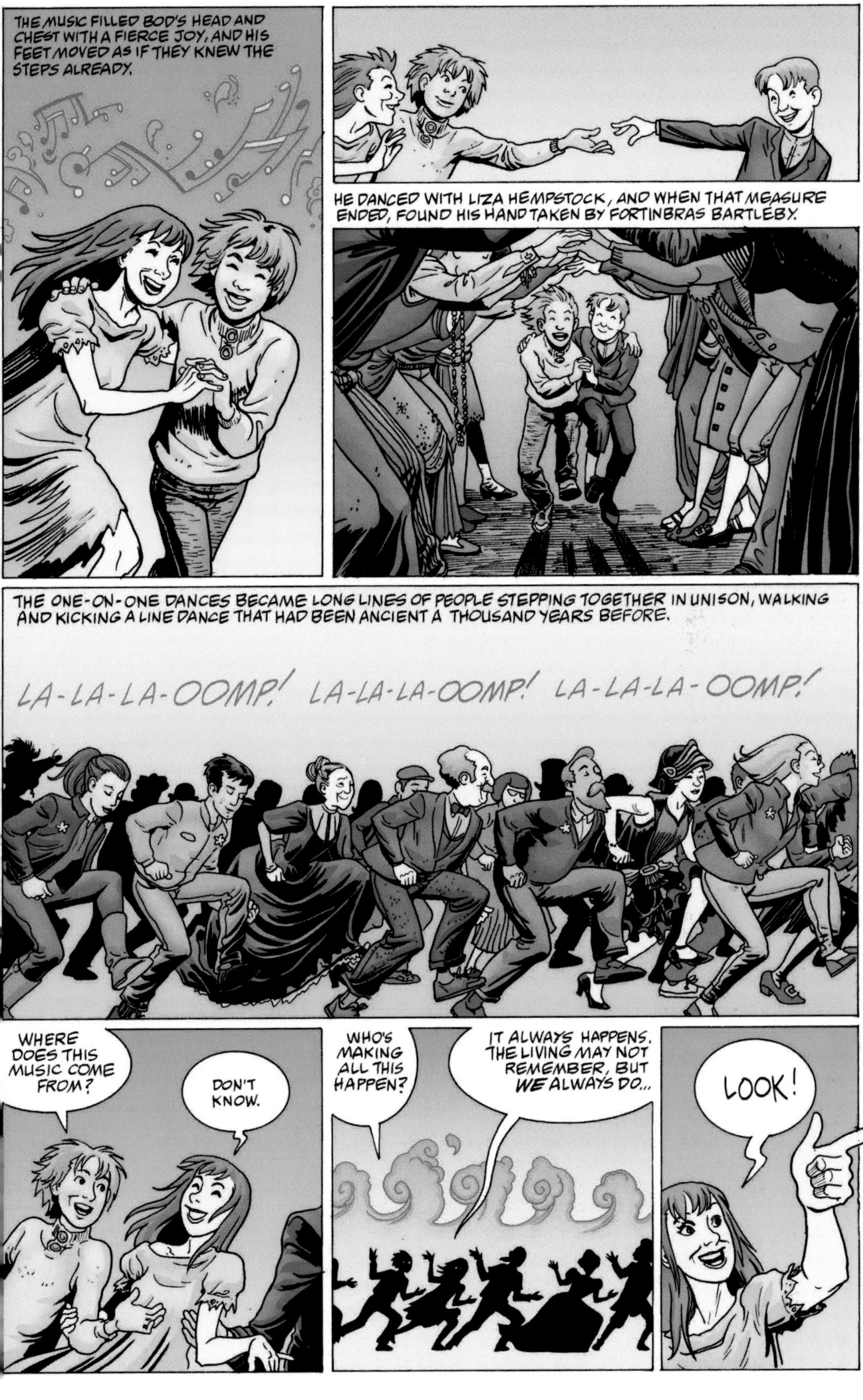
THE MUSIC FILLED BOD'S HEAD AND CHEST WITH A FIERCE JOY, AND HIS FEET MOVED AS IF THEY KNEW THE STEPS ALREADY.
HE DANCED WITH LIZA HEMPSTOCK, AND WHEN THAT MEASURE ENDED, FOUND HIS HAND TAKEN BY FORTINBRAS BARTLEBY.
THE ONE-ON-ONE DANCES BECAME LONG LINES OF PEOPLE STEPPING TOGETHER IN UNISON, WALKING AND KICKING A LINE DANCE THAT HAD BEEN ANCIENT A THOUSAND YEARS BEFORE.
LA-LA-LA-OOMP! LA-LA-LA-OOMP! LA-LA-LA-OOMP!
WHERE DOES THIS MUSIC COME FROM?
DON'T KNOW.
WHO'S MAKING ALL THIS HAPPEN?
IT ALWAYS HAPPENS. THE LIVING MAY NOT REMEMBER, BUT *WE* ALWAYS DO...
LOOK!

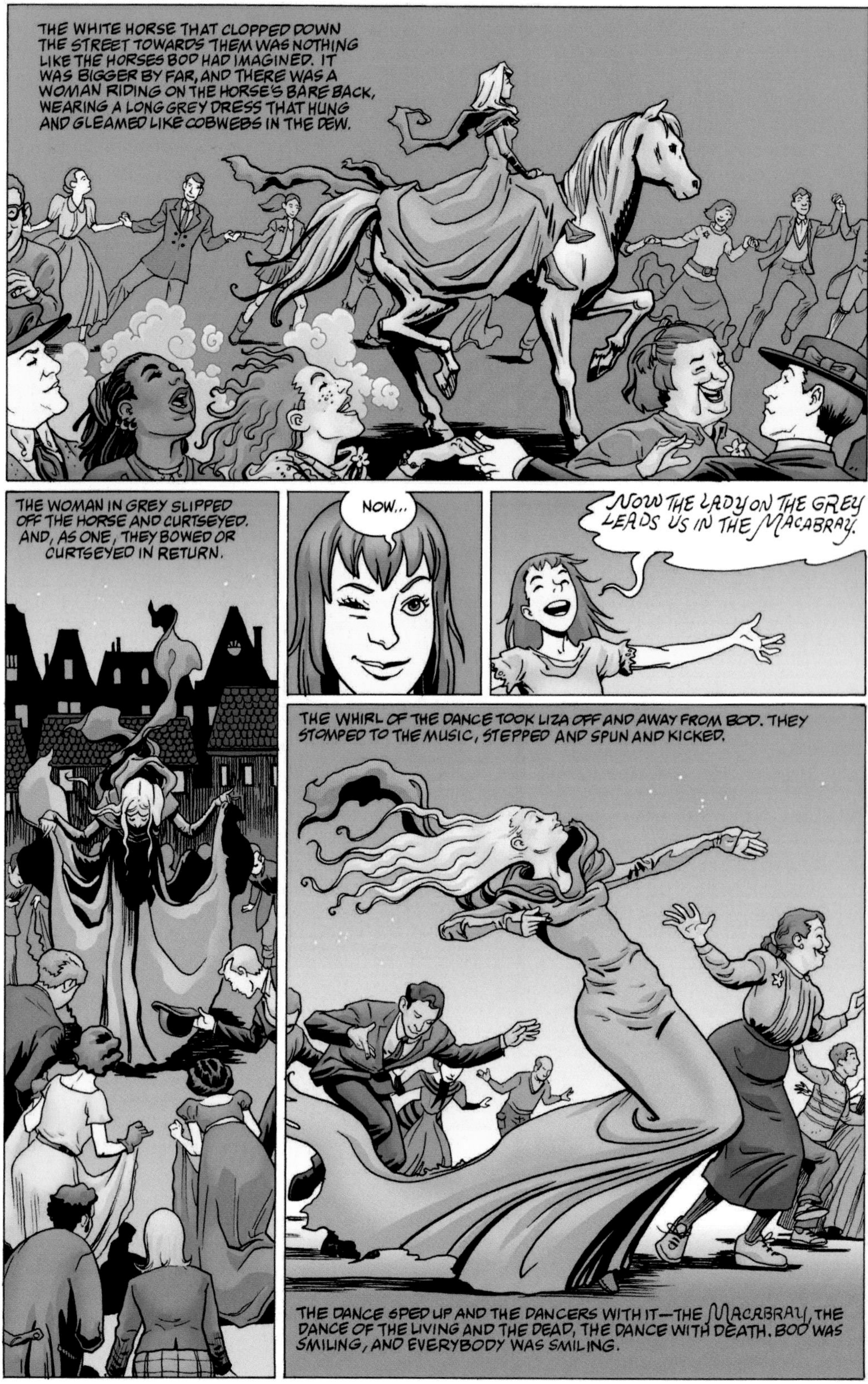
THE WHITE HORSE THAT CLOPPED DOWN THE STREET TOWARDS THEM WAS NOTHING LIKE THE HORSES BOD HAD IMAGINED. IT WAS BIGGER BY FAR, AND THERE WAS A WOMAN RIDING ON THE HORSE'S BARE BACK, WEARING A LONG GREY DRESS THAT HUNG AND GLEAMED LIKE COBWEBS IN THE DEW.
THE WOMAN IN GREY SLIPPED OFF THE HORSE AND CURTSEYED. AND, AS ONE, THEY BOWED OR CURTSEYED IN RETURN.
NOW...
NOW THE LADY ON THE GREY LEADS US IN THE MACABRAY.
THE WHIRL OF THE DANCE TOOK LIZA OFF AND AWAY FROM BOD. THEY STOMPED TO THE MUSIC, STEPPED AND SPUN AND KICKED.
THE DANCE SPED UP AND THE DANCERS WITH IT—THE MACABRAY, THE DANCE OF THE LIVING AND THE DEAD, THE DANCE WITH DEATH. BOD WAS SMILING, AND EVERYBODY WAS SMILING.

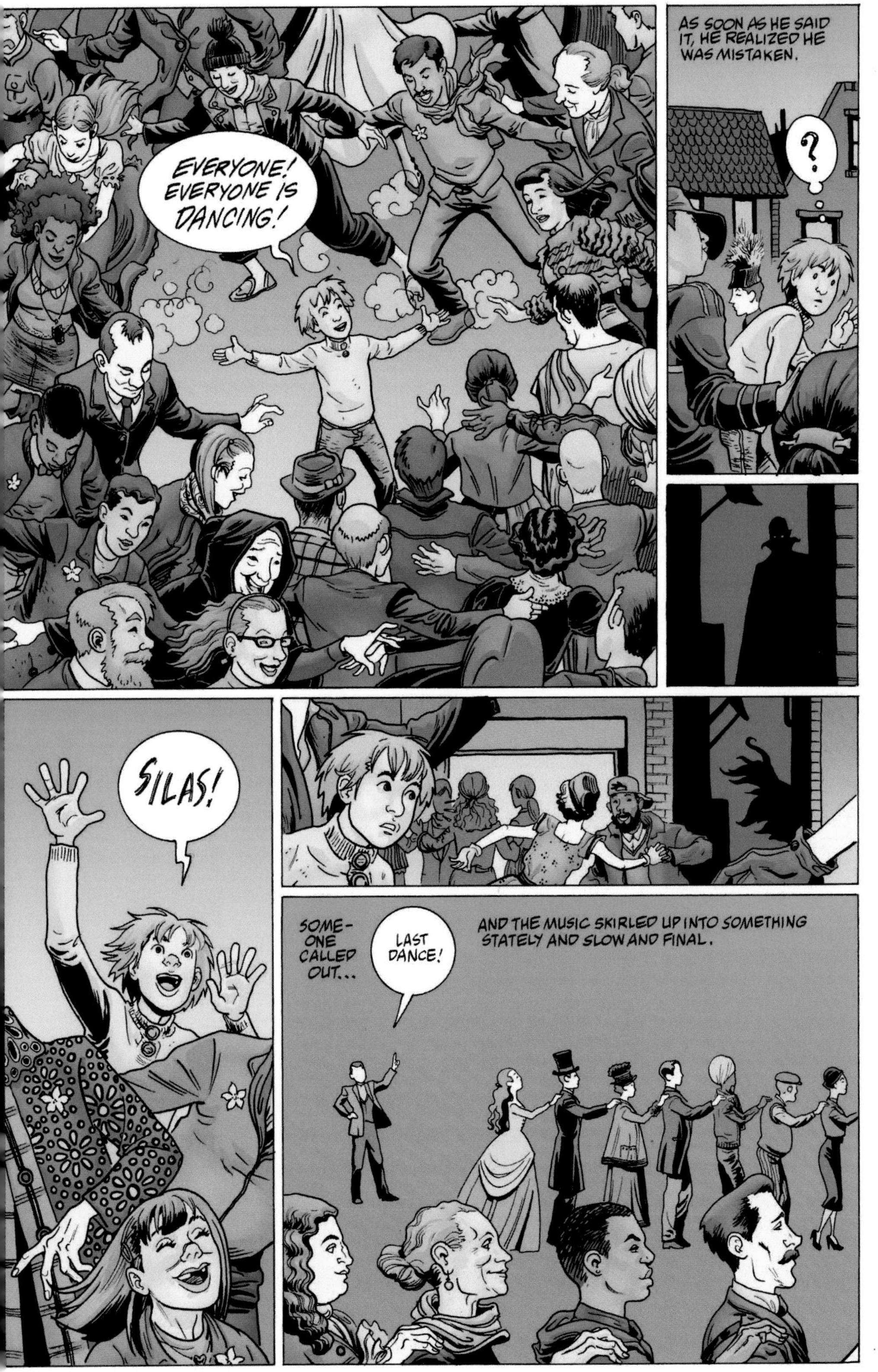
EVERYONE! EVERYONE IS DANCING!
AS SOON AS HE SAID IT, HE REALIZED HE WAS MISTAKEN.
?
SILAS!
SOME-ONE CALLED OUT...
LAST DANCE!
AND THE MUSIC SKIRLED UP INTO SOMETHING STATELY AND SLOW AND FINAL.

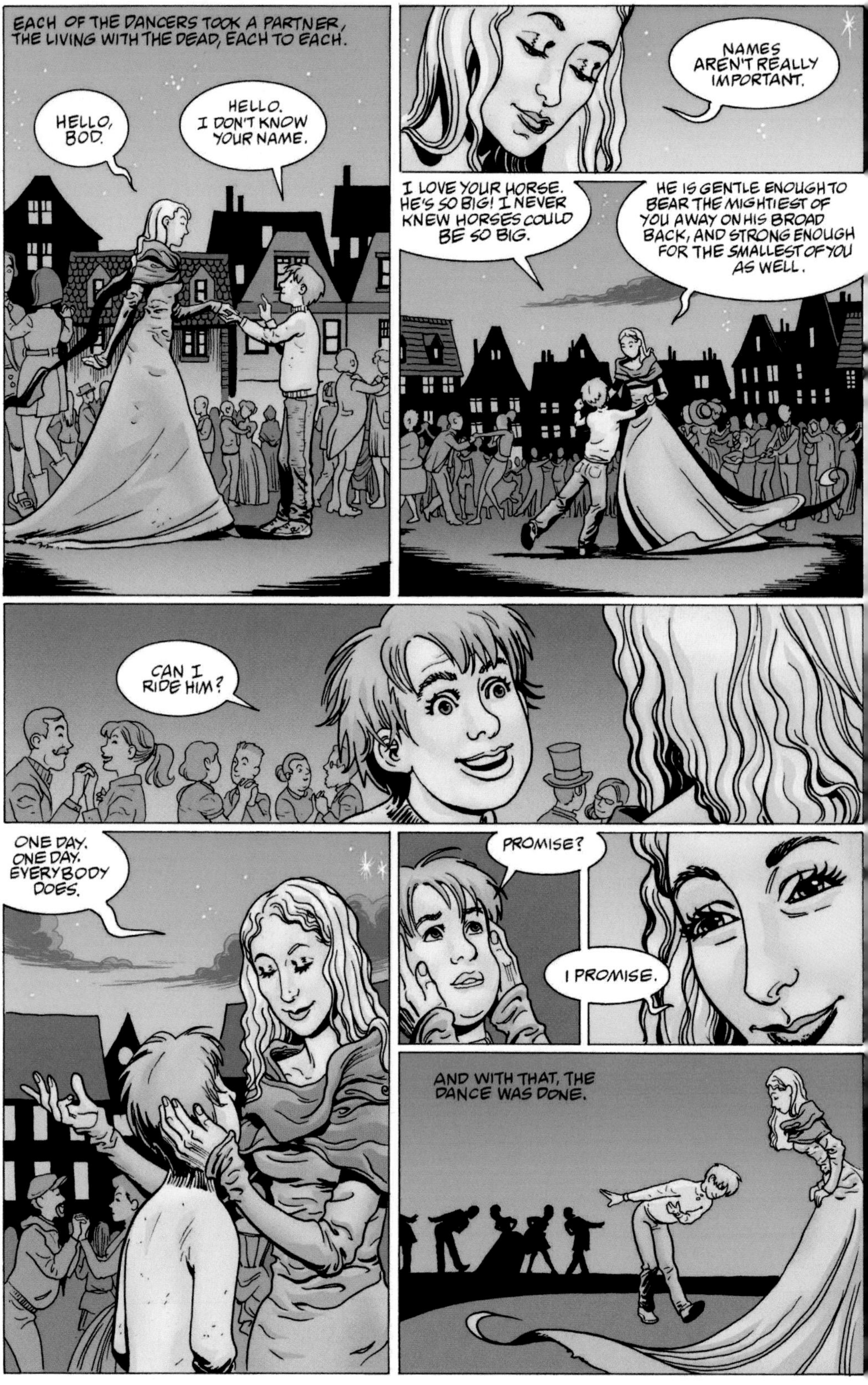
EACH OF THE DANCERS TOOK A PARTNER, THE LIVING WITH THE DEAD, EACH TO EACH.
HELLO, BOD.
HELLO. I DON'T KNOW YOUR NAME.
NAMES AREN'T REALLY IMPORTANT.
I LOVE YOUR HORSE. HE'S SO BIG! I NEVER KNEW HORSES COULD BE SO BIG.
HE IS GENTLE ENOUGH TO BEAR THE MIGHTIEST OF YOU AWAY ON HIS BROAD BACK, AND STRONG ENOUGH FOR THE SMALLEST OF YOU AS WELL.
CAN I RIDE HIM?
ONE DAY. ONE DAY. EVERYBODY DOES.
PROMISE?
I PROMISE.
AND WITH THAT, THE DANCE WAS DONE.

THEN, AND ONLY THEN, DID BOD FEEL EXHAUSTED, FEEL AS IF HE'D BEEN DANCING FOR HOUR AFTER HOUR.

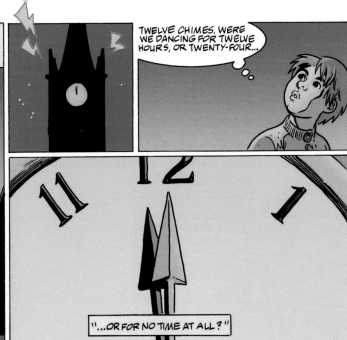
TWELVE CHIMES. WERE WE DANCING FOR TWELVE HOURS, OR TWENTY-FOUR...

"...OR FOR NO TIME AT ALL?"

HE LOOKED AROUND HIM. THE DEAD HAD GONE, AND THE LADY ON THE GREY. ONLY THE LIVING REMAINED, AND THEY WERE LEAVING THE SQUARE STIFFLY, LIKE PEOPLE WHO HAD WAKENED FROM A DEEP SLEEP. THE TOWN SQUARE WAS LITTERED WITH TINY WHITE FLOWERS.

IT LOOKED AS IF THERE HAD BEEN A WEDDING.

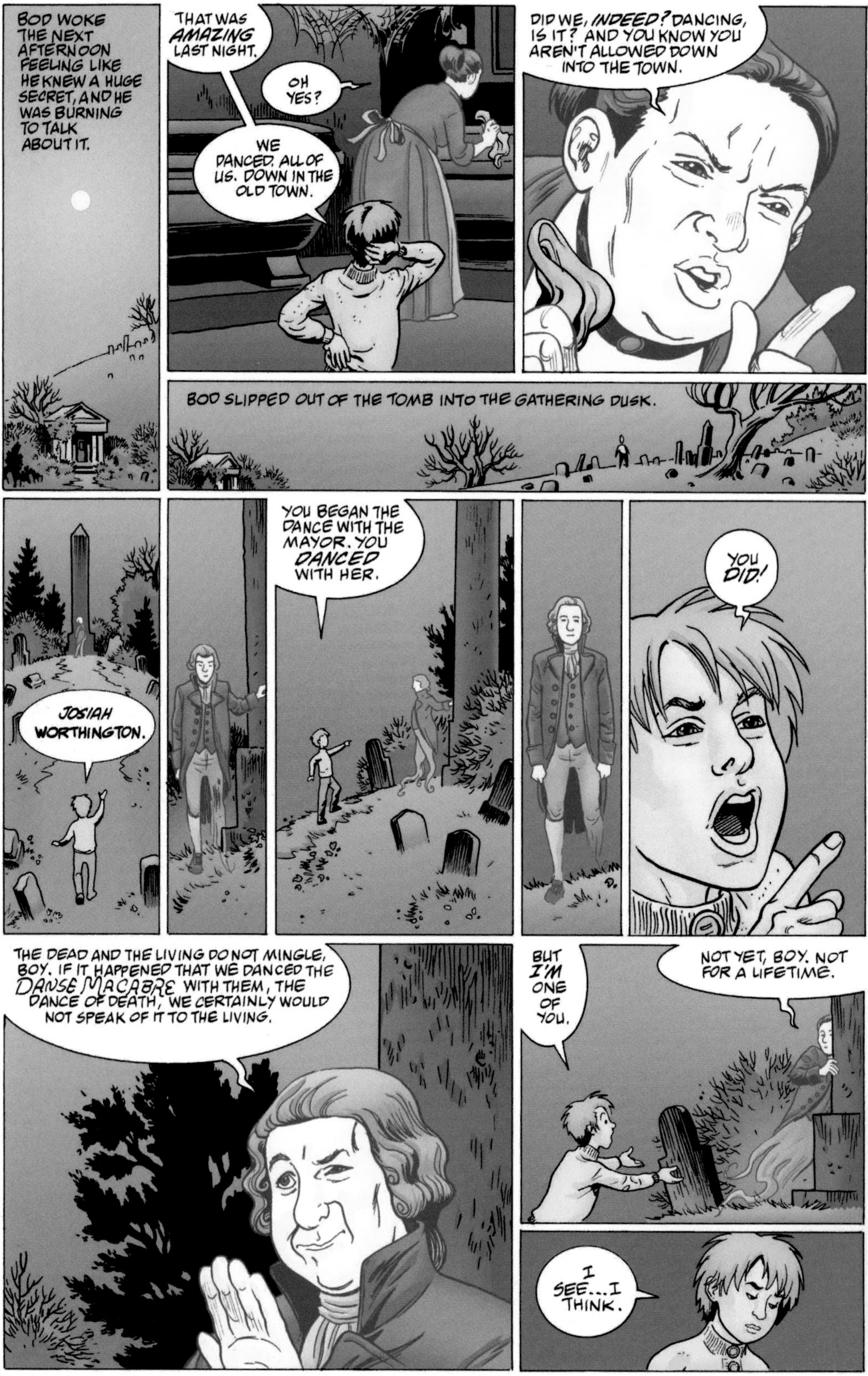
BOD WOKE THE NEXT AFTERNOON FEELING LIKE HE KNEW A HUGE SECRET, AND HE WAS BURNING TO TALK ABOUT IT.
THAT WAS AMAZING LAST NIGHT.
OH YES?
WE DANCED, ALL OF US. DOWN IN THE OLD TOWN.
DID WE, INDEED? DANCING, IS IT? AND YOU KNOW YOU AREN'T ALLOWED DOWN INTO THE TOWN.
BOD SLIPPED OUT OF THE TOMB INTO THE GATHERING DUSK.
JOSIAH WORTHINGTON.
YOU BEGAN THE DANCE WITH THE MAYOR. YOU DANCED WITH HER.
YOU DID!
THE DEAD AND THE LIVING DO NOT MINGLE, BOY. IF IT HAPPENED THAT WE DANCED THE DANSE MACABRE WITH THEM, THE DANCE OF DEATH, WE CERTAINLY WOULD NOT SPEAK OF IT TO THE LIVING.
BUT I'M ONE OF YOU.
NOT YET, BOY. NOT FOR A LIFETIME.
I SEE... I THINK.

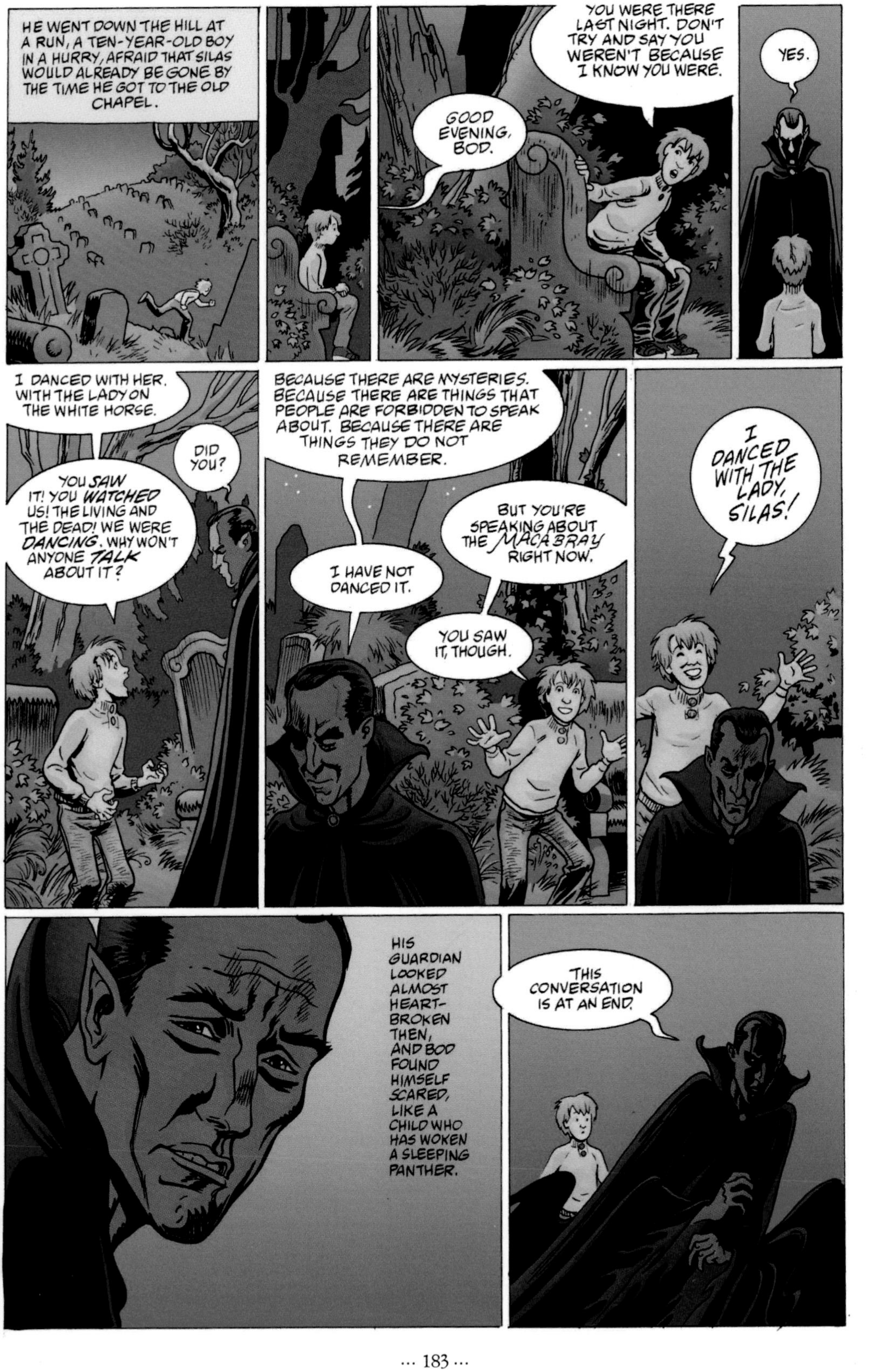
HE WENT DOWN THE HILL AT A RUN, A TEN-YEAR-OLD BOY IN A HURRY, AFRAID THAT SILAS WOULD ALREADY BE GONE BY THE TIME HE GOT TO THE OLD CHAPEL.
GOOD EVENING, BOD.
YOU WERE THERE LAST NIGHT. DON'T TRY AND SAY YOU WEREN'T BECAUSE I KNOW YOU WERE.
YES.
I DANCED WITH HER. WITH THE LADY ON THE WHITE HORSE.
DID YOU?
YOU SAW IT! YOU WATCHED US! THE LIVING AND THE DEAD! WE WERE DANCING. WHY WON'T ANYONE TALK ABOUT IT?
BECAUSE THERE ARE MYSTERIES. BECAUSE THERE ARE THINGS THAT PEOPLE ARE FORBIDDEN TO SPEAK ABOUT. BECAUSE THERE ARE THINGS THEY DO NOT REMEMBER.
BUT YOU'RE SPEAKING ABOUT THE MACABRAY RIGHT NOW.
I HAVE NOT DANCED IT.
YOU SAW IT, THOUGH.
I DANCED WITH THE LADY, SILAS!
HIS GUARDIAN LOOKED ALMOST HEART-BROKEN THEN, AND BOD FOUND HIMSELF SCARED, LIKE A CHILD WHO HAS WOKEN A SLEEPING PANTHER.
THIS CONVERSATION IS AT AN END.

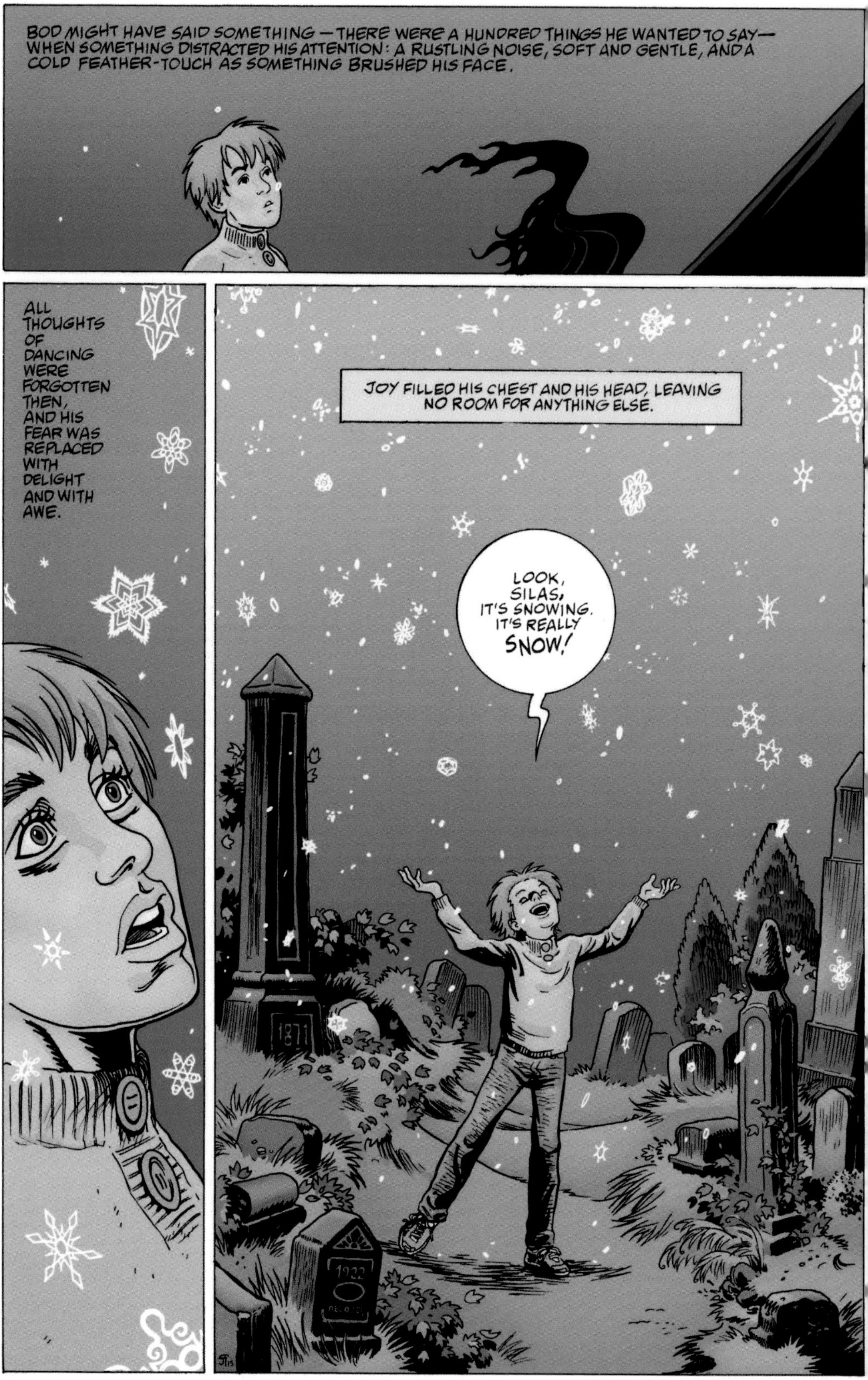
BOD MIGHT HAVE SAID SOMETHING — THERE WERE A HUNDRED THINGS HE WANTED TO SAY — WHEN SOMETHING DISTRACTED HIS ATTENTION: A RUSTLING NOISE, SOFT AND GENTLE, AND A COLD FEATHER-TOUCH AS SOMETHING BRUSHED HIS FACE.
ALL THOUGHTS OF DANCING WERE FORGOTTEN THEN, AND HIS FEAR WAS REPLACED WITH DELIGHT AND WITH AWE.
JOY FILLED HIS CHEST AND HIS HEAD, LEAVING NO ROOM FOR ANYTHING ELSE.
LOOK, SILAS, IT'S SNOWING. IT'S REALLY SNOW!

INTERLUDE

Illustrated by Stephen B. Scott

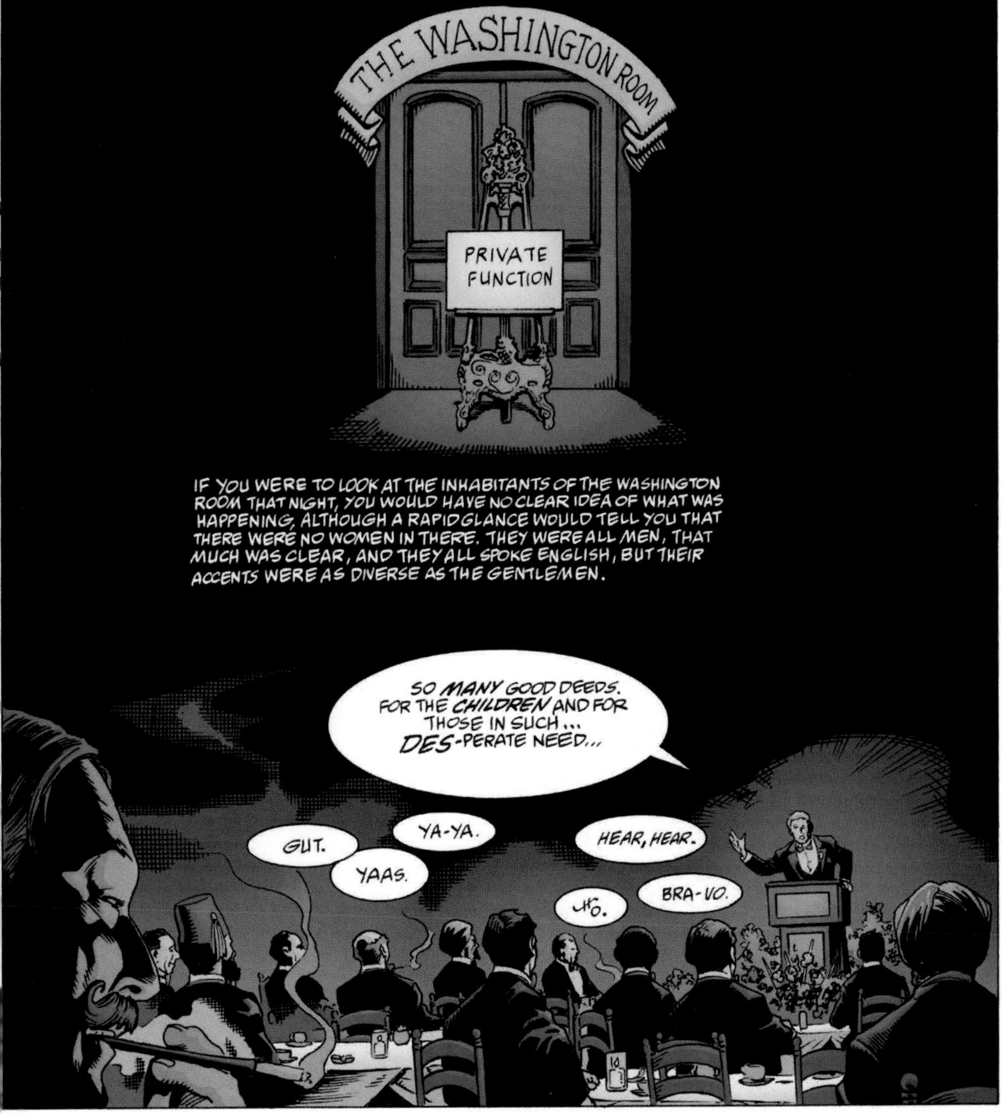
THE WASHINGTON ROOM
PRIVATE FUNCTION
IF YOU WERE TO LOOK AT THE INHABITANTS OF THE WASHINGTON ROOM THAT NIGHT, YOU WOULD HAVE NO CLEAR IDEA OF WHAT WAS HAPPENING, ALTHOUGH A RAPID GLANCE WOULD TELL YOU THAT THERE WERE NO WOMEN IN THERE. THEY WERE ALL MEN, THAT MUCH WAS CLEAR, AND THEY ALL SPOKE ENGLISH, BUT THEIR ACCENTS WERE AS DIVERSE AS THE GENTLEMEN.
SO *MANY* GOOD DEEDS. FOR THE *CHILDREN* AND FOR THOSE IN SUCH... *DES*-PERATE NEED...
GUT.
YA-YA.
YAAS.
HEAR, HEAR.
BRA-VO.

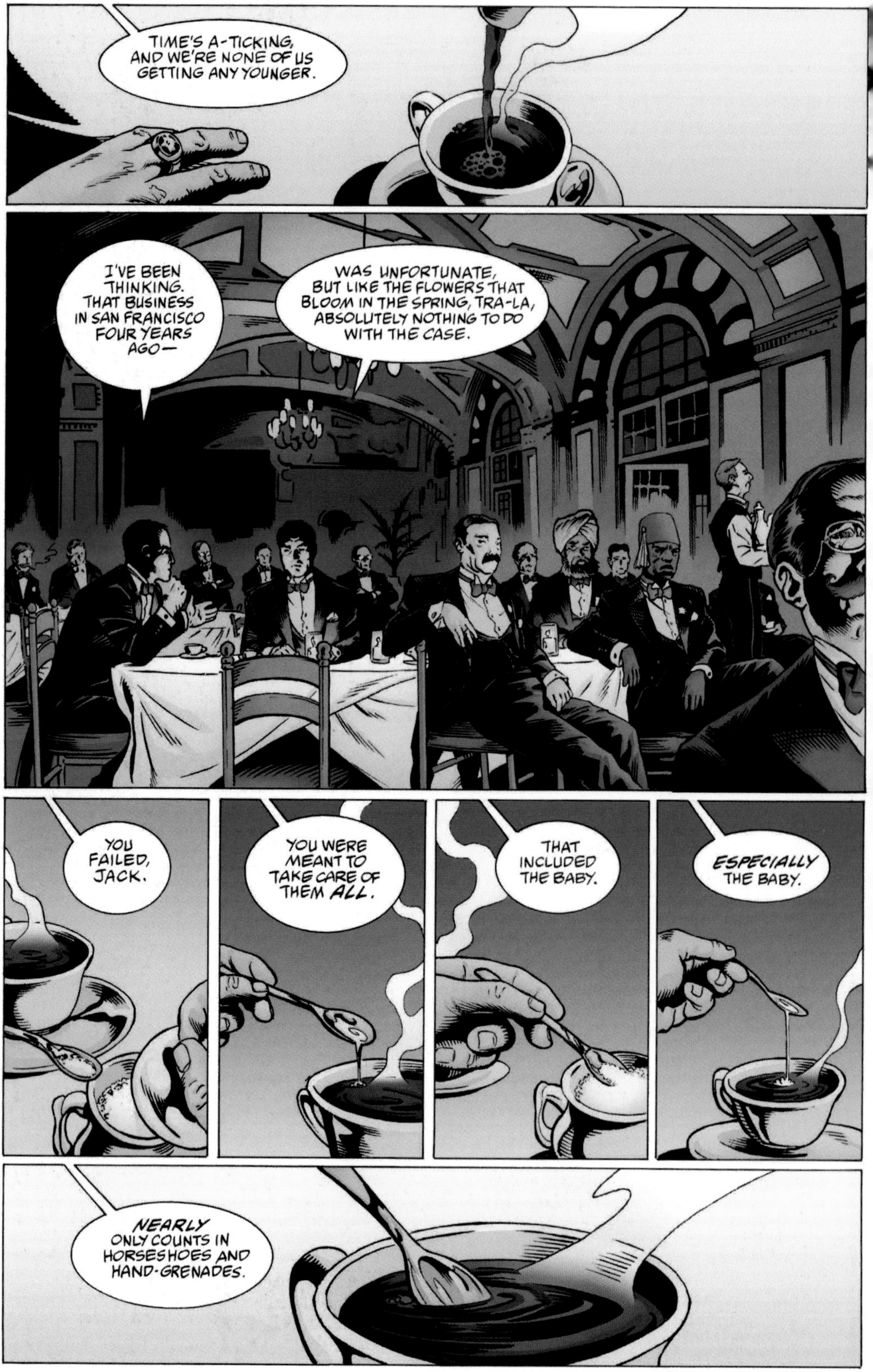
TIME'S A-TICKING, AND WE'RE NONE OF US GETTING ANY YOUNGER.
I'VE BEEN THINKING. THAT BUSINESS IN SAN FRANCISCO FOUR YEARS AGO—
WAS UNFORTUNATE, BUT LIKE THE FLOWERS THAT BLOOM IN THE SPRING, TRA-LA, ABSOLUTELY NOTHING TO DO WITH THE CASE.
YOU FAILED, JACK.
YOU WERE MEANT TO TAKE CARE OF THEM ALL.
THAT INCLUDED THE BABY.
ESPECIALLY THE BABY.
NEARLY ONLY COUNTS IN HORSESHOES AND HAND-GRENADES.

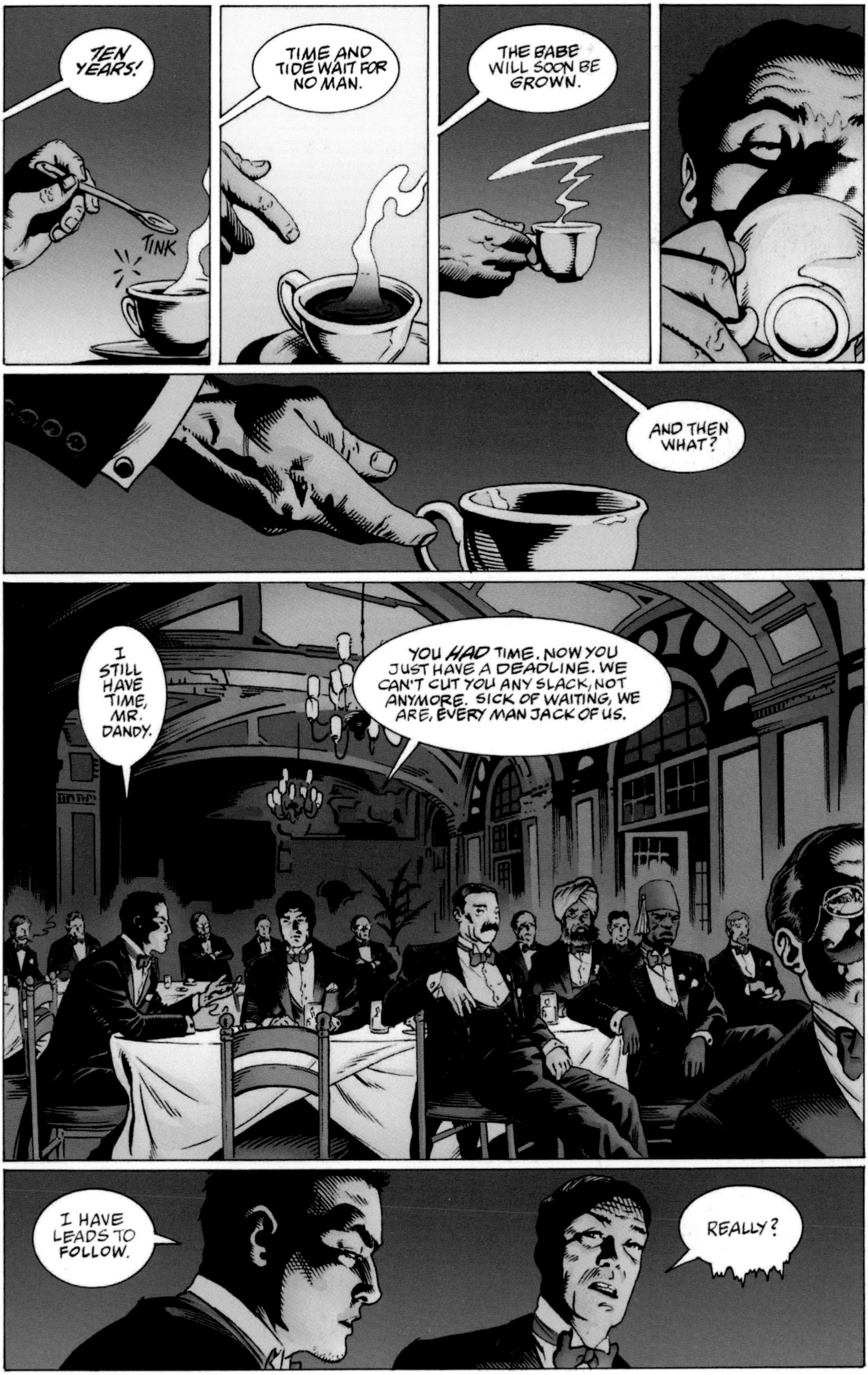
TEN YEARS!
TINK
TIME AND TIDE WAIT FOR NO MAN.
THE BABE WILL SOON BE GROWN.
AND THEN WHAT?
I STILL HAVE TIME, MR. DANDY.
YOU HAD TIME. NOW YOU JUST HAVE A DEADLINE. WE CAN'T CUT YOU ANY SLACK, NOT ANYMORE. SICK OF WAITING, WE ARE, EVERY MAN JACK OF US.
I HAVE LEADS TO FOLLOW.
REALLY?

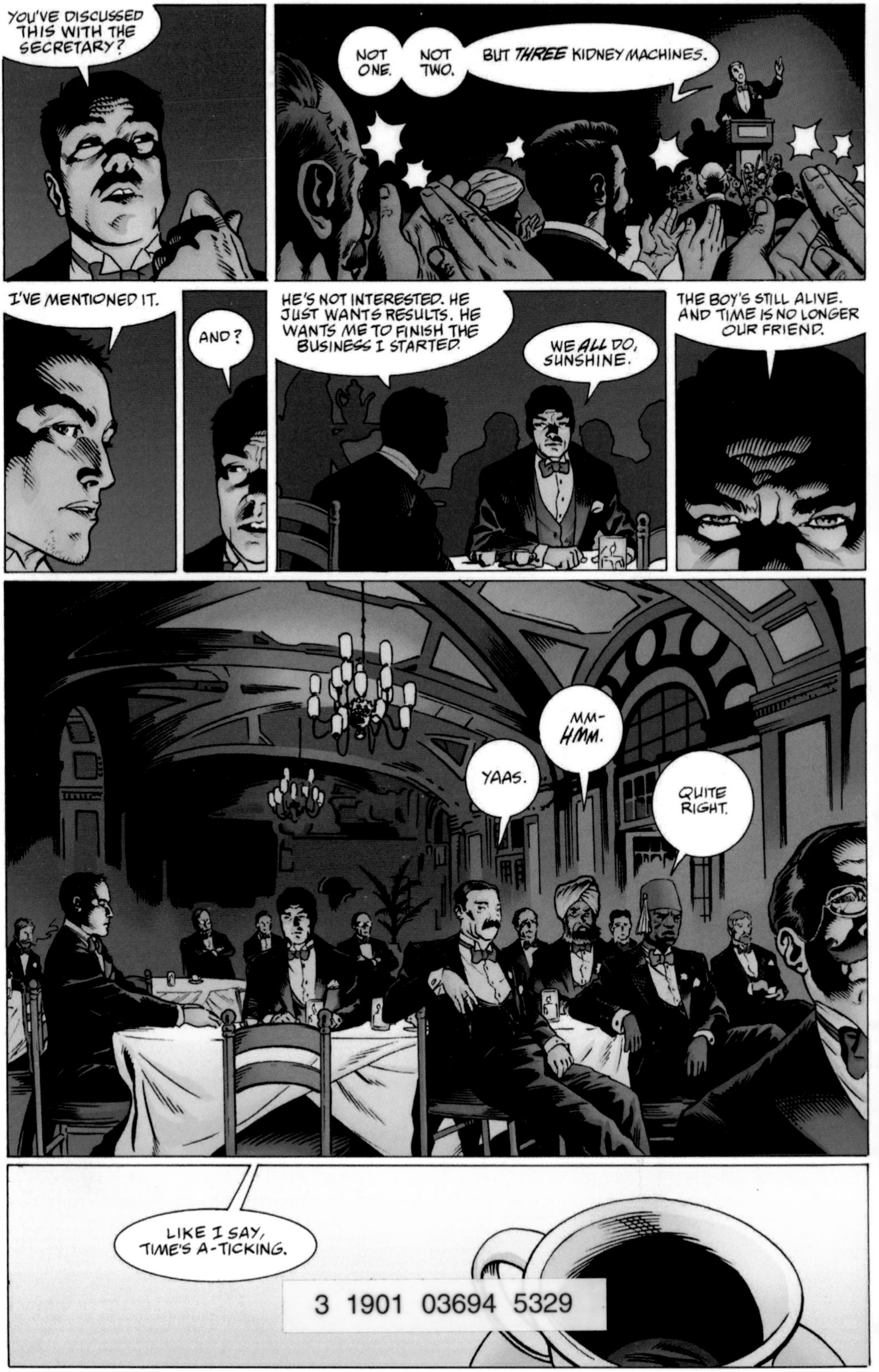
YOU'VE DISCUSSED THIS WITH THE SECRETARY?
NOT ONE.
NOT TWO.
BUT THREE KIDNEY MACHINES.
I'VE MENTIONED IT.
AND?
HE'S NOT INTERESTED. HE JUST WANTS RESULTS. HE WANTS ME TO FINISH THE BUSINESS I STARTED.
WE ALL DO, SUNSHINE.
THE BOY'S STILL ALIVE. AND TIME IS NO LONGER OUR FRIEND.
YAAS.
MM-HMM.
QUITE RIGHT.
LIKE I SAY, TIME'S A-TICKING.